PENGUIN BOOKS

LAND OF THE LIVING

'The most tightly plotted of French's thrillers to date, *Land of the Living* is also the most petrifying . . . don't read it at home alone' *Independent on Sunday*

'The best crime book you will come across this year' *The Good Book Guide*

'A rollercoaster of a read . . . the novel leaves you emotionally exhausted – desperate to reach the conclusion but reluctant to let the thrill end' *Sunday Express*

'The novel never loses pace or interest . . . *Land of the Living* is one of her most enjoyable' *The Spectator*

'Steel yourself for a gripping tale of obsession, madness and fear' *Sunday Mirror*

'A dark and gripping thriller' *Heat*

'Right up there with the suspense novels of Minette Walters, Frances Fyfield and Val McDermid' *Irish Times*

'Dark and menacing, the tension never lets up for a moment' *Woman and Home*

'This thriller will grip you to the gruesome end . . . Powerful stuff' *Family Circle*

Land of the Living

NICCI FRENCH

PENGUIN BOOKS

PENGUIN BOOKS

Published by the Penguin Group
Penguin Books Ltd, 80 Strand, London WC2R ORL, England
Penguin Putnam Inc., 375 Hudson Street, New York, New York 10014, USA
Penguin Books Australia Ltd, 250 Camberwell Road,
Camberwell, Victoria 3124, Australia
Penguin Books Canada Ltd, 10 Alcorn Avenue, Toronto, Ontario, Canada M4V 3B2
Penguin Books India (P) Ltd, 11, Community Centre,
Panchsheel Park, New Delhi – 110 017, India
Penguin Books (NZ) Ltd, Cnr Rosedale and Airborne Roads,
Albany, Auckland, New Zealand
Penguin Books (South Africa) (Pty) Ltd, 24 Sturdee Avenue,
Rosebank 2196, South Africa

Penguin Books Ltd, Registered Offices: 80 Strand, London WC2R ORL, England

www.penguin.com

First published by Michael Joseph 2002
Published in Penguin Books 2003

1

Typeset by Rowland Phototypesetting Ltd, Bury St Edmunds, Suffolk
Printed in England by Clays Ltd, St Ives plc

To Timmy and Eve

Part One

Darkness. Darkness for a long time. Open my eyes and close, open and close. The same. Darkness inside, darkness outside.

I'd been dreaming. Tossed around in a black dark sea. Staked out on a mountain in the night. An animal I couldn't see sniffed and snuffled around me. I felt a wet nose on my skin. When you know you're dreaming you wake up. Sometimes you wake into another dream. But when you wake and nothing changes, that must be reality.

Darkness and things out there in the darkness. Pain. It was far away from her and then closer to her and then part of her. Part of *me*. I was filled to the brim with hot, liquid pain. Although the darkness remained, I could see the pain. Flashes of yellow and red and blue, fireworks exploding silently behind my eyes.

I started to search for something without really knowing what it was. I didn't know where it was. I didn't know what it was. Nightingale. Farthingale. It took an effort, like hauling a package out of the water of a deep dark lake. That was it. Abigail. I recognized that. My name was Abigail. Abbie. Tabbie. Abbie the Tabbie. The other name was harder. There were bits missing from my head and it seemed to have got lost among the missing bits. I remembered a class register. Auster, Bishop, Brown, Byrne, Cassini, Cole, Daley, Devereaux, Eve, Finch, Fry. No, stop. Go back. Finch. No. Devereaux. Yes, that was it. A rhyme came to me. A rhyme from long, long ago. Not Deverox like box. Nor Deveroo like shoe. But Devereaux like show. Abbie Devereaux. I clung to the name as if it was a life-ring that had been thrown to me in a stormy sea. The stormy sea was in my head mostly. Wave after wave of pain rolling in and dashing itself against the inside of my skull.

I closed my eyes again. I let my name go.

Everything was part of everything else. Everything existed at the same time as everything else. How long was it like that? Minutes. Hours. And then, like figures emerging from a fog, things resolved and separated. There was a taste of metal in my mouth and a smell of metal stinging my nostrils but the smell became a mustiness that made me think of garden sheds, tunnels, basements, cellars, damp dirty forgotten places.

I listened. Just the sound of my own breathing, unnaturally loud. I held my breath. No sound. Just the beating of my heart. Was that a noise or just the blood pumping inside my body, pushing against my ears?

I was uncomfortable. There was an ache down my back, my pelvis, my legs. I turned over. No. I didn't turn over. I didn't move. I couldn't move. I pulled up my arms as if to fend something off. No. The arms didn't move. I couldn't turn. Was I paralysed? I couldn't feel my legs. My toes. I concentrated everything on my toes. Left big toe rubbing against the toe beside. Right big toe rubbing against the toe beside. No problem. I could do it. Inside a sock. No shoe. I wasn't wearing shoes.

My fingers. I drummed them. The tips touched something rough. Cement or brick. Was this a hospital? Injured. An accident. Lying somewhere, waiting to be found. A railway accident. The wreckage of a train. Machinery on top of me. Wreckage. In a tunnel. Help coming. Heat-seeking equipment. I tried to remember the train. Couldn't remember. Or a plane. Or a car. Car more likely. Driving late at night, headlights on the windscreen, falling asleep. I knew the feeling, pinching myself to stay awake, slapping my cheeks, shouting, opening the window so the cold air hit my eyeballs. Maybe this time I failed. Veered off the road, down an embankment, rolled over, the car lost in undergrowth. When would I be reported missing? How do you look for a lost car?

I mustn't wait to be rescued. I might die of dehydration or blood loss just yards from people driving to work. I would have to move. If only I could see the way. No moon. No stars. It might only be twenty yards to safety. Up an embankment. If I could feel my toes, then I could move. Turn over first. Ignore the pain. I turned but this time I felt something hold me back. I flexed my legs and arms, tightened and loosened the muscles. There were restraints. Over my forearms and just above my elbows. My ankles and thighs. My chest. I could lift my head, as if in the feeble beginning of an attempt at a sit-up. Something else. Not just dark. It was dark but not just that. My head was covered.

Think clearly. There must be a reason for this. Think. People in prison were restrained. Not relevant. What else? Patients in hospitals can have restraints placed on them in order to prevent them harming themselves. Lying on a trolley. Restrained on a trolley prior to being wheeled in for an operation. I've been in an accident. Say, a car accident, which is most likely. Statistically. Severe but not life-threatening. Any sudden movement could cause, and the phrase came to me out of nowhere, severe internal bleeding. The patient could fall off the trolley. It's just a matter of waiting for the nurse or the anaesthetist. Perhaps I had been given the anaesthetic already. Or a pre-anaesthetic. Hence the vacancies in my brain. Strange quiet, but you do hear of people in hospitals lying around on trolleys for hours waiting for a free operating theatre.

Problems with the theory. I didn't seem to be lying on a trolley. The smell was of darkness, mildew, things that were old and decaying. All I could feel with my fingers was concrete, or stone. My body was lying on something hard. I tried to think of other possibilities. After famous disasters bodies were stored in improvised morgues. School gymnasiums. Church halls. I could have been in a disaster. The injured could have been placed wherever there was room. Restrained to prevent them injuring themselves. Would they be hooded as well? Surgeons were hooded. But not their eyes. Perhaps to prevent infection.

I raised my head again. With my chin I felt a shirt. I was wearing clothes. Yes. I could feel them on my skin. A shirt, trousers, socks. No shoes.

There were other things at the edge, clamouring to be admitted to my brain. Bad things. Restrained. In the dark. Hooded. Ridiculous. Could it be a joke? I remembered stories of students. They get you paralytically drunk, put you on a train at Aberdeen. You wake up in London dressed only in your underwear with a fifty-pence piece in your hand. Everyone will jump out in a minute, pull off the blindfold and shout, 'April fool.' We'll all laugh. But was it April? I remembered cold. Had summer been? Was summer still to come? But of course a summer had always been and there was always another summer to come.

All the alleys were blind. I had gone up them all and found nothing. Something had happened. I knew that.

One possibility was that it was something funny. It didn't feel funny. Another possibility, possibility number two, was that something had happened and it was in the process of being officially dealt with. The hood – or bandage, yes, very possibly a bandage. That was a thought. I might have received a head wound, eye or ear damage and my entire head was bandaged and hooded for my own protection. They would be removed. There would be some stinging. The cheery face of a nurse. A doctor frowning at me. Don't worry, nothing to worry about. That's what they'd say. Call me 'dear'.

There were other possibilities. Bad ones. I thought of the stone under my fingers. The damp air, like a cave. Until now, there had been only the pain and also the mess of my thoughts, but now there was something else. Fear in my chest like sludge. I made a sound. A low groan. I was able to speak. I didn't know who to call or what to say. I shouted more loudly. I thought the echoing or harshness of the sound might tell me something about where I was but it was muffled by my hood. I shouted again so that my throat hurt.

Now there was a movement nearby. Smells. Sweat and scent. A sound of breathing, somebody scrambling. Now my mouth was full of cloth. I couldn't breathe. Only through my nose. Something tied hard around my face. Breath on me, hot on my cheek, and then, out of the darkness, a voice, little more than a whisper, hoarse, strained, thick so I could barely make it out.

'No,' it said. 'Make another sound and I'll block your nose as well.'

I was gagging on the cloth. It filled my mouth, bulged in my cheeks, rubbed against my gums. The taste of grease and rancid cabbage filled my throat. A spasm jerked my body, nausea rising through me like damp. I mustn't be sick. I tried to take a breath, tried to gasp through the cloth but I couldn't. I couldn't. I was all stopped up. I tugged with my arms and my ankles against the restraints and tried to take a breath and it was as if my whole body was twitching and shuddering on the rough stone floor and no air inside me, just violent space and red behind my bulging eyes and a heart that was jolting up through my throat and a strange dry sound coming from me, like a cough that wouldn't form. I was a dying fish. A fish thrashing on the hard floor. I was hooked and tied down, but inside me I was coming loose, all my innards tearing apart. Is this what it's like? To die? To be buried alive.

I had to breathe. How do you breathe? Through your nose. He'd said so. The voice had said he'd block my nose next. Breathe through my nose. Breathe now. I couldn't take enough air in that way. I couldn't stop myself trying to gasp, trying to fill myself up with air. My tongue was too big to fit in the tiny space left in my mouth. It kept pushing against the cloth. I felt my body buck again. Breathe slowly. Calmly. In and out, in and out. Breathe like that until there's nothing except the sense of it. This is how to keep alive. Breathe. Thick, musty air in my nostrils, oily rottenness running down my throat. I tried not to swallow but then I had to and again biliousness flowed through me, filled my mouth. I couldn't bear it. I could bear it, I could, I could, I could.

Breathe in and out, Abbie. Abbie. I am Abbie. Abigail Devereaux. In and out. Don't think. Breathe. You are alive.

The pain inside my skull rolled back. I lifted my head a bit and the pain surged towards my eyes. I blinked my eyes and it was the same deep darkness when they were open and when they were closed. My eyelashes scraped against the hood. I was cold. I could feel that now. My feet were chilly inside the socks. Were they my socks? They felt too big and rough; unfamiliar. My left calf ached. I tried to flex my leg muscles to get rid of the crampy feeling. There was an itch on my cheek, under the hood. I lay there for a few seconds, concentrating only on the itch, then I turned my head and tried to rub the itch against a hunched shoulder. No good. So I squirmed until I could scrape my face along the floor.

And I was damp. Between my legs and under my thighs, stinging my skin beneath my trousers. Were they my trousers? I was lying in my own piss, in the dark, in a hood, tied down, gagged. Breathe in and out, I told myself. Breathe in and out all the time. Try to let thoughts out slowly, bit by bit, so you don't drown in them. I felt the pressure of the fears dammed up inside me, and my body was a fragile, cracking shell full of pounding waters. I made myself think only of breathing, in and out of my nostrils. In and out.

Someone – a man, the man who had pushed this cloth into my mouth – had put me in this place. He had taken me, strapped me down. I was his prisoner. Why? I couldn't think about that yet. I listened for a sound, any sound except the sound of my breath and the sound of my heart and, when I moved, the rasp of my hands or feet against the rough floor. Perhaps he was here with me, in the room, crouching somewhere. But there was no other sound. For the moment I was alone. I lay there. I listened to my heart. Silence pressed down on me.

An image flitted through my head. A yellow butterfly on a leaf, wings quivering. It was like a sudden ray of

9

light. Was it something I was remembering, a moment rescued out of the past and stored away till now? Or was it just my brain throwing up a picture, some kind of reflex, a short circuit?

A man had tied me in a dark place. He must have snatched me and taken me here. But I had no memory of that happening. I scrabbled in my brain, but it was blank – an empty room, an abandoned house, no echoes. Nothing. I could remember nothing. A sob rose in my throat. I mustn't cry. I must think, but carefully now, hold back the fear. I must not go deep down. I must stay on the surface. Just think of what I know. Facts. Slowly I will make up a picture and then I'll be able to look at it.

My name is Abigail; Abbie. I am twenty-five years old, and I live with my boyfriend, Terry, Terence Wilmott, in a poky flat on Westcott Road. That's it: Terry. Terry will be worried. He will phone the police. He'll tell them I have gone missing. They'll drive here with flashing lights and wailing sirens and hammer down the door and light and air will come flooding in. No, just facts. I work at Jay and Joiner's, designing office interiors. I have a desk, with a white and blue laptop computer, a small grey phone, a pile of paper, an oval ashtray full of paperclips and elastic bands.

When was I last there? It seemed impossibly far off, like a dream that disappears when you try to hold on to it; like someone else's life. I couldn't remember. How long had I lain here? An hour, or a day, or a week? It was January, I knew that – at least, I thought I knew that. Outside, it was cold and the days were short. Maybe it had snowed. No, I mustn't think of things like snow, sunlight on white. Stick only to what I knew: January, but I couldn't tell if it was day or night. Or perhaps it was February now. I tried to think of the last day I clearly remembered, but it was like looking into a thick fog, with indistinct shapes looming.

Start with New Year's Eve, dancing with friends and everyone kissing each other on the stroke of midnight. Kissing people on the lips, people I knew well and people I'd met a few times and strangers who came up to me with arms open and an expectant smile because kissing is what you do on New Year's Eve. Don't think of all that, though. After New Year's Eve, then, yes, there were days that stirred in my mind. The office, phones ringing, expense forms in my in-tray. Cups of cooling bitter coffee. But maybe that was before, not after. Or before and after, day after day. Everything was blurred and without meaning.

I tried to shift. My toes felt stiff with cold and my neck ached and my head banged. The taste in my mouth was foul. Why was I here and what was going to happen to me? I was laid out on my back like a sacrifice, arms and legs pinned down. Dread ran through me. He could starve me. He could rape me. He could torture me. He could kill me. Maybe he had already raped me. I pressed myself against the floor and whimpered deep down in my throat. Two tears escaped from my eyes and I felt them tickle and sting as they ran down towards my ears.

Don't cry, Abbie. You mustn't cry.

Think of the butterfly, which means nothing but which is beautiful. I pictured the yellow butterfly on its green leaf. I let it fill my mind, so light on the leaf it could be blown away like a feather. I heard footsteps. They were soft, as if the man was barefooted. They padded closer and stopped. There was a sound of someone breathing heavily, almost panting, as if he was climbing or scrambling towards me. I lay rigid in the silence. He was standing over me. There was a click, and even from beneath the hood I could tell he had switched on a torch. I could hardly see anything, but I could at least see through the grain of the fabric that it was no longer entirely dark. He must be standing over me and shining a torch down on my body.

'You're wet,' he murmured, or maybe it sounded like a murmur through my hood. 'Silly girl.'

I sensed him leaning towards me. I heard him breathing and I heard my own breathing getting louder and faster. He pulled the hood up slightly and, quite gently, pulled out the cloth. I felt a fingertip on my lower lip. For a few seconds, all I could do was pant with the relief of it, pulling the air into my lungs. I heard myself say, 'Thank you.' My voice sounded light and feeble. 'Water.'

He undid the restraints on my arms and my chest, so that only my legs were tied at the ankle. He slid an arm under my neck and lifted me into a sitting position. A new kind of pain pulsed inside my skull. I didn't dare make any movements by myself. I sat passively, and let him put my arms behind my back and tie my wrists together, roughly so that the rope cut into my flesh. Was it rope? It felt harder than that, like washing line or wire.

'Open your mouth,' he said in his muffled whisper. I did so. He slid a straw up the hood and between my lips. 'Drink.'

The water was tepid and left a stale taste in my mouth.

He put a hand on the back of my neck, and started to rub at it. I sat rigid. I mustn't cry out. I mustn't make a sound. I mustn't be sick. His fingers pressed into my skin.

'Where do you hurt?' he said.

'Nowhere.' My voice was a whisper.

'Nowhere? You wouldn't lie to me?'

Anger filled my head like a glorious roaring wind and it was stronger even than the fear. 'You piece of shit,' I shouted, in a mad, high-pitched voice. 'Let me go, let me go, and then I'm going to kill you, you'll see –'

The cloth was rammed back into my mouth.

'You're going to kill me. Good. I like that.'

For a long time I concentrated on nothing but breathing. I had heard of people feeling claustrophobic in their own bodies, trapped as if in prison. They became tormented by the idea that they would never be able to escape. My life was reduced to the tiny passages of air in my nostrils. If they became blocked, I would die. That happened. People were tied up, gagged, with no intention to kill them. Just a small error in the binding – the gag tied too close to the nose – and they would choke and die.

I made myself breathe in one-two-three, out one-two-three. In, out. I'd seen a film once, some kind of war film, in which a super-tough soldier hid from the enemy in a river breathing just through a single straw. I was like that and the thought made my chest hurt and made me breathe in spasms. I had to calm myself. Instead of thinking of the soldier and his straw and what would have happened if the straw had become blocked, I tried to think of the water in the river, cool and calm and slow-moving and beautiful, the sun glistening on it in the morning.

In my mind, the water grew slower and slower until it was quite still. I imagined it starting to freeze, solid like glass so that you could see the fish swimming silently underneath. I couldn't stop myself. I saw myself falling through the ice, trapped underneath. I had read or heard or been told that if you fall through ice and can't find the hole, there is a thin layer of air between the ice and the water and you can lie under the ice and breathe the air. And what then? It might be better just to have drowned. I had always been terrified of drowning above all things, but I had read or heard or been told that drowning was in fact a pleasant way to die. I could believe it. What was unpleasant and terrifying was trying to avoid drowning. Fear is trying to avoid death. Giving yourself up to death is like falling asleep.

One-two-three, one-two-three, I was becoming calmer. Some people, probably about two per cent of the population at least, would have died already of panic or asphyxiation if they'd had done to them what I was having done to me. So I was already doing better than someone. I was alive. I was breathing.

I was lying down now, with my ankles tied and my wrists tied, my mouth gagged and a hood over my head. I wasn't tied *to* anything any more. I struggled into a squatting position, then very slowly stood up. Tried to stand up. My head bumped against a roof. It must be just under five foot high. I sat down again, panting with the effort.

At least I could move my body. Wriggle and hump along, like a snake in the dust. But I hardly dared. I had the sense that I was somewhere up high. When he came into the room, he was underneath me. The footsteps and his voice came from down below. He climbed to get at me.

I stretched my feet in one direction and felt only the floor. I swivelled painfully around, my T-shirt riding up and bare skin on my back scraping along the roughness beneath me. I stretched my feet. Floor. I humped forward. Slowly. Feet feeling. Then not feeling – not feeling the hardness underneath. Stretched over a space, a blank. Nothing underneath. I lay down and moved forward again, bit by bit. Legs hanging over, bent at the knee. If I sat up now, I'd be sitting over a fall, a cliff. My breath juddered in my chest with panic. I started shifting backwards. My back hurt. My head crashed and banged. I kept wriggling and scraping backwards until I was pressed up against a wall.

I sat up. I pressed my bound hands against the wall. Damp coarse brick against my fingertips.

I shuffled upright along the wall in one direction, until I met the corner. Then in the other direction, my muscles burning with the effort. It must be about ten feet wide. Ten feet wide and four feet deep.

It was hard to think clearly because the pain in my head kept getting in the way. Was it a bang? A scrape? Something in my brain?

I was shivering with cold. I had to keep thinking, keep my mind busy, keep it off things. I had been kidnapped in some way. I was being held against my will. Why did kidnaps happen? To take hostages, for money or for a political reason. My total wealth, once credit card and storecard debts were deducted, amounted to about two thousand pounds, half of it bound up in my rusty old car. As for politics, I was a working-environment consultant not an ambassador. But then I didn't remember anything. I could be in South America, now, or Lebanon. Except that the voice was clearly English, southern English as far as I could tell from the soft, thick whisper.

So what other reasons were there? I had argued myself towards an area where everything looked really, really bad. I felt tears bubbling up in my eyes. Calm down. Calm down. I mustn't get all snotty, blocked up.

He hadn't killed me. That was a good sign. Except it wasn't necessarily all that good a sign – in the long run it might be a bad sign in a way that made me feel sick even to think about. But it was all I had. I flexed my muscles very gently. I couldn't move. I didn't know where I was. I didn't know where I'd been captured, or when, or how. Or for what reason. I couldn't see anything. I didn't even know anything about the room I was lying in. It felt damp. Maybe it was underground or in a shed. I didn't know anything about the man. Or men. Or people. He was probably close by. I didn't know if I knew him. I didn't know what he looked like.

That might be useful. If I could identify him, he might . . . Well, that might be worse. Professional kidnappers wore hoods so that the hostage never saw them. Putting a hood over my head might be the same thing, the other way round. And he was doing something to his voice, muffling it somehow, so that he didn't sound like a human at all. It might even be that he was planning to hold me for just a little while and let me go. He could dump me in some other part of London and it would be impossible for me ever to find him again. I would know nothing – nothing at all. That was the first bit of remotely good news.

I had no idea how long I had been here but at the very outside it couldn't be more than three days, maybe even two. I felt dreadful but I didn't feel especially weak. I felt hungry but not ill with hunger. Maybe two days. Terry would have reported me missing. I wouldn't have turned up at work. They would phone Terry, he would be baffled. He would have tried my mobile phone. Where was that? The police might have been called within hours. By now there would be a huge hunt. Lines of people scouring wasteland. All leave cancelled. Sniffer dogs. Helicopters. Another promising thought. You can't just grab an adult off the street and hide them somewhere without creating some sort of suspicion. They would be out there, knocking at doors, marching into houses, shining torches into dark places. Any time now I'd hear them, see them. All I had to do was stay alive as long as . . . Just stay alive. Stay alive.

I had shouted at him before. I'd said I'd kill him. That was the only thing I could remember having said to him, except I'd said, 'Thank you,' when he gave me water. I hated the fact I'd said thank you. But when I'd shouted, I'd made him angry. What were his words? 'You kill me? That's a good one.' Something like that. That's not promising. '*You* kill *me*?' That might seem good to him because in fact he's going to kill me.

I tried to seize some other kind of comfort. It might just seem funny to him because I was so much in his power that the idea of me getting back at him was completely ludicrous. I was taking a risk being rude to him. I'd made him angry. He could have tortured me or hit me or anything. But he hadn't done anything. That might be useful to know. He had kidnapped me, he had me tied down and I'd threatened him. It could be that if I stand up to him he feels weakened and unable to do anything to me. If I don't give in to him, that may be the best way of playing him along. He might have kidnapped a woman because he's frightened of women and this is the only way to control at least one woman. He might expect me just to be begging pathetically for my life and that would give him the control he wants. But if I don't yield, then it's not going according to his plan.

Or it might be the opposite. It might have shown nothing more than that he's in control. It doesn't matter to him what I say. He just finds it funny and is proceeding with his plan, whatever that is. Surely the point is to be as much of a flesh-and-blood person for him as possible so that he finds it harder to do anything to me. But if that is threatening to him, then it might make him angrier. I couldn't do anything. I couldn't fight, I couldn't escape. All I could do was slow him up.

What was the best way of doing that? Making him angry? Happy? Scared? I lay on the floor and stared into the stifling darkness of my hood.

There was a change of texture in the blackness around me. There was a sound and a smell. Once again there was that hoarse, croaking whisper. 'I'm going to take your gag out. If you shout I'll bleed you like an animal. If you've heard and understood what I've said, nod your head.'

I nodded frantically. The hands – large, warm hands – fiddled behind my neck. The knot was untied, the cloth pulled roughly from my mouth. As soon as I was free I coughed and coughed. A hand held my head down and I felt the straw pushed into my mouth. I sucked the water until a bubbling sound told me it was gone.

'There,' he said. 'There's a bucket here. Do you want to use it?'

'What do you mean?' Get him talking.

'You know. Toilet.'

He was embarrassed. Was that a good sign?

'I want to go to a proper one.'

'It's the bucket or you can lie in your own piss, sweetheart.'

'All right.'

'I'll put you by the bucket. You can feel it with your feet. I'll stand back. You try anything funny I'll cut you up. All right?'

'Yes.'

There was the sound of him going down some steps, and then I felt his arms under my armpits, then as I slithered towards him, around me. Hard, strong hands. I was pressed against him. An animal smell, sweat, something else. One arm under my thighs. Nausea in my throat. Swung across and put down lightly on a rough floor, gritty. I raised myself up straight. My legs and back felt terribly sore. My hair was seized by a hand and I felt something hard against my neck.

'You know what this is?'

'No.'

'It's a blade. I'm going to untie the wire holding your hands together. Try anything and I'll use it.'

'I won't. I want you to leave me alone.'

'It's dark. I'll step back.'

I felt pressure as he freed a knot behind my back. He stepped away. For just a second I thought of trying something until I saw the absurdity of it. Partially tied up, hooded, in a dark room with a man carrying a knife.

'Go ahead,' he said.

I hadn't really meant it. I just wanted to be moved. I felt my clothes. T-shirt, slacks. I couldn't do this.

'You'll have the bucket again tomorrow morning.'

Tomorrow morning. Good. Some information. All right, all right. He said it was dark. I unfastened my trousers, pulled them and my knickers down and sat on the bucket. Nothing but a dribble. I stood up again, pulled the trousers up.

'Can I say something?'

'What?'

'I don't know what this is about. But you mustn't do this. You won't get away with it. You may not realize what'll happen when they find me. But you can let me go. Drive me somewhere. Turn me loose. That'll be it. I'll have been reported missing, they'll be looking for me. I know you can do what you like to me and it probably won't do me any good but you'll be caught. If you let me go, we can just go back to our lives. Otherwise, you'll be caught.'

'That's what they all say. When they say anything.'

'What?'

'Stand still.'

'All?'

The sensation of knots being refastened. The sensation of being lifted up high, set down like a small child being put up on a high shelf. Like a doll. A dead animal.

'Stay there,' he said. 'Right there.'

I sat there, thinking he would go away now.

'Open your mouth.'

He was beside me. The rag was pushed in, another cloth tied hard around my face. I heard footsteps then felt a new pressure around my neck. Tight. I was pulled back. I could feel the wall behind my back.

'Listen,' the voice said. 'This is a wire looped around your neck. It goes through a loop behind you and fastens on a bolt in the wall. Understand? Nod your head.'

I nodded.

'You're on a platform. Understand?'

I nodded.

'If you move, you'll slip off the ledge, the wire will throttle you and you'll die. Understand?'

I nodded.

'Good.'

And there was silence. Just silence. And my heart,

pounding like the sea. The wire burned my neck. I breathed, in and out, in and out.

I was standing on a wooden jetty and the lake around me was still as a mirror. Not a ripple of wind. I could see smooth pebbles far beneath me, pink and brown and grey. I bent my knees slightly and brought up my arms to dive into the cool, quiet water, and then suddenly something caught me round the neck, and I was falling with a sickening lurch but being held back at the same time, and the water disappeared, became inky darkness instead. The noose was digging into my neck. I sat up straight. For a moment I was a blank, then fear rushed in, filling all the spaces in my body. My heart was pounding and my mouth dry. Sweat ran down my forehead, under the hood, and I could feel wisps of hair sticking to my cheeks. I was clammy with fear, itchy and sticky and sour. My fear was so real now it was something I could smell.

I had fallen asleep. How could that be? How could I sleep when I was trussed up like a chicken waiting for its neck to be snapped? I'd always wondered how prisoners could sleep before the day of execution, but I'd slept. How long for? I had no idea – perhaps a few minutes, nodding off on this ledge before the noose woke me; or perhaps several hours, longer. I didn't know if it was night still or morning. Time had stopped.

Except that time hadn't stopped. It was marching on. It was running out. Silence roared around my ears. Something was going to happen, and I didn't know what and I didn't know when, but I knew something was going to happen. It could be now, as soon as I stopped this thought, or it could be ages away, through the sludge of days. His words came back to me, and with them came a burning sensation in my stomach. It was as if there was an animal inside me, a scabby rodent with sharp yellow teeth eating away at me. 'That's what all the others said.' What did that mean? I knew what it meant. It meant that there had been others before me. They were dead and I was the next here on a ledge with a noose round my neck, and then after me – after me . . .

Breathe and think. Make plans. Plans of escape were futile. All I had was my brain and the words I spoke to him – when he pulled this foul rag out of my mouth. I counted in my head. Seconds into minutes into hours. Was I counting too fast or too slowly? I tried to slow down. I was thirsty and the inside of my mouth felt soft and rotten. My breath must stink by now. I needed water, ice-cold water. Gallons of clean water pulled up from a well deep in the earth. I was no longer hungry at all. Eating food would be like eating twigs or gravel. But clean cold water in a tall glass tumbler, chinking with ice, that would be good. I kept on counting. I mustn't stop.

One hour, twenty-eight minutes, thirty-three seconds. How many seconds was that altogether? I tried to continue counting while doing the sum in my head, but everything scrambled, and I lost the time and I lost the sum. Tears were rolling down my cheek.

I shuffled forward and stretched my body out as far as I could, leaning back my neck until the noose cut in just under my chin. I balanced myself on the ledge, its edge sharp in the small of my back and my lower body hanging over. The wire must be about three feet long. I was like a see-saw. I could tip backwards again, and go on sitting and waiting and counting seconds and minutes and hours, or I could tip forwards into the darkness. He would find me hanging there, the wire noose around my neck. That would be one way of beating him; beating time. It would be that easy.

I shuffled myself back into a sitting position. My whole body was trembling with the effort. I concentrated on breathing, in and out. I thought of the lake in my dream, with its still water. I thought of the river and its fish. I thought of the yellow butterfly on the green leaf. It quivered there, almost as light as the air around it. One whisper of wind would dislodge it. That's like life, I thought; my life is that fragile now.

My name is Abbie. Abigail Devereaux. Abbie. I repeated my name to myself; I tried to hear the sound out loud. But the sound quickly lost its meaning. What did it signify, to be Abbie? Nothing. Just a collection of syllables. Two syllables. Two mouthfuls of air.

'I had this dream,' I said. My voice sounded hoarse and feeble, as if the noose had already damaged my windpipe. 'I slept and I had this dream. Did you have a dream? Do you dream?' I'd rehearsed this sentence while waiting for him – I didn't want to tell him personal things about myself, because somehow that felt risky. And I didn't want to ask him anything specific about himself, because if I knew anything about him he could never let me go. I asked about dreams, because they are intimate but abstract; they feel important but their meanings are vague, insubstantial. But now, speaking my sentence out loud with him beside me, it sounded fatuous.

'Sometimes. Finish your water and then you can use the bucket.'

'Did you dream last night?' I persisted, though I knew it was futile. He was a few inches from me. If I put out an arm I could touch him. I resisted the sudden urge to grab hold of him and wail and howl and plead.

'You can't dream if you haven't slept.'

'You didn't sleep?'

'Drink.'

I took a few more sips, making the water last as long as I could. My throat was sore. It had been night, and yet he hadn't slept. What had he been doing?

'Do you have insomnia?' I tried to appear sympathetic; my voice sounded horribly artificial.

'That's crap,' he said. 'You work and then you sleep when you need to. Day or night. That's all.'

There was a faint grainy light showing through the hood. If I lifted my head up high and peered downwards, perhaps I would see something; his outstretched legs beside mine, his hand on the ledge. I mustn't look. I mustn't see anything. I mustn't know anything. I must stay in the dark.

I did exercises. I pulled my knees up and let them down again. Fifty times. I lay down and tried to sit up. I couldn't do it. Not even once.

People in solitary confinement often went mad. I had read about that. I must have imagined briefly what it would be like, to be locked up and all alone. Sometimes they recited poetry to themselves, but I didn't know any poetry, or if I did I could remember none of it. I knew nursery rhymes. Mary had a little lamb. Hickory dickory dock. The cheery, insistent rhythm felt obscene and mad, like someone inside my sore head, tapping away. I could make up a poem. What rhymed with dark? Stark, hark, lark, park, bark. I couldn't make up poems. I'd never been able to.

I tried once more to reach back into my memory –

not my long memory, the memory of my life and my friends and my family, not the things that made me into who I am, the passage of time like rings in a tree trunk, not all of that, don't think of that. My recent memory, the memory that would tell me how I came to be here, now. There was nothing. A thick wall lay between me here and me there.

I recited tables inside my head. I could do the two times table, and the three, but after that I got muddled. Everything became jumbled up. I started to cry again. Silently.

I shuffled forward until I found the drop. I struggled into a sitting position. It couldn't be that high. He had stood beneath me and lifted me down. Four feet, maybe five. Not more, surely. I wriggled my feet in their bindings. I took a deep breath and shuffled forward a few inches more, so I was teetering on the edge. I would count to five, then I'd jump. One, two, three, four . . .

I heard a sound. A sound at the other end of the room. Wheezing laughter. He was watching me. Squatting in the dark like a toad, watching me writhing around pathetically on the platform. A sob rose in my chest.

'Go on, then. Jump.'

I wriggled backwards.

'See what happens when you fall.'

Back a bit more. Legs on the ledge now. I shifted myself back against the wall and lay slumped there. Tears rolled down my cheeks, under my hood.

'Sometimes I like watching you,' he said. 'You dunno, do you? When I'm here and when I'm not. I'm quiet, like.'

Eyes in the darkness, watching me.

*

'What time is it?'

'Drink your water.'

'Please. Is it still morning? Or afternoon?'

'That doesn't matter any more.'

'Can I . . . ?'

'What?'

What? I didn't know. What should I ask for? 'I'm just an ordinary person,' I said. 'I'm not good but I'm not bad either.'

'Everyone has a breaking point,' he said. 'That's the thing.'

Nobody knows what they would do, if it came to it. Nobody knows. I thought of the lake, and the river, and the yellow butterfly on the green leaf. I made myself a picture of a tree with silver bark and light green leaves. A silver birch. I put it on the top of a smooth green hill. I made a breeze to rustle through its leaves, turning them so that they glinted and shone as if there were lights among the branches. I put a small white cloud just above it. Had I ever seen a tree just like that? I couldn't remember.

'I'm very cold.'

'Yes.'

'Could I have a blanket? Something to cover me.'

'Please.'

'What?'

'You have to say please.'

'Please. Please give me a blanket.'

'No.'

Once again I was filled with wild anger. It felt strong enough to suffocate me. I swallowed hard. Beneath the hood, I stared, blinked. I imagined him looking at me, sitting with my arms behind my back and my neck in a noose and my head in a hood. I was like one of those people you see in newspaper pictures, being led out into a square to be shot by a line of men with guns. But he couldn't see my expression beneath the hood. He didn't know what I was thinking. I made my voice expressionless.

'All right,' I said.

When the time came, would he hurt me? Or was he just going to let me die bit by bit? I was no good with pain. If I was tortured, I would crack and give up any secret, I was sure of that. But this was much worse. He would be torturing me and there would be nothing I could do to stop him, no information to give. Or perhaps he would want sex. Lying on top of me in the dark, forcing me. Pull my hood off, naked face, the rag from my mouth, push in his tongue. Push in his . . . I shook my head violently, and the pain in my head was almost a relief.

I had once read or heard or been told how soldiers who wanted to join the SAS were ordered to run a long distance with a heavy pack on their back. They ran and ran, and at last they arrived at the end, near to collapsing. And then they were ordered to turn round and run the distance back again. You think you can't bear any more, but you can.

There is always more in you than you think. Hidden depths. That's what I told myself. For what was my breaking point?

I was woken by slaps on my face. I didn't want to wake. What was the point? What was there to wake for? Just curl up and sleep. More slaps. Hood pulled up, the gag pulled out of my mouth.

'You awake?'

'Yes. Stop.'

'I've got food. Open your mouth.'

'What food?'

'What the fuck does that matter?'

'Drink first. Mouth dry.'

There was muttering in the dark. Steps going away and down. That was good. A tiny victory. A minuscule bit of control. Steps came back up. The straw in my mouth. I was desperately thirsty but I also needed to rinse away the lint and fluff of the awful old rag I'd been choking on for so long.

'Open your mouth.'

A metal spoon was pushed into my mouth with something soft on it. Suddenly the idea of eating something I couldn't see, pushed into my mouth by this man who was going to kill me, was so disgusting that I imagined chewing on raw human flesh. I started to retch and spit. More swearing.

'Fucking eat or I'll cut the water off for a day.'

A day. That was good. He wasn't planning to kill me today.

'Wait,' I said, and took several deep breaths. 'All right.'

The spoon scraped in a bowl. I felt it in my mouth. I licked the food and swallowed it. It was something porridgy, but blander and smoother and slightly sweet. It tasted like one of those powdery bland mushes for babies. Or it might have been one of those concoctions that is given to convalescents, the sort you buy in a chemist's. I thought of gibbering glassy-eyed people sitting in hospital beds being spoon-fed by bored nurses. I swallowed and more food was pushed into my mouth. Four spoonfuls altogether. I wasn't being fattened, just kept alive. When I was finished I sucked more water through a straw.

'Pudding?' I said.

'No.'

I had an idea. An important idea.

'When did we meet?'

'What do you mean?'

'Since I woke up here, I've had the most terrible headache. Was it you? Did you hit me?'

'What are you on about? Are you fucking me around? Don't you fuck me around. I could do anything to you.'

'I'm not. I don't mean anything like that. The last thing I remember . . . I'm not even sure. It's all so blurred. I can remember being at work, I can remember . . .' I was going to say 'my boyfriend' but I thought that making him jealous, if that's what it would do, might not be a good idea. 'I remember my flat. Doing something in my flat. I woke up here and I've no idea how I got here or how we met. I wanted you to tell me.'

There was a long pause. I almost wondered if he had gone but then there was a whinnying sound, which I realized with a shock was a wheezing laugh.

'What?' I said. 'What did I say? What?'

Keep talking. Maintain communication. I was thinking all the time. Thinking, thinking. Thinking to stay alive, and thinking to stop feeling, because I knew dimly that if I allowed myself to feel I would be throwing myself off a cliff into darkness.

'I've got you,' he said.

'Got me?'

'You're wearing a hood. You're not seeing my face. You're being clever. If you can make me think you never saw me, then maybe I'll let you go.' Another wheezing laugh. 'You think about that, do you, while you're lying there? Do you think about going back to the world?'

I felt a lurch of misery that almost made me howl. But it also made me think. So we did meet. He didn't just grab me from behind in a dark alley and hit me over the head. Do I know this man? If I saw him, would I know his face? If he spoke naturally, would I recognize his voice?

'If you don't believe me, then it doesn't matter if you tell me again, does it?'

The rag was jammed into my mouth. I was lifted down and led over to the bucket. Carried back. Dumped on the ledge. No wire. I took that to mean that he wasn't going out of the building. I felt his breath close on my face, that smell.

'You're lying in here trying to work things out. I like that. You're thinking that if you can make me believe that you can't identify me, I'll play with you for a while, then I'll let you go. You don't understand. You don't see the point. But I like it.' I listened to his scraping whisper, trying to recall if the voice was in any way familiar. 'They're different. Like Kelly, for example. Take Kelly.' He rolled the name round in his mouth as if it was a piece of toffee. 'She just cried and fucking cried all the time. Wasn't a bloody plan. Just crying. It was a bloody relief just to shut her up.'

Don't cry, Abbie. Don't get on his nerves. Don't bore him.

The thought came to me out of the darkness. He's been keeping me alive. I didn't mean that he hadn't killed me. I had been in this room now for two or three or four days. You can live for weeks without food but how long can a human being survive without water? If I had just been locked in this room, unattended, I would be dead or dying by now. The water I'd gulped down had been his water. The food in my gut was his food. I was like an animal on his farm. I was his. I knew nothing about him. Outside this room, out in the world, this man was probably stupid, ugly, repulsive, a failure. He might be too shy to talk to women, workmates might bully him. He could be the silent, weird one in the corner.

But here I was his. He was my lover and my father and my God. If he wanted to come in and quietly strangle me, he could. I had to devote every single waking second to thinking of ways to deal with him. To make him love me, or like me, or be scared of me. If he wanted to break down a woman before killing her, then I had to remain strong. If he hated women for their hostility, then I had to reassure him. If he tortured women who rejected him, then I had to . . . what? Accept him? Which was the right choice? I didn't know.

Always and above all I had to stop myself believing that it probably didn't matter what I did.

I didn't count the time without the wire. It didn't seem to matter. But after a time he came back in. I felt his presence. A hand on my shoulder made me start. Was he checking I was still alive?

Two choices. I could escape in my mind. The yellow butterfly. Cool water. Water to drink, water to plunge into. I tried to re-create my world in my head. The flat. I walked through the rooms, looked at pictures on the wall, touched the carpet, named the objects on shelves. I walked around my parents' house. There were odd blanks. My father's garden shed, the drawers in Terry's desk. But still. So much in my head. So many things. In there and out there. But sometimes as I was wandering through these imaginary rooms, the floor would disappear from beneath my feet and I would fall. These mind games might be keeping me sane but I mustn't just keep sane. I must also keep alive. I must make plans. I wanted to kill him, I wanted to hurt, gouge, mash him. All I needed was an opportunity but I couldn't see any possibility of an opportunity.

I tried to imagine that he hadn't really killed anybody. He might be lying to scare me. I couldn't make myself believe it. He wasn't just making an obscene phone call. I was here, in this room. He didn't need to make up stories. I knew nothing about this man but I knew he had done this before. He had practised. He was in control. The odds against me were bad. They were as bad as they could be. So any plan I could come up with didn't have to have a particularly good chance of success. But I couldn't think of any plan at all that had any chance of success. My only plan was to stretch it out as long as I could. But I didn't even know if I was stretching it out. I had a horrible feeling – another horrible feeling, all my feelings were horrible – that this was all on his timetable. All talk, all my feeble plans and strategies, was just noise in his ear like a mosquito buzzing around his head. When he was ready, he would slap it.

'Why do you do this?'
    'What?'
    'Why me? What have I done to you?'
    A wheezing laugh. A rag stuffed in my mouth.

More knee pull-ups. I couldn't do more than sixteen. I was getting worse. My legs hurt. My arms ached.
    Why me? I tried to stop myself asking the question

but I couldn't. I've seen pictures of murdered women, in newspapers and on TV. But not murdered. Hardly ever. No. I'd seen them when they thought their lives were going to be ordinary. I suppose that when the families give the photos to the TV companies they choose the prettiest, smiliest pictures. They're probably from high-school yearbooks most of the time. But they're blown up larger than they were meant to be. It gives them a slightly blurry, creepy feel. They don't know what's going to happen to them and we do. We're not like them.

I couldn't believe that I was going to be one of them. Terry would go through my stuff and find a picture. Probably that stupid one I got for my passport last year in which I look as if I've got something trapped in one of my eyes and I'm smelling a bad smell simultaneously. He'll give it to the police and they'll blow it up so it looks all blurry and I'll be famous for being dead and it's so unfair.

I went through the unlucky women I knew. There was Sadie, who was left a month before Christmas by her boyfriend when she was nearly eight months pregnant. Marie has been in and out of hospital for her chemo-therapy and has been wearing a headscarf. Pauline and Liz were made redundant from the firm when Laurence did the belt-tightening the year before last. He told them on a Friday evening when everybody had left, and when we came in on Monday morning they were gone. Even six months later Liz was still crying about it. They're all luckier than me. And some time in the next few days they'll know it. They'll hear about it and they'll each become mini-celebrities in their own right. They'll be saying to acquaintances, colleagues at work, with excitement covered with a thin layer of deepest sympathy,

'You know that woman, Abbie Devereaux, the one in the papers? I knew her. I can't believe it.' And they'll all be shocked and they'll all tell themselves secretly that they might have had their problems but at least they weren't Abbie Devereaux. Thank God that the lightning had struck her and not them.

But I am Abbie Devereaux and it's not fair.

He came in and slipped the wire around my throat. I was going to count this time. I'd been thinking about this, planning it. How would I stop myself losing count? I worked out a plan. Sixty seconds in a minute, sixty minutes in an hour. That's 3,600 seconds. I would imagine walking up a hill in a town beginning with A. A hill with 3,600 houses and I would count the houses as I walked past them. I couldn't think of a town beginning with A, though. Yes, Aberdeen. I walked up the hill in Aberdeen. One, two, three, four . . . When I got to the top of the hill in Aberdeen, I began again in Bristol. Then Cardiff, then Dublin, Eastbourne, Folkestone and then, when I was half-way up the hill in Gillingham, he was back in the room, the wire was slipped off my neck. Six and a half hours.

If you are in a hole, stop digging. A stitch in time saves nine. Don't cross a bridge till you come to it. Don't burn your bridges. Was that right, two sets of bridges? What else? Think, think, think. No use crying over spilt milk. Look before you leap. Too many cooks spoil the broth and many hands make light work and don't put all your eggs in one basket and birds of a feather flock together and one swallow doesn't make a summer. Red sky at night, shepherd's delight. My delight. But red sky in the morning, shepherd's warning. How many roads must a man walk down, before . . . ? No, that was something else. A song. A song not a saying. What was the tune? I tried to remember, to put music in my brain and to hear the sound in this dense and silent dark. No use.

Pictures were easier. A yellow butterfly on a green leaf. Don't fly away. A river, with fish in it. A lake of clear, clean water. A silver tree on a smooth hill, with its leaves furling in the breeze. What else? Nothing else. Nothing. I was too cold.

'Hello. I was hoping you would come soon.'

'You haven't finished your water.'

'There's no hurry, is there? There are so many things I wanted to ask you.'

He made a faint guttural sound. I was shaking, but perhaps that was because I was so chilled. I couldn't imagine ever being warm again, or clean. Or free.

'I mean, here we are, two people alone in this place. We should get to know each other. Talk to each other.' He said nothing. I couldn't tell if he was even listening. I drew a breath and continued: 'After all, you must have chosen me for a reason. You seem like a man who has reasons, is that right? You're logical, I think. I like that. Logical.' Was logical a word? It sounded all wrong.

'Go on,' he said.

Go on. Good. What should I say next? There was a sore patch above my lip. I put out the tip of my tongue to touch it; it felt like a cold sore. Perhaps my whole body was breaking out in sores and blisters. 'Yes. Logical. Purposely.' No. Definitely the wrong word. Try again. 'Purposeful. You're someone who is strong. Am I right?' There was a silence. I could hear him breathing hoarsely. 'Yes. I think I'm right. Men should be strong, though many are weak. Many,' I repeated. 'But I think you're

35

lonely as well. People don't recognize your hopes. No, your strengths, I meant strengths, not hopes. Are you lonely?' But it was like dropping stones into a deep well. I spoke the stupid words and they disappeared into the darkness. 'Or do you like being alone?'

'Maybe.'

'We all need someone to love us, though,' I said. 'No one can be all alone.' I would do anything to survive, I thought. I'd let him hold me and fuck me and I'd even pretend I liked it. Anything, to live. 'And there must have been a reason you chose me, rather than somebody else.'

'Do you want to hear what I think? Eh? Do you?' He put a hand on my thigh. He rubbed his hand up and down.

'Yes. Tell me.' Oh, don't let me be sick and don't let me scream out loud.

'I think you haven't got a clue what you look like at the moment.' He gave his wheezy laugh. 'You think you can flirt with me, eh? Trap me like that, as if I'm stupid? But you've no idea what you look like, sweetheart. You don't look like a person at all. You haven't even got a face. You look like a–a–a *thing*. Or an animal. And you smell, too. You smell of piss and shit.' He laughed once more, and his hand on my thigh tightened until he was pinching me hard and I cried out in pain and humiliation.

'Abbie, who tried so hard,' he whispered. 'Kelly who cried and Abbie who tried. I can make you into a rhyme. Cried, tried, died. It's all the same to me, in the end.'

Cried, tried, died. Rhymes in the dark again. Time was running out. I knew it was. I imagined an hourglass with the sand falling through it in a steady stream. If you looked at it, the sand always seemed to fall faster as it reached the end.

He was lifting me off the ledge again. My toes buzzed with pins and needles and my legs felt as if they did not belong to me any more. They were stiff, like sticks, or not like sticks, like twigs that might snap at any moment. I stumbled and lurched and he held on to my arm to keep me upright. His fingers dug into my flesh. Perhaps they were leaving bruises there, four on top and one underneath. I could tell there was a light. It was dark grey not black inside the hood. He dragged me along the floor, then said: 'Sit. Bucket.'

He didn't bother to untie my wrists. He tugged down my trousers himself. I felt his hands on my flesh. I didn't care. I sat. I felt the metal rim under me and behind my back. I curled my fingers round it and tried to breathe calmly. When I'd finished, I stood up and he pulled up the trousers again. They were loose on me now. I took a kick at the bucket and sent it flying. I heard it hit his legs and tip. He grunted and I launched myself blindly in the direction of the grunt, screaming as hard as I could with the rag stuffed in my mouth. It didn't sound like a scream, but a shallow croaking noise. I hurtled into him, but it was like running into a solid wall. He put up an arm to stop me and I brought up my head and butted him in the chin. Pain filled my head; there was red behind my eyes.

'Oh,' he said. Then he hit me. And hit me again. He held me by the shoulder and he punched me in the stomach. 'Oh, Abbie,' he said.

I sat on the ledge. Where did I hurt? Everywhere. I could no longer tell which bit of me was which. Where the pain in my head stopped and the pain in my neck began; where the cold in my legs became the cold in my body; where the taste in my ulcerous mouth became the bile in my throat and the nausea in my stomach; where the sound ringing in my ears became the silence packed in around me. I tried to flex my toes but couldn't. I twisted my fingers together. Which fingers belonged to my right hand and which to my left?

I tried the times tables again. I couldn't even make it through the two times table. How was that possible? Even tiny children can do the two times table. They chanted it in class. I could hear the chanting inside my head but it didn't make any sense.

What did I know? I knew I was Abbie. I knew I was twenty-five. I knew it was winter outside. I knew other things too. Yellow and blue makes green, like the blue summer sea meeting the yellow sand. Crushed shells make sand. Melted sand makes glass; water in a glass tumbler, ice chinking. Trees make paper. Scissors, paper, stone. There are eight notes in an octave. There are sixty seconds in a minute, sixty minutes in an hour, twenty-four hours in a day, seven days in a week, fifty-two weeks in a year. Thirty days have September, April, June and November – but I couldn't finish that one off.

I mustn't sleep. And yet I slept, falling into a shallow, muttering dream. Then I woke with a jerk because he was there beside me. There was no light this time. And no water. At first he said nothing, but I could hear him breathing. Then he began his muffled whispering in the darkness.

'Kelly. Kath. Fran. Gail. Lauren.'

I sat quite still. I didn't move at all.

'Kelly. Kath. Fran. Gail. Lauren.'

It was a shuffling drone. He repeated the five names over and again, and I sat there, with my head hung forward a bit as if I was still asleep. There were tears sliding over my cheeks, but he couldn't see that. They stung. I imagined them making tracks down my skin, like snail tracks. Silver.

Then he stood up and left and I went on crying silently in the dark.

'Drink.'

I drank.

'Eat.'

Four more spoonfuls of sweet sludge.

'Bucket.'

My name is Abbie. Abigail Devereaux. Please help me, someone. Please.

Nobody will help me.

Yellow butterfly. Green leaf. Please don't fly away.

He slipped the wire around my neck almost with a kind of tenderness. For the third time, or was it the fourth?

I felt his fingers around the neck checking the position. If I was thinking about him all the time, then I must always be in his mind. What did he feel towards me? Was it a kind of love? Or was he like a farmer with a pig that must be kept penned and fed in the days before it is slaughtered? I imagined him in a day or two coming in and tightening the wire around my neck or cutting my throat as a weary duty.

When he was gone, I began counting again. I did countries this time. I walked along a hot sunny street in Australia counting the houses. It was raining as I climbed a winding medieval lane in Belgium. It was hot in Chad. Cold in Denmark. Blustery in Ecuador. Then at number

2351 in a long, tree-lined avenue in France I heard a door close outside, footsteps. He had been away for about five hours forty minutes. A shorter time than before. He was anxious about me. Or his time away varied at random. What did it matter?

More of the gruel fed to me with a spoon. Not as much as before. I wasn't being fattened. I was being thinned while being kept alive. The bucket. Carried back to the ledge.

'You're feeling tired,' he said.

'What?'

'You're not talking as much.'

I decided to make the effort once more to be bright and charming and strong. It was like dragging an enormously heavy sack up a steep hill.

'Do you miss my talk?' My voice seemed to come from a long way off.

'You're fading.'

'No. Not fading. Just a bit sleepy at the moment. Tired. You know how it is. Very tired. Echoes in my head.' I tried to concentrate on what I was saying, but words didn't seem to fit together properly any more. 'Can you cope with that?' I said, meaninglessly.

'You don't know what I can cope with. You don't know anything about me.'

'There are things I know. Things I don't know, of course, more things. Most. I know you've grabbed me. But why me? I'd like to know why me. I don't know that. Soon they'll catch you. They will. I listen for footsteps. They'll rescue me.'

There was his wheezy laughter beside me. I shivered. Oh, I was cold all over. Cold, dirty, aching, scared.

'It's not a joke,' I said, with an effort. 'They'll save

me. Someone. Terry. I have a boyfriend, you know. Terence Wilmott. He'll come. I have a job. I work at Jay and Joiner's. I tell people what to do. They won't let me go.' That was a mistake, to tell him things like that. I tried to force the words in a different direction. My tongue was thick and my mouth dry. 'Or the police. They'll find me. You should let me go before they find me. I won't tell. I won't tell and I have nothing to tell. There is nothing to tell, after all.'

'You talk too much.'

'Then you talk. Talk to me now.' All I knew was that he mustn't stuff my mouth with a rag and tie a wire round my throat. 'What are you thinking?'

'You'd no way understand what I'm thinking, even if I told you.'

'Try me. Talk to me. We could talk. Find a way out. Find a way for me to go.' No, I shouldn't be saying that. Keep thoughts silent. Concentrate.

A long silence in the darkness. I thought of him sitting out there, a foul, wheezing thing.

'You want me to talk to you?'

'Yes. Can't you tell me your name? No, no, not your real name. Another name – something I can call you.'

'I know what you're trying to do. Do you know what you're trying to do?'

'I want to talk to you.'

'No, you don't, sweetheart. You're trying to be clever. You're trying to be a clever girl. You're trying to be, like, all psychological.'

'No. No.'

'You reckon that you can become my friend.' He chuckled. 'You're tied up and you know you can't escape. You know you can't get at me. I'm in control. The only reason you're alive at this moment is because I want you to be. So you wonder what you can do. You reckon that maybe I'm a sad, lonely man and I'm scared of girls. And if only you can be all friendly with me that I'll let you go. You see, you don't understand at all.'

'I just want to talk. Too much silence.'

'You see, some of them just snivel. They're just like an animal that's been half run over and it's flapping around on the road and it's just waiting to be put out of its misery, to be stamped on. And others tried to bargain with me. Like Fran. She said she'd do anything I wanted if I let her go. As if she had anything to bargain with. What do you think of that?'

I felt sick.

'I don't know.'

'Gail used to pray. I heard her when I took the gag off. Didn't do her any good.'

'How do you know?'

'What do you mean?'

'How do you know it didn't do her any good? You don't know.'

'I know, I promise you. Funny, isn't it? Some whined, some tried to be all seductive. You did a bit of that. Some prayed. Lauren, she fought and fought and never let up. Had to do her in quick. It all amounts to the same thing in the end.'

I wanted to cry. I wanted to sob and sob and be held and comforted and I knew that was the one thing I must never do. Then I would be the flapping wounded animal and he would stamp on me.

'Is this real?' I said.

'What?'

'These women.'

That coughing laugh.

'You'll be with them in a few days. Ask them yourself.'

He went away but things seemed different. He was back again in a few minutes as if he couldn't stay away. He had thought of something else. He had inserted the gag and now he removed it again. I felt his lips near my ear, wet wool and sweet meaty oniony breath.

'One day soon,' he said, 'and you won't know in advance, I'll come in here and I'll give you a piece of paper and a pen and you can write a letter. A goodbye letter. You can write to anybody you want. I'll post it. You can say anything you want, unless I don't like it. I don't want any moaning. It can be like a will if you want. You can leave your favourite teddy bear to somebody or whatever. And then when you've written the letter, I'll do the deed. Did you hear what I said? Yes or no.'

'Yes.'

'Good.'

He pushed the gag into my mouth. He was gone.

I wondered what Gail had prayed for. Did I love life as much as those other women? Kelly, who cried for her lost life. Fran, who desperately offered herself. Lauren who fought. Gail who prayed. For what? Maybe just for peace. For release. I doubted that I was as good as Gail. If I prayed, it wouldn't be for peace. I would pray for a gun and my hands untied. Or a knife. Or a stone. Or a nail. Anything to do damage.

A last letter. No last meal but a last letter. Who would I write to? Terry? What would I say? If you find someone else, be better to them than you were to me. Not exactly. To my parents? I imagined writing a noble letter full of wise thoughts about life that would make everybody feel better. When somebody dies it's important for the people who knew them to find ways of comforting themselves. She didn't suffer. Or, she did suffer, but at least it's over and she is at rest. Or, she showed her spirit to the end. That might make people feel better. Good old Abbie, she managed to crack a few jokes even when she was about to be murdered. What a lesson to us all. What a fucking lesson to us all in how to deal with the problem of being murdered. Pay attention, children. If ever you're captured by a psychopath and he's about to kill you, here's this letter by Abigail Devereaux. That's exactly the spirit in which to be murdered. Brave and forgiving and at the same time not taking herself too seriously.

But I'm not wise and I'm not forgiving and I'm not brave and I just want it all to go away. People talk about what you would have for your last meal as if it were some little game like your desert island discs. Well, if there were a last meal I wouldn't be able to swallow it. And if there's a last letter – a brilliant bit of writing to sum up my life – I won't be able to write it. I can't write a howl in the darkness.

When I was first here, all that time ago, I was tormented by the thought of ordinary people a few hundred yards or a mile away. People in a hurry somewhere, wondering what they were going to watch on TV tonight, feeling for their change, deciding what bar of chocolate to buy. Now it all seems far away. I don't belong to that world any more. I live in a cave deep down in the earth where light has never penetrated.

When I was first here I had a dream about being buried alive. It was the most frightening thing I could think of. I was shut in a dark box. I was pushing at the lid of the box but the lid couldn't be opened because above the lid was thick, heavy earth and above the earth was a stone slab. It seemed the most frightening thing that my brain could think of. Now I think of it and it doesn't seem the most frightening thing at all, because I'm already in that grave. My heart is beating, my lungs are breathing, but it doesn't really matter. I'm dead. I'm in my grave.

'Did I fight back?'

'What are you on about?'

'I don't remember. I want you to tell me. Did I come peacefully? Did you have to force me? I was banged on the head. I don't remember.'

The laugh.

'Still trying that on? It's so too late for that. But if you want to play that game, all right, yeah, you did fight back. I had to smash you up a bit. You fought worse than anybody. I had to give you a few thumps, quieten you down.'

'Good.'

'What?'

'Nothing.'

Do the knee-ups. Don't give up. One, two, three, four, five. Have to do ten. Try. Try harder. Six, seven, eight, nine. One more. Ten. Horrible sickness rising up in me. Don't give up. Breathe, in and out. Never give up.

All right, then. My last letter. It's not to anyone. Well, maybe it's to someone who doesn't exist, whom I might have met in the future. Like writing a diary. I used to write a diary when I was a teenager, but it always had this embarrassing tone. It made me into a stranger, and one I didn't particularly like. I never knew who it was for, or to.

Where was I? Yes. My letter. When did I last write a

letter? I can't remember. I write lots of emails, and every so often I send postcards, you know the kind of thing, the rain is raining or the sun is shining and I'm thinking of you, here, now. But real letters, well, it's been ages. I had a friend called Sheila who went and lived in Kenya in her gap year, doing voluntary work and living in a thatched hut in a small village. I wrote her letters every so often, but I never knew if they were going to arrive, and I discovered when she came home that only a couple of them ever did. It's a strange feeling you get when you're writing to someone and not knowing if they'll ever read it. Like those times when you're talking to someone, really talking, I mean, and you turn round and they've left the room. What happens to those words and thoughts? Things that don't ever arrive.

My mouth felt horrible, full of blisters. My gums were soft and swollen. When I swallowed, it was like swallowing poison, the taste of the rag and the taste of my own decay, so I tried not to do it, but it was very hard.

I sat in the dark, I twisted my hands together. My nails had got longer. One of the facts that everyone knows is that nails go on growing after you've died, but I've heard or read or been told that's not true. It's just the skin shrinks, or something. Who told me that? I couldn't remember. There's a lot I'd forgotten. It was as if things were falling away, one by one, the things that bound me to life.

The letter. Who would I leave my things to? What have I got to leave? I don't have a house, or a flat. I've got a car that's rusty round the edges. Terry tuts when he looks at it, but in a pleased kind of way, as if he's saying, 'Women!' A few clothes, not so many. Sadie can have those except she's bigger than me after having a baby. Some books. A few bits of jewellery, nothing expensive, though. Not much. They could all be sorted out in a couple of hours.

What was it like outside, I wondered. Perhaps it was sunny. I tried to picture sunlight falling on roads and houses, but it was no use. Those pictures had gone – the butterfly, the lake, the river, the tree. I tried to put them in my mind, but they dissolved, wouldn't hold together. Maybe outside it was foggy instead, all the shapes shrouded. I knew it wasn't night yet. At night – for six hours, five hours – he put a noose round my neck and left.

I thought I heard a sound. What was it? Him, padding towards me? Was this it, then? I held my breath, but my heart pounded so fast and blood roared round my head that for a moment all I could hear was the rushing inside my own body. Could you die of fear? No, there was no one there. I was still all alone on my ledge, in the dark. It wasn't time yet. But I knew it would be soon. He watched me. He knew I was coming apart, bit by bit. That was what he wanted. I knew that was what he wanted. He wanted me to stop being me, and then he could kill me.

And I watched myself blindly in the darkness. How can the brain know that it is failing, the mind feel itself disintegrate? Is that what it is like to go mad? Is there a period of time when you know, with the bit of you that is going mad, that you're going mad? When do you give up and, with a ghastly kind of relief, let yourself fall into the abyss? I imagined a pair of hands gripping on to a ledge, hanging on, and then very slowly the fingers relax, uncurl. You fall through space and nothing can stop you.

The letter. Dear anyone, help me, help me, help me, I can't do it any more. Please. Oh, Jesus, please.

My eyes stung and prickled. My throat was sore, sorer than usual, I mean. As if there were bits of grit in it. Or glass. Maybe I was getting a cold. Then I would gradually stop being able to breathe. All blocked up.

'Drink.'

I drank. Just a few sips this time.

'Eat.'

Four spoonfuls of mush. I could barely swallow.

'Bucket.'

I was lifted down, lifted back up. I felt like a rubbishy plastic doll. For a brief moment, I thought about writhing and kicking, but I knew he could squeeze the life out of me. I felt his hands holding me around my ribcage. He could snap me.

'Noose.'

'Piece of shit,' I said.

'What?'

'You. Rubbish. Piece of shit.'

He hit me in the mouth. I could taste my blood. Sweet, metallic.

'Garbage,' I said.

He stuffed the gag into my mouth.

Five hours perhaps, and some minutes. How many was it last time I counted? I couldn't remember any more. Then he'd come back. Perhaps he would be carrying a piece of paper and a pen. Outside, it must be dark now; probably it had been dark for hours. Perhaps there was a moon, stars. I imagined pricks of light in the black sky.

Here I was, alone inside my hood, inside my head. Here I was and nothing else seemed real any more. At first, I had not let myself think of life beyond this room, of ordinary life as it had been. I had thought that would be a way of taunting myself and going mad. Now that I wanted to remember things, I couldn't, or not properly. It was as if the sun had gone in and a storm was brewing and night was coming. It was coming.

I tried to put myself in the flat, but I couldn't. I tried to see myself at work, but I couldn't. Memories lay in gathering darkness. I remembered this, though: I remembered swimming in a loch in Scotland, I couldn't recall when, years ago, and the water was so brackish and murky that you couldn't see through it. I couldn't even see my hands clearly when I stretched them out in front of me. But when I did the crawl, I could see silver bubbles of air in the dark water. Cascading bubbles of silver air.

Why do I remember that when other memories were shutting down? The lights were going out, one by one. Soon there would be nothing left. Then he would have won.

I knew what I was going to do. I wasn't going to write any letter. I wasn't going to wait for him to come into the room with his piece of paper. It was the only power I had left. The power of not waiting for him to kill me. It wasn't much, but it was all I had. No memory, no hope. Just that. And it was perfectly simple, really. If I went on sitting here, sooner or later – and probably sooner, tomorrow or the next day, I could sense the moment was near – he would murder me. Any doubt of that had gone. I was quite sure that he had murdered the other women and he would do the same to me. I wasn't going to outwit him. I wasn't going to escape when he lifted me down. I wasn't going to persuade him that he should set me free after all. The police weren't going to burst into the room and rescue me. Terry wasn't going to come. Nobody was. I wasn't going to wake up one morning and discover it had all been a nightmare. I was going to die.

I told myself this at last. If I waited, he would kill me, as sure as anything was sure. I felt no hope at all. My pitiful attempts to change that had been like hurling myself against a solid wall. But if I threw myself off this ledge, the noose would hang me. That's what he had told me, and I could feel the wire round my neck if I leant forward. He must have known that I wouldn't try. Nobody in their right mind would kill themselves in order not to die.

Yet that is exactly what I was going to do. Throw myself off. Because it was the only thing left I could do. My last chance to be Abbie.

And I didn't have much time. I would have to do it before he came back, while I still could. While I had the will.

I breathed in and held my breath. Why not now, before I lost courage? I breathed out again. Because it's impossible to do it, that's why. You think: Just one more second of life. One more minute. Not now. Any time that isn't now.

And if you jump, then you're saying no more breath and no more thought; no more sleeping and knowing you'll wake, no more fear, no more hope. So, of course, you hold off, like when you climb up to the high diving board and all the time you think you can do it until you reach the top step and walk along the springy platform and look down at the turquoise water and it all seems so horribly far away and you know you can't, after all. Can't. Because it is impossible.

But then you do. Almost without knowing in advance, while in your mind you are turning round and heading back to safety, you step off and you're falling. No more waiting. No more terror. No more. And maybe in any case it would be better to die. If I'm going to die, better to kill myself.

And I do what I know I can't. I do jump. I do fall.

Terrible pain around my neck. Flashes of colour behind my eyes. A small interested corner of my brain looked on and said to itself: This is what it is like to die. The last gulps of air, the final pumps of blood before the fading into death and not existing.

The lights did fade but the pain became sharper and more localized. My neck. A scraping on a cheek. One leg felt as if it had been bent backwards. My face, my breasts, my stomach were so hard on the ground it felt for a moment as if I'd pulled the wall down with me and it was lying on top of me, weighing me down.

And I wasn't dead. I was alive.

Then a thought came into my mind like a jab of steel right through me. I wasn't tied down. He wasn't here. How long had he gone? Think. Think. This time I hadn't counted. Quite a long time. My wrists were still tied behind my back. I tugged at them. Useless. I almost sobbed. Had I done this just to lie helpless on the floor? I swore to myself that if I could do nothing else I would kill myself by smashing my head on the stone. If I had no other power, I could at least deny him that pleasure.

My body felt sore and starved into weakness. And there was a new fear. I had virtually abandoned myself to death and there had been peace in that. It had been a form of anaesthetic. But now I had a chance. That knowledge brought feelings back into my limbs. I was able to be very, very frightened again.

I swung my body around. Now my back was resting on my tethered arms. If I could push them over my feet so they were in front of me. It was a gymnast's trick and I'm so far from being a gymnast. I raised my feet off the ground and stretched them back as if I were going to touch the ground behind my head. Now the pressure was off my wrists. I made an exploratory attempt to pull my hands round. They wouldn't go round. I pushed and pushed. No. I groaned. Then I spoke to myself. Silently. It went like this: Some time soon, in one minute or three hours or maybe five, he will come back and he will kill you. There will absolutely definitely never be another chance after this one. You know this can be done. You have seen children doing it as a game. You probably did it when you were a girl. You would cut your hands off, if that would get you out of these knots. You don't have to do that. You just have to get your hands in front of you. If it means you need the strength to dislocate your shoulders, then do it. Strain yourself. Get ready. Five, four, three, two, one.

And I pushed with all the force in my body. I thought my arms would come away from my shoulders and I pushed harder and my hands were behind my thighs. If my ankles hadn't been tied together it would have been easier. Now I was trussed up like a pig ready to have a bolt shot into its head. I made myself think of that as I pulled my knees down on to my chest, back as far as I could, and worked my hands round my feet. The muscles in my back, my neck, my arms and shoulders were screaming but suddenly my arms were in front of me and I was gasping and felt the sweat running off me.

I sat up and pulled the hood off my head with my tied hands, thinking as I did so that he would be there looking at me when I did it. I pulled the gag out of my mouth and drank air as if it were cold water. It was dark. No, not entirely dark. Very dim light. I looked at my wrists.

They were secured by some sort of wire. It wasn't knotted. The ends were twisted around each other. With my teeth it was really quite easy to undo. It just took time. Ten horrible seconds for each twist and my lips were bleeding now. And then, with the last twist, it came away and my hands were free. I freed my ankles within a couple of minutes. I stood up and then fell immediately, shouting in pain. My feet felt as if they were being pumped up and were going to burst. I rubbed and scratched at my ankles until I could stand again.

I looked around. In the near darkness I could see brick walls, the dirty cement floor. There were some rough shelves, broken pallets on the floor. I could see the ledge where I had spent the past days. Then I remembered. I lifted the wire noose over my head. One end was attached to a bolt that my fall had pulled out of the wall. How lucky had I been? I felt my neck with the tips of my fingers.

I looked in the direction the man had always come from. There was a closed wooden door with no handle on the inside. I tried to grasp it with my fingers but I couldn't get any purchase. I needed something quick. On the other side of the room there was a dark doorway. I walked across and looked through it. I couldn't see anything. The idea of walking into the dark seemed horrible. The only way out I was sure of was the closed wooden door. Maybe it was the only way out. Was there any sense in getting further away from that possible means of escape?

I was panting and shivering and sweating. The beating of my heart was echoing in my ears but I tried to stop and make myself think. What could I do? I could hide somewhere in the darkness. He might think I'd gone and run out, leaving the door open. It seemed hopeless. He would probably just switch a light on and catch me straight away. I could find some weapon. I could hide by the door and really smash him when he came in. That was so tempting. Even if it failed, and it surely would fail, I would have a chance to damage him and that was what I wanted to do more than anything. I wanted to rip the flesh off his bones.

No, the best chance must be to try to get out through that door while he was away. I didn't know if the door was actually locked. I felt around on the floor for something I could use to lever it open. I touched some useless pieces of wood and then felt a strip of metal. If I could hook that on to the door, I could pull it. Or if there was a latch on the other side, then I might be able to push the strip through the crack in the door and raise it. I came close to the door and felt for the crack. I was about to slip the strip through when I heard a sound. I stopped breathing and listened. There was no doubt. I heard the rattle of a door opening, footsteps. I almost sank down on the floor in tears. .

The whole idea of staying by the door and wrestling with him was just stupid. I tiptoed across the room into the awful darkness. If it were just a closed storeroom I would be trapped like an animal. I ran through into what seemed like a corridor. There were entrances on either side. Get further away. Buy myself some time. He might have to search them. I ran along to the back where there was a wall. There was a doorway on either side. I looked through the left. Nothing but dark. Through the right. There really was something. I could see a light. Up in the wall across the floor. Through some sort of glass. Behind me, far behind me in the darkness, I heard a noise, a shout, a door, footsteps, and from then on everything was like one of those nightmares in which things happen in the wrong order, in which you run as fast as you can but the ground has become like soup and you don't get anywhere, you are pursued and don't get away. I left it to some primitive, instinctive part of my brain to make the decisions and save my life. I know that I grabbed something and there was the sound of shattering glass and I was pushing myself through a gap that felt too small for me but I was through and there was a raking pain along my body and there was something wet. There was a banging noise somewhere. It was behind me. And shouting.

I ran up some steps. I could feel wind. Air. I could feel outside. There were lights in the distance. I ran and ran towards them. Running in a dream. Running past objects and not seeing what they were. Running because if I stopped I was dead. My feet, in their socks, stumbled and tripped on the cold ground. Pebbles and sharp objects bit into them. He would be fast. I had to run randomly in different directions. I wasn't able to see properly. Those days underground. The lights hurt my eyes like a flare through frosted glass. I heard my own footsteps, unnaturally loud even without shoes. Just keep on running. Don't think about where it hurts; don't think about anything. Run.

Somewhere inside me I knew that I needed to find something moving. A car. A person. I mustn't run into anywhere deserted. People. Get to people. But I couldn't run and concentrate. Mustn't stop. Mustn't. And then there it was, a light in a window. I was in a street of houses. Some were boarded up. More than boarded up. They had heavy metal grilles across the doors and windows. But there was a light. I had a moment of great lucidity. I wanted to run to the door and scream and shout and bang on it but I had this fear – among all the other fears – that if I did that, the person inside would turn the television up higher and he would come and find me and take me back.

So in a mad way I just pressed the doorbell and heard a chime somewhere far inside. Answer answer answer answer. I heard footsteps. Slow, quiet shuffling. Finally, after a million years, the door opened and I fell on it and through and on to the floor.

'Police. Please. Police. Please.'

And even as I was lying there clawing at someone's lino, I knew it just sounded like 'please please please please please'.

Part Two

'Do you want me to make a proper statement?'

'Later,' he said. 'For the moment I'd just like us to talk.'

I couldn't see him properly at first. He was a silhouette against the window of my hospital room. My eyes were sensitive to the glare and I had to look away. When he came closer to the bed I was able to make out his features, his short brown hair, dark eyes. He was Detective Inspector Jack Cross. He was the person I could now leave everything to. But first I had to explain it all to him. There was so much.

'I've already talked to somebody. A woman in a uniform. Jackson.'

'Jackman. I know. I wanted to hear it for myself. What do you remember first?'

That was how I told the story. He asked questions and I tried to answer them and after more than an hour I answered one of his questions and he was silent and I felt I had said everything I could possibly say. He was silent for several minutes. He didn't smile at me or even look at me. I saw different expressions move across his face. Confusion, frustration, deep thought. He rubbed his eyes.

'Two more things,' he said finally. 'Your memory. The last thing you remember is what? Being at work? At home?'

'I'm sorry. That's all blurry. I've spent days thinking and thinking. I remember being at work. Bits of my flat. I don't have a definite last moment.'

'So you have no memory of encountering this man.'

'No.'

He took a small notebook out of a side pocket, and a pen.

'And those other names.'

'Kelly. Kath. Fran. Gail. Lauren.'

He wrote them down as I spoke them.

'Do you remember anything about them? A second name? Any suggestion of where he found them, what he did to them?'

'I told you everything.'

He shut the notebook with a sigh and stood up. 'Wait,' he said, and walked away.

I'd already become used to the pace of hospital life, the slow motion with long pauses in between, so I was surprised when barely five minutes later the detective returned with an older man, dressed in an immaculate pin-striped suit. A white handkerchief protruded from his breast pocket. He picked up the clipboard on the end of my bed as if it was all a bit boring. He didn't ask me how I felt. But he looked at me as if I were something he had stumbled over.

'This is Dr Richard Burns,' said DI Cross. 'He's in charge of your case. We're going to move you. You're going to have a room of your own. With a TV.'

Dr Burns replaced the clipboard. He took off his spectacles.

'Miss Devereaux,' he said. 'We're all going to be rather busy with you.'

The cold air hit me in the face, as if someone had slapped me. I gasped and my breath plumed up in the air. My eyes stung with the cold glare of light.

'It's all right,' said Jack Cross. 'You can get back into the car if you want.'

'I like it.' I tipped my head back and breathed in deeply. The sky was completely blue, not even a wisp of cloud, and the sun was a washed-out disc, casting no heat. Everything sparkled with frost. Dirty old London looked wonderful.

We were in a street of terraced houses. Most of them were boarded up with planks, some had metal grilles across their entrances and windows. The small front gardens were thick with nettles and brambles and rubbish.

'It was here, wasn't it?'

'Number forty-two,' said Cross, pointing across the street. 'This is where you fetched up and scared Tony Russell half to death. You remember this at least?'

'It's all a bit of a daze,' I said. 'I was in a blind panic. I thought he was right behind me. I was running as randomly as possible to shake him off.'

I looked across at the house. It hardly looked less abandoned than the rest of the street. Cross leant back into the car and retrieved an anorak. I was dressed in a strange assemblage of other people's clothing that had been found for me in the hospital. I tried not to think of the women who might have worn them before. Cross's manner was affable and relaxed. We might have been strolling to a pub.

'I hoped we could retrace your footsteps,' he said. 'Which direction did you come from?'

That was easy. I pointed down the street, away from where we'd come.

'That makes sense,' he said. 'Let's go there, then.'

We walked down the street.

'That man I said,' I said. 'The one in number forty-two.'

'Russell,' said Cross. 'Tony Russell.'

'Did he see him?'

'He's not much of a witness,' said Cross, 'old Tony Russell. In any case, he slammed the door shut and dialled 999.'

At the end of the street I expected more rows of terraced houses but instead we were faced with one corner of a huge, almost completely derelict housing estate whose windows were smashed and doors boarded up. There were two archway entrances immediately ahead and others further down.

'What's this?' I said.

'The Browning estate,' said Cross.

'Does anybody live here?'

'It's due for demolition. It's been due for demolition for twenty years.'

'Why?'

'Because it's a shithole.'

'This must have been where I was kept.'

'Do you remember?'

'I know I came from this direction.' I looked up and down desperately. 'I ran under one of those archways. I must have been in that estate.'

'You reckon?'

'I suppose so.'

'Do you remember which archway you came through?'

I walked across the road. I looked so hard that it hurt. 'They're quite similar. It was dark, I was running desperately. I'm so sorry. I'd had a hood over my eyes for days. I was almost hallucinating. I was in such a state.'

Cross took a deep breath. He was obviously disappointed.

'Maybe we can narrow down the possibilities.'

We walked up and down the street and into the courtyards through the archway. It was awful. I could just about see what must have been in the architect's head when he designed it. It would have been like an Italian village, piazzas, open spaces for people to sit and walk and talk. Lots of little passageways so that people could walk through and around it. But it hadn't worked out. Cross pointed out to me how the passageways had been perfect for all different kinds of concealment, for shooting up, for mugging, for getting away. He showed me where a body had been found in a skip.

I became more and more miserable. All the spaces and arcades and terraces looked the same. And in the daylight it looked like nothing I'd ever seen before. Cross was patient with me. He just waited, his hands thrust into his pockets and his breath curling up into the air. He started asking me about time instead of direction. Did I remember how long it had taken me to run from the building to Tony Russell's house? I tried to recall it. I couldn't get it to make sense. He kept trying. Five minutes? I didn't know. More? Less? I didn't know. Had I run all the way? Yes, of course I had. As fast as I could? Yes, I'd thought he might be behind me. I had run so fast that it hurt. So how far would I be able to run at top speed? I didn't know. A few minutes? I couldn't tell. It wasn't normal. I was running for my life.

Gradually the day seemed colder, greyer.

'I'm not helping, am I?' I said.

Cross seemed distracted and hardly heard me. 'What?' he said.

'I wanted to do better.'

'Take your time.'

Jack Cross barely spoke on the short journey back to the hospital. He stared out of the window. He murmured a few routine words to the driver.

'Are you going to search the estate?' I asked.

'I wouldn't know where to start,' he said. 'There's over a thousand derelict flats there.'

'I was underground, I think. Or in a basement. Or at least on the ground floor.'

'Miss Devereaux, the Browning estate is about a quarter of a mile square. Or more. I don't have the men.'

He walked back with me to my new special room. That was something, a room of my own. He stopped at the door.

'I'm sorry,' I said. 'I thought it would go better.'

'Don't worry,' he said, with a smile that quickly faded. 'We're depending on you. You're all we've got. If there's anything else . . .'

'There's the other women – Kelly, Kath, Fran, Gail and Lauren. Can't you check them out?'

Suddenly Jack Cross looked weary of it all.

'I've got someone on it. But I've got to say, it's not as simple as you think.'

'What do you mean?'

'How do you imagine I can check for the names? We don't have a last name, any location, a date, even an approximate one. We have nothing. We've got a bunch of common first names.'

'So what can you do?'

He shrugged.

A nurse wheeled a telephone into my room and gave me a small handful of change. I waited until she was out of the room and then fed in a twenty-pence piece.

'Mum?'

'Abigail, is that you?'

'Yes.'

'Is everything all right?'

'Mum, I wanted to tell you . . .'

'I've had the most terrible time.'

'Mum, I just needed to talk to you, to tell you something.'

'It's the pains in my stomach. I've not been sleeping.'

I paused for a moment. I took a deep breath. 'I'm sorry,' I said. 'Have you been to the doctor?'

'I'm always going to the doctor. He gave me some pills, but he doesn't take it seriously. I've not been sleeping.'

'That's awful.' My hand tightened round the phone. 'You couldn't come to London for the day, could you?'

'To London?'

'Yes.'

'Not at the moment, Abigail. Not the way I've been feeling. I can't go anywhere.'

'It's less than an hour on the train.'

'And your father's not been well.'

'What's wrong?'

'His usual. But why don't you come and see us? It's been ages.'

'Yes.'

'Give us some notice, though.'

'Yes.'

'I should go,' she said. 'I'm making a cake.'

'Yes. All right.'

'Ring again soon.'

'Yes.'

'Goodbye, then.'

'Goodbye,' I said. 'Goodbye, Mum.'

I was woken by a large machine being pushed through the door. It was a monstrous floor-cleaning machine with a revolving circular contraption and nozzles releasing soapy water. It would quite obviously have been far better to use a bucket and a mop and this machine was especially useless in the confined space of my room. It couldn't reach into the corners and it couldn't go under the bed and it didn't like tables very much so the man behind it pushed it along the few exposed spaces. He was followed by another man. This man didn't look like a cleaner or a nurse or even a doctor since he was dressed in black shoes, baggy brown trousers, a navy blue jacket that looked as if it was made out of sacking, and an open-necked checked shirt. He had wiry all-over-the-place grey hair. He was carrying a stack of files under his arm. He was trying to speak. I could see his mouth moving. But the noise of the cleaning machine drowned everything so he stood rather awkwardly by the wall until the machine had passed him and headed down the ward. He looked dubiously after it.

'One day somebody's going to check one of those machines and discover it doesn't do anything,' he said.

'Who are you?' I said.

'Mulligan,' he said. 'Charles Mulligan. I've come to have a word with you.'

I got out of the bed.

'Have you got any identification?'

'What?'

I walked past him and shouted for a passing nurse. She looked reluctant but she saw that I meant business. I said that a stranger had come into my room. There was a brief argument and she led him away to make a phone call. I went back to bed. A few minutes later the door of my room opened and the man was led back in by a more senior-looking nurse. 'This man has permission to see you,' she said. 'He will be with you for a very short time.'

She left with a suspicious glance at Charles Mulligan. He took some horn-rimmed glasses from his jacket pocket and put them on.

'That was probably sensible,' he said. 'It was very boring but probably sensible. What I was in the middle of saying was that Dick Burns rang me and asked me to have a word with you.'

'Are you a doctor?'

He put down his files on the table and pulled a chair over towards the bed. 'Is it all right if I sit down?'

'Yes.'

'I am a doctor. I mean, I'm qualified as a doctor. I don't spend much of my time in the hospital.'

'Are you a psychiatrist? Or a psychologist?'

He gave a nervous, chopping ha-ha laugh.

'No, no, no, I'm a neurologist, really, more or less. I study the brain as if it were a thing. I work with computers and cut up mouse brains, that sort of thing. I talk to people as well, of course. When necessary.'

'I'm sorry,' I said. 'But what are you doing here?'

'I said. Dick rang me up. Fascinating case.' A sudden expression of alarm appeared on his face. 'I know it was awful as well. I'm terribly sorry. But Dick asked if I could come and have a look at you. Is that all right?'

'What for?'

He rubbed his face with his hands and looked almost excessively sympathetic. 'Dick told me something of what you've gone through. It's horrible. I'm sure somebody will be coming to talk to you about that. About the trauma. And all of that.' His sentence had trailed off and he looked lost. Now he pushed his fingers through his curly hair. It didn't do much to neaten it. 'Now, Abigail, is it all right if I call you that?' I nodded. 'And call me Charlie. I'd like to talk to you about your amnesia.

Do you feel up to that?' I nodded again. 'Good.' He gave a faint smile. He had got on to his real subject and his talk, his whole manner, was more assured. I liked that. 'Now, this is the only time I'm going to behave like a real doctor, but I'd like to have a look at your head. Is that all right?' More nodding. 'I looked at your notes. Plenty of bruising all over, but no particular reference to headaches, soreness on the head, that sort of thing. Is that right?'

'My very first memory, from after the bit where I lost my memory, if you know what I mean. I woke up and I had a terrible pain in my head.'

'Right. Do you mind if I take some notes?' He took a mangy little notebook out of his pocket and began writing. Then he put it on the bed and leant forward. 'They're going to pop you into a machine later for a quick look at your brain. But this is a different sort of examination. Do you mind?' As he said this, he leant forward and very gently touched my face and all over my head. I love my head being touched. It's my secret fetish. The main thing I love about getting my hair cut is having my hair washed by a stranger, those fingers on my scalp. Terry as well. Sometimes we'd sit in the bath together and he'd wash my hair. That's what relationships are for, little things like that. Charles Mulligan gave a little murmuring sound as his fingertips pattered over my head. I gave a little cry when he touched above my right ear. 'That hurt?'

'It's just sore.' He looked more closely. 'Is there a problem?'

'Swollen and bruised – but I can't see anything significant.' He sat back. 'There. That's all done.' He reached over for a file. It took some rummaging to find the right one. 'Now I'm going to ask you some questions. They might seem a bit silly, but bear with me. They'll take a bit of time. Are you up to it? I could come back later, or tomorrow, if you need a rest. I know you've had a hard day.'

I shook my head. 'I just want to do anything I can as quickly as possible.'

'Great.' He opened a large printed booklet. 'You ready?'

'Yes.'

'What's your name?'

'Is this part of the test?'

'That's sort of a philosophical question. Do you want to bear with me?'

'Abigail Elizabeth Devereaux.'

'When were you born?'

'The twenty-first of August, 1976.'

'What's the name of the Prime Minister?'

'Are you serious? I'm not *that* bad.'

'I'm testing various kinds of memory. It'll get harder.'

So I told him the name of the Prime Minister. I told him the day of the week and that we were in St Anthony's Hospital. I counted backwards from twenty. I counted forwards in threes. I counted backwards from a hundred in sevens. I was rather proud of myself. Then it started to get hard. He showed me a page of different shapes. He chatted to me for a moment about something stupid and then showed me another page of shapes. I had to remember which were on both sheets. He got a bit embarrassed as he read me a story about a boy taking a pig to the market. I had to tell it back to him. He showed me stars and triangles paired with colours, word pairs. He showed me four increasingly complicated shapes. The fourth one looked like a vandalized electricity pylon. It made me dizzy even to look at, let alone draw from memory.

'This is giving me a bloody headache,' I said, as I struggled with it.

'Are you all right?' he said, with concern.

'It makes my head spin.'

'I know what you mean,' he said. 'I get stuck at the counting backwards. Don't worry, there are just a couple more.'

He started to recite sequences of numbers. Groups of three and four were a doddle. He stopped at eight, which I could just about manage. Then I had to recite the sequences backwards – that really made my brain ache. After that he brought out a sheet of coloured squares. He tapped them in an order which I had to repeat. Again up to eight. And then backwards.

'Fuck,' I said, when he put the sheet away.

'Yes,' he said. 'That's all. We're done.'

'So, did I pass? Am I brain-damaged?'

He smiled cheerfully. 'I don't know. I have no tests for the pre-morbid period. Sorry, that sounds grim. I mean for the period before the onset of amnesia. But I can't believe that it was much better than this. You've got a remarkably good memory. Your spatial recall in particular is excellent. I'd swap you any time.'

I couldn't help blushing. 'Well, thanks, um, Charlie, but . . .'

He looked serious for a moment and peered at me closely. 'What do *you* think?' he said.

'I feel fine. I mean, I don't feel fine. I have bad dreams and I keep going over and over things in my head. But I can think clearly. It's just that gap in my memory. I keep trying and trying to remember but it's like staring into pitch darkness.'

He began putting the papers back into files.

'Try looking at the boundaries,' he said. 'Take your

image of an area of darkness. You could say that there is an area that's entirely dark and another that's entirely light. You could try concentrating on where the two areas meet.'

'I've done that, Charlie. Oh, God, I've done it. There's no problem for the afterwards bit. I woke up and I was there in that place. I didn't know how I'd got there, didn't remember being grabbed. Before it's different. I can't remember the last thing I did or anything like that. There's no cut-off point. I just have vague recent memories of being at work. It was like I went into the darkness slowly without noticing.'

'I see,' Charles said, and wrote something more. It made me nervous when he did that.

'But isn't there something ridiculous about it? The one thing I need to remember is gone. I don't want to know who the bloody Prime Minister is. I want to remember how I was grabbed, what he looks like. What I've been thinking is, could it be something that happened that was so disturbing that I've suppressed it?'

He clicked his pen shut. When he replied it was almost as if he were trying to hide a faint smile. 'And that maybe I could dangle my watch in front of your face and it would all come flooding back?'

'That would be very useful.'

'Maybe,' he said. 'But I'm sure your amnesia is unrelated to any form of post-traumatic stress. Or indeed any psychological symptom.'

'When I'm talking to Cross – I mean the police – it just feels so ridiculous.'

'It's unfortunate and frustrating,' he said. 'But it's not ridiculous. Post-traumatic amnesia after a closed head injury such as yours isn't uncommon. It usually happens in car crashes. They bang their head during the smash.

When they wake up after the injury they don't remember the crash, but often they don't remember the hours or even days leading up to it either.'

I touched my head gently. Suddenly it felt so fragile.

'Post-traumatic,' I said. 'I thought you said it wasn't something psychological.'

'It isn't,' he said. 'Psychogenic amnesia – I mean amnesia caused by psychological influences, rather than an injury to the brain – is rarer in cases like yours. And also – how shall I say? – more dubious.'

'What do you mean?'

He gave a wary cough. 'I'm not a psychologist, so maybe I'm biased. But, for example, a substantial percentage of murderers claim to have no memory of committing their murders. These are not people who have received physical injuries. There could be various explanations. They are often very drunk, which can result in memory black-outs. Committing a murder is, presumably, an extremely stressful thing to do, more than almost anything else that can be imagined. That could affect memory. Some of us sceptics might also say that there is often an incentive for a murderer to claim he has no memory of what happened.'

'But being kidnapped and threatened with death must be pretty bloody stressful. Couldn't that have made me forget for psychological reasons?'

'Not in my opinion, but if I were standing in court and you were a lawyer, you could get me to admit that it was possible. I'm afraid you're going to have a few other people prodding you like a lab rat to answer questions like that.'

He stood up and mustered his files under his arm with some difficulty. 'Abigail,' he said.

'Abbie.'

'Abbie. You're a fascinating case. I don't think I'm going to be able to resist coming back.'

'That's all right,' I said. 'I seem to have lots of time on my hands. But I've got one question: is there any chance of my memory coming back?'

He paused for a moment and pulled an odd face, which must have been some sort of indication that he was thinking. 'Yes, it's possible.'

'Could I be hypnotized?'

Suddenly he looked shocked and rummaged in his pocket, which was a particularly awkward operation with his armful of files. He extracted a card and gave it to me. 'That's got various numbers on it. If anybody comes in here and starts dangling things in front of your eyes or talking to you in a soothing voice, call me straight away.'

With that he was gone, and I lay on the bed with my sore, vulnerable head. My head with a black hole in it.

'Have you talked to your boyfriend?'

I only managed to murmur something. I wasn't entirely awake and DI Cross leant closer over me in concern.

'Shall I call someone?' he asked.

'No. And, no, I haven't.'

'We're having a bit of difficulty tracking him down at the moment.'

'Me too,' I said. 'I've left three messages on the answering-machine. It'll be because of his work.'

'Does he go away often?'

'He's an IT consultant, whatever that means. He's always flying off to Belgium or Australia or wherever on special projects.'

'But you can't remember when you last saw him?'

'No.'

'Do you want to talk to your parents?'

'No! No, please.'

There was a pause. I was doing so badly. I tried to think of something I could give Cross. 'Would it help if you could have a look at our flat? I'll be back there in a day or two, I guess, but there might be something there. Maybe that's where I was grabbed. I might have left a note.'

Cross's blank expression barely altered. 'Do you have a key you can give me?'

'As you know I've got nothing except the clothes I escaped in. But in the front garden, to the left of the front door, there are two things that look like ordinary stones. But they're these crazy mail-order gimmicks and one of them is hollowed out. Inside there's a spare key. You can use that.'

'Do you have any allergies, Miss Devereaux?'

'I don't think so. I came up in hives once with some shellfish.'

'Do you suffer from epilepsy?'

'No.'

'Are you pregnant?'

I shook my head so hard it hurt.

'It doesn't mean anything but we're legally obliged to tell you that a CAT scan can have side effects, but the likelihood is extremely small, negligible. Would you sign this consent form? Here and here.'

Suddenly the nurse was sounding like an air stewardess. I thought of those demonstrations with the lifejacket. In the unlikely event of a landing on water.

'I don't even know what a CAT scan is,' I said, as I signed.

'Don't worry. The technologist will explain it all to you in a minute.'

I was led into a large, fiercely bright room. I saw the high-tech trolley where I was going to lie, padded and concave in the middle, and, behind it, a white tunnel into the heart of the machine. It looked like a toilet bowl turned on its side.

'Ms Devereaux, my name is Jan Carlton. Won't you sit down for a minute?' A tall spindly woman in an overall gestured to a chair. 'Do you know what a CAT scan is?'

'It's one of those names you hear,' I said cautiously.

'We like you to be prepared. Is there anything you're unsure about?'

'Everything, really.'

'It's really just an X-ray enhanced by a computer, which is in another room. Think of your body as a giant loaf of bread.'

'A loaf?'

'Yes. The CAT scan looks at a particular area of your body in slices, you see, then it puts together the slices into a three-dimensional view.'

'Oh, you meant a *sliced* loaf?'

'It's just a comparison.'

'I thought scans were for cancer.'

'They are. It's just a way of looking inside the body. It's a standard procedure for anyone who has had an injury, severe headaches, trauma.'

'What do I have to do?'

'We'll just pop you on the table and slide you into that thing that looks like a white doughnut. You'll hear humming, and you'll probably see the track spinning around. It won't last long at all. All you have to do is lie completely still.'

I had to put on a hospital robe again. I lay down on the table and stared at the ceiling.

'This will feel a little cold.'

She rubbed gel into my temples, smearing it over my newly washed hair. She slid a hard metal helmet under my skull.

'I'm tightening these screws. It might feel a bit uncomfortable.' She fastened some straps over my shoulders, arms and stomach, pulling them taut. 'The table is about to start moving.'

'Table?' I said feebly, as I slid slowly away from her and through the tunnel. I was lying inside a metal chamber and, yes, there was that humming. I swallowed hard. It wasn't quite dark in here. I could see lines moving round above me. Out there, a few feet away, was a bright room with a competent woman in it, making sure everything was as it should be. Beyond that was another room with a computer showing pictures of my brain. Upstairs there were wards, patients, nurses, doctors, cleaners, porters, visitors, people carrying clipboards and pushing trolleys. Outside, there was a wind coming in from the east and it might well snow. And here I was, lying in a humming metal tube.

I thought that some people, having gone through what I had gone through, might find it difficult to be confined like this. I closed my eyes. I could make up my own pictures. I could remember the blue sky that I'd seen this morning; the electric-blue that stretched from horizon to horizon and sparkled so. I could imagine the snow falling gently out of the dull, low sky and settling on houses, cars, bare trees. But in the darkness the sound of humming seemed to change. It sounded more like a kind of wheezing. And I could hear footsteps. There were footsteps coming towards me. Footsteps in the darkness. I opened my mouth to call out, but I couldn't speak or make a sound, except for a strangled whimper.

What was happening? I tried again but it was as if something was blocking my mouth. I couldn't breathe properly. I couldn't draw air through my mouth; I was gasping but nothing was happening. I was going to suffocate in here. My chest was hurting. I couldn't draw breath, not properly. It came in ragged bursts that gave me no relief. The footsteps came closer. I was trapped and I was drowning. Drowning in the air. A roaring built up in my head and I opened my eyes and it was still dark and I closed them and there was red behind my eyes. My eyes were burning in my sockets. Then the roaring split apart, as if my head had burst open to let out all the horror.

I was screaming at last. The tube was filled with the sound of my howling. My ears throbbed and my throat tore with it and I couldn't stop. I tried to make the screams into words. I tried to say, 'Help!' or 'Please,' anything, but all the sounds crashed and bubbled and streamed together. Everything was shaking and then there were bright lights in my eyes and hands on me. Hands that held me down, that wouldn't let me go. I screamed again. Wailed. Screams were pouring out of me. I couldn't see in the light. Everything stung. Every-thing around me bore down on me. There were new sounds, voices somewhere, someone calling my name. Eyes looking at me out of the dazzling light; watching me and there was nowhere to hide because I couldn't move. Fingers touching me. Cold metal on my skin. On my arm. Something wet. Something sharp. Something piercing my skin.

Then suddenly everything was quiet and it was as if

the light that hurt and the terrible sounds were gradually
fading away from me. Everything was fading and going
grey and far off, like night falling, and you just want it
to be day. Just want it to be snow.

When I woke up, I didn't know if it was the next morning
or many mornings later. The world was in black and
white but I knew that it wasn't the world. It was me. I
felt like there was a grey filter over my eyes, bleaching
the colour out. My tongue felt dry and fluffy. I felt
fidgety and irritable. I wanted to scratch myself or scratch
somebody else. I wanted to get up and do something,
but I didn't know what. Breakfast tasted of cardboard
and cotton wool. Every noise made me wince.

I lay in the bed and thought dark thoughts and then
made plans, which involved getting up and finding someone, anyone, in authority and telling them that it was
time for me to go home, and then finding Detective
Inspector Cross and telling him to bloody get on with
his inquiry, and somewhere in the middle of this a
woman came in. No nurse's uniform, no white coat. She
must have been in her fifties. Red-haired, pale freckly
skin, rimless glasses. She wore a honey-coloured sweater,
shiny grey trousers. She smiled at me.

'I'm Dr Beddoes,' she said. There was a pause. 'Irene
Beddoes.' That was Irene rhyming with 'sheen' and
'clean' rather than with 'eenymeeny'. 'I saw you yesterday afternoon. Do you remember our conversation?'

'No.'

'You were drifting in and out of sleep. I wasn't sure
how much you were taking in.'

I had slept and still I felt tired. Tired and grey.

'I've been seen by a neurologist,' I said. 'He tested
my memory. I've been put into a machine. I've been

78

examined for physical injuries and been patched up a bit. What are you here for?'

Her concerned smile only wavered a little. 'We thought you might like someone to talk to.'

'I've talked to the police.'

'I know.'

'Are you a psychiatrist?'

'Among other things.' She gestured at the chair. 'Do you mind if I sit down?'

'No, of course not.'

She dragged it over and sat by the bed. She smelt nice; subtly fragrant. I thought of spring flowers.

'I talked to Jack Cross,' she said. 'He told me your story. You've been through a terrifying ordeal.'

'I'm just happy to have escaped,' I said. 'I don't want you to see me as some sort of victim. I think I'm doing OK, you know. For several days I was dead. It may sound stupid but it was true. I was above ground, I was breathing and eating, but I knew I was dead. I didn't exist in the same world that everyone else occupied. What do you call it? The land of the living. The place where people worry about money and sex and paying bills. Mainly through luck I escaped and I'm alive again and I just think every day is something I never thought I'd be allowed.'

'Yes,' Dr Beddoes said, but still looking concerned for me.

'The other thing is that I'm not ill. I know I was knocked around a bit. I know that I've got a problem with my memory because I got a bang on the head. But I feel fine on the whole. A bit unreal, maybe. And this isn't how I imagined it would be.'

'What would be?'

'Being free. I'm lying in this bed in an old itchy nightie

that doesn't belong to me and people bringing me awful food on a trolley and people coming and sitting next to my bed and looking at me with anxious expressions on their faces and talking to me in a soft voice as if they were trying to talk me off a window-sill. What I really want is to get back to my flat and get on with my life. See my friends. Go to a pub again, to a café, walk down ordinary streets in my own clothes, go dancing, lie in bed on a Sunday morning with the sun streaming in through the windows, eat what I want when I want, go for a walk at night down by the river . . . But he's still out there, in the world I want to be in. If you want to know, that's what I really can't get out of my mind, the idea that he's still walking the streets.'

There was a silence and I felt a bit embarrassed by my outburst. But she didn't look too disconcerted.

'Your flat,' she said. 'Where's that?'

'It's not exactly mine,' I said. 'It actually belongs to my . . . to the guy I live with. Terry.'

'Has he been in to see you?'

'He's away. I've tried calling but he must be working somewhere – he travels a lot.'

'Have you seen anyone else? Family or friends?'

'No. I just want to get out of here and then I'll call them.' She looked at me and I felt a need to explain. 'I guess I'm putting off telling my story,' I admitted. 'I don't know where to begin. I don't know how to tell it because it's still not finished. I want there to be a proper ending to it before I begin, if you see what I mean.'

'You want him to be caught first?'

'Yes.'

'But maybe, in the meantime, you could talk to me.'

'Maybe,' I said cautiously. 'What I really want to do, though – the one thing I know I need – is to get out of here. It's as if this hospital is a half-way house between being in prison and being free. I'm in limbo here.'

Dr Beddoes contemplated me for a moment. 'Something terrible happened to you, Abbie. You're being dealt with by about five different specialities at the hospital and that's not to mention the police. It's quite a logistical struggle to get everybody to communicate. But as far as I understand there is a general agreement that you should stay here for at least a couple more days. For a start, I know that the neurologists want to keep you under observation for a time, just in case. And the police obviously are very worried indeed. The man you encountered must be exceptionally dangerous and they would rather have you in a more secure environment while they make certain decisions.'

'Do they think I might be under threat?'

'I can't speak for them, but I think it's extremely difficult to assess. That's part of the problem. What I want to say is that I would like to use the next couple of days to talk to you. Obviously it's up to you but I think I could be helpful to you. Not just that. It's possible that if we talk things over we might come up with details that could assist the police, but that would only be by the way. You talk about just wanting to get back to your normal life.' There was now a sudden, long pause that I found disconcerting. 'I'm thinking about how to put this. You might not find it as easy to return to your life as you assume. It may be that you take things with you from an experience like this.'

'You think I'm contaminated by it?'

'Contaminated?' She looked for a moment as if she were smelling the contamination, or trying to sniff it out. 'No. But you had a normal life, then suddenly you were thrown out of it into a terrible horror. Now you have to return to normality. You have to decide what to do with this thing that happened. We all need to find ways of accommodating things that have happened to us. I think that if we talked, I could help you do that.'

I looked away from her and I saw the greyness of the world again. When I spoke it was as much to myself as to her. 'I don't know how I'm supposed to accommodate someone wanting to kidnap and kill me. That's the first thing. The second is that my life wasn't as smooth as all that before it happened. But I'll give it a try.'

'We'll meet for a chat,' she said. 'And you aren't going to have to lie on a couch. We can do it in more pleasant surroundings, if you like.'

'That would be great.'

'I may even be able to find somewhere that serves proper coffee.'

'That would be the most therapeutic thing of all.'

She smiled and stood up and shook my hand and left. When Dr Beddoes arrived, I had wanted to turn my back to her and close my eyes. Now that she had gone, I was shocked to realize that I already missed her.

'Sadie?'

'Abbie!' Her voice was warm and clear, and relief spread through me. 'Where are you calling from?' she said. 'Are you still on holiday?'

'Holiday? No. No, I'm in hospital, Sadie.'

'My God! What's wrong?'

'Can you come and see me? I can't talk about it over the phone.'

'How do I know he didn't rape me?'

Jack Cross was sitting on the chair by my bed, fiddling with the tight knot of his tie. He nodded at the question,

then said: 'We can't know for sure, but there's no suggestion of that.'

'How do you know?'

'When you were admitted to hospital, you were, well,
examined, et cetera, et cetera.'

'And?'

'And there was no evidence of sexual assault.'

'That's something, at least.' I felt curiously blank. 'So
what else has happened?'

'We're building up a picture,' he said carefully.

'But . . .'

'One of the people we obviously want to talk to is
your boyfriend, Terence Wilmott.'

'And?'

'How would you describe your relationship with him?'

'Why on earth should I say anything about it at all?
What's Terry got to do with anything?'

'As I said, we're building up a picture.'

'Well, we're fine,' I said defensively. 'We have our
ups and downs, of course.'

'What sort of downs?'

'It wasn't Terry, if that's what you're thinking.'

'What?'

'He didn't do this. I know the man concealed his voice
and I didn't see him but it wasn't Terry. I know Terry's
smell. I know him backwards and forwards. He'll be
back soon from wherever he's gone off to and then you
can talk to him.'

'He's not abroad.'

'Oh?' I looked at him then. 'Why do you say that?'

'His passport's still in his flat.'

'Is it? Well, he must be in the UK, then.'

'Yes. Somewhere.'

★

I stood in front of the mirror and saw a stranger there. I was no longer me. I was someone else. A thin woman with matted hair and a bruised face. Chalky-grey skin. Sharp bones. Glassy, frightened eyes. I looked like a dead person.

I met Dr Beddoes in a courtyard in the hospital because, although it was so cold, I had a longing to be outside. The nurses had found me a giant strawberry-pink quilted coat. The courtyard had clearly been designed to be soothing to neurotic patients. It was too shady for grass, but there were plants with huge dark green fronds and the centrepiece was a water feature. A large bronze pot was full and permanently overflowing with water running down the outside. I was alone for a few minutes, so I wandered over and examined it. It looked like a machine for wasting water but I noticed an opening around the base, so I supposed that it was sucked back up again. Round and round for ever.

Irene Beddoes had brought us both mugs of coffee and biscuits wrapped in Cellophane. We sat on a slightly damp wooden bench. She gestured at the wet ornament.

'They got that because I thought it would be relaxing in a Japanese, Zen sort of way,' she said. 'I find it rather creepy.'

'Why?'

'Wasn't there someone in hell who was condemned to spend the whole of eternity trying to fill a huge earthenware jar with water – a jar that had a hole in it?'

'I didn't know that.'

'I shouldn't have told you. I may have spoiled it for you.'

'I like it; I like the sound. It's a happy sound.'

'That's the spirit,' she said.

It felt wonderful but a bit strange to be sitting outside on this sunny winter day. I only sipped at my mug of coffee. I had to be careful. I already felt on edge. Too much caffeine would turn me into a basket case.

'How are you doing?' she asked. It seemed a fairly inept beginning.

'You know what I hate about being in hospital? People are being nice and everything and I've got my own room and a TV, but still there's something about being in a room where people don't have to knock before they come in. People I've never seen before come in and clean or bring food and the nice ones give me a nod and the others just get on with it.'

'Do you get scared?'

I didn't answer at first. I took another sip of coffee and a bite of my biscuit. Then I said, 'Yes, of course. I mean, I think I get scared in different ways – I'm scared thinking about what it was like; remembering it all over again, almost as if I was still inside it and had never got away. The whole thing kind of closes in on me, like I'm underwater or something. Drowning in it. Most of the time I try not to let myself remember. I try and push it away from me. Perhaps I shouldn't do that. Do you think it's healthier to go over it?' I didn't give her time to answer. 'And the other thing I get scared about is the idea that he hasn't been caught. And that maybe he's just waiting for me to come out and then he'll grab me again. When I let myself think of that I can't breathe properly. Everything in my body seems to be breaking up with fear. So, yes. I get scared. Not always, though. Sometimes I just feel very, very lucky to be alive. But I wish they'd catch him. I don't suppose I'll be able to feel safe again, until that happens.'

Irene Beddoes was the first person I'd met whom I

could talk to about what had happened to me in that room, and what I had felt. She wasn't a friend. I could tell her about my sense of losing myself, of being turned, bit by bit, into an animal, or an object. I told her about his laugh, his whisper, the bucket. I told her I'd wet myself. I told her about how I would have done anything, let him do anything to me, in order to stay alive. And she listened, saying nothing. I talked and I talked until my voice grew weary. Then I stopped and leant towards her. 'Do you think you can help me remember my lost days?'

'My concern, my job, is what's happening in your head, what you've been going through and what you are still going through. If it results in anything that helps the investigation, then that's a bonus. The police are doing everything they can, Abbie.'

'I'm not sure I've given them much to go on.'

'Your job is to get better.'

I sat back in my chair. I looked up at the floors of the hospital surrounding us. One floor up a small boy with a high forehead and a solemn face was looking down at us. I could hear the hum of traffic outside, the sound of horns.

'You know one of my nightmares?' I said.

'What?'

'I've got lots of them, actually. Like being back in that room again. And I hate being in this limbo, I feel trapped. But sometimes I fear that I'm going to leave hospital, go back to my life and it'll just go back to normal and the man will never be found and the only trace there'll be will be the bits of memory of him like a worm crawling around in my head eating me up.'

Irene Beddoes looked at me; her eyes were keen. 'Didn't you like your life?' she said. 'Don't you like the idea of getting it back?'

'That's not what I mean,' I said. 'I mean that I can't bear the idea of nothing coming of all this. And I'll never be able to get rid of the idea as long as I live. You know the people who get that sort of deafness, except it's not deafness. It's not silence. It's a noise in their ears and it never goes away and it drives people mad until sometimes they kill themselves just to shut it up.'

'Could you tell me about yourself, Abbie? Before all of this.'

I took a sip of my coffee. From being too hot, it was now too cold. 'Where do I start? I'm twenty-five. Um . . .' I stopped, at a loss.

'Where do you work?'

'For the last couple of years I've been working like a lunatic for a company that furnishes offices.'

'What do you mean?'

'If some company is setting up a new office, we can do as little or as much as people want. Sometimes it's just designing the wallpaper, sometimes it's everything from the pens to the computer system.'

'Do you enjoy it?'

'Kind of. I can't believe I'll still be doing it in ten years' time – or even in one year's time, when I come to think of it. I just kind of wandered into it and discovered I was quite good at it. Sometimes we're sitting around, but when the pressure's on we work all night. That's what people pay us for.'

'And you have a boyfriend?'

'Yes. I met Terry through work. That's the way most people meet, isn't it? I don't know where else I'd meet anyone. He works with company computer systems and I moved in with him about a year ago.'

She just sat and waited for me to say more, so of course I did, because I've always talked too much, especially when there's a silence – and because I wanted to talk, I suppose, about things I'd never put into words before. So now I took the plunge in a gabble.

'Actually, the last few months haven't been exactly brilliant. Well, they've been awful in many ways. I was working too hard and he was working too hard – and when he works hard, he drinks hard. I don't think he's an alcoholic or anything, he just drinks when he wants to unwind. But the trouble is, he doesn't unwind, or not for long. He gets weepy or he gets angry.'

'Angry about what?'

'I don't know, really. Everything. Life. Me. He gets angry with me, because I'm there, I think. And he, well, he –' I stopped abruptly. This was very hard to say.

'Is he violent?' Irene Beddoes asked.

I felt I was slipping down a slope towards things I had never properly told anyone.

'Sometimes,' I muttered.

'Does he hit you?'

'He's lashed out a couple of times. Yes. I always thought I was the kind of woman who would never let myself be hit more than once. If you'd asked me a few months ago, I'd have said that I would just walk if a man hit me. But I didn't. I don't know why. He was always so very sorry, and I guess I felt sorry for him. Does that sound stupid? I felt he was doing something that hurt him much more than it hurt me. When I talk about it – well, I've never really talked about it before now, actually, but now, I feel that this isn't me I'm describing. I'm not like the woman who stays with a man who treats her badly. I'm more – well, more the kind of woman who escaped from a cellar and now just wants to get on with life.'

'And you did terrifically,' she said warmly.

'I don't think of it like that. Really. I just did the best I could.'

'By the sound of it that was very good indeed. I've made something of a study of these sort of psychopaths . . .'

'You didn't tell me that,' I said. 'You said you were a psychiatrist and that you weren't interested in all that side of it.'

'The way you handled yourself was first amazingly resilient, just to survive at all. Then there was your remarkable escape. That is almost unprecedented.'

'You've only heard my version. Maybe I exaggerated it to make myself seem more heroic.'

'I don't see how that's possible,' she said. 'After all, you're here. You're alive.'

'That's true,' I said. 'Anyway, now you know all about me.'

'I wouldn't say that. Maybe over the next day or two we can meet again.'

'I'd like that,' I said.

'I'm going to get us lunch in a minute. You must be starving. First I'd like to ask a favour.'

'What?'

She didn't answer. Instead she started rummaging in her shoulder-bag. While she did this I thought about her. I had to make an effort to prevent myself feeling that she was the sort of mother I would have invented for myself: warm where my mother was detached, assured where my mother was nervous, intelligent where my mother was, well, not exactly Einstein, and just sort of deep and complicated and interesting.

She pulled a file out of the bag. She put it on the table and removed a piece of paper, a printed form, which she put in front of me.

'What's this?' I asked. 'Are you trying to sell me insurance?'

She didn't smile. 'I want to help you,' she said, 'and I want to make a proper assessment and in order to do that I want to build up as complete a picture as I possibly can. I'd like to have access to your medical records, and for that I need your permission. I need you to sign this.'

'Are you serious?' I said. 'It's just bundles of stuff about injections for going on holiday and antibiotics when I had a chest infection.'

'It would be useful,' she said, offering a pen.

I shrugged and signed. 'I don't envy you,' I said. 'So, what do we do now?'

'I'd like to talk,' she said. 'Or, rather, I'd like you to talk. Just talk and see where it takes you.'

And I did. I gave myself up to it. Irene Beddoes went into the building and returned with sandwiches and salad and fizzy water and tea and biscuits, and the sun moved across the sky and I talked, and sometimes, as I thought of the sheer tiredness that my life had been over the last year, I cried, but mainly I talked and talked and talked until I was exhausted and the courtyard had become dark and cold and she led me through echoey corridors back to my room.

There was a large bunch of daffodils on my bed, and a note scribbled across the back of a used envelope. 'Sorry you weren't here. I waited as long as I could. I'll come back as soon as I can. Loads of love and I'm thinking of you, Sadie.'

I sat on the bed, weak with disappointment.

'How's the investigation going?'

'We're short of anything to investigate.'

'There's the women.'

'There's five female names.'

'Six. Including me.'

'If you . . .' Cross paused and looked awkward.

'If I remember anything,' I said, 'you'll be the first to know.'

'This is your brain.'

'My brain.' I looked at the scan spread out on the light board in front of us and then touched my temples. 'How odd to look at your own brain. Well, is it all right?'

Charlie Mulligan smiled at me. 'It seems pretty good to me.'

'It's a bit shadowy.'

'It's the way it's meant to look.'

'But I still can't remember. There's a hole in my life.'

'Maybe there always will be.'

'A disaster-shaped hole.'

'Or perhaps memory will gradually return and fill it in.'

'Can I do anything about it?'

'Don't fret away at it. Relax.'

'You don't know who you're talking to.'

'There are worse things than forgetting,' he said mildly. 'Anyway, I ought to be getting on.'

'Back to your mice.'

He held out his hand and I grasped it. It was warm and firm. 'Back to my mice. Get in touch if you need anything.'

If I need something you can do anything about, I thought. But I just nodded and tried to smile.

'I read somewhere that you only really fall in love twice, maybe three times, in your life.'

'Do you think that's true?'

'I don't know. Maybe. But, then, I've either fallen in love lots of times, or hardly ever. There's the bit where you can't sleep and you can't eat and you feel sick and breathless, and you don't know if you're very happy or completely wretched. You just want to be with him and the rest of the world can go hang.'

'Yes.'

'I've had that feeling quite a lot of times. But it doesn't last long. Sometimes just a few days; sometimes until the moment after you've had sex. It settles down and then you have to see what you're left with. And usually it's not much. Like ashes after the fire's gone out. You think: God, what was that all about? And sometimes you still care, feel affection, desire. But is that love? The time I was most intensely in love was when I was at university. God, I adored him. But it didn't last.'

'Did he leave you?'

'Yes. I cried for weeks. I thought I'd never get over it.'

'What about Terry? Has the relationship with him been stronger than other ones?'

'Longer, at least, which must count for something, some kind of commitment. Or endurance.' I gave a laugh that didn't sound quite like my normal laugh. 'I mean, I feel I know him really well, now. I know him in a way that I hardly know anyone. All the intimate little things, all the things he hides from other people . . . And the more I know him the more reason there is to leave him, but the harder it gets to do it. If that makes sense?'

'You make it sound as if you're trapped.'

'Lots of people feel trapped in their relationships at times, don't they?'

'So you feel trapped at work and trapped at home?'

'That's a bit dramatic. I've just let things get into a rut.'

'Which you've wanted to escape from?'

'You get into things gradually, and you don't realize quite where you are until it's a crisis and you suddenly see.'

'So you're saying . . . ?'

'This is my crisis.'

The next day when Irene came to my room . . . My room. I would catch myself saying that. As if it was where I was going to spend the rest of my life. As if I wouldn't be able to cope with a world outside where I would have to buy things for myself, make decisions.

She was as composed as always. She smiled and asked me how I'd slept. In the real world, people might sometimes ask you how you were, but they didn't really want to know. You were just meant to answer, 'Fine.' They didn't ask you how you'd slept, how you were eating, how you were feeling, and really want to know the answer. Irene Beddoes wanted to know. She would look at me with her intelligent eyes and wait for me to speak. So I said I'd slept fine, but it wasn't true. That was yet another thing about hospital. I had my own private room, of course, but unless your room was on an island in the middle of the Pacific you were always going to be woken at about two thirty in the morning by some woman screaming. Someone would come and deal with her but I'd be left staring at the dark, thinking about dying and being dead and about that cellar and the voice in my ear.

'Yes, fine,' I said.

'Your file arrived,' she said.

'What file?'

'From your GP. Your basic NHS file.'

'Oh, God,' I said. 'I'd forgotten about that. I suppose

it's full of stuff that's going to be taken down and used in evidence against me.'

'Why do you say that?'

'It was just a joke. Now you're going to say that there's no such thing as "just a joke".'

'You didn't tell me you'd been treated for depression.'

'Have I?'

She glanced down at her notebook. 'You were prescribed an SSRI in November 1995.'

'What's that?'

'An antidepressant.'

'I don't remember that.'

'Try.'

I thought for a moment. 1995. University. Wreckage.

'That must have been when I split up with Jules. I told you about that yesterday. I got into a terrible state; I thought my heart was broken. Well, I suppose it was. I wasn't getting out of bed in the morning. I was crying all the time. I couldn't seem to stop. Strange how much water there is inside you. So a friend of mine made me go to the college doctor. He prescribed some pills, but I can't even remember taking them.' I caught myself and laughed. 'When I say I can't remember, I don't mean more amnesia. It just never seemed important.'

'Why didn't you mention it to me before?'

'When I was about eight I was given a penknife for my birthday. Unbelievable, but true. About eight minutes later I was trying to carve a bit of wood in the garden and the knife went into my finger.' I held up my left hand. 'Look, there's still quite a nice scar. It bled like anything. I may be imagining it, but when I look at the scar I can feel what it was like when the knife slipped and went in. I didn't mention that either.'

'Abbie, we've been talking about your mood. We've

been talking about how you react to stress. But you didn't mention it.'

'Are you saying that I forgot it, the way I can't remember being grabbed by this man? But I did mention it. I told you about it when we talked yesterday.'

'Yes, but you didn't mention that you received medical treatment.'

'Only because I didn't think of it as relevant. I had an affair with someone at university then got depressed when it went wrong. Oh, OK, maybe it's relevant. Everything's relevant, I suppose. Maybe I didn't mention it because it was so sad and I felt so abandoned.'

'Abandoned?'

'Yes. Well, of course. I was in love and he wasn't.'

'I was interested, looking through your files, in how you had reacted to other episodes of stress in your life.'

'If you want to compare me being held prisoner by someone who wanted to kill me with bits of my life where I broke up with a boyfriend or where I had some kind of eczema that took about two years to go away – have you reached that bit of the file? – well, then, all I can say is that there is no comparison.'

'There is one thing they all have in common, which is that they happen to you. And I look for patterns. This has become an event in your life. Like everything that happens in your life it will change you in some way. I hope I can help you to make sure it doesn't affect you in a bad way.'

'But there are things that happen in life that are just bad and that is one of them. It's always going to be bad. I can't turn it to good. The only thing I can think of that's really important is for this incredibly dangerous man to be found and locked away where he can never do this again to anyone else.' I looked out of the window.

Over the buildings I could see a clear blue sky. I couldn't feel the cold outside but somehow I could see it. Even looking at it made this hateful room unbearably stuffy. 'There's another thing.'

'What?' said Irene.

'I need to leave here. I really do, or I'll never be able to. I need to be in ordinary life again. I suppose I can't just get up and put on these borrowed clothes – though, come to think of it, I don't know why not – but I'm going to track down Dr Burns, or leave a message with his secretary, and tell him that I'm leaving tomorrow. I'll leave a forwarding address with Jack Cross. And if you still feel that it's worth talking to me, then I can come and meet you at any place you suggest. But I can't stay here any longer.'

Irene Beddoes always reacted as if it was always just what she had been expecting me to say, and that she quite understood.

'That may be right,' she said. 'Could you do us one favour? As we've talked about before, you're being seen by all sorts of different people and departments. I'm sorry about all the delays but as you can imagine it's a logistical nightmare getting everybody together at the same time to agree on a decision. I've just heard that there's going to be a meeting tomorrow morning with absolutely everybody. We're going to talk about where we go from here. One of the obvious issues is about you leaving.'

'Can I come?'

'What?'

'Can I come to the meeting?'

For the first time ever Irene looked at a loss. 'I'm sorry, that's not possible.'

'You mean there are things I might not want to hear?'

She smiled her reassuring smile. 'Not at all. Patients don't attend case conferences. It's just one of those things.'

'It's just that I think of it more as an investigation in which I'm involved.'

'There's nothing cloak-and-dagger about it. I'll come and see you straight away.'

I wasn't looking at her. My gaze was drawn to the window once more. 'I'll have my bag packed,' I said.

I didn't get Jack Cross that afternoon. He was too busy. I got a less important detective called Detective Constable Lavis. He was one of those men who was so tall that he was constantly ducking as if he was about to bump his head, even if he was in a room like mine that was about nine feet tall. He looked very much a stand-in, but he was friendly too, as if it was me and him against every-body else. He sat down on the chair next to my bed, which looked ridiculously small under him.

'I tried to contact Cross,' I said.

'He's out of the office,' Lavis said.

'That's what they told me,' I said. 'I hoped he'd give me a call.'

'He's a bit busy,' Lavis said. 'He sent me.'

'I was going to tell him that I'm leaving the hospital.'

'Right,' said Lavis, as if he had hardly heard what I'd said. 'I'll pass that on. I've just been sent along to talk about a couple of things.'

'Like what?'

'Good news,' he said cheerfully. 'Your boyfriend. Terry Wilmott. We were getting a bit worried about him, but he's turned up.'

'Was he working or was he on a binge?'

'Bit of a drinker, is he?'

'From time to time.'

'I met him yesterday. He looked a bit pasty but he was all right.'

'Did he say where he'd been?'

'He said he'd been ill. He'd been staying in some cottage in Wales that a friend of his owns.'

'That sounds like Terry. Did he say anything else?'

'There was nothing much he had to contribute.'

'So the mystery is cleared up,' I said. 'Idiot. I'll give him a ring.'

'So he hasn't been in touch?'

'Obviously not.'

Lavis looked ill at ease. He reminded me of the sort of adolescent who blushed when you asked him the time.

'The boss has been sending me out on some inquiries,' he said. 'I called at your company, Jay and Joiner's. Nice people.'

'If you say so.'

'We were attempting to establish the sort of period when you disappeared.'

'Did you?'

'I suppose.' He gave a sniff and looked around as if checking out an escape route. 'What are your plans?'

'I already said. I'm planning to leave tomorrow.'

'What about work?'

'I'll get in touch with them. I haven't really felt up to it but I suppose I'll go back in the next week or two.'

'You'll go back to work?' he said. He sounded surprised.

'What else? I've got a living to earn. And it's not just that. I've got to get back to normal life while there's a life for me to get to.'

'Yes, right,' said Lavis.

'I'm sorry,' I said. 'I know that my personal problems aren't really your business.'

'No,' said Lavis.

'I suppose you've got your hands full with the investigation.'

'Pretty much.'

'I know that I haven't been giving you much to go on.'

'We're doing what we can.'

'I'm really sorry that I couldn't find the place where I'd been held. I'm not exactly the greatest witness in criminal history. But I feel completely in the dark. Have there been any other developments? I suppose they must have checked out those names I gave Cross. The names of the other victims. I was hoping that would give them a clue. Have they found anything? I assume they haven't because if they had they would have told me. Except that nobody tells me anything. That's one of the problems about being in this bed, in this room. I think that if nothing else I've gained some kind of insight into what it's like to be old and ill. People just treat you as if you were slightly thick. Do you know what I mean? They come in here and they talk slowly and ask extremely simple questions as if I have a mental problem. And they don't believe I need to be told anything. I honestly think that if I didn't have a tantrum every so often, they would forget me altogether.'

The reason I was babbling on and on was that Lavis was shifting in his seat looking trapped and not answering, and the longer I babbled on the more trapped he looked. I felt that I'd become like one of those people in the street who walk along muttering to themselves and every so often they manage to stop someone and rant to them about their problems and about how everybody is out to get them.

'I haven't been able to tell you very much,' I said. 'I mean, I've said loads but it hasn't been much use.'

'No, that's fine,' said Lavis, as he stood up. He was about to make a break for it. 'I just needed to check a couple of things. As I said.'

'I'm sorry that I've been going on and on and on,' I said. 'I'm a bit stir crazy.'

'That's fine,' said Lavis, as he edged away from me towards the safety of the open door. But he didn't contradict me.

The St Anthony Hospital NHS Trust

Date: 28 January 2002
Subject: Case Conference – Abigail Elizabeth
Devereaux, Room 4E, Barrington Wing. Hosp.
No. 923903
Cc. Detective Chief Superintendent Gordon Lovell,
Laurraine Falkner (Chief Executive), Professor Ian
Burke (Medical Director).
Record made by Susan Barton (Medical Administration
Assistant).

NB: RESTRICTED CIRCULATION

Present: Detective Chief Superintendent Lovell,
Detective Inspector Cross, Dr Burns, Dr Beddoes,
Prof. Mulligan.

Detective Inspector Cross began the meeting with an
account of the case and the progress of related
investigation. On 22 January Ms Devereaux was
brought by ambulance from Ferdinand Road.
Interviewed the following day, she claimed to have
been kidnapped and threatened with death. The

investigation has been hampered by lack of independent evidence. Ms Devereaux is unable to recall her capture. She was kept hooded and bound. Her only significant memory was a list of female first names, the names her captor claimed to be previous victims.

Ms Devereaux escaped from this captivity but, on being escorted back to the area, was unfortunately unable to locate the place she had escaped from.

Dr Beddoes asked if such escapes were unusual. DI Cross said his experience of such cases was limited. She asked if the investigation had made any progress at all. DI Cross said it was still in a preliminary stage.

Dr Burns described the mostly superficial injuries suffered by Ms Devereaux. He stated that her dehydrated, malnourished state, while not dangerous, was consistent with some form of physical ordeal.

Dr Beddoes asked if there was any physical evidence of violence or torture. Dr Burns said that there were bruises around neck and wrists suggesting physical restraint.

Dr Burns reported that the CAT scan showed no obvious cerebral lesions.

Professor Mulligan described his evaluation of Ms Devereaux. He announced his conclusion that her account of her post-traumatic amnesia was consistent with his examination.

Dr Beddoes asked if he had found any objective, physical evidence of such injury and such amnesia. Professor Mulligan said that such findings were not relevant. There was an animated discussion between them not detailed here.

Dr Beddoes gave her report on her assessment of Ms Devereaux. She found Ms Devereaux an articulate, intelligent, attractive subject. Her account of her ordeal was compelling and convincing. Further examination revealed that Ms Devereaux had been undergoing considerable stress in the months before the alleged ordeal. She had been under considerable pressure at her employment culminating in her being compelled to take a period of leave for stress-related reasons. This period of leave began shortly before, by Ms Devereaux's account, her period of imprisonment began. Her relationship with her boyfriend had also been a source of considerable strain, due to his excessive drinking and violent behaviour.

Dr Beddoes reported that, on further examination, other relevant factors had come to light. Contrary to her own account, Ms Devereaux had a history of mental instability, and had indeed received medical treatment in the past. This she had failed to mention during her first interviews. She also had a history of reporting violence. Records showed that on one occasion she had called the police in response to a domestic disturbance. This was with her boyfriend.

She also had apparent difficulty in recalling these events. This was obviously comparable to her current reported amnesia. When these doubts began to appear in Dr Beddoes' mind, she had consulted widely with others on the case in search of any independent, objective confirmation of Ms Devereaux's claim. There was none. Dr Beddoes said it was her conclusion that Ms Devereaux's disorders were psychological in origin and that the best course of action was a course of cognitive therapy and medication.

Professor Mulligan asked about the marks found on Ms Devereaux's body and about her having been found in an emaciated state in an area of London distant from her home and work. Dr Beddoes replied that Professor Mulligan was there for his expertise in certain narrow neurological matters.

Detective Chief Inspector Lovell asked if Dr Beddoes was stating that no crime had been committed. Dr Beddoes said that she was not certain of what might or might not have occurred between Ms Devereaux and her boyfriend. But she was certain that the kidnap was a fantasy. In her view, not a fabrication. It was a cry for help.

DCI Lovell said the immediate question was whether Ms Devereaux should be charged with wasting police time.

There was loud discussion. DI Cross stated that he was not yet ready to dismiss Ms Devereaux's account. Professor Mulligan asked Dr Beddoes if she was aware that if she was wrong then the result would be to cut Ms Devereaux loose and expose her to mortal danger. There followed more agitated discussion not summarized here.

Professor Mulligan stated that he wished it to be entered into the record that he dissented from the prevailing decision of the meeting. He stated that if anything happened to Ms Devereaux it would be on the consciences of everybody at this meeting. (Susan Barton excepted. Inserted on Professor Mulligan's instructions.) Professor Mulligan then left the meeting.

There was discussion as to how to proceed. DCI Lovell ordered DI Cross to halt the inquiry. Dr Beddoes said she would immediately visit Ms Devereaux and discuss a therapeutic regime.

Dr Beddoes thanked the other members of the meeting for their co-operation. She described it as a model of how medical and legal organizations should work together. Dr Burns asked when Ms Devereaux's bed would be available.

Part Three

One

Walk. Just walk. One foot in front of the other. Don't stop, don't pause, don't look round. Keep your head up and your eyes ahead of you. Let faces blur. Pretend you know where you are going. People calling your name, but it's an echo of an echo, bouncing off the white walls. They're calling a stranger, not you. Don't listen. That's all over now, the listening and talking and doing what you're told. Being good. Keep walking. Not running, walking. Through those double doors, which slide silently open as you approach. No tears now. Don't cry. You are not mad, Abbie. You are not mad. Past the ambulances, the cars, the porters with their trolleys. Don't stop now. Step into the wide world. This is freedom, except you are not free. Not free, not safe. But not mad. You are not mad. And you are alive. Breathe in and out and walk forward now.

The sky was startlingly blue and the ground icy. The world glittered with cold. My cheeks burned with it, my eyes stung, and my fingers were numb where they gripped the plastic bag I was carrying. My feet, in their stupid slipshod shoes, crunched on the gravel. I stood outside the tall Victorian house, at the top of which was our flat – well, Terry's, really, but I'd lived in it for nearly two years now. It was me who'd painted our bedroom, opened up the fireplace, bought second-hand pieces of furniture and large mirrors and pictures and rugs and vases and the general clutter that made a place feel like home.

I tipped my head carefully to look up. The movement seemed to make pain spill over in my skull. The flat didn't appear particularly homely right now. It looked chilly and empty. The bathroom window was still cracked, and there were no lights on. The curtains in our bedroom were drawn, which meant either that Terry was sleeping off the kind of hangover that made him pasty-faced and sour-tempered, or that he'd not bothered to open them when he staggered out of bed that morning, late for work. I hoped it was the latter.

I tried the bell anyway. If I put my ear to the door, I could hear it far above me – a spluttery ring because the battery was running out. It seemed to have been running out for months. I waited then tried again. I pushed open the metal letter-box and squinted inside to see if anyone was coming down the stairs, but could only see an empty strip of maroon carpet.

I retrieved the spare key hidden under the stone but I dropped it a couple of times before I managed to fit it into the lock with my frozen fingers. Even inside, in the hall, my breath steamed in the air. I hoped Terry had left the heating on, or that at least the water was hot enough for a bath. I was grubby and cold, and my body still felt as if everything had come loose inside. It was a poor kind of homecoming. The poorest, really.

It was an effort to go up the flights of stairs, past the flat on the first floor, where I could hear the sound of a television. My legs felt heavy and I was panting by the time I reached our door on the next floor up. I called out, as I turned the key. 'Hello? Hello, it's me. I'm back.' Nothing. 'Terry? Hello?'

Silence, except for the noise of a tap dripping in the bathroom. Suddenly, without warning, fear flooded me and I had to stop quite still, holding on to the door to steady my crumbling legs. I breathed deeply, in and out, until the fear had ebbed again, then stepped inside and pushed the door closed behind me.

I don't know what I noticed first. Probably it was just the mess: the muddy shoes on the living-room floor, unwashed dishes piled up in the sink, dead tulips drooping on the kitchen table, next to several empty bottles and an overflowing ashtray. Grimy surfaces, stale air. But then I saw that there were odd spaces here and there, where things should be but weren't. My CD player, for a start, which we'd always kept on a low table in the living room next to the little television. Except it wasn't a little television any longer, but a new big one. Automatically I looked next at the small desk in the corner of my room for my laptop and it, too, was gone. It was an old one, a dinosaur in computer terms, but I groaned to think of the things stored in there that were lost – all the email addresses, for a start, which I'd never made a note of anywhere else.

I sat down on the sofa, next to a pile of old newspapers and Terry's overcoat. Had we been robbed? Books seemed to be missing as well – there were gaps all along the shelves. I tried to remember what had been there: a giant encyclopedia from the lower shelf; several novels from the shelf above; an anthology of poetry; the *Good Pub Guide* perhaps. Certainly a couple of cookery books.

I went into our bedroom. The bed was unmade; the jumbled-up duvet still held the shape of Terry's body. There was a pile of dirty clothes on the floor, along with two empty wine bottles. I opened the curtains to let in the dazzling sunshine, opened the window to feel the fierce, clean air blasting into the room, and then stared around. It's always hard to see what isn't there; to notice absence. But the alarm clock was gone from my side of the bed. My wooden box of jewellery was gone too, from the top of the chest of drawers. There wasn't anything valuable in it – just a few earrings, bangles, a couple of necklaces, things given to me over the years – but they were mementoes and gifts and could never be replaced.

I opened the drawers. My underwear was gone, except for an old pair of black knickers stuffed at the back. Several of my T-shirts were missing, a couple of pairs of jeans and smarter trousers and at least three of my jumpers, including the expensive one I'd succumbed to in the January sales. I pulled open the wardrobe doors. All of Terry's things were in there, as far as I could see, but some of the hangers on my side were empty. A couple of dresses were missing. My black coat wasn't in the cupboard, or my leather jacket. Neither were most of my shoes – just a couple of pairs of sandals and some scuffed trainers remained on the wardrobe floor. Most of my work clothes seemed to be still there, though. I looked around, bewildered, and I saw that some of the missing clothes had been stuffed into a bulging bin-bag at the base of our bed.

'Terry,' I said aloud. 'You bastard.'

I went into the bathroom. The lavatory seat was up and I banged it down. No Tampax, no makeup, no moisturizing cream, no perfume, no body spray, no deodorant. I'd been cleared away. Even my toothbrush was gone. I opened the cabinet. All the first-aid stuff was still there. I unscrewed the bottle of paracetamol and poured two into my palm. I swallowed them without water. My head banged.

This was a dream, I thought. A nightmare, in which I was being rubbed out of my own life. I'd wake up soon. But that was the difficulty – where had the nightmare begun, and at which point would I wake? Back in my old life, and nothing had happened and everything was just a feverish concoction inside my head? Back on the ledge, a rag stuffed into my mouth, my mind clouding over, waiting to die? Back in hospital, still thinking the doctors were going to cure me and the police were going to save me?

I went into the kitchen and put on the kettle. While I was waiting for it to boil, I rooted around in the fridge for I was suddenly dizzy with hunger. There wasn't much in there, apart from several bottles of beer and three or four oven-ready meals stacked on top of each other. I made myself a Marmite and lettuce sandwich on white bread, plasticky like the hospital bread, and poured boiling water over a tea bag.

But mid-bite, still standing by the fridge and with a strip of lettuce dangling from my lower lip, a thought came to me. Where was my bag, with my purse, my money, my cards and my keys? I picked up cushions, looked behind coats on hooks, opened drawers. I looked in places it wouldn't be and places I had already searched.

I must have been carrying it when I'd been snatched. Which meant that he had my address, keys, everything, while I had nothing at all. Nothing. I didn't have a single penny. I had been so furious and so ashamed when Dr Beddoes told me about the 'treatment regime' she was going to begin that would help me to 'move on', I shouted something incoherent at her and said that if she wanted me to listen to a single further word from her or anybody connected with the hospital she would have to have me strapped down and sedated. Then I had marched out of the hospital in the clothes I'd been found in, trying not to let my knees buckle under me, trying not to weep, rant, beg. I'd refused all offers of a lift, some money, proper explanations, a follow-up session with a psychiatrist, help. I didn't need help. I needed them to catch him and make me safe. And I needed to punch Dr Beddoes in her smug face. I didn't say any more. There was no point. Words had become like vicious traps, springing shut on me. Everything I had said to the police, the doctors and to that fucking Irene Beddoes had been turned against me. I should have taken the money, though.

I didn't want my sandwich any more. I chucked it into the bin, which looked as if it hadn't been emptied since I was last here, and took a sip of cooling tea. I walked over to the window and looked out, pressing my forehead against the icy pane and almost expecting to see him standing there on the pavement below, looking up at me, laughing.

Except I wouldn't know that it was him. He could be anyone. He could be that old man dragging a resistant dachshund with stiff legs, or that young guy with a pony-tail, or that nice-looking father in a bobble hat with a red-cheeked child beside him. There was a thin layer of snow on the trees and on the roofs of houses and cars, and the people who passed were muffled up in thick coats and scarves, and had their heads bent against the cold.

No one raised their heads to see me standing there. I was completely at a loss. I didn't even know what I was thinking. I didn't know what to do next, or whom to turn to for help. I didn't know what help I would be asking for: tell me what happened, tell me what to do, tell me who I am, tell me where to go from here, only tell me . . .

I shut my eyes and tried for the thousandth time to remember something, anything. Just a tiny chink of light in the darkness would do. There was no light, and when I opened my eyes again I was staring once more into the street, made unfamiliar by winter.

I went to the phone and dialled Terry's number at work. It rang and rang. I tried his mobile number and got voicemail.

'Terry,' I said. 'Terry, it's me. Abbie. I urgently need to speak to you.'

I phoned Sadie's number next, but only got an answering-machine and I didn't want to leave a message. I thought about calling Sheila and Guy but then I would have to explain it all and I didn't want to do that, not now.

I had imagined coming home and telling my story. Friends would sit round me with wide eyes, listening. It would be a horror story with a happy ending, a story of despair, then hope; of ultimate triumph. I would be a kind of heroine, because I'd survived and was telling them the tale. The awfulness of what had happened would be redeemed by the ending. What could I say now? The police think I'm lying. They think I made it all up. I know about suspicion: it spreads. It is like an ugly stain.

What do you do when you're feeling lost, angry, depressed, scared, a bit ill and very cold? I ran a bath, very hot and deep, and took all my clothes off. I looked at myself in the mirror. There were hollows in my cheeks and my buttocks; my pelvic bones and my ribs jutted out sharply. I was a stranger to myself. I stood on the scales that were under the sink: I'd lost over a stone.

I lowered myself into the scalding water, held my nostrils together between finger and thumb, took a deep breath and disappeared under the surface completely. When I finally emerged, spluttering into the steamed-up air, someone was shouting. They were shouting at me. I blinked and a face came furiously into focus.

'Terry!' I said.

'What the fuck do you think you're doing in there? Have you gone mad?'

He was still in his thick jacket and his face was blotchy with cold. I pinched my nose and slid under the water again, to shut out the sight of him, to stop the voice that was calling me mad.

Two

I scrambled out of the bath with Terry glaring at me, wrapped myself in a towel, and went into the bedroom. I grabbed clothes from wherever I could find them – a pair of old jeans from the bin-bag, an itchy, dark-blue sweater from the drawer, some scuffed trainers, that old pair of scrunched-up black knickers. At least they were clean. On the shelf above the bath I found a hairband, so I was able to tie up my wet hair with trembling hands.

Terry was sitting in the wicker chair in the corner of the living room. In the wicker chair I'd bought in a second-hand shop in the high street one rainy Sunday morning. I'd even carried it back myself, using it as an umbrella. He leant forward and stubbed out his cigarette in the ashtray. The ashtray I'd taken with me as a souvenir from a café where I'd once waitressed. He took another cigarette from the packet lying on the table and lit it. With his copper hair, his pale skin, he looked beautiful, the Terry I had first met. It was when he started to talk that problems began.

'Aren't you going to ask me if I'm all right?' I said. Though, of course, it was too late for that. If I had to ask him to ask me, it wasn't going to work as an expression of concern. Like when you ask someone if they love you – if you have to ask them, they don't. Or not enough. Not the way you want them to.

'What?' he said. He made it sound more like a statement than a question.

'What's going on?'

'That's what I want to know. You look dreadful. And that cut . . . What's wrong with you?'

'You know I've been in hospital?'

He took a long slow drag on his cigarette and blew out the smoke slowly, savouring it, as if it was of far more interest than I was. There were two bad-tempered Terrys. There was angry, shouty Terry. The one I'd briefly glimpsed in the bathroom. And there was quiet, calm, sarcastic Terry, the one sitting in the wicker chair smoking his cigarette.

'Yes, I heard,' he said. 'Eventually. I heard from the police. They came here.'

'I tried to phone you,' I said. 'You weren't here. Well, you know you weren't here, of course.'

'I've been away.'

'Terry,' I said, 'I've been having the most – well, the most terrible, terrible time. I want to . . .' I stopped, I didn't know what I wanted or what to say. I certainly did not want to be sitting in a chilly room with an angry man. A hug, I thought. A hug, a cup of cocoa, someone saying they're glad I'm home, someone saying they missed me, someone making me feel safe. That's what I need right now. 'I can't remember things,' I said at last. 'I'm all in the dark and I need your help to sort things out.' No reaction. 'I should be dead,' I said.

Another bloody slow drag at the cigarette. Was he on something? There seemed to be an extra beat before everything he said, as if there was some ironic subtext that I was missing. People talk about being able to feel when a storm is coming. Their old war wound starts to ache or something. I've never been able to manage it myself. My own war wounds ache all the time. But whenever a row is coming with Terry, I can feel it. I can feel it all over my skin and in the hairs on the back of my neck and in my spine and my stomach and behind my eyes, and I can feel it in the air. But this time my own anger stirred inside me, too.

'Terry,' I said, 'did you hear what I said?'

'Am I missing something?'

'What?'

'Is this some weird way of coming back?'

'They discharged me from the hospital. That's all. What did they tell you? Haven't you heard anything about it? I've got so much to tell you. Oh, God, you'll never believe it.' I gave a gulp when I heard myself say that, and hurried to correct myself. 'Except it's true, of course.'

'Isn't it a bit late for that?'

'Sorry? I guess you've got a few things to tell me about as well. Where were you?'

Terry gave a barking kind of laugh then looked around as if he was worried that someone else might be looking at him. I closed my eyes then opened them again. He was still there in the wicker chair, smoking, and I was still here, standing over him.

'Are you drunk?' I asked.

'This is some kind of put-on, right?'

'What do you mean?'

'Is this some way of getting back at me?'

I shook my head to clear it, and it throbbed violently. I felt as if I was seeing everything through a grey mist.

'Listen, Terry. OK? I was grabbed by a madman. He hit me on the head and I blacked out. I don't know what happened, only some of it. But I could have died. I nearly did. I was in hospital. You weren't around. I tried to call you, but you never answered. Probably you were on a binge, is that it? But I've come home.'

Now Terry's expression changed. He looked puzzled,

completely thrown. His cigarette burned between his fingers as if he'd forgotten about it.

'Abbie . . . I just don't get this.'

I sat down on the sofa. The sofa was Terry's. I think his mother had passed it on to him years before. I rubbed my eyes. 'I know the police talked to you,' I said warily. I wanted to tell as little as I could to Terry. And that was part of the problem, wasn't it? 'What did they say?'

Now it was Terry's turn to look wary. 'They wanted to know when I'd last seen you.'

'And what did you tell them?'

Another slow drag on the cigarette. 'I just answered their questions.'

'And they were satisfied?'

'I told them where I'd been staying. I think they made a couple of calls to check. That seemed to be enough for them.'

'What did they tell you about me?'

'They said you'd been injured.'

' "Injured"?' I said. 'That was their word?'

He gave a shrug. 'Something like that.'

'I was attacked,' I said.

'Who by?'

'I don't know. I never saw his face.'

'You what?' He gawped at me. 'What happened?'

'I don't know. I've got no memory of it. I was hit. Hard. On the head. I can't remember anything for days and days.'

I had his attention now. He clearly had so many questions, he could hardly think of which one to ask.

'If you don't remember anything, how do you know you didn't just fall over and hit your head?'

'He took me prisoner, Terry. He was going to kill me. I escaped.'

At this point, I suppose, pathetically, I felt that any human being would come over and hold me and say, 'How awful,' but Terry just carried on with his interrogation, as if he hadn't really heard what I was saying.

'I thought you didn't see him.'

'I was blindfolded. It was in the dark.'

'Oh,' he said. There was a long pause. 'Christ.'

'Yes.'

'I'm sorry, Abbie,' he said awkwardly. It was far too little and it came too late to mean anything; awareness of this was written all over his face. Then he asked: 'So what are the police doing?'

This was the question I had been dreading. This was why I hadn't wanted to get into a detailed discussion. Even though I knew I was right, I felt ashamed even in front of Terry and at the same time I felt bitterly angry with myself for that.

'They don't believe me,' I said. 'They think it never happened.'

'But what about the injuries? Those bruises?'

I pulled a face. I wanted to cry but I absolutely was not going to cry in front of bloody Terry. Which was another part of the trouble.

'From what I understand, the people who are on my side think I imagined it. The people who aren't on my side think I made it up. They all think they're doing me a favour by not charging me with wasting police time. So they've turned me loose. I'm out in the open again, with no protection.' I waited for him to come over to me. He didn't move. His face had a blank look to it. I took a deep breath. 'So what's happened with my stuff ? Who took it?'

'You did.'

'What? Me?'

'Two weeks ago.'

'I took it?'

'Yes.' Terry shifted in his chair. He looked at me closely. 'Is this true? Do you not remember anything?'

I shook my head.

'It's all fuzzy. There's a whole dark cloud over the last few weeks. I've got a vague memory of being at work, of being here. Then it all fades. But what are you talking about? What do you mean *I* took it?'

Now it was Terry who looked embarrassed. His eyes were flickering, as if he was thinking quickly, trying to come up with something. Then he looked calm again.

'You left,' he said.

'What do you mean?'

'It's not as if you haven't threatened to about a million times. And don't look at me as if it's something that's my fault.'

'I'm not looking at you in any way at all.'

He narrowed his eyes. 'You really don't remember?'

'Not a thing.'

He lit another cigarette. 'We had a row,' he said.

'What about?'

'I don't remember. What are rows ever about? Something stupid. Maybe it was the final straw.'

'What a cliché that is.'

'Well, there you are. Maybe I used a cliché that offended you or picked up the wrong spoon. We had a row. You said that that was it. I thought you were joking and I, well, I went out. But when I got back you were gathering up your stuff. Most of it, anyway. You took everything you could fit into your car and then you drove off.'

'Is this true?'

'Look around you, Abbie. Who else would want your CD player apart from you?'

'So you're saying it was just one of our rows.'

'One of our worse rows.'

I felt bleak and cold. There seemed no reason for concealing anything now.

'I've forgotten a lot of things,' I said. 'But I remember that our worse rows usually ended with you lashing out at me.'

'That's not true.'

'Did you hit me?'

'No,' said Terry. But the expression on his face was both defensive and ashamed.

'You know, that was one of the reasons why the police didn't believe me. I'm a victim. I've got a history. I'm a woman who has been hit. I called the police before. Do you remember that evening? Maybe you don't remember it. You'd been drinking and there was some sort of row. I don't remember what that one was about either. Was it the one where I'd washed a shirt of yours that you wanted to wear and it was still wet? And I said if it was a problem, why didn't you wash it yourself? Was it that one? Or was it one of the ones where you said I ruined your life by going on at you? There were a lot of those. It's hard to tell those ones apart. But it ended with you grabbing the kitchen knife and me calling the police.'

'No, I don't remember that,' Terry said. 'You're exaggerating.'

'No! I'm not exaggerating, I'm not making it up. I'm saying what happens when you get drunk. First you get cheerful, then aggressively cheerful, then maudlin and self-pitying, and by the fourth drink you're angry. And if I'm there, you're angry with me. And I'm not going to sit here like some vengeful woman and list the things

I've seen you do when you're drunk. But for some reason that I've never been able to work out, you get off on it. And then, for some reason I've also never been able to fathom, I believe you when you cry and say it'll never, not ever, happen again.'

Terry stubbed out his cigarette and lit another. Was that his fourth, or his fifth?

'Abbie, this is a pretty good fucking imitation of the row we had.'

'Then I wish that I remembered it, because I rather like the woman I was who pulled herself together and walked out.'

'Yes,' said Terry, sounding suddenly almost as tired as I was. 'I rather liked her as well. You know, I'm sorry I didn't come and see you in the hospital. I was going to when I heard about it, and then stuff came up and then suddenly you were in my bath.'

'That's all right,' I said. 'So where are my things?'

'I don't know.'

'What do you mean?'

'You left me, remember?'

'When did I leave you?'

'When?'

'What date?'

'Oh. On Saturday.'

'Which Saturday?'

He cast me a glance, as if he suspected this was some elaborate charade. 'Saturday January the twelfth. Around midday,' he added.

'But that was sixteen days ago! I don't remember it.' Once again, I felt close to tears. 'Didn't I leave a forwarding address?'

'You went to stay with Sadie, I think. But that was just for a night.'

'And after that?'

'No idea.'

'Oh, my God,' I said, and just held my head in my hands. 'So where do I go now?'

'You could stay here for a bit, if you want. It would be all right. Just until you got things sorted out. We could talk things over . . . You know.'

I looked at Terry sitting there in his cloud of cigarette smoke. And I thought of that woman, the woman I couldn't remember, me, who had taken the decision and walked out sixteen days earlier.

'No,' I said. 'No. I've got things to sort out. All sorts of things.'

I looked around. Didn't someone say that if you leave something somewhere, it shows you want to come back? For sort of the same reason, I felt I had to take something away. Anything. There was a small globe on the mantelpiece. Terry had given it to me on the only birthday of mine we had spent together. I took hold of it. He looked quizzical.

'It's mine,' I said. 'You gave it to me. It was my birthday present.'

I moved towards the door and then I remembered something. 'Sorry, Terry,' I said. 'I haven't got my purse. I haven't got anything. Could you lend me some money? Ten pounds. Twenty. Anything.'

With a vast sigh, Terry got up and walked across to where his jacket was hanging over the back of the sofa. He searched through his wallet. 'I can give you fifteen,' he said. 'I'm sorry. But I'll need the rest tonight.'

'That's all right.'

And he counted the money out as if he were paying the paper bill. A ten-pound note, three pound coins and then a mass of silver and copper. I took it all.

Three

I spent £2.80 on the Underground, and put a twenty-pence piece into the open violin case of a busker who was standing at the bottom of the escalator, playing 'Yesterday' and trying to catch people's eyes as they flowed past him on their way home from work. I spent another fiver on a bottle of red wine when I reached Kennington. Now I had just seven pounds left, stuffed into my back pocket. I kept feeling it to make sure it was still there, one folded note and five coins. I had a plastic bag full of the unfamiliar clothes I'd been found in six days ago; only six days. I had a globe. As I stumbled along the street, head down against the wind and nose turning red, I felt dangerously unencumbered. It was as if without all the ordinary stuff of my previous life I was weightless and inexplicable and could drift away like a feather.

I had let myself dream of this: walking down the cold street with a bottle of wine to see a dear friend. Now I kept glancing around to see who was walking beside me, behind me. Why had I never noticed before how strange people look, especially in winter when they're muffled and buttoned up into themselves? My old shoes kept slipping on the ice. At one point a man put out his hand to steady me as we crossed the road. I wrenched my arm away and he stared at me in surprise.

'Be in, be in, be in,' I said, as I pressed the bell to Sadie's basement flat and waited. I should have phoned in advance. What if she was out somewhere, or away?

But she was never out at this time of day. Pippa was only six or seven weeks old and Sadie was euphorically housebound. I pressed the bell again.

'Coming!' called a voice. I could see her figure through the frosted glass. 'Who is it?'

'Me. Abbie.'

'Abbie! I thought you were still in hospital! Hang on.'

I heard her cursing and fiddling with the locks and the door swung open and there she was, with Pippa in her arms, swaddled in thick towels and only a section of wrinkled pink face showing.

'I was just giving her a bath –' she began, then stopped. 'Jesus! Look at you!'

'I should have phoned in advance. I just . . . sorry, I needed to see you.'

'Jesus!' she said again, stepping back to let me inside.

A sour-sweet heat hit me as Sadie closed the door behind us. Mustard and talcum powder and milk and vomit and soap. I closed my eyes and took a deep breath.

'Bliss,' I said, and put my face towards Pippa. 'Hello, sweetie, do you remember me?' Pippa opened her mouth and I could see right down her clean pink tunnel of throat to her tonsils. She gave a single thin yell. 'No?' I said. 'Well, that's not surprising, really. I'm not sure I remember me either.'

'What on earth's happened to you?' asked Sadie. She pulled Pippa more firmly towards her and jiggled her slightly, in that instinctive way that all mothers seem to have. 'You look –'

'I know. Awful.' I put the globe on the kitchen table. 'This is for Pippa.'

'What can I get you? Here, sit down. Move those baby clothes.'

'Can I have a biscuit or a bit of bread or something? I feel a bit wobbly.'

'Of course. God, what's been going on with you?' Pippa began to grizzle and Sadie lifted her up higher until she was bunched under her chin. 'Sssh, it's all right now,' she crooned in her new sing-song voice, which none of us had heard until Pippa was born. 'There, there, my little poppet.'

'You need to deal with her. I've come barging in at just the wrong time.'

'She wants her feed.'

'Go on. I can wait.'

'Are you sure? You know where everything is. Make us both some tea. There are some digestives, I think. Have a look.'

'I brought wine.'

'I'm breast-feeding, I shouldn't, really.'

'You have a glass and I'll manage the rest.'

'I'll just change her, then I'll feed her in here. I want to hear everything. God, you're so thin. How much weight have you lost, anyway?'

'Sadie?'

'Yes?' She turned in the doorway.

'Can I stay?'

'Stay?'

'Just for a bit.'

'Sure. Though I'm surprised you want to, really. It's just the sofa, mind, and the springs are gone and you know how Pippa wakes in the night.'

'That doesn't matter.'

'You said that last time, until it happened.'

'Last time?'

'Yes.' She looked at me strangely.

'I can't remember.'

'What?'

'I can't remember,' I repeated. I felt so tired I thought I'd fall over.

'Look, make yourself comfortable,' Sadie said, 'I'll be back. Five minutes, max.'

I opened the bottle of wine and poured two glasses. I took a sip from mine and at once felt dizzy. I needed something to eat. I rummaged in the cupboards and found a packet of salt and vinegar crisps, which I ate standing up, cramming them into my mouth. I took another cautious sip of wine, then sat down on the sofa again. My head throbbed, my eyes burned with fatigue and the cut on my side was prickling. It felt so wonderfully warm and safe in here, down in the basement, with baby clothes draped over radiators and a big vase of dark orange chrysanthemums on the table, like flames.

'OK?' Sadie was back. She sat beside me, unbuttoned her shirt and undid her bra. She held Pippa to her breast, then sighed and settled back. 'Tell me, then. It was bloody Terry, wasn't it? Your poor face, it's still bruised. You shouldn't have gone back. I thought you'd gone on holiday.'

'Holiday?' I repeated.

'You said you were going to book one,' she said.

'There was no holiday,' I said.

'What did he do this time?'

'Who?'

'Terry.' She peered at me. 'Are you all right?'

'What makes you think it was Terry?'

'It's obvious. Especially after what happened last time. Oh, Abbie.'

'What do you mean, "last time"?'

'When he hit you.'

'So he did hit me.'

'Yes. Hard. Abbie? You must remember.'

'Tell me anyway.'

She looked at me, puzzled, wondering if this was some kind of joke.

'This is weird. You argued, he hit you, you left him and came here. You said it was over for good this time. You were very determined. Almost excited, really. Happy, even. So you went back?'

'No.' I shook my head. 'At least, I don't know. But it wasn't him.'

'You're not making sense.' She stared at me, frowning, and then turned back to Pippa.

'I got hit over the head,' I said. 'Now I can't remember things. I can't remember leaving Terry, or coming here, or anything.'

She made a whistling sound between her teeth. I couldn't tell if it was shock or incredulity. 'You mean, you were concussed or something?'

'Something like that.'

'So you really can't remember?'

'I really can't.'

'You can't remember leaving Terry?'

'No.'

'Or coming here?'

'No.'

'Or moving out again?'

'Did I move out again? I suppose I must have done – nothing of mine's here, is it? Where did I go?'

'You really can't remember?'

'No.' I felt tired of saying it.

'You went to Sheila and Guy's.'

'So I went there on the Sunday?'

'I guess. Yes, that must be right. Days of the week seem to merge for me at the moment.'

'And you didn't see me again, till now, I mean?'

'No. I thought you were away.'

'Oh, well.'

'Abbie, tell me what happened. The whole story.'

The whole story: I took a sip of my wine and looked at her, while she whispered endearments to her baby. I badly needed to talk to someone, to pour it all out, everything that had happened, the terror in the dark, the shame, the horrible, terminal loneliness, the sense of being dead. I needed to tell someone about the police and the way they'd taken all those emotions and turned them back on me – and I needed that someone to be solid as a rock in their faith in me. If they weren't . . . I drained the wine in my glass and poured myself some more. If not Sadie, then who? She was my best friend, my oldest friend. I'd been the one she'd turned to after Bob dumped her, when she was eight months pregnant. If Sadie didn't believe me, who would? I took a deep breath.

I told Sadie everything. The ledge, the noose, the hood, the bucket, the wheezy laugh in the darkness. How I knew I would die. She listened without interrupting, though occasionally she made little sounds of amazement or muttered expletives. I didn't cry. I had thought I would cry and she would hold on to me and stroke my hair the way she stroked Pippa's. But I felt absolutely dry-eyed and dispassionate and told my account calmly, right up to this moment. 'I'm not going mad, am I?' I finished.

'They didn't believe you! How could they not believe you? The bastards!'

'They thought I was in a vulnerable state and fantasizing.'

'How could you make up something like that? Why would you, for God's sake?'

'I don't know. To run away, to get attention. Whatever.'

'But *why*? Why didn't they believe you?' she persisted.

'Because there's no evidence,' I said flatly.

'None at all?'

'No. Not a shred.'

'Oh.' We sat there in silence for a few seconds. 'So, what on earth are you going to do now?'

'I don't know that either. I don't know where to begin, Sadie. I mean, I literally don't know what to do next. When I get up tomorrow morning, I don't have a clue where I should go, who I should see, who I should *be* even. It's like I'm starting from zero. A blank. I can't tell you how odd it feels. How truly horrible. It's like an experiment designed to drive me insane.'

'You must be furious with them.'

'Yes, I am.'

'And scared.'

'Right.' The warm room suddenly felt chilly.

'Because,' said Sadie, following her thoughts, 'because if what you say is really true then he is still out there. He may still be after you.'

'Yes,' I said. 'Exactly.' But we'd both heard her say it. *If.* If what I said was true, if I hadn't made the whole thing up. I looked at her and she dropped her eyes and started talking to Pippa again in her baby voice, though Pippa had fallen asleep by now, her head tipped back like a drunkard's and her small mouth half open, a milk blister on her top lip.

'What do you fancy for supper?' she asked. 'You must be famished.'

I wasn't going to let it drop. 'You don't know whether to believe me, do you?'

'Don't be ridiculous, Abbie. Of course I believe you. Of course. One hundred per cent.'

'Thanks.' But I knew, and she knew I knew, that she was unsure. Doubt had been planted, and it would grow and flourish. And who could blame her? It was my hysterical Gothic tale against everyone else's measured, everyday sanity. If I was her, I'd doubt me.

I made supper while Sadie put Pippa to bed. Bacon sandwiches, with fat white slices of bread that I dipped in the fat first, chewy and salty, and big mugs of tea. Being here should have felt like a refuge from all that had happened and might again, but that night on Sadie's lumpy sofa I slept fitfully and several times I lurched awake from dreams of running, tripping, falling, with my heart racing and sweat pouring off my forehead. Pippa woke often, too, howling angrily. The walls in the flat were thin and it was as if we were in the same room. In the morning I'd leave. I couldn't stay here another night.

'That's what you said last time,' remarked Sadie cheerily, when I told her at six the next morning. She seemed remarkably fresh. Her face was rosy under her mess of soft brown hair.

'I don't know how you manage. I need at least eight hours, preferably ten, twelve on Sundays. I'll go to Sheila and Guy's; they've got room. Just till I work out what to do.'

'And you said that too.'

'So it must be a good idea.'

I made my way to Sheila and Guy's in the dawn. It had snowed some more in the night, and everything – even the dustbins, even the burnt-out cars – looked eerily beautiful in the soft light. I walked, but I stopped at a baker's on the way to buy three croissants as a peace-offering, so I now had exactly £5.20 left. Today I'd phone my bank. What was my account number? I had a flash of panic that I wouldn't be able to remember it, and that lots of bits of my life were disappearing now, as if there was a delete cursor randomly at work in my brain.

It wasn't even seven o'clock when I rapped at their door. The curtains upstairs were all drawn. I waited for a decent interval, then rapped again, longer and louder. I stood back from the door and looked up. A curtain twitched. A face and bare shoulders appeared in the window.

Sheila and Sadie and I have known each other for more than half our lives. We were a quarrelsome threesome at school, breaking up and re-forming. But we went through our teenage years together: exams, periods, boyfriends, hopes. Now Sadie has a baby and Sheila has a husband, and I . . . well, I don't seem to have much right now, except a story. I waved furiously at the window and Sheila's face changed from scowling grumpiness to surprise and concern. It disappeared, and a few moments later, Sheila was standing at the door in a voluminous white towelling robe, her dark hair in rats' tails round her bleary face. I thrust the bag of croissants into her hands.

'Sorry,' I said. 'It was too early to ring in advance. Can I come in?'

'You look like a ghost,' she said. 'What's happened to your face?'

I edited the story down this time, just the highlights. I was vague about the police. I think Sheila and Guy were obviously confused, but they were effusively supportive and welcoming, fussing over me with coffee and offers of a bath, a shower, money, clothes, the use of their phone, of their car, of their spare bedroom for as long as I liked.

'We'll be at work, of course. Just treat the place like your own.'

'Did I leave any of my things here?'

'Here? No. There might be odds and ends floating around.'

'How long did I stay then? Just one night?'

'No. Well, kind of, I suppose.'

'What do you mean, "kind of"?'

'You stayed here Sunday and then you didn't come back on Monday. You phoned to say you were staying somewhere else. And then you picked up your stuff on Tuesday. You left us a note. And two very expensive bottles of wine.'

'Where did I go after that, then?'

They didn't know. All they could tell me was that I had been rather hyped-up, had kept them up till the early hours of Monday, talking and drinking and making fine plans for the rest of my life, and then had left the next day. They glanced at each other surreptitiously as they were telling me this and I wondered what they weren't telling me. Had I behaved disgracefully, thrown up on the carpet? At one point, I came back into the kitchen just as they were getting ready to leave for work. They were talking urgently in low voices, their heads close together, and when they saw me they stopped and smiled at me and pretended they'd simply been making arrangements for the evening.

Them too, I thought, and I looked away as if I hadn't noticed anything. It was going to be like this, especially after Sheila and Guy had talked to Sadie, and they'd all talked to Robin, and then to Carla and Joey and Sam. I could imagine them all ringing each other up. Have you heard? Isn't it terrible? What do you think, I mean, *really* think, just between us?

The trouble is, friendships are all about tact. You don't want to know what friends say about you to other friends or to partners. You don't want to know what they really think or how far their loyalty goes. You want to be very careful before you test it. You might not like what you find.

Four

I had no embarrassment. I was down to about five pounds and I just had to borrow money from Sheila and Guy. They were very nice about it. Of course, being 'very nice' meant a lot of huffing and puffing and gritting of teeth and rummaging in purse and wallet and saying that they would be able to get to the bank later. At first I felt like saying it didn't matter and I could manage without the money, but it did matter and I couldn't manage without it. So fifty-two pounds in assorted notes and coins was dropped into my open hands. Then I borrowed a pair of knickers from Sheila and a T-shirt and threw mine into her dirty-washing basket. She asked if she could give me anything else and I asked if she had an old sweater that I could take for a day or two. She said, 'Of course', and went and found me a lovely one that didn't look old at all. Sheila was rather larger than me, especially now, but I was able to roll up the sleeves and didn't look too ridiculous. Even so, she couldn't keep an entirely straight face.

'I'm sorry,' she said. 'You look great but . . .'

'Like someone living rough,' I said.

'No, no,' she insisted. 'I'm used to you seeming, I don't know, more grown-up, maybe.'

As they left for work, I thought they looked a little concerned about the idea of leaving me alone in their house. I don't know whether they thought I would raid the drinks cabinet or the fridge or make international calls. In fact I raided the medicine cabinet for some paracetamol, and I made four calls, all local. I ordered a cab because there was no way I was going to wander around the streets on my own. I rang Robin at work. She said she couldn't meet me for lunch. I said she had to. She said she was already having lunch with someone. I said I was sorry but she had to cancel it. There was a pause and she said, 'All right', with a sigh.

I was calling in a lifetime of favours. I rang Carla and leant on her to meet me for coffee in the afternoon. I rang Sam and arranged to meet him for another coffee, forty-five minutes after my meeting with Robin. He didn't ask why. Neither did Carla. It seemed worrying. They must know something. What had Sadie said? I knew the feeling. I, too, had been feverish with some amazingly hot piece of gossip and had run around spreading it like Typhoid Mary. I could imagine it. Hey, listen, everybody, did you hear what happened to Abbie? Or was it simpler than that? Hey, everybody, Abbie's gone mad. Oh, and by the way, she'll want to take all of your loose change.

I looked out of the window until I saw the cab draw up. I reached for my bag and realized I didn't have a bag. I had nothing except a small amount of Sadie's money and quite a bit more of Sheila and Guy's crammed into my pockets. I told the cab driver to take me to Kennington Underground station. The cab driver wasn't exactly ecstatic. And he was puzzled as well. It was probably the first time in his career that he had taken a passenger to a tube station a few streets away. It cost three pounds fifty.

I took the train to Euston and walked across the platform, where I changed on to the Victoria Line. I got off at Oxford Circus and walked to the Bakerloo Line platform. I looked across the rails at the map. Yes, this train led to places satisfyingly remote from anywhere I'd ever heard of. A train arrived and I got on. Then, as the doors started to close, I stepped off. The train pulled out and for a second or two, until other people arrived on the platform, I was alone. Anyone looking at me would have thought I was a lunatic. And obviously I had known that nobody was following me. Nobody *could* be following me. But now I really knew and that made me feel better. A bit. I went to the Central Line and took the tube to Tottenham Court Road.

I walked to a branch of my bank. I felt a great weariness as I pushed through the doors. All the simple things had become so hard. Clothes. Money. I felt like Robinson Crusoe. And the worst bit was that I had to tell almost everybody I met some version of my story. I gave a very truncated version to the woman behind the counter and she sent me to the 'personal banker', a larger woman in a turquoise blazer with brass buttons, sitting at a desk in the corner. I waited for some time while she opened a bank account for a man who apparently spoke no English. When he left, she turned to me with an expression of relief. Little did she know. I explained that I wanted to withdraw some money from my account but I had been the victim of a crime and I didn't have my cheque book, credit card or debit card. No problem, she said. Any form of photographic identification would be perfectly acceptable.

I took a deep breath. I didn't have any form of identification. I didn't have anything. She looked puzzled. She almost looked afraid. 'Then I'm sorry –' she began.

'But there must be some way of getting at my money,' I said. 'And I need to cancel my old cards and get new ones. I'll sign anything you want, give you any information you want.'

She still looked doubtful. More than doubtful. She seemed almost paralysed. Then I remembered Cross. Of all the people who had ejected me back into the world, Cross had looked the most unhappy. He had muttered something about how if there was any help I needed he would do what he could.

'There's a policeman,' I said. 'He was in charge of the case. You can check it with him.'

I wrote down the number for her and was immediately worried. If Cross was too co-operative, I might be worse off than before. She frowned at the number and said she would have to talk to the assistant branch manager. He was a balding man in a decidedly smart grey suit and he looked worried as well. I think they would have been relieved if I had got into a temper and stormed out but I didn't give up. They had to let me back into my life.

It took a long time. There were phone calls. They asked me lots of questions about my life, about my account, bills I'd paid recently, they asked my mother's maiden name. I signed lots of pieces of paper and the woman typed and typed into the computer on her desk. In the end, with obvious reluctance, they gave me two hundred pounds and told me that they would send new credit cards and a cheque book to me within two working days, maybe even the following day if I was very lucky. I suddenly realized that this meant that it would all be sent to Terry's flat. I was going to get them to send it somewhere else, but I thought if I tried to change my address as well, they would probably throw me out on to the street. So I left with the wad of cash stuffed into two trouser pockets. I felt as if I were coming out of a betting shop.

*

Robin hugged me hard as soon as she saw me, but if she was concerned she was also wary. I could see why. We looked like members of a different species. She's beautiful, dark-skinned, groomed, besuited. I looked like what I was, which was someone with nowhere to live and nowhere particularly urgent to go. She met me outside the travel agent's where she works. She hadn't booked anywhere for us to eat. I said I didn't mind. I *didn't* mind. We went to an Italian sandwich bar where we sat at a counter. I ordered a large coffee and a sandwich that looked like an entire delicatessen counter between two slices of bread. I felt ravenously hungry. She just had coffee. She started to pay and I didn't stop her. I needed to husband my money carefully for the moment. I didn't know what things I would have to pay for in the vagrant existence I was leading.

'Sadie called me,' she said.

'Good,' I mumbled, my mouth full of sandwich.

'I can't believe it. We're so appalled for you. If I can do anything, anything at all . . .'

'What did Sadie say?'

'Just the bare bones.'

And then Robin gave me a version of my story. It was a relief to be hearing it, rather than telling it.

'Are you seeing someone?' she asked, when she had finished.

'You mean a man?' I said.

'I meant a doctor.'

'I've been in hospital.'

'But Sadie said you had a head injury.'

I'd just taken a large bite of my sandwich and there was a pause in the conversation as I chewed and swallowed.

'That's part of what I wanted to talk to you about, Robin. As Sadie said, I got this concussion thing, and that was the problem with the doctors and the police. So one of the things I'm trying to do is to reconstruct what happened in the time where my memory is blank. For example, and I feel a bit embarrassed even telling you this, I didn't realize I had walked out on Terry. It's stupid, isn't it? I finally get it together to make one of the best decisions of my life, then forget all about it. So, basically, if I were a policeman and I were missing and I said to you, "When did you last see Abbie Devereaux?" what would you say?'

'What?'

'When did you last fucking see me, Robin? That's not such a difficult question.'

'No, that's right.' She thought for a moment. 'I knew you'd left Terry. We met the next day. Sunday, late morning.'

'Hang on. Sunday January the thirteenth?'

'Right. We went shopping over on Kensington high street. You must remember that.'

'Not a thing. What did I buy?'

She looked at me aghast.

'Is this for real? Well, I bought some fantastic shoes. They were reduced to thirty-five pounds from something ridiculous like a hundred and sixty.'

'But what about me?'

Robin smiled. 'I remember now. We'd talked on the phone the previous evening. You were a bit manic then. But that morning you were fine. Really good. The best I'd seen you in ages. You said you felt really positive and you said you were going to equip yourself for your new life. You bought a lovely short brown dress. Crushed velvet. Some tights and knickers. Shoes to go with the dress. And a spectacular coat. Long, navy blue. You spent a fortune. It was good, though. Money well spent. You were rather giggly about spending so much when you'd just walked out of your job.'

'Oh, God! Don't tell me I've left work as well as Terry!'

'Yes. Didn't you know? You didn't seem to mind, though.'

'So I don't have a job any more?'

The ground seemed to sway under my feet. The world appeared changed again. Greyer, colder.

'Abbie?' Robin looked concerned.

I fumbled for something to say. 'Was that the last you saw of me?'

'We had lunch and we arranged to meet for a drink. I think it was on the Thursday evening. But the day before you rang and cancelled.'

'Why?'

'You said something had come up. You were very apologetic.'

'Was it something good? Did I sound upset?'

'You sounded . . . well, a bit hyper, maybe. It was very brief.'

'And that was it?'

'Yes.' Robin looked at me now, as I finished the last of my sandwich. 'This couldn't all have been some sort of misunderstanding?'

'You mean being captured and held prisoner by some-one who said he was going to kill me and that he had already killed other women? You mean that bit?'

'I don't know.'

'Robin,' I said slowly. 'You're one of my oldest friends and I want you to be honest with me. Do you believe me?'

At that, Robin took my head between her slim fingers, kissed me on both cheeks, and then pushed me back and looked at me. 'The thing is,' she said, 'if it's true, and I'm sure it is, I just can't bear the idea of it.'

'You should try it from where I'm sitting.'

My meeting with Carla consisted of hugs and tears and assurances of friendship but it basically boiled down to the fact that she had been away for those days and all she could say was that I had left a message on her answering-machine asking her to call and when she got back she had left a message on Terry's answering-machine and that was that.

Sam is another of my oldest friends and I can't believe that the boy I remember with a joint in his hand upstairs at various parties in south London is now a solicitor who wears a suit and a tie and has to impersonate a grown-up between nine and five on weekdays. And yet, at the same time, I had started to see what this rather good-looking, trendy twenty-six-year-old was going to look like when he was forty.

'Yes, we met,' he said. 'We had a drink on Sunday evening.' He smiled. 'I feel a bit pissed off that you don't remember it. You were staying with Sheila and Guy. You talked a bit about Terry. But not that much. I thought that we were meeting so you could sound off about that ungrateful bastard. I mean, ungrateful for living with you. But you seemed excited more than anything else.'

Oh, yes. I remembered. I didn't remember our meeting but I sort of knew what must have happened. Sam and I had always been friends, never been out together. I sometimes wondered if he had regretted that and maybe he might have seen my break-up with Terry as an opportunity. It was something that had crossed my mind too. But clearly the Abbie who had had a drink with him had decided against him. He was better as a friend.

I took a sip of about the fourth coffee I'd had that afternoon. I was buzzing with caffeine and strangeness. I hadn't learnt much, but maybe that was what was interesting. I now knew that I had chosen not to spend those last days before it happened with my closest friends. So who had I spent them with? What had I done? Who had I been?

'What are you going to do?' Sam asked, in his forensic style.

'What do you mean?'

'Because if what you say . . . I mean, from what you say, he must be out there, and *he* knows that *you*'re out there, so what are you going to do?'

I took another sip of coffee. This was the question that my brain had been screaming at me and that I had been trying to ignore.

'I don't know,' I said. 'Hide. What else can I do?'

Five

I hadn't made an appointment, and they told me that I would have to wait for at least fifty minutes before they could do it, but I didn't mind that. I didn't have anywhere else to be, and it was warm in here. And safe. I sat in an easy chair near the door and leafed through last year's glossy magazines. Penny, the woman who was going to cut my hair, told me to pick out styles that I thought I might like, so I examined film stars and musicians and grinning celebrities and tried to imagine my face under their hair. The trouble was, I'd still look like me.

It was just beginning to get dark. Outside the window, people trudged by, wrapped in coats and scarves, wincing in the cold. Cars and lorries thundered past, throwing up muddy slush. Inside, it was bright and still and quiet, just the sound of scissors snipping through hair, the swoosh of the broom on the floor, gathering locks up into soft piles, an occasional murmur of conversation. There were six people already having their hair cut, all women. They sat up straight in their chairs, black robes draped around them, or lay back against the sink, having shampoo and conditioner massaged into their scalps. I could smell coconut, apple, camomile. I closed my eyes. I could sit here all day.

'Have you decided?'

'Short,' I said, snapping open my eyes. She led me to a seat in front of a large mirror and stood behind me, running her hands through my hair, her head to one side speculatively.

'You're sure about that, are you?'

'Yes. Really short. Not a bob or anything. You know, cropped. Short, but not too brutal.'

'Choppy, perhaps, mussed up. A bit soft round here, maybe?'

'Yes. That sounds fine. I'm having a different colour put in first, as well.'

'That'll take a good hour more.'

'That's all right. What colour do you think I should have?'

'You've got pretty hair as it is.'

'I want a change. I was thinking about red. Bright red.'

'Red?' She lifted my long pale hair and let it fall through her fingers. 'Do you think red would suit your colouring? What about something softer – a kind of dark caramel colour maybe, with interesting highlights?'

'Would it look very different?'

'Oh, definitely.'

I've never had really short hair. When I was a girl I refused to have it cut at all. I wanted to be like my friend Chen, who could sit on her blue-black hair. She used to wear it in a single plait, fastened at the bottom with a velvet bow. It snaked down her back, thick and gleaming, as if it were alive. I put up a hand and stroked the top of my head, took a last look.

'OK, then,' I said. 'Let's go, before I change my mind.'

'I'll be back after the colour's in.'

Another woman dyed my hair. First, she applied a thick, brownish paste that smelt unpleasantly chemical. I sat under a lamp and baked. Then she put some lighter dollops on to slabs of hair and wrapped them with bits of tin-foil. I looked as if I was about to be trussed and put into the oven. I closed my eyes once more. I didn't want to see.

Fingers combed through my hair, warm water ran over my scalp. Now I smelt of fruit, of humid tropical forests. A towel was wrapped round my head like a turban. Someone put a cup of coffee down in front of me. Outside, more snow started to fall.

I closed my eyes when Penny began cutting. I heard the scissors crunch and a piece of hair slid down my cheek. The back of my neck felt strangely exposed, my ear-lobes too. Penny sprayed more water on to my head; she cut steadily, not talking except to tell me to sit this way or that; she leant forward and blew away prickles of hair. I opened my eyes and saw in front of me a small, pale, naked face. My nose and mouth looked too big, my neck looked too thin. I closed my eyes again and tried to think about other things. Food, for instance. After this I'd go and buy a pastry from the deli I'd spotted down the road, something sweet and spicy. Cinnamon and pear, maybe. Or a slice of carrot cake. Perhaps an apple, big and green and tart.

'What do you think?'

I forced myself to look. There were smudges under my eyes and my lips were pale and dry. I put up a hand and touched the soft bristle on top of my head. 'Fine,' I said. 'Great.'

Penny angled the mirror behind me. From the back, I looked like a young boy.

'What do you think?' I said.

She looked at me appraisingly. 'Very edgy,' she said.

'Just what I wanted.'

A brush was flicked round my neck and over my face, the mirror was tipped so I caught every variation of my new profile, I was handed my jacket and posted into the outside world, where tiny flakes of snow whirled through the gathering darkness. My head felt weirdly light. I kept seeing myself in shop windows and being startled. I bought a giant chocolate-chip cookie and ate it while I made for the shops.

For the past three years, I've dressed pretty smartly. It was part of the job and I guess I got used to it. Suits. Skirts and jackets and sheer tights, with an extra pair in my bag in case they got snagged. Things that were tailored and trim. So now I used up the rest of the money that Sheila had lent me, and then rather a lot more, on a pair of baggy black trousers, several T-shirts, some leather biker boots, a hooded, fleecy sweatshirt, black as well, a long stripy scarf and a black woollen hat, some warm gloves. I nearly bought a long leather coat, except I didn't have enough money left, which was probably fortunate. But I did have enough money for six pairs of knickers, two bras, several pairs of thick socks, a toothbrush and toothpaste, and some lipstick, mascara, deodorant and shampoo.

I stood in front of the long shop mirror. I turned round slowly, looking at myself over my shoulder. I lifted my chin. I was no longer Abbie the businesswoman, hair drawn up in a sleek bun and sensible shoes. I looked thin and almost feral, with sharp collar-bones. The new black clothes made my face seem paler than ever, though the bruise on my cheek had faded to a jaundiced yellow stain. My hair was spiky and the colour of birchwood. I thought I looked a bit like an owl. And about sixteen, a schoolgirl. I smiled at myself, the newness I saw there, and nodded.

'Good,' I said, aloud. 'Perfect.'

Six

'Christ!' said Sheila, as she opened the door.

'What do you reckon?'

'It's certainly a change of image. I hardly recognized you.'

'That's the general idea. Can I come in, then? I'm freezing out here!' Icy flakes were landing on my cheeks and nose, trickling down my neck. My new haircut was flat and wet.

She stood back and let me into the warmth. 'Sure. God, you look . . .'

'What?'

'I dunno. Younger.'

'Is that good?'

'Yes,' she said dubiously. 'You look littler, too, some-how. Tea? Drink?'

'Drink. I bought us some beer.'

'Thanks, but you shouldn't have bothered.'

'Don't thank me. It was your money. I'll be able to pay you back soon, though, when my credit card is sent to Terry's, which should be any day.'

'Whenever. That reminds me, Terry rang.'

'Here?'

'No, Sadie's. He thought you'd be there. So Sadie rang me to say that Terry says can you go and collect this big bag he forgot to give you yesterday, with all your mail and stuff. And the rest of your clothes.'

'Fine. I'll go tomorrow.'

'Or he'll throw it away.'

'Charming. I'll go now.'

'Now? Don't you want something to eat? We're having these friends round. A couple, very nice, he works with Guy and she does something with antiques, I think. Nothing smart, just the four of us. Or five, that is,' she said bravely.

'It's OK, Sheila. Four's a better number. Maybe I'll be back for the cheese course.'

'No cheese. Lemon tart.'

'You made lemon tart?'

'Yes.' She looked self-conscious and virtuous at the same time.

'Save some for me. Can I use your phone to book a cab?'

'Of course. You don't have to ask.'

I kissed her on both cheeks. 'You're being very nice to me. I promise I won't stay here for long.'

It costs a lot of money to go across London in a taxi, make it wait, then come all the way back again. I watched the meter nervously as it clicked into double figures. I'd had £257 this morning, from Sheila and Guy and from the bank, but after my haircut and shopping spree and various coffees and cabs, it was down to seventy-nine. By the end of the evening I'd have about sixty again.

The lights were on in our flat. Terry's flat, that is. I rang the bell and waited, then heard footsteps running down the stairs and a light went on in the hall.

'Hello?'

'Hi, Terry.'

'Abbie?' He peered at me. 'What have you gone and done to yourself? Your hair, it's –'

'Gone. I know. Can I come in and collect my stuff? I'm in a bit of a hurry. A cab's waiting.'

'I'll go and get it. I've put everything in bags. Wait here.' He turned and dashed back up the stairs again. But I wasn't going to wait in the freezing cold, so I followed him and we arrived simultaneously. There was a lovely smell coming from the flat, garlicky and pungent. On the table was a bottle of wine, but only half drunk, two glasses, two plates of chicken covered with sprigs of rosemary and whole garlic cloves. That was my recipe, my standby. Candles – that I'd bought. A woman was sitting there, twiddling her glass, her long fair hair falling forward and shining in the soft light. She was wearing a charcoal-grey suit and had tiny gold studs in her ears. I stood there in the doorway, in my baggy trousers, with my tufty hair, and stared at her.

'I'll get all your stuff,' said Terry.

'Aren't you going to introduce us?'

He muttered something and disappeared.

'I'm Abbie,' I said brightly to the woman.

'Nice to meet you,' she said faintly. 'Sally.'

'Here.' Terry dragged in two bin-bags with my remaining clothes, then put a bulging plastic bag of mail into my hands. He was red-faced.

'Must go,' I said. Then I turned to the woman. 'Do you know what's odd? You look rather like me.'

She smiled, polite but incredulous. 'I really don't think so.'

They were still on the fish when I backed into the kitchen, dragging my bags after me.

'Abbie, back already! This is Paul and Izzie. Are you going to join us?'

'Hi.' I could tell by the way Paul and Izzie looked at me that they'd heard the full story. 'Don't worry, I'm not really hungry. I'm going to go through my post.'

I lifted up the splitting plastic bag. 'Get some clues, eh?' They all laughed nervously and glanced at each other. Sheila flushed, and leant forward to refill their glasses.

'I'd love some wine, though.'

Most of the post was junk, January sales catalogues, stuff like that. There were two postcards: one from Mary, who was in Australia for the whole of the month; one from Alex in Spain. He must be back by now. I wondered if he'd heard. There were two invitations to parties. One had been and gone, but one was this weekend. Maybe I'd go to that, dance and flirt, I thought, and then, But what shall I wear? And what shall I say? And who on earth would flirt with someone who looked like a vagrant schoolgirl? Perhaps I wouldn't go, after all.

There was a strange, formal letter from Laurence Joiner at Jay and Joiner's, confirming that I was on unpaid leave, but that my pension and National Insurance would still be paid. I frowned and put it to one side. Clearly I needed to go into the office sometime. Maybe tomorrow.

Then there was a bank statement. At the beginning of the month I had been a glorious and uncharacteristic £1810.49 in credit but now I had only £597 left. I squinted at the row of figures. What on earth had I spent £890 on, on 13 January? Fuck, those must be the clothes that Robin had told me about. What on earth had possessed me? I must have been drunk or something. And I didn't even have the clothes to show for it. Then, three days later, I'd withdrawn five hundred pounds in cash, which was very odd. I usually take out about fifty.

I drank some wine and opened an official-looking letter, which informed me that the tax disc on my car was due to run out. This didn't concern me too much because I didn't have a clue where my car was – except

I suddenly did, because I opened the next envelope and discovered that it was being held in a police pound in Bow.

'Yes!' I said aloud. 'At last!'

I looked more closely at the letter. Apparently it had been towed away from an illegal parking place on Tilbury Road, E1, wherever Tilbury Road was. Wherever bloody E1 was. I could collect it between nine and five. I'd go tomorrow, first thing.

I raced to the kitchen. 'I've found my car!' I said to them.

'Good,' said Guy, a little startled. 'Great. Where is it?'

'In a police pound in Bow apparently. I'll get it tomorrow morning. Then I won't need all those cabs.' I picked up the bottle of wine and poured myself another large glassful.

'How?' asked Guy.

'What do you mean, how?'

'How will you get it? You don't have the key.'

'Oh.' I felt winded by disappointment. 'I hadn't thought of that. What shall I do?'

'You could get a locksmith out,' suggested Izzie kindly.

'No, I know. There's a spare key at Terry's, somewhere, God knows where, though. In a safe place I've forgotten. I'll have to go back again. Shit. I thought tonight was the end of it.'

'At least you'll have your car again. That's something.'

'It's a start.'

I was falling, falling from a great height. Nothing could stop me and there was silent black air all around me and I was plunging through it. I heard myself call out, a wild cry in the night. I heard it echo.

Then I woke with a violent lurch and lay as if winded

on the pillow. The pillow was damp from sweat. I felt sweat trickle down my cheeks and neck like tears. I opened my eyes but it was still dark. Quite dark. There was a heaviness over my heart, as if a great weight had been dropped on to me. I was trapped in the darkness, I heard myself breathing, but the sound was hoarse, like a rusty gasp. Something was wrong. I couldn't catch my breath properly; it was stuck in my chest and my throat kept closing against it in spasms. I had to remember how to do it. I had to remember how to breathe. I had to count, yes, that was it. Breathe in and then out. Slowly. One-two, one-two. Pulling air into my lungs, holding it for a second, letting it out again.

Who was there? Someone was nearby. A board creaked. I wanted to sit up but my body wouldn't move, and I wanted to call out but my voice was frozen inside me. Another board creaked. There was breathing. I could hear it, just outside the door. I lay flattened against my pillow. I could feel my mouth pulled back in a scream, but still no sound came, and there was the breathing again, footsteps, a quiet, stifled cough.

'No,' I said at last. 'No.' I spoke louder. 'No, no, no, no.' The words filled up my head. They ricocheted around the room, crashed around my skull, tore at my throat. 'No, no, no, no.'

The door opened and in the slab of light I could see a black shape.

'No!' I screamed again, even louder. There was a hand on my shoulder, fingers on my hair. I thrashed on the bed. 'No, no, no, no. Oh, please, no!'

'Abbie. Abbie, wake up. It's all right. You're having a dream. It's just a dream.'

'Oh, Jesus.'

'Abbie.'

'God, God, God,' I whimpered.

'You were having a nightmare.'

I took hold of Sheila's hand and pressed it against my forehead.

'You're soaked through! You must have a fever.'

'Sheila. Oh, Sheila. I thought . . .'

'You were having a nightmare.'

I sat up. 'It was terrible,' I said.

'You poor thing. Listen, I'm going to get you a towel to put over your pillow. You'll be all right now.'

'Yes. Sorry. I woke you.'

'You didn't. I was going to the bathroom anyway. Hang on.'

She went away and returned a few moments later with a large towel. 'All right now?' she asked.

'Yes.'

'Call if you need me.'

'Thanks. And, Sheila – leave the door open, will you? And the light in the corridor on?'

'It's very bright.'

'It doesn't matter.'

'Good night, then.'

'Night.'

She left and I lay back in bed. My heart was still pounding like a drum. My throat hurt from screaming. I felt weak and shaky and clammily sick. The light flooded in through the door. I lay and watched it and waited for it to be morning.

'Where would I have hidden it?'

'No idea,' said Terry. He was still in his dressing-gown, the one I'd given him for his last birthday, drinking thick black coffee and smoking cigarette after cigarette. A blue fug clouded the room, which smelt of ash and the garlic from last night. There was no sign of the other woman, though.

'I mean, it's not in any of the little cabinet drawers. It's not in the wooden bowl that every bit of crap ends up in. It's not in the bathroom.'

'Why would it be in the bathroom?'

'It wouldn't be. That's what I said, it's not.'

'Oh.' He lit another cigarette. 'Well, I've got to get dressed and go. I'm running late as it is. Will you be long?'

'As long as it takes to find the key. Don't worry, I can let myself out.'

'Well, not really.'

'Sorry?'

'You don't live here any more, Abbie. You walked out on me, remember? You can't just come and go like this.'

I stopped rummaging and stared at him. 'Are you serious?'

'I'll get dressed while you look,' he said. 'But, yes, I am.'

I opened all the drawers in the kitchen and living room and banged them shut again, opened cupboards and slammed them closed. Not with the cutlery; not with the bills; not with the tins of food, the bags of flour and rice, the cereal packets, the packets of coffee and tea, the bottles of oil, vinegar, soy sauce. Not on one of the mug hooks. Not on the lintel of the door between the two rooms. Not on the bookshelves, or with the stationery, or in the glass bowl where I put – used to put – things like rubber bands, paper clips, spare buttons and hairbands, stamps, tampons.

Terry came back into the room. He put his hands into his coat pockets and jangled change impatiently.

'Look,' I said, 'you don't want me here and I don't

want to be here. Go to work and when you come back I'll have gone. I won't steal anything. I won't remove the things that are mine. You can have them. I might as well start over with a completely blank slate. I won't scribble obscenities on the bathroom mirror with my lipstick. I'll find the key and I'll leave. OK?'

He jangled the coins some more. 'Is this really the way it's going to end?' he asked eventually, which took me by surprise.

'The woman who was here last night seemed nice,' I said. 'What was her name? Sarah?'

'Sally,' he said, giving up. 'OK. I'll leave you to it.'

'Thanks. 'Bye, then.'

''Bye Abbie.' He hovered by the door for a few seconds, then was gone.

I made myself a last cup of coffee. I took the mug and wandered round the flat. Part of me was wondering if the key would be hidden inside this cup, that cubby-hole. Part of me was just looking, remembering. I found the key under the pot of basil. The earth was all dried out and the leaves had wilted. I watered it carefully. I washed up my mug, dried it, put it back on the hook and left.

Bow was a long way. By the time I arrived I had forty-eight pounds left and a few coppers. I asked in a post office for directions to the car pound. It turned out to be a mile away from the nearest Underground station. You'd have thought that if they towed away your car, they'd at least put it somewhere near public transport. I would have taken a taxi if I'd seen one, but I didn't. There were just lots and lots of cars and vans spraying water up from the wide puddles in the road.

So I walked, past the garages selling BMWs, the factories making lights and catering equipment and car-

pets; past the building sites where cranes topped with
snow stood motionless. I saw the pound as I came over
the hill; row upon row of cars surrounded by a high
fence, with double-locked gates. Most of them were old
and dented. Perhaps their owners had simply abandoned
them. I couldn't see my car, which was also old and
dented, anywhere.

I took my letter to the office in the corner and a man
rummaged around in the filing cabinet, came out with a
piece of printed paper, scratched his head and sighed
heavily.

'So can I just take it?' I asked.

'Hang on, not so fast. You have to pay, you know.'

'Oh, yes, of course, sorry. How much?' I felt anxiously
in my pocket for the dwindling wad of notes.

'That's what I'm working out. There's the fine for
parking illegally, then there's the cost of towing it away,
then you have to add on the time it's been here.'

'Oh. That sounds like rather a lot.'

'It is, yes. A hundred and thirty pounds.'

'Sorry?'

'A hundred and thirty pounds,' he repeated.

'I don't have that much money.'

'We take cheques.'

'I don't have a cheque book.'

'Cards.'

I shook my head.

'Oh dear, oh dear,' he said. He didn't sound too sad.

'What shall I do?'

'I couldn't tell you.'

'Can I take the car, drive to a friend's to get money,
then come back here?'

'No.'

There was nothing for it but go away again. I slogged

back to Bow and sat in a little café with another cup of bitter, tepid coffee. Then I went to a payphone, called Sam and asked him, begged him, really, to send sixty pounds – no, make that eighty, ninety even – by courier to the police pound, where I'd be waiting. 'Please, please, please,' I said. 'I'm really sorry but this is an emergency.' I knew about the courier service because once he'd got his jacket collected from a club we'd been to because he couldn't be bothered to go back for it. Perk of the job, he'd said.

I finally got my car. At just after twelve thirty, I paid over the £130 and he gave me a printout of where it had been towed away from and a breakdown of the charges. Then he pointed out where it was parked, and unlocked the double gates. I had nineteen pounds left.

I climbed in and turned the key in the ignition. It started at once. I turned up the heating and rubbed my hands together to get rid of their cold stiffness. There was a Maltesers packet lying on the passenger seat. I pushed the tape that was in the machine and didn't recognize the music that came on. Something jazzy and cheerful. I turned up the volume and drove through the gates. Then I pulled over and looked at the official receipt. The car had been towed away from outside 103 Tilbury Road, E1 on 28 January – which I worked out was my last day in hospital. The road must be near here, surely.

The road map was in the glove compartment. I found Tilbury Road and drove there, through an area of London that was quite unfamiliar to me. It was a long, dismal street of boarded-up houses, dimly lit newsagents and twenty-four-hour shops selling grapefruit and okra and dented tins of tomatoes. I parked outside number

103 and sat in my car for a few minutes. I put my head on the steering-wheel and tried to remember. Nothing happened, no glimmer in the darkness. I put the map back in the glove compartment, and felt a rustle of papers. There were three receipts pushed in there too. One was for petrol: £26, on Monday 14 January. The second was for £150-worth of Italian lire on Tuesday 15 January. The third was for an Indian takeaway delivery for that same day: £16.80 for two pilau rice, one vegetable biryani, one king prawn tikka, one spinach, one aubergine, one garlic naan. To be delivered to 11b Maynard Street, London NW1. I'd never heard of Maynard Street and I couldn't remember when I'd last been in that corner of north London.

I stuffed the receipts back into the glove compartment and something fell on the floor. I leant down and picked up a pair of sunglasses and a key on a loop of string. Not my key. A key I had never seen before.

It was not quite four. I drove off again, through the drawn-out London outskirts, in the growing dusk. Everything seemed more frightening in the dark. I felt ragged with tiredness, but I still had things to do before going back to Sheila and Guy's.

Seven

'You know what you need, don't you?'

'No, Laurence, what do I need?'

'A rest.'

Laurence didn't know what I needed. I was standing in the office of Jay and Joiner's looking at the spot where my desk used to be. That was the funny thing. The office looked just as it had always looked. It's not a place that is anything special, which is pretty ironic for a company that designs offices. The only real attraction is that it is in a back alley, which is right in the middle of Soho, a couple of minutes' walk from the delicatessens and the market. When I say that the office looked the same, I mean the same except that all traces of me had vanished. It wasn't even as if someone else had just been sitting at my desk. The rest of the office seemed to have been repositioned very subtly so that the space I had once occupied wasn't there any more.

Carol had led me through. That was strange as well, being led through my own office. I didn't get the casual nods and greetings I was used to. There were double-takes, stares, and one new woman who looked at me curiously, assuming I was a customer, until Andy leant over and whispered something to her, and she looked at me even more curiously. Carol was breathlessly apologetic about the lack of all my stuff. She explained that people were falling over it and it had been put in boxes and stowed away in the storeroom, wherever that was. My mail was being opened and either redistributed around the office to relevant people or sent on to me at Terry's. But, then, I'd arranged all that, hadn't I? When I'd left. I nodded vaguely.

'Are you all right?' she asked.

That was a big question. I didn't know whether she just meant my appearance. She had certainly flinched when I had walked into Reception in my civilian clothes. Very civilian clothes. Then there was my hair. Also I had lost over a stone since she had last seen me. Plus, my face was still a bit yellow from the bruising.

'I've had a bit of a difficult time,' I said.

'Yes,' said Carol, not catching my eye.

'Did the police come here? Asking about me?'

'Yes,' she said. She was looking at me now. Warily. 'We were worried about you.'

'What did they ask?'

'They wanted to know about your work here. And why you'd left.'

'What did you say?'

'They didn't ask me. They talked to Laurence about it.'

'What do *you* think?'

'What do you mean?'

'About why I left.'

I didn't tell her that I had no idea myself about why I'd left, no memory of leaving. I was hoping that there might be at least one person to whom I could avoid telling my story. I felt I couldn't bear looking at another face showing those signs of growing puzzlement. Should they pity me? Should they believe me?

Carol looked thoughtful. 'I think you were right,' she said. 'You couldn't go on the way you were going. You were burning yourself out.'

'So you think I did the right thing?'

'I envy you your six months off. I think it's very brave.'

Another shock. Six months. And I noticed her use of the word 'brave': 'brave' as a euphemism for 'dumb'.

'But you're looking forward to me coming back?' I said jokingly. She looked wary again and that really did alarm me. What the fuck had I been up to?

'Obviously things got a bit frazzled at the end,' she said. 'And people said things they shouldn't have.'

'I always had a big mouth,' I said, when what I really wanted to say was, 'What is all this about?'

'I think you were mainly right,' Carol said. 'It's always a matter of tone, isn't it? And timing. I think it's good you've come in to talk things over.' We were at the door of Laurence's office now. 'By the way,' she said, too casually, 'that stuff with the police. What was it about?'

'It's complicated,' I said. 'Wrong place at the wrong time.'

'Were you . . . you know . . . ?'

Oh, so that was it. The gossip was that I might have been raped. Or not really raped.

'No, nothing like that.'

So I found myself being told by Laurence Joiner what I needed. It was all very awkward. On the spur of the moment I decided not to launch into a detailed account of my recent medical and psychiatric history. It was obvious that my last days at Jay and Joiner's hadn't been brilliant, and if there was going to be any prospect of my coming back, I ought to try not to make things worse.

'Good idea,' I said. 'In fact, I'm trying to get as much rest as I possibly can.'

'I don't need to tell you, Abbie, how important you are to us.'

'You do,' I said. 'It's always good to hear that.'

Laurence Joiner had forty-two suits. There had once

been a party at his house and one of the girls in the office had wandered into his bedroom and counted them. They had taken up three cupboards. And that had been a year earlier so there were probably more by now. And they were beautiful. As he talked, he stroked the knee of the lovely dark green one he was wearing today, as if it were a pet lying in his lap.

'We've all been worried about you,' he said.

'I've been a bit worried about myself.'

'First, we have . . . well, I needn't go over it again.'

Oh, please, go over it again, I said silently. If the apple wouldn't fall, I'd have to give the tree a little shake.

'One of the things I wanted to make sure,' I said desperately, 'was that everything was still all right from your point of view.'

'We're all on the same side,' Laurence said.

It was all so polite.

'Yes, but I want to know, explicitly, how you saw it. I mean my taking time off. I want to hear your view of it.'

Laurence frowned. 'I'm not sure if it's healthy to rake over it again. I'm not angry any more, I promise. It's clear to me now that you had been overworking for some time. It's my fault. You were so productive, and so effective, I just overloaded you. I think if we hadn't had the row over the Avalanche job we would have had it over something else.'

'Is that all?'

'If you mean, have I forgiven you for badmouthing the company to clients *after* you had taken time off, for going round London encouraging them to complain, the answer is yes. Just about. Now look, Abbie, I don't want to sound like someone out of *The Godfather* but I really don't think you ought to take sides with clients against the company. If you feel they've been badly advised or overcharged, you take it up with me, rather than informing them behind my back and in your own time. But I think we're all agreed on that.'

'When, um – just for my own records, I mean – when did I make these complaints?' I didn't need to ask what the complaints had been: I had a clear enough memory of the Avalanche project to know that.

'You're not going to start raking over everything again, are you, just when we've smoothed it all out?'

'No, no. But I'm a bit unclear about chronology, that's all. My diary's here and . . .' I stopped because I couldn't think how to finish the sentence.

'Shall we just draw a veil over the sorry affair?' said Laurence.

'I left on Friday, didn't I? Friday the eleventh.'

'Right.'

'And I complained to people, um . . .' I waited for him to fill in the gap.

'After the weekend. I don't know the dates myself. I just heard gradually, on two occasions by solicitors' letters. You can imagine how let down I felt.'

'Quite,' I said. 'Could I have a look through the Avalanche file?'

'What on earth for? That's all behind us. Let sleeping dogs lie.'

'Laurence, I absolutely promise I'm not going to make any trouble for you. But I want to talk to a couple of the people involved with it.'

'You must have the numbers.'

'I'm in a bit of chaos, I'm afraid. I've moved.'

'Do you mean moved out?'

'Yes.'

'I'm sorry to hear that. You can get any information you need from Carol.' Now he looked even more concerned. 'I don't want to butt in. But as I said, we've been worried. I mean, your problems here, you've split up with Terry, and then there were the police coming round. Can we do anything? Would you like us to arrange for you to go somewhere?'

I was puzzled for a moment then couldn't help laughing.

'You think it's drink or drugs?' I said. 'I wish.' I leant over and kissed Laurence's forehead. 'Thank you. Laurence, I've got one or two things to sort out and I'll be in touch.'

I opened the door of his office.

'Listen,' he said, 'if there's anything at all we can do . . .'

I shook my head. 'Just listening to you has made me think of how much you've already done. I hope I haven't been too much of a handful.' A thought came to me. 'I'd say that I was a different person then, but that might sound as if I wasn't taking proper responsibility.'

Laurence looked deeply puzzled, and no wonder.

On the way out I asked Carol for the Avalanche file.

'Are you serious?' she said.

'Why shouldn't I be?'

She looked doubtful. 'I'm not sure,' she said.

'The job's done with.'

'Yes, but –'

'It'll just be a few days,' I said. 'I'll be very careful.'

She started to yield. Maybe the idea that I would go away if she gave it to me was just too tempting.

'Do you want the drawings as well?'

'Just the correspondence will be fine.'

She fetched a bulky file and gave me a Marks & Spencer plastic carrier bag to put it in.

'One more thing,' I said. 'Has anybody called me here in the last couple of days?'

Carol rummaged around on her desk and gave me two sheets of paper covered with names and numbers. 'Only fifty or sixty people. Mostly the usual suspects. Do you want to give me a number I can give them?'

'No. This is important. Don't give anyone my numbers. Nobody.'

'Fine,' she said, looking rather startled by my urgent tone.

'I'll just take these numbers with me, I think. You don't need them, do you?' I folded up the sheets of paper and put them into my back pocket. 'I'll call you every so often. And one last thing.'

'What?'

'What do you think of my hairstyle?'

'Amazing,' she said. 'A bit extreme maybe, but amazing.'

'Does it make me look different?' I said.

'I didn't recognize you. Well, not at first.'

'Great,' I said, and she looked worried all over again.

I sat in the car and tried to clarify my thoughts. Avalanche. I felt like I'd been dropped on to a new planet. A foggy new planet. What did I actually know? The people at Jay and Joiner's saw me as a traumatized crazy. I'd left my job – temporarily, at least – after a row. And I'd left my boyfriend. At some point in the next few days I'd gone around visiting people who'd been involved in the project, apparently encouraging them to make complaints about the way our company had dealt with them. And I had met someone mad and murderous. Or could it possibly have been someone I already knew? It couldn't, could it?

An image came into my mind of an animal out in the open. I wanted to run for cover, but I didn't know which direction to run in. There were people who didn't know what had happened to me and there were other people who didn't believe what had happened to me. But there was one person who knew I was telling the truth. Where was he? I looked around reflexively and shuddered. Maybe I could escape somewhere very far away and never come back. Australia. The North Pole. No, it was hopeless. What was I going to do, initiate the process of emigration? What did that involve? Or should I just go on holiday to Australia and refuse to leave? It didn't sound very feasible.

I took the takeaway receipt from the glove compartment: 11b Maynard Street, NW1. It meant nothing to me. At one end of the spectrum, it might have been left there by someone else and have nothing important to do with me at all. Or it might be where he lived. But as soon as the thought came to me I knew I had to go there.

This was turning into the longest day of my life. I looked in the A–Z. It wasn't so far away. And I look completely different. I could pretend I had the wrong place. It would probably amount to nothing.

The flat was on the first floor of a smart stuccoed house just off Camden high street. I found a parking meter and crammed change into it to give me thirty-six minutes. It had its own entrance down the side. I stood in front of it and took a deep breath. I reached into the glove compartment and found the sunglasses. The cold winter evening was now as dark as the grave but it would complete my disguise. If a woman answered, I would have a proper conversation. If a man answered, I would play it safe. I would just say, 'Sorry, I must have the wrong address,' and start walking decisively away. There were enough people in the street for me to be safe.

But nobody answered. I pressed the bell again. And again. I could hear the bell ring, far inside. Somehow you can tell when a doorbell is ringing inside somewhere empty. I took my car keys out of my pocket and juggled them in my hand. I could go to one of the other flats in the building. But what would I ask? I walked back to the car. The meter showed that I had thirty-one minutes left. What a waste. I opened the glove compartment to replace the takeaway bill. There among the other stuff, the log book, a brochure, an RAC membership card, was that key, the key that wasn't the key to my old flat.

Feeling ridiculous, I took the key and walked back to the flat. With a sense of utter unreality, I pushed it gently into the lock and opened the door. As I pushed it wider, I saw a pile of mail. I picked up a letter. Josephine Hooper. I'd never heard of her. She was obviously away. There were stairs and I climbed them slowly. It could hardly have felt stranger if I had walked through the wall. I looked inside. I saw stripped pine, pictures, photographs pinned to the wall in the entrance hall, photographs I didn't recognize. Rich colours. I pushed the door shut. Yes, I could smell the mustiness of absence. Something had gone off somewhere.

I had no memory of the house, the street. I had barely even been to the area before. But I had had the key to the door in my car, so maybe I shouldn't have been surprised when I walked into the living room and turned on the lights and there, along with Josephine Hooper's pictures, table, rug, sofa, was my stereo, my television, my books. I felt as if I was going to faint. I sank back into a chair. My chair.

Eight

I wandered round the main room, finding traces of myself everywhere. At first I just looked at them, maybe touched them with one finger, as if they might dissolve and disappear. My small television set on the floor. My stereo and my CDs. My laptop on the coffee table. I lifted the lid and pressed the shift bar, at which it emitted a bleep and sprang to life. My green glass vase on the table, with three dead yellow roses rotting over its side and a scatter of black petals at its base. My leather jacket lying on the sofa, as if I'd just popped out for some milk. And there, stuck into the mirror over the fireplace, was a photograph of me. Two, to be precise: passport photos in which I was trying to suppress a smile. I looked happy.

But this was someone else's flat, full of unfamiliar furniture – apart from my chair – and books that I'd never read or even heard of, except the book of recipes that lay on the surface near the hob. Here was all the foreign clutter of someone else's life. There was a framed photograph on one of the shelves and I picked it up and examined it: a young woman with curly windswept hair, hands thrust into the pockets of her padded jacket, grinning widely, and hills spread out behind her. It was a lovely, carefree image, but I had never seen the face before. At least, I couldn't remember seeing it. I gathered up the mail that was lying on the floor and leafed through it. All the letters were to Jo Hooper, or Josephine Hooper, or Ms J Hooper. I put them in a neat pile on the kitchen table. She could open them later. But when I looked at the dead flowers on the table, or the amount of mail that had stacked up on the floor, I wondered when she was last here herself.

I opened the 'Mail' file on my laptop, clicked on the 'send and receive' button and waited while a little clock shimmered on the screen. There was a melodic bleep and I saw I had thirty-two new messages. I scrolled down them quickly. Nothing but messages from organizations I'd never heard of, alerting me to things I didn't want to know about.

I hesitated in the quiet room. Then I went across the hall and pushed open the first of the doors. It swung open and I was in a bedroom, with open curtains and a radiator that was warm. I turned on the light. The double bed was made, three velvet cushions scattered at the base and a pair of red checked pyjamas on the pillow. There was a lavender-coloured dressing-gown hanging on a hook on the door, and some moccasin slippers on the floor. On the top of the chest of drawers there was an ancient, balding teddy, a bottle of perfume, a little pot of lip balm, a silver locket, and another photograph – this time a close-up of a man's stubbly face. He had an Italian look to him, dark with absurdly long eyelashes. There were fine lines around his eyes and he was smiling. I opened the wardrobe. That black dress, that soft woollen shirt, this thin grey cardigan were someone else's. I lifted the lid of the laundry basket. It was empty, except for a pair of white knickers and some socks.

The next door opened on to the bathroom. It was clean, warm, white-tiled. My blue-and-white toothbrush was in a glass beaker, next to her black one; my toothpaste, with the lid off, was next to hers, with the lid on. There was my deodorant, my moisturizing cream, my makeup case. My green towel was on the radiator, next to her multicoloured one. I washed my hands, dried them on my own towel, stared at my unaccustomed face in the mirror. I half expected to see her standing behind me, with that smile. Josephine Hooper. Jo.

When I went into the third room I knew at once it was mine – not, at first, because of individual objects that I recognized, but because of the peculiar, powerful sense I had of coming home. Perhaps it had something to do with the smell, or the vague, controlled mess of the room. Shoes on the floor. My suitcase lying open underneath the sash window, with shirts and jerseys and underwear still packed inside. A thick deep-pink jersey thrown across the chair. A small pile of dirty washing in the corner. A tangle of jewellery on the bedside table. The long rugby shirt I wear at night hung over the bed head. I pulled open the cupboard door and there were my two smart suits, my winter dresses and skirts. And there was the blue coat I'd heard about from Robin, and the brown, crushed-velvet dress. I leant forward and sniffed its soft folds, wondering if I had ever got round to wearing it.

I sat down on the bed and for a few moments I just sat there, gazing around me. My head buzzed lightly. Then I slipped off my shoes and lay down and closed my eyes and listened to the hum of the central heating. It was quiet in here. Every so often I heard a faint shuffle from the upstairs flat, or a car driving along on an adjacent road. I pulled the rugby shirt towards me, and put my head on it. Somewhere, a car door banged and someone laughed.

I must have dozed off because when I jerked awake, with a strange taste in my mouth, it was raining outside. The street lamps were glowing orange and the tree outside my window shimmered in its orange glow. I was chilly, so I picked up the pink jersey and discovered, underneath it, my bag. There it was, bulging and securely fastened. I fumbled with the zip. On the top there was my wallet. I opened it and found four crisp, twenty-pound notes and quite a bit of change. My credit cards were in there too, and my driving licence, a book of stamps, my National Insurance number written out on a bit of paper, several visiting cards. Nothing seemed to be missing at all.

I wandered back into the kitchen-living room, clutching my bag. I drew the curtains properly, and turned on the standard lamp and the light above the cooker. It was nice here, homely. I'd obviously made a good move. I peered into the fridge. It was full of food: fresh pasta, bags of salad, a cucumber, spring onions, milk, butter, cheese – Cheddar, Parmesan and feta – individual pots of yoghurt, eggs, half a loaf of seeded brown bread, the remains of a bottle of white wine. No meat or fish – perhaps this Jo was a vegetarian. Most things were past their sell-by date; the milk, when I sniffed it, was sour, the bread was stiff, the salad in its bag limp and faded. That wine must need drinking, though, I thought.

Without thinking, I went to a cupboard and took out a tall wineglass. Then just as I was lifting the bottle, I stopped dead in my tracks: I had known where the glasses were kept. A tiny, buried part of my mind had known. I stood quite still and tried to let that shred of buried memory grow, but it was no use. I poured myself a generous glass of wine – after all, maybe I had bought it myself – and put on some music. I was half expecting Jo to walk in through the door, and the thought made me both nervous and excited. Would she be alarmed to see me or happy? Would she greet me casually or with disapproval and shock? Would she raise her eyebrows or give me a hug? But, really, I knew she wouldn't come. She'd gone away somewhere. Nobody had been here for days.

There was a light flashing on the phone and after some hesitation, I pressed the playback button. The first message was from a woman, saying she hoped everything was all right, and that she was going to cook supper, if Jo would wait in. The voice sounded familiar but it took a few moments to realize that she was me. I shivered and rewound, listened once more to my unfamiliar voice in this unfamiliar place. I sounded very cheerful. I drank a gulp of vinegary wine. There was a long, bossy message from a woman about the delivery date of a piece of work, and how it was being brought forward; a man's voice simply saying, 'Hi, Jo, it's me, shall we meet soon? Give me a bell.' A different woman, saying she'd be in town tomorrow and how about a drink; another woman saying, 'Hello? Hello?' until the line went dead. I saved the messages and took another sip of sharp yellow wine.

I didn't quite know what to do with myself. Was I an intruder here, or was this where I lived now? I wanted to stay, to have a hot bath and climb into my rugby shirt and eat pasta and watch TV – my TV – curled up on my chair. I didn't want to be staying with friends who were being very kind and polite but who thought I was crazy. I wanted to stay here and meet Jo and find out about the self I'd lost.

Whatever I was going to do later, I had to find out as much as I could now. First things first. I sat down on the chair and tipped the contents of my bag on to the coffee table. The largest item was a thickish brown A5 envelope with my name on it. I shook out the contents: two passports, one old and one brand new. I turned to the back and found my photograph, the replica of the pair stuck into the mirror. An airline ticket: ten days ago I was meant to have flown to Venice, returning the day before yesterday. I've always wanted to go to Venice.

A pair of black gloves, balled up into each other. My address book, coming apart at the spine. Four black pens, one leaking. Mascara. Two tampons. Half a packet of Polo mints – I put one into my mouth absentmindedly, which at least covered up the taste of the wine. A pack of tissues. One sucking sweet. One bead bangle. Three thin hairbands, which I didn't need any longer. A comb and a tiny mirror. And a bit of tin-foil that had fallen on the floor. I picked it up and it wasn't tin-foil after all, but a stiff silver strip, holding two pills, except one pill had been pressed out. I tilted it up to the light to make out the words printed on the back of the strip. Levonelle, 750 microgram tablets, levonorgestrel. I had an absurd impulse just to pop the other round white tablet into my mouth, just to see what would happen.

I didn't, of course. I made myself a cup of tea, then called Sheila and Guy's number and got the answering-machine. I told them I wouldn't be back tonight, but thanks so much for everything and I'd be in touch very soon. I put on my leather jacket, put the key and the tablet into the inside pocket, and went outside. My car was still there, except now it had a ticket wrapped in polythene, tucked under its iced-up windscreen wipers.

I'd deal with that later. I jogged in the darkness on to Camden high street and kept going until I came to a chemist's. It was about to close. I went up to the prescription counter, where a young Asian man asked me if he could help me.

'I hope so. I just wondered if you could tell me what

this is for.' I produced the silver strip and passed it across to him.

He glanced at it briefly and frowned at me. 'Does it belong to you?'

'Yes,' I said. 'That is, no, no, it doesn't. Because if it was mine I'd know, wouldn't I? I found it. I found it in my – my little sister's room and I just wanted to make sure it was safe. Because, you see, one's gone.'

'How old is your sister?'

'Nine,' I said wildly.

'I see.' He laid the strip down on the counter and took off his glasses. 'This is emergency contraception.'

'What?'

'The morning-after pill.'

'Oh,' I said.

'And you say your sister is only nine?'

'Oh, God.'

'She ought to see a doctor.'

'Well, as a matter of fact . . .' I petered out nervously. Another customer was standing behind us, listening eagerly.

'When do you think she took it?'

'Ages ago. Ten days, something like that.'

He looked very disapproving and then a rather ironic expression appeared on his face. I think he knew.

'Normally,' he said, 'you should take two pills. The first no later than seventy-two hours after intercourse has taken place, preferably earlier than that, and the second twelve hours after that. So your sister could be pregnant.'

I grabbed the strip and waved it. 'I'll deal with it, I promise, thank you, but I'll make sure it's all right. Thank you.' I made for the street. The cold rain felt wonderful on my burning cheeks.

Nine

I knew what had happened. I bloody knew. It was one of those ludicrous things that I'd heard of other people doing. Even friends. How pathetic. As soon as I got back to the flat, I phoned Terry. He sounded as if he had been asleep. I asked him if any mail had arrived for me that morning. He mumbled that there were a couple of things.

'They might have sent my new credit card. They said they'd try to.'

'I'll send it on, if you'd prefer.'

'It's desperately urgent. And I'm just in the neighbourhood, so is it all right if I drop by?'

'Well, all right but –'

'I'll be there in half an hour.'

'I thought you were in the neighbourhood.'

I tried to think of a clever explanation but couldn't.

'Look, the longer we talk the longer it will be until I get there.'

When I arrived, he had a bottle of wine open. He offered me a glass and I accepted. I had to be subtle about this. I had to work my way round to it. He looked at me with the appraising expression I knew so well, as if I was a slightly dodgy antique and he was putting a value on me.

'You've found your clothes,' he said.

'Yes.'

'Where were they?'

I didn't want to tell him. This wasn't just bloody-mindedness. I thought that, just for these few days, it would be good to create the maximum amount of confusion. If the people who knew who I was didn't know where I was and the people who knew where I was didn't know who I was, then maybe I'd be safer for a while. At least I'd be more of a moving target.

'I'd left them with someone,' I said.

'Who?'

'It's no one you know. Have you got my mail?'

'I put it on the table.'

I wandered over and looked at the two envelopes there. One was a questionnaire about shopping habits, which I chucked immediately into the bin, the other an envelope marked 'special delivery'. I picked it up and it felt promisingly firm. I ripped it open. A brand-new shiny credit card. A. E. Devereaux. I had a place to sleep, my clothes, some CDs and now a credit card. I was really coming back to life. I looked around.

'Of course, some of my stuff is still here, bits and pieces,' I said.

I sipped at my wine and Terry gulped at his. I was going to say something about his drinking and then I remembered with relief that I didn't have to do that any more. That was Sally's job now. But maybe he didn't drink with her.

'You can collect it any time you want,' he said.

'I haven't exactly got anywhere to put it,' I said. 'Is there a rush? Is Sally moving in?'

'I've only known her a couple of weeks. She's just –'

'You know, Terry, if there's one thing I don't want to get into it's a discussion about how she really doesn't mean anything to you.'

'That's not what I meant. I was talking about you. I

just wanted to say that I wasn't happy about what happened when you left.' He tried to take a sip from an empty glass. He looked down at the floor, then up at me. 'I'm sorry, Abbie. I'm sorry I hit you. Really. I've got no excuse to offer at all. It was my fault completely and I hate myself for it.'

I knew this Terry very well. This was the apologetic Terry. The one who admitted everything and said he would never do it again and from now on it would all be different. I'd believed that Terry too often but, then, he always believed himself too.

'It's OK,' I said at last. 'You don't need to hate yourself.'

'I was terrible to live with.'

'Oh, well, I was probably difficult too, in my own way.'

He shook his head ruefully. 'That's the thing, you weren't difficult at all. You were happy and generous and fun. Except for the first few minutes after your alarm went off in the morning. All my mates thought I was the luckiest man in the world. And you didn't give up on me.'

'Oh, well . . .' I said uncomfortably.

'Except you are now, aren't you? Giving up on me.'

'It's over, Terry.'

'Abbie . . .'

'Don't,' I said. 'Please. Listen, Terry, I wanted to ask you something.'

'Anything.' He was on his second glass of wine now.

'For some reason, my own sanity mainly, I'm trying to reconstruct this period that I can't remember. I'm investigating myself as if I were someone else. Now, from what I understand we had a massive row on the Saturday and I walked out.'

'As I've said, it wasn't really a row. It was all my fault. I don't know what came over me.'

'Terry, I'm completely uninterested in that. I just want to know where I was. And various other things. So I left, and went to stay with Sadie. But if I stormed out, I presumably wasn't carrying my CD player and my TV with me.'

Terry shook his head.

'No,' he said. 'You walked out with nothing except your bag. I thought you'd be back later that evening. The next day you rang and I tried to talk you out of it but I couldn't. You wouldn't tell me where you were. Then a couple of days later, you rang again. You said you'd be over to collect some things. You came on Wednesday and you took quite a lot of stuff.'

Now I was getting to the difficult bit. 'Was there anything else?'

'What do you mean?'

'Well, when we talked . . . when we rowed, you know, did we also, um . . . ?'

'We didn't really talk, as such. We had a row. You left. I asked if you wanted to come back. You refused. You wouldn't tell me where you were. I tried to reach you on the phone but I couldn't.'

'What about when I came round here to collect my stuff ? What about then?'

'We didn't meet. You came when I was out.'

I felt a lurch in my stomach.

'I'm sorry,' I said. 'I know I'm being stupid about this, but you're saying that we didn't have any contact after I walked out?'

'We talked on the phone.'

'I don't mean that. We didn't meet?'

'No. You wouldn't let me.'

'So who the fuck . . . ?'

I'd begun a sentence that I couldn't possibly finish.

'Look, Abbie, I really want to . . .'

At that moment the doorbell rang so I never learnt what it was that Terry really wanted, although I could make a fair guess at it. I saw Terry clench his teeth and I saw that he knew who was at the door, so I knew as well.

'This is a bit awkward,' he said, as he moved across to the door.

I wasn't in a condition to deal with anything at all. I could hardly speak.

'It's not at all awkward. Go and let her in. I'll come down with you. I'm going now.'

We trooped down the stairs in single file. 'I'm just on my way,' I said to Sally, on the doorstep. 'I was collecting my mail.' I waved the single envelope.

'It's fine,' Sally said.

'I won't make a habit of this,' I said.

'It doesn't matter at all,' she said.

'That's fantastic,' I said, as I moved past her. 'I can honestly say, with complete sincerity, that you and Terry make a better couple than Terry and I ever did.'

Her expression turned frosty. 'What are you talking about? You don't know me at all.'

'No,' I said. 'But I know me.'

I stopped off on the way home at one of those mini-supermarkets that compensate for the wrinkled fruit and veg they keep out on the pavement by never closing. I got milk, a bottle of white wine and the ingredients for a basic salad. Back in Jo's flat I locked the door with the chain then threw the salad together. I was so tired that I'd gone beyond the desire to sleep. My eyes felt sore, my head buzzed, my limbs ached. I swallowed a couple of pills and washed them down with a gulp of cold white wine, then I ate the salad alone and in silence, trying to clarify my thoughts. I looked at the small pyramid of Jo's mail. There was nothing necessarily sinister about that. She might have invited me to flatsit while she was on holiday or working abroad or almost anything. I flicked through her letters. There were a few red letters. I didn't know if that meant anything. Jo might be the sort of person who always leaves bills until the last minute. Or she might just have forgotten. Or she might be arriving back from her holiday at any second. I decided to give it a couple of days and then I would start to find out about Jo. First I had to find out about myself.

I sat cross-legged on Jo's pine floor and arranged things around me. There was the Avalanche file, the mail I'd collected from Terry out of the bag. There were the phone messages from Carol, the receipts I'd found in the glove compartment of my car. I went to the bureau in the corner of the room and pulled it open. I took a pen from a mug with a London Underground map on in it. From a drawer I took a handful of white A4 paper.

What did I know about the days that I couldn't remember? I took one of the pieces of white paper and wrote 'Lost Days' at the top. At the far right-hand side I wrote Tuesday 22 January. Right at the end of the day, just before midnight, I had collapsed on the doorstep of Tony Russell. How many days had I been held captive? Three? No, it must have been more than that. Four, five, six, maybe more. The last piece of information I was absolutely sure of was the evening of Tuesday 15 January when I had ordered a takeaway to be delivered to this very flat. I needed to fill in the days. What had I been doing? I knew I hadn't been seeing my friends.

A thought occurred to me. I went to the kitchen. I had to open a number of cupboard doors before I found the rubbish bin. An awful smell, sweet and rotting, hit me as I leant over it. But I forced myself to look into it. There were horrible things down there, mouldy, rancid, slimy, but no tin-foil containers left over from a takeaway meal. Which meant that the bin had been emptied at least once and then there had been enough time for more rubbish to be thrown into it. Which meant that Jo or I, or Jo and I, or someone else had been here for at least some time after the Tuesday. Unless the takeaway meal had been thrown directly into an outside bin. How likely was that?

My head hurt. Hadn't Robin said something about me phoning her to cancel our evening drink? I scribbled 'Wednesday' in the margin of the page and put a question mark beside it.

I began with Carol's list of telephone messages. More than anything those scrawled reminders took me back to my old life, those urgent communications, brief responses. One by one, I crossed out the ones I recognized. At the end I was left with three I couldn't remember. One with no name beside it, but a phone number. One saying, 'Pat called.' Pat? I knew about twelve people called Pat, male and female. One of them I'd been at nursery school with. She had the loudest scream I've ever heard. The other message was 'a guy called'. Thanks, Carol.

I sat down again and selected another blank sheet of paper. I wrote 'Things To Do' at the top of the page. My general motto in life was, when in doubt write a list. First I wrote, 'phone the numbers'. Under that I wrote: 'Avalanche'. Laurence had said that after I had stormed out of Jay and Joiner's I had used up my own time to go and speak to people involved in the project, and encouraged them to complain. It was one of the only real clues I had to what I'd been doing during the lost days.

I opened the Avalanche file and took out the contact sheet on top. They were all familiar names, the people I'd been dealing with during those frenetic days at the beginning of January. I flicked through the file. I wrote down names, put some in brackets and underlined others. It made me tired just to think about the work I'd done.

I came to the accounts at the back of the file. I stared at the figures until they blurred. As if shapes were sliding out of a thick fog, I remembered some of the arguments I'd had with Laurence. Or, at least, I remembered why I would have had them: the shoddy behaviour of our company towards its subcontractors, the creative accounting that had gone on under my nose. And then I remembered Todd.

Actually, Todd was a part of my life that I'd never forgotten, just pushed to the back of my mind. I had wondered afterwards if I should have seen the signs earlier. He had been running the Avalanche project. It was a hugely complicated task that needed a mixture of finesse and banging heads together. I had learnt very quickly that everybody on a job has a grievance against someone else and everybody has an excuse for their own failings. If you step too far in one direction, you provoke a revolt. Too far in the other direction and nothing gets done. Because Todd and I were using some of the same people I started to hear that the work was going slowly. Work always goes slowly. But if the builders say it's going slowly, they mean it's going backwards. I mentioned this a couple of times to Todd and he said it was all coming along fine. I started to feel something was seriously wrong and mentioned it to Laurence.

The next I heard was that Todd had been fired and that I was in charge of the Avalanche job. Laurence told me that Todd had apparently had a breakdown without telling anybody and that part of this meant that he had done absolutely nothing and that Jay and Joiner's was facing the prospect of litigation. I was appalled and said that I hadn't meant to betray Todd. Laurence said that Todd was a psychotic, that he needed medical help, but that the immediate problem was to save the company. So I walked into Todd's office and I worked solidly for forty hours. For a week after that I never slept for more than four hours a night. So if I was partly responsible for what had happened to Todd, then Todd was partly responsible for what had happened to me.

I wrote his name on the sheet of paper. I thought, then added a question mark. I'd consider that one. I drew a square around the question mark. I added more lines to make it look as if the question mark were inside a cube. I shaded the sides of the cube. I drew lines radiating from the cube to make it look as if the cube were shining or exploding.

Another thought occurred. Oh, fuck, oh, fuck, oh, fuck, oh, fuck. Underneath 'Todd' I wrote 'pregnancy test' and underlined it. I had had sex with someone and I clearly hadn't taken any precautions. Who with? I started to think of writing another list of potential candidates, but I had nobody to put on it. Which men had I definitely met during my lost week? Guy. Unlikely. The person who delivered the takeaway was probably a man. And, of course, there was him.

Next I started to write 'What' and then stopped. I'd been thinking: What are you doing? And I'd started to write it automatically. But what *was* I doing? The idea of these forgotten dark days was horrible and it was somewhere in my brain tormenting me every second of the day and night. Sometimes I fantasized that that was what was causing the pain in my head. If I could fill in all the blanks, discover everything I had been doing, the pain would go. Was it worth putting myself at risk for that? And was I even at risk? Was he out there somewhere in London looking for me? He might have found me already. He might be outside Jo's flat right now, waiting for me to come out. Or I could be wrong about all this. The man might have vanished. He knew that I didn't remember how he'd first met me. I didn't know what he looked like. If he sat tight, he would be safe. He would be safe to go off and kill other women and forget about me. But could he feel sure?

I drew a large question mark around 'What'. I turned it into a three-dimensional question mark, then shaded it. If I could prove that I really had been kidnapped . . . That was the best I could hope for. If I could find some piece of evidence, then the police would believe me and they would protect me and go and find the man and I could have a life again.

But what would that evidence be like? Where would I look? I decorated my giant question mark with a filigree of baby question marks that ran down its back, round its tail, back up along its stomach then up to its head until it was entirely surrounded by a cloud of fluttering bemusement.

Ten

I woke with a start and for a moment I couldn't remember where I was. The room was dark and there was no sound at all. I lay in bed and waited for memory to return. I waited to hear something; a sound in the blackness. My heart was hammering fast and my mouth felt suddenly dry. Then I heard it, a gentle shuffling outside. Perhaps that was what had woken me. But who was there, outside my window? I turned and looked over at my radio-alarm clock on the table. It was ten minutes to five, and cold.

I heard it again, the shuffling, scraping sound. I couldn't move, but lay pressed up against my pillow. It was difficult to breathe properly and my head hammered relentlessly. I let myself remember the hood and the gag, but then I pushed away the thought. I made myself get out of bed and go over to the window. I opened the curtains a crack and looked outside, through the flowers of frost on the glass. The newly fallen snow made everything brighter, and by the light of the street lamp I could make out a dark shape beneath me. A fat tabby cat was rubbing itself against the shrub by the front door, winding its thick tail round the dead leaves. I almost laughed in relief, but then it raised its head and seemed to gaze straight at me with its unblinking yellow eyes. A feeling of dread seized me. I looked down the street, dark between its puddles of orange light. It was empty. Then a car a few yards away started up; its headlights illuminated the street and I caught the glimpse of a shape in the distance. There were footprints in the new snow.

I let the curtains drop and turned away. I was being ridiculous, I told myself sharply. Paranoid. In London someone is always awake. There are always cars and cats and figures on the street. Whatever time I woke in the night I could press my face against the window and see someone standing there.

I climbed back into bed and curled up, wrapping my arms around myself. My feet were freezing and I tried to tuck them inside the rugby shirt to warm them, but they kept slipping out. After a few minutes, I got out of bed again and went to the bathroom. I'd seen a hot-water bottle hanging on the door. I boiled the kettle, filled it, took two pills for my head, then climbed back into bed. I lay there for a while, hugging the bottle against myself and trying to go back to sleep. Thoughts whirled round in my head, like a wild snowstorm, and tasks piled up in drifts: the phone calls I had to make, the names in the file I had to go to see, and I must try to find out where Jo was, find out more about her at least, and what about the bloody morning-after pill? Someone must know what on earth I'd been up to, and was I looking for one man or was I looking for two, and what if I was pregnant? I remembered my old life and it seemed very far away, like a picture behind glass, while this new life was sinister and insistent, and shifted whenever I looked at it.

The radiator crackled and hummed, and after a few minutes the edge was gone from the cold. Outside, through the chink in the curtain, I could see the darkness was beginning to lift. It was no good. I couldn't sleep any more. While I lay there, dread squatted on my chest like a great toad. To shift it, I had to get started on sorting things out. That was the only thing to do.

I had a bath, almost too hot to bear so that when I

got out my skin was pink and my fingers wrinkled. I dressed in my baggy trousers and black hooded fleece and put on two pairs of socks. I made myself a cup of coffee, heating the milk for it. I boiled an egg, toasted a slice of the stale bread and buttered it liberally. I was going to look after myself. I made myself eat the breakfast at the table, dipping the toast into the yolk and chewing it slowly between gulps of milky coffee. Then I went into the bathroom and stood in front of the mirror. I still got a mild shock when I saw myself, my naked white face. I wet my hair and combed it, so that it wasn't so tufty and brushed my teeth vigorously, watching myself as I did so. No makeup. No jewellery. Ready for action.

It was still only just past seven; most people would probably be still in bed. It was certainly too early to get a pregnancy-testing kit. I'd do that later. I settled down with my pieces of paper, going through the lists I had made last night, adding notes to myself. I rummaged through drawers, looking for Blu-Tack. I didn't find any, but there was some Sellotape in a drawer full of screwdrivers, string, fuses and batteries. I stuck the pieces of paper along the wall, leaving gaps that I hoped to fill in later. It was oddly satisfying, a bit like tidying a desk and sharpening pencils before starting real work.

I wrote down the names and addresses of the men I planned to visit today. They were all names I knew well, and I assumed they were the men I'd gone to visit after I'd left Jay and Joiner's. I had phoned them, or their staff, daily during the last weeks at work and I knew we had mistreated them. Some of them I'd met, but that frantic period was a blur, a time of abstract urgency, as if I'd been moving too fast to see, or as if the amnesia had somehow oozed backwards. Perhaps, I thought, my memory loss is like ink spilt on to blotting paper. It has a central point of greatest darkness, and it gets gradually lighter as it spreads outwards, until finally the stain is imperceptible.

I looked up each address in the road map, planning my route and which person to go to first. I lifted the phone and started to dial the first number – then put it down again. I should arrive unannounced. I had no advantage except unpredictability. I put on my woollen hat and drew it down low over my brow, I wrapped my stripy scarf round the lower half of my face and then I turned off all the lights, and drew the curtains in my bedroom, as they'd been before I arrived.

The long day yesterday, and the unsatisfactorily short night, had made me extra jumpy this morning. There was no back way out, so I had to use the front door. Just before opening it, I put on my dark glasses; now there was scarcely a strip of my face showing. I took a deep breath and marched out, into the blasting wind. It was the coldest day yet, a cold to scour the skin and ache in the bones. The parking ticket was still under iced wipers on my car but that didn't matter. Today I'd be using public transport.

Ken Lofting's shop wasn't open yet, but when I pressed my face to the glass doors I could see that the lights were on at the back. There didn't seem to be any kind of bell, so I pounded with my fist and waited. At last I saw a shape appear. The lights in the shop went on – and when I say they went on, I mean they lit up in a dazzling display and suddenly it was like Christmas all over again – and the bulky figure of Ken came walking ponderously towards me, frowning at my impatience. He didn't immediately open the door. He looked at me through the glass then recognition dawned slowly on his heavy, florid face. He unlocked one set of bolts, then the next, and pulled open a door. My mouth went dry with apprehension but I kept on smiling steadily at him.

'Abbie?'

'I just had my hair cut, that's all. Can I have a word with you?'

He stood back, still staring at me until I felt self-conscious. 'I was hoping to see you,' he said. I listened to his voice. Was the accent right? 'You've been on my mind.'

'I thought you'd be open by now,' I said, glancing around nervously. The lamps and chandeliers and spot-lights shone, but there seemed to be no one else here.

'In five or ten minutes' time.'

'Can we talk?'

He stood aside and I stepped into the shop. He locked and bolted the door behind us. The sound made me shiver. I couldn't stop myself.

Ken isn't just any old electrician who puts wires behind skirting boards; he's a maestro. He's competent with wires but he's obsessed with lights – the way light falls, the depth of its field, the quality of contrast. In his shop in Stockwell you can buy weird discontinued Norwegian bulbs, and he can spend hours discussing up-lighting and down-lighting and over-head lighting; sharp beams and soft diffusions. He often did. The lights we put into Avalanche's office were works of art. Each desk was brightly lit, and each individual office, but there were areas between that were more shaded. 'Contrast,' he'd said, over and over again. 'You've got to have contrast, give shape and depth to a room, bring it to life. The golden rule is never make lighting flat and glaring. Who can live with that?' The Avalanche directors loved that kind of talk.

'Why were you hoping to see me, Ken?'

'First things first. Tea?'

'Lovely.'

He made tea in his back office, which was full of cardboard boxes. I sat in the chair and he sat on a box. It was very cold in there, and I kept on my coat although he was in shirt-sleeves.

'Why did you want to see me?'

'Biscuit? Ginger nut?'

'No, I'm fine. Thanks.'

'To thank you.'

'Thank you for what?'

'For saving me from losing three grand, that's what.'

'I did that?'

'Yep.'

'How?'

'What?'

'Sorry, Ken. Bear with me. There's just some things at work that need clearing up.'

He seemed satisfied with that. 'You told me I'd been underpaid and I should make a fuss.'

'And you did?'

'Oh, yes.'

'When did I tell you, Ken?'

'It must have been the Monday morning. Early like this.'

'Which Monday?'

'Well, the one three weeks back or so.'

'Monday the fourteenth?'

He thought, then nodded. 'That would be the one.'

'And I haven't seen you since?'

'Seen me? No. Should you have done?' A little glimmer of comprehension appeared on his heavy face. 'Do you want to have seen me for your company records, to make up the hours, is that it? Because I owe you, so you just tell me when you saw me and for how long.'

'It's not that. I just want to clear up a muddle. Have I really not seen you since?'

He seemed disappointed. 'No. Though I've been wanting to say thank you.' He leant forward and put one hand on my shoulder. 'You put your neck on the block for me, didn't you?'

I shuddered at that, then said, 'So you're sure? Monday the fourteenth? You remember it clearly?'

'I remember you could hardly stay still for a single second, you were that angry.' He laughed a bit chestily.

'You need to be opening up soon,' I said. 'I should go. You've been very helpful, Ken.'

'Yes,' he said. He didn't move from his box, but perhaps that was simply because he was a big, slow man. And he looked at me in a way that might have been entirely friendly. But I didn't know. Doubt crawled through my entrails.

'So maybe you could unlock the doors for me, please?'

He lifted himself up and we walked very slowly through the dazzling shop. He opened the doors and I was out into the cold day. There were beads of sweat on my forehead and my hands were trembling.

'Oh, no! What now? Something not working? Something gone wrong, something crashed? Some idiot who doesn't know how to use the system? I tell you this.' He practically jabbed me in the chest with his forefinger. 'I am not doing any work for your company ever again. I've already told your lot that. Not ever. Not if you went down on your bended knee. It's not worth it. First that man who looked like he was about to cry every time he saw me and then that blonde woman who seemed to have a rocket up her arse, pardon my language, even though she did turn out all right in the end. You've probably got rid of her, haven't you, just for having a sense of justice?' He was a skinny, hot-tempered man. I liked him at once.

'It was me who told you about being underpaid, Mr Khan,' I interrupted.

'No, no, no. No way I'm having that. It was her. The one with long blonde hair. Abbie something, that was her name. I've never met you.'

Was it really true that he didn't recognize me? I took off my black woollen cap. His expression didn't alter. So I gave in and pretended to be someone else. Abbie's friend.

'When did you last see her?' I asked, trying to sound businesslike.

'Friday January the eleventh,' he answered promptly.

'No, I mean when did you really see her?'

'I just told you.'

'It won't get her into any more trouble than she's already in, Mr Khan.'

'So she is in trouble? I knew it. I told her she would be. She didn't seem to care at all.'

'Did you see her afterwards?'

He gave a shrug and glared at me. I wanted to hug him.

'I'm Abbie's friend,' I persisted. At any moment he'd recognize me and then he'd think I was fraudulent, malevolent or quite simply mad. 'I'm on her side.'

'That's what other people say too,' he said.

What did he mean by that? Bewildered, I just stared at him and he continued, 'All right, then. I saw her the next Monday. And then I went straight to my lawyers. She did me a big favour.'

'Monday the fourteenth.'

'Yes. If you see her, thank her from me.'

'I'll do that. And, Mr Khan . . .'

'What?'

'Thanks,' I said. For a brief moment his expression wavered. He looked at me more closely and I turned away, putting the glasses back over my eyes and the cap back on my head. 'Goodbye.'

I had lunch in a warm, dimly lit Italian café in Soho. They gave me a table tucked into the corner, at the back. I could see anyone who came in, but felt invisible. The café was full of tourists. I could hear people speaking Spanish, French and German, just from where I was sitting. A shudder of happiness ran through me. I took off my coat, hat, scarf, dark glasses, and ordered spaghetti with clams and a glass of red wine. I ate slowly and spent nearly an hour there, listening to fragments of conversation, breathing in the smell of cigarettes, coffee, tomato sauce and herbs. I had a cappuccino and a slice of lemon cheesecake. My toes thawed out and my head stopped aching. I could do this, I thought. If I can find out what happened to me, make people believe it, if I can make myself safe again, then I can come to places like this and sit among the crowds and be happy. Just to sip a cup of coffee and eat some cake and feel warm and safe, that's happy. I'd forgotten about such things.

I left the café and went and bought a pregnancy test.

I couldn't remember ever meeting Ben Brody before, though I'd been to his workshop in Highbury once. I made my way there now, through a fine icy drizzle. I could feel my nose – the only bit of me that was exposed – turning red again. His workshop was up a small alleyway off the arterial road. His name was on the door: 'Ben Brody, Product Designer'. How do people become product designers? I wondered. Then I felt stupid. How do people become office-space consultants, for God's sake? It struck me what a ludicrous job I'd been doing. If I ever got through this, I could become a gardener, a baker, a carpenter. I could actually *make* things. Except I'm useless with my hands.

Ben Brody did make things. Or, at least, he made prototypes. He'd designed the office desks and chairs for Avalanche, and the screens that made the vast open space of the floor less intimidating. And we'd underpaid him then overcharged our clients.

I didn't knock. I just opened the door and went in. The large room was lined with workbenches. Two men were standing near the skeleton of a bicycle. There was a drilling sound from the far end. The place smelt of sawdust. It reminded me of the way Pippa smells when she wakes up and her crinkly pink face stretches and yawns. Sweet and woody.

'Can I help you?'

'Mr Brody?'

'No. Ben's out the back.' He jerked his thumb towards a door. 'Doing accounts. Shall I fetch him?'

'I'll do it.'

I opened the door and the man sitting at the desk looked up. I kept my woollen hat on but removed my dark glasses. In the dark little room, I could hardly see with them on.

'Yes?' he said. He stared at me. For a moment he looked as if he'd sucked on a lemon. He took off his glasses and laid them on the desk. He had a thin face, but I saw that his hands were large and strong. 'Yes?' he said once more.

'You probably don't remember me. We've only met a couple of times. My name's Abbie Devereaux and I'm from Jay and Joiner's.'

He looked at me blankly. 'I haven't entirely forgotten you,' he said. 'What are you doing here?'

His manner was almost rude. I pulled up a chair and sat down opposite him. 'I won't take up your time. I'm just trying to clear up some confusion with the office.'

'I don't understand,' he said. Indeed, he looked grimly baffled. 'Why are you here?'

'I just want to sort things out.' He just looked at me. I tried again. 'There are some dates I don't understand, it's too complicated to go into the reasons.'

'Too complicated?'

'Don't ask. You don't want to know, I promise. I just wanted to ask you when we met. The last time we met.'

The phone rang behind him, and he swivelled round in his chair to pick it up. 'Absolutely not,' he said firmly. 'Rubber. No. No. That's right.' He put the phone down and turned back to me. 'You came here on Monday, three weeks ago, to tell me about concerns you had with the Avalanche contract.'

'Thank you,' I said. The back of my neck prickled for I was starting to feel that I recognized his voice. Not the tone of it, something about the intonation maybe. I dug my nails into my palms. 'You're quite sure I came on that day?'

'Yes,' he replied, in imitation of me. 'It's too complicated to go into the reasons, but I'm quite sure.'

I felt myself flushing. I got up and he stood too.

'I'm sorry to have taken your time,' I said formally.

'Not a problem,' he said. 'Goodbye. And I hope you get better soon.'

'Better?'

'Yes. You've been ill, haven't you?'

'I'm all right now,' I said hurriedly, and left.

I had not seen Molte Schmidt, the plumber, on the fourteenth, but I had called him on the phone. I had been very helpful, he said.

I must have had quite a day of it on that Monday, I thought – and then it occurred to me that in fact today was its replica and I was playing Grandmother's Footsteps with myself.

I quite enjoyed my twenty minutes with Molte because he was young and beautiful and friendly, with long hair tied back in a pony-tail and startling blue eyes. And because, as he told me, he was half Finnish and half German, and had an extremely thick accent.

And here, in the half-dusk, was my final stop of the day. The thin drizzle had turned to spitting snow, which flickered down out of the grey sky. But the lights were all on in the greenhouses and when I entered I smelt resin and heard running water. Occasionally a wind chime jingled in a gust of air.

It was like stepping out of my world and into another dimension. The greenhouse wasn't vast, yet a panoramic view was spread before me, as if I could see for miles and miles. There were trees everywhere, old and beautiful, with twisted trunks and spreading boughs. I bent down and touched one delicately.

'Chinese elm,' said a voice behind me. 'Over a hundred years old.'

I straightened up. Gordon Lockhart was stocky and balding. He was wearing bright red braces over a thick blue jersey.

'It's an indoor plant,' he continued. 'This one,' he

pointed to a tiny tree with leaves the colour of flame, 'that's a Japanese maple. Outdoor, except we've brought it in for winter.'

'It's lovely,' I said. 'God, it's odd and lovely here. Peaceful.'

'It is,' he said. 'I come in here and I step off the dirty, noisy street and I'm in another world. An ancient forest in the middle of London. See here, that's a banyan tree. See those aerial roots.'

'Lovely,' I repeated. 'Like a dream.'

'Take your time. It's not easy to choose the tree that's right for you. Or is it for a gift? Very popular gift, especially for weddings and anniversaries.'

'I've really come here to ask you something,' I said. 'I think we've met before.'

'I meet a lot of people.'

'I'm from Jay and Joiner's. You provided twenty bonsai trees for the Avalanche offices at Canary Wharf. I think I came here to tell you that you should charge more for your labour.'

'Abbie? Abbie Devereaux? You've cut off all your nice hair.'

'Yes.'

'I got more money out of them. And I gave you a present, if I remember rightly.'

'Yes,' I repeated, remembering nothing, not wishing to offend him. My head buzzed. Behind me, water gurgled like laughter. I said, 'It was a Chinese elm, wasn't it?'

'An elm, because you wanted it for the inside, you said. Ten years old, as I recall. Nice fat trunk already. You said it was a present.'

'A present,' I repeated. 'Yes. It was a perfect present. Well, I just came here to ask you if you could remember when we met. The date, I mean.'

It turned out we'd met twice, on the Monday and then on Wednesday the sixteenth. I felt winded and elated at the same time. I had leapt two days on in my schedule. I thanked him and then, on an impulse, I bought the banyan tree. I could give it to Jo when we met.

Eleven

As I approached Jo's flat with the banyan tree, I saw that my car had been clamped. Apart from the original ticket, there was now a large sticker on the windscreen telling me not to try to move it. It also gave the phone number I had to call to get it released, on payment of a large amount of money. I felt in my pockets but I couldn't find a pen. The car hardly looked worth releasing. I'd deal with it some other time. At least I knew where it was for the moment.

I had more important things to do. The pregnancy-testing kit I had bought was on special offer, so that was some good news. Fifteen per cent off. First there was much fumbling with my cold, trembling fingers to get the polythene wrapper off. I looked at the end of the box. The expiry date was 20.04.01. That was why I had got it cheap. It was nine months past its sell-by date. Did this matter? Once it was past the expiry date, did it start getting the results wrong?

I went into Jo's bathroom and ripped open the inner wrapper. I pulled apart an object that looked like a pen with a giant felt-tip at the end. I looked at the instructions on the box. 'Hold the pink urine absorber in your urine stream for at least one second.' That was no problem. I replaced the stick in the cartridge. I looked at the instructions. 'Now wait four minutes before reading the result.' Four minutes. An irritating amount of time. After I'd pulled my knickers and trousers up, I didn't have long enough to go and do anything. I stared at the three holes.

They duly went pink. Now I just had to wait for the pink to go away in the middle window. Who designs something like that? A man, probably. Someone like that Ben guy at the design company. What a way to earn a living. I could imagine all the meetings that had been held to decide on the optimum shape. I had spent the last couple of years going to meetings like that. I rotated it so that I couldn't see the window. It was an obvious scientific fact that if I continued to look at the pink stain in the middle window, then it would be unable to fade away and I would be pregnant.

It was possible. I had looked in my diary and found my period had been due around 24 January, when I was in hospital. Today it was Friday 1 February, so I was a week overdue. Of course, that might have been because I'd been practically starved for several days, and continuously terrified out of my wits. The body is quite wise. But what if I was pregnant? I devoted a huge psychological effort into not trying to imagine what that would be like. Obviously, putting an effort into not thinking about something is like having a hippopotamus in your living room and trying not to look at it but I only had to do it for about two minutes, or maybe even one minute. You probably didn't need the full four minutes, so I turned the cartridge round and I wasn't pregnant. I checked the package again just to make absolutely sure I was right. I was right.

I opened a bottle of Jo's wine to celebrate. With my first sip I wondered if this was wrong. The next day I would buy some wine to replace it. I still felt guilty and I thought of those red-edged bills. Men would be coming soon to cut off her gas, electricity and phone. I was living in the house. I had to take some responsibility. For all I knew I might have arranged with Jo to run the house while she was away. I imagined her coming through the door and finding a pile of unpaid bills and me sitting in the kitchen disposing of her wine. I topped up my glass – really topped it up, almost to the rim – and went to take responsibility for Jo's mail.

In the end, there really wasn't much to deal with. Once I'd thrown away the envelopes, then winnowed out the magazines, the catalogues, the offers of insurance, the invitations to events that had already taken place, there was not much more than a handful of letters that were really for her. There were the bills: phone, gas, electricity, credit card. I flicked through. They were all very small. No problem. I did a rough calculation in my head and concluded that it would be less than a hundred pounds to pay the lot of them. I'd even pay her credit-card bill, since that added up to a measly twenty-one pounds. Among her other talents, Jo clearly had a Zen Buddhist control over her finances. No storecards. For the rest there were three letters with handwritten addresses and two postcards. I didn't look at these, just propped them up on the mantelpiece.

The phone rang. I didn't answer. I'd thought about this and in the end I'd given Jo two more days. If she hadn't returned by then, I would start intercepting calls. In the meantime, I left the answering-machine on and listened as, every few hours, a friend left a message. Hi, I'm Jeff or Paul or Wendy, call me.

I went to sleep thinking of who I needed to see next. He was almost the last person I wanted to meet. Almost.

Todd Benson was visibly surprised to see me on his doorstep. I hadn't phoned ahead, but I thought he'd probably be home. 'Abbie,' he said, as if he was confirming that it was me, or hoping it wasn't.

'Carol gave me your address,' I said. 'I just rang her

and told her I was coming to see you at home. To check if it was all right.' That was untrue. 'I was in the neighbourhood, I thought I'd drop by for a word.'

That was untrue as well. Todd lived in a basement flat in a smart square just south of the river. It was a tube journey and a fairly hefty walk. I had got Todd's address out of the file and I had said nothing to Carol about coming to see him, or anything else. Pretending I had made me feel a bit safer.

Todd shrugged and asked me in. I thought he'd either be very rude to me or very depressed, but he was just polite. He asked me if I wanted some coffee then made it while I stood and looked at him.

In a grey T-shirt, purple tracksuit bottoms and moccasins, he wasn't exactly dressed for the office. The last trace of Jay and Joiner's was his designer spectacles, so thick-framed they looked like welder's glasses. He handed me a mug of coffee and we stood together, awkwardly, in his kitchen. I held it in both hands – they were still cold from the northerly wind outside.

'You look worse than I do,' he said.

'I've had a bit of a bad time,' I said. 'I went on leave.'

'Like me,' he said.

I wasn't sure of the extent to which he was joking. 'Sort of,' I said warily. 'That's not why I'm here. Somebody attacked me.'

'Who?'

'I don't know. Nobody's been caught. I was quite badly hurt and one result of that is that I've got very vague memories of the last few weeks.'

He sipped his coffee. 'I don't take pleasure in that,' he said.

'Well, of course you don't,' I said, alarmed rather than reassured.

'I don't feel any anger against you.'

'I'm sorry about what happened –'

'No,' he interrupted. 'You did me a favour. I think I went mad.'

'I'm not sure –'

'In the last weeks I was almost outside my body looking at myself as I laid waste to my life. You see I've always wanted to be a success, and to a certain extent I've always been a success. I've been thinking about it in the last couple of weeks and I've come up with an answer. I felt that people would only love me if I succeeded. Love was a reward for achievement. I think that I needed to make a complete fuck-up in order to make a total separation between my work life and my emotional life. It's me who should apologize to you. I put you in the position of having to do my dirty work for me. So I'm sorry, Abbie, I'm so sorry.'

And standing there in his own kitchen, Todd cried until his face shone with tears. I put my coffee mug on his kitchen table. I wasn't going to hug Todd, I just wasn't. It would be hypocritical. On the other hand I couldn't just stand there. So I took a couple of steps forward and put my hand on his shoulder. The problem was quickly resolved because he threw his arms around me and held me tight to him, sobbing. One side of my neck was wet with his tears. It was impossible for me to avoid some sort of reciprocal embrace. I didn't give him a full hug. I moved my arms round and gave him not much more than a light tap on his shoulder-blades.

'Todd,' I said feebly. 'I'm sorry about this.'

'No, no, Abbie,' he sobbed. 'You're really a good person.'

I slightly increased the pressure of my hug then eased myself free. I went over to his sink and tore off a bit of paper towel. I handed it to him and he blew his nose and dabbed his face with it. 'I've been doing a lot of thinking,' he said. 'It's really been a positive time.'

'That's good,' I said. 'I'm glad about that. But if it's all right with you, I'd like to talk to you about what I was saying about these really vague memories of the last few weeks. For example, I remembered nothing at all about taking time off from Jay and Joiner's. What I'm doing is talking to people I know and seeing if they can tell me anything about that time. Stuff that I've forgotten.' I looked Todd in the eyes. 'Some people might say that we parted on pretty bad terms. I wondered if we had any contact after you . . . well, left.'

Todd rubbed his eyes. His face was puffy and red. 'I felt pretty bad for a few days,' he said. 'I was bitter. I felt I'd been shafted. But then, as I thought about it, I felt different. By the time you got in touch I was fine.'

'Got in touch? What do you mean?'

'You rang me.'

'When was this?'

'Two, three weeks ago.'

'I mean, exactly.'

Todd stopped and thought. He ran his hand over his stubbly hair.

'It was one of the days I go to the gym. They kept up my membership, you know. That was good. So it must have been a Wednesday. Afternoon.'

'Wednesday afternoon, right. What did I say?'

'Nothing much. You were being nice. You rang me to ask if I was all right.'

'Why?'

'Because you were being nice. You said you had things on your conscience and you wanted to sort them out. I was one of them.'

'Did I say anything?'

'You talked about your time off. You told me about the Avalanche job. You were lovely. You sounded happy. I mean in a good way.'

I stopped for a minute, thinking, going over the lost days in my head. Then I looked up at Todd. 'You mean there's a bad way of being happy?'

I rewrote my 'Lost Days' very neatly, underlining dates. It went something like this:

<u>Friday January 11</u>: showdown at Jay and Joiner's. Storm out.

<u>Saturday January 12</u>: row with Terry. Storm out. Go to Sadie's for night.

<u>Sunday January 13</u>: leave Sadie a.m. Go to Sheila and Guy. Meet Robin for shopping spree and spend too much money. Meet Sam for drink p.m. Go back to Sheila and Guy's.

<u>Monday January 14</u>: see Ken Lofting, Mr Khan, Ben Brody and Gordon Lockhart. Phone Molte Schmidt. Fill car with petrol. Phone Sheila and Guy to say not coming back for night.

<u>Tuesday January 15</u>: go to Sheila and Guy and leave note saying found somewhere to stay. Collect stuff from there. Phone Terry and arrange to collect stuff next day. Book holiday in Venice. Order Indian takeaway p.m.

<u>Wednesday January 16</u>: buy bonsai tree. Phone Robin. Collect stuff from Terry's. Phone Todd.

<u>Thursday January 17</u>:

But Thursday was a blank. I wrote, in capital letters, 'MORNING AFTER PILL', and then I wrote 'JO'. I made myself coffee and then I stared at my piece of paper and let it grow cold.

Twelve

As long as I had things to do, I was all right. I just had to keep busy, keep myself from thinking, from remembering, for then memories engulfed me like icy waters and I was back in the dark, and eyes were staring at me, fingers touching. No. I mustn't go there.

I tackled the fridge first, throwing out all the old food and wiping down the shelves. Then, of course, I had to do a shop to refill it. I walked to Camden high street, where I went to the bank and withdrew £250 from my account, which was shrinking rapidly with no immediate prospect of being replenished. Then I bought satsumas, apples, salad stuff, cheese, coffee and tea, milk, bread, butter, eggs, yoghurt, honey, two bottles of wine, one red and one white, six bottles of wheat beer, some crisps and olives. I didn't get any meat, because maybe Jo was a vegetarian. I got washing powder as well, and toilet paper. Even though I felt precarious and strange in Jo's flat, I was making myself at home there – lying in the bath, washing my clothes, adjusting the central heating, cooking myself comforting meals, lighting candles as the dark closed in. But I was always waiting for a key to turn in the lock and for Jo to walk through the door. And I was always fearing that she wouldn't. She was like a ghost in her own home and she haunted me.

I staggered back there now, weighed down by plastic bags that bit into my gloveless fingers. I had to stop every now and then to rest and get a firmer grip. At one point, a man came up and offered to help me as I stood bent over the bags, getting my breath back.

'I'm fine,' I snapped, and watched the benign expression on his face fade.

Back in the flat, I took three envelopes from Jo's desk, and put fifteen pounds into one, for Terry, fifty-five into another, for Sheila and Guy, and a further ninety into the third, for Sam. Later, I promised myself, I'd make a pilgrimage, paying off my debts and saying thank you.

It occurred to me that I should report my mobile phone missing; I should have done it immediately. I started to dial a number, but another thought clamped itself round my guts and I banged down the phone hurriedly, as if it might bite me.

I went outside again and walked up Maynard Street, then down another road, until I came to a public phone box that was working. Inside, it smelt of piss and the booth was covered with cards offering massages and very strict French lessons. I inserted twenty pence and dialled. It rang three times, and was picked up.

'Hello?' I said.

There was no answer, but I could hear breathing at the other end.

'Hello, who is this, please? Hello. Hello.'

The breathing went on. I thought about wheezy laughter in the darkness, a hood, hands lifting me off a ledge on to a bucket. Suddenly, the realization of what I was doing winded me. I managed to stutter out, 'Can I speak to Abbie, please?'

The voice at the other end – a voice I didn't know whether or not I recognized – replied, 'She isn't here now.' Sweat trickled down my forehead and the receiver felt slippery in my hand. The voice continued, 'I can say you called. Who's speaking?'

'Jo,' I heard myself say. I was going to be sick. Bile rose in my throat.

The line went dead. I stood for a few seconds, holding the phone in my hand. A man on crutches stopped outside the booth and tapped on the glass with the end of one of them. I put the receiver down, pushed open the door and ran back to the flat as if someone was chasing me. I'd put the bag of stuff I'd taken with me when I left the hospital – the clothes I'd been found in, and the few odds and ends I'd picked up while I was there – inside the wardrobe. I rummaged through it now, and to my relief found the card that Inspector Cross had given me. I dialled the number and he answered immediately.

It wasn't much fun talking to Cross again. He had been embarrassed and quite sympathetic at our last meeting at the hospital. Or perhaps compassionate is the right word – but it was a compassion that had made me feel ill with rage and shame and terror then, and even now gave me a queasy feeling. I said I had something urgent to tell him, but that there was no way I could set foot in the police station, and could he come to me. He said that it was probably better anyway for him to see me when he was off-duty, which made me feel that I was illicit business. We arranged for him to come to the flat shortly after five in the afternoon.

The conversation lasted for about one gruff minute and when I put the phone down I felt so strange that I took two pills, drank a tumbler of water then went into my room and lay on the bed for a few moments, face down and eyes shut.

Had I spoken to him? I didn't know, but the sensation that I'd felt in the phone booth – the kind of feeling you have in a nightmare just before you jerk awake, a sensation of falling, of wheeling through the darkness – had been so strong that even now I felt dizzy and appalled.

I had two hours before he came. Two hours is a long time when you feel ill with dread and loneliness. I poured myself a glass of wine, then poured it down the sink before I could drink it. I made myself a piece of toast and spread it with Marmite. When I'd finished that, I spooned yoghurt into a bowl and stirred in some honey. It was soothing. I finished off with a large cup of tea. I decided to change my clothes. I should wear something understated and respectable – something that would make me look rational and sane, not a woman who'd go around making up stories about being grabbed and held underground by a murderer. I picked out some beige trousers and a cashmere V-necked sweater – the outfit I used to put on for meetings with the financial department.

The trouble is, I wasn't the same person any more. My clothes still hung off me, making me look a bit like a child dressing up in adult things. My haircut was emphatically spiky and short, and neither its colour nor its style went with cashmere and smartly creased beige. I stared at myself in the mirror, nervously dissatisfied. In the end, I put on an old pair of jeans, with a belt to keep them up, and a red flannel T-shirt that I'd found hanging in the cupboard, though I had no recollection of buying it.

I wondered about my mobile phone. Should I cancel it, or should I leave it, knowing that perhaps the person who now had it was him? I couldn't decide. In my mind, it was an invisible thread stretching between us. I could snap it or I could try to follow it – but was I following it out of the labyrinth, or back in again?

I examined the pieces of paper that I had stuck to the wall. At the very earliest, I had been grabbed on Wednesday late afternoon or evening. Where did that get me? Nowhere. I called Sadie, just to say hello, really, just to hear a friendly voice from a life that seemed to have gone, but she was out and I left no message. I thought about calling Sam, or Sheila and Guy, but didn't. Tomorrow; I'd do it tomorrow. I went to the window and stood there for a few minutes, just gazing out idly at the people who walked by. Perhaps he knew where I was, because perhaps this was just where I'd been before. Was I hiding in the only place he knew to look?

I didn't know what to do with myself until Cross arrived. I needed to keep busy, to keep on the move, to give myself urgent tasks and unmissable deadlines, to persuade myself that I was one step ahead of him. I wandered into Jo's room. It was very well ordered. I opened her chest of drawers and everything was folded neatly. Even her knickers were laid out, one pair on top of another. I opened the square leather box on her chest of drawers and looked at the few pairs of earrings, the thin gold necklace, the brooch in the shape of a fish. There was a square piece of white card as well; when I turned it over it had a four-leafed clover sellotaped to it. I looked at the books on her bedside table. There was a Thai cookbook, a novel by a man I'd never heard of, and an anthology of 101 *Happy Poems*.

There was a video as well, with a blank label. I went back into the living room and inserted it into the video-machine. Nothing, just a blank. I pressed the fast-forward button. A blurred shoulder appeared, then the camera jerked to a leg. It was obviously a home video made by a first-timer. I leant forward and waited.

I saw Jo's face, half smiling. It gave me the most peculiar sensation. Then the camera moved backwards and she was standing in the kitchen, by the oven, stirring something, looking back at the camera and making a face at whoever was behind it. She was wearing the dressing-gown that was hanging on the back of her bedroom door, and her moccasin slippers. Maybe it was morning, or late in the evening, it wasn't possible to tell. The screen went blank again, then fuzzy. A few lines ran down it, and then, suddenly, I was looking at me. Me before it happened. I was sitting cross-legged on the armchair, and had a glass of wine in my hand. I was in a pair of sweatpants, wearing no makeup, and my hair – my old, long hair – was piled up on top of my head. I was grinning. I raised my glass in a toast and blew a kiss. The camera moved towards me until my face went out of focus.

The screen was blank for a few minutes, and then I was watching a black-and-white film, with a woman in a plumed hat riding a horse side-saddle. I reeled fast forward, but the film just went on until the credits. I rewound and stared once more at Jo's smiling face. Then at mine again. I looked happier than I could remember having been for a long time. I put my fingers up to my cheek and found that I was crying.

I turned off the television, ejected the video, and put it back in Jo's room, on her book of happy poems. I saw that on top of her wardrobe there was a video camera, as well as a pair of binoculars and a tape-recorder. In the living room, the phone rang twice, before it was picked up by the answering-machine. After a pause a voice said, 'Hi, Jo, it's me. Just checking about tonight. If I don't hear from you, I'll assume it's still on.' He didn't leave a name. Somewhere, someone would be waiting for Jo to turn up; a friend, or a lover. On an impulse, I dialled 1471, but couldn't find out the caller's number. He was probably phoning from an office.

A few minutes later, the phone rang again, and I picked it up at once.

'Hello?' I said.

'Jo?' said the voice at the other end. Then, before I had time to answer, it gathered in strength and anger. 'Jo, it's Claire Benedict. As you probably know, I've left dozens of messages by now and you haven't replied, but –'

'No, it's –'

'You realize that your work should have been sent to the printers by now.'

'Listen, this isn't Jo, it's a friend. Abbie. Sorry.'

'Oh. Can you tell me where Jo is, then? As you probably gathered, I urgently need to contact her.'

'I don't know where she is.'

'Oh. Well, when you see her can you tell her I called? Claire Benedict of ISP. She'll know what it's about.'

'Yes, but that's the thing. She seems to have just disappeared. When was she supposed to have delivered her work?'

'Disappeared?'

'Well, maybe.'

'She was due to give us her formatted text by Monday the twenty-first of January, at the latest. She never said she was having a problem finishing it. She just went quiet on us.'

'Was she usually reliable?'

'Yes. Very. Look, are you serious about her being missing?'

'I'll let you know what happens, OK? Give me your number.'

I scribbled it down on the back of one of the unopened envelopes, and put the phone down.

Then the doorbell rang.

For a startled second, I thought Cross was someone else. I'd only seen him in a suit, with his hair neatly brushed, and an inscrutable air about him. Now he was in worn brown corduroys, a thick jumper, and a padded blue jacket, whose hood was pulled up over his head. He looked as if he should be out in the garden, poking a bonfire. Or playing with his children. Did he have children? But his frown remained the same.

'Hello,' I said. I stood back to let him in. 'I appreciate this.'

'Abbie?'

'My new look. Don't you like it?'

'It's certainly bold.'

'It's my disguise.'

'I see,' he said, looking uncomfortable. 'You're looking better anyway. Healthier.'

'Do you want a cup of tea?'

'All right.' He looked around. 'This is a nice place you've got yourself.'

'I'm not quite sure how I got it.'

Cross looked puzzled but didn't pursue it. 'How have you been?' he asked instead.

'Scared shitless.' I poured water over the tea bags, keeping my back to him. 'Among other things, of course. But that's not why I asked to see you. I've got some new information. Do you take sugar?'

'One, please.'

'I should offer you a biscuit but I don't think there are any. I could make you some toast.'

'I'm fine. Have you remembered something?'

'It's not that.' I handed him the tea and sat down opposite him, in my armchair. 'The thing is, well, there are two things, really. First, I think I've just talked to him.'

His expression didn't alter. 'Him?' he said politely.

'The man who grabbed me. *Him.*'

'You say you talked to him.'

'On the phone.'

'He rang you?'

'No. I rang him – I mean, I rang my mobile phone, because it's gone, and someone answered. I knew at once. And he knew I knew.'

'Let me get this straight. You rang the number of your lost mobile phone, and someone answered and you're now saying that the person who answered is the person who you claim grabbed you.'

'I don't *claim*,' I said.

Cross sipped his tea. He looked rather tired. 'What was his name, the man who answered?'

'I don't know. I didn't ask – well, he wouldn't have told me, and I felt all of a sudden so very terrified. I thought I was going to keel over. I asked to speak to myself.'

He rubbed his eyes. 'Oh,' was all that he managed to say.

'I didn't want him to know it was me, but I think he did anyway.'

'Abbie, mobile phones get stolen all the time. It's a crime epidemic.'

'And then he asked me who was calling, and I said, "Jo."'

'Jo,' he repeated.

'Yes. You see, this flat belongs to someone called Jo. Josephine Hooper. I must have met her, but I can't remember that. I just know I moved in here when she was here too. In that week, just before I was grabbed and held prisoner.' I said this last fiercely. He just nodded and looked into his tea. 'And that's the second thing: she's gone missing.'

'Missing.'

'Yes. She's gone missing and I think the police should take it seriously. I think it may have something to do with what happened to me.'

Cross put his mug of tea down on the table between us. He reached into his trouser pocket and pulled out a large white handkerchief. He blew his nose loudly, folded the handkerchief and put it back in his pocket. 'You want to report her missing?'

'She's not here, is she?'

'You say you can't remember meeting her?'

'No.'

'Though you're living in her flat.'

'That's right.'

'Presumably this woman has family, friends, work colleagues.'

'People keep ringing up. I've just spoken to someone she was doing a job for. She was some sort of editor, I think.'

'Abbie, Abbie,' he said, infuriatingly, as if he were trying to calm me down. 'In what sense is this woman missing?'

'In the sense that she's not here and she should be.'

'Why?'

'She hasn't paid her bills for a start.'

'If you haven't met her, then how the hell did you come to be here?'

So I told him. I told him about Terry, and the car in the pound, and the receipt and the key; about the rotting garbage, the dead flowers, the cross publisher shouting down the phone. My story didn't sound as authoritative as I'd expected it to, but I didn't falter. I ended with the video footage of Jo and myself.

'Perhaps you're flat-sitting for this woman you can't remember,' he said.

'Maybe.'

'Perhaps she asked you to deal with the rubbish and the bills.'

'I have dealt with them.'

'There you are.'

'You don't believe me.'

'What's there to believe?'

'She's gone missing.'

'Nobody's reported her missing.'

'I'm reporting her missing now.'

'But . . . but . . .' He seemed baffled and unable to find the right word. 'Abbie, you can't report someone missing if you don't know anything about who they are or where they're meant to be or anything.'

'I know,' I insisted. 'I know something is wrong.'

'Abbie,' he said gently, and my heart sank. I forced myself to meet his eyes. He didn't look irritated or angry, but grave. 'First you reported yourself missing, with no evidence. Now you are reporting Josephine Hooper missing.' He paused. 'With no evidence. You're not doing yourself any favours, Abbie.'

'So that's it, is it? But what if I'm right and she's in danger, or worse?'

'I tell you what,' he said kindly. 'Why don't you let me make a couple of calls to establish if anyone else has expressed concern over her disappearance? All right?'

'All right.'

'May I use your phone?'

'Jo's phone. Go ahead.'

I left the room while he was making his calls, went into Jo's bedroom again and sat on her bed. I very badly needed an ally; someone who would believe in me. I'd called Cross because I thought in spite of everything that had happened he might be on my side. I couldn't do this on my own.

I heard him put down the phone and went back to join him. 'Well?'

'Someone has already reported Josephine Hooper missing,' he said.

'See?' I said. 'Was it a friend?'

'It was you.'

'Sorry?'

'You did. On Thursday January the seventeenth, at eleven thirty in the morning, you rang the Milton Green station.'

'There you are,' I said defiantly.

'Apparently, she hadn't even been gone for a full day then.'

'I see.'

I did see – I saw several things at once: that Cross wasn't going to be my ally, however nice he was trying to be to me; that in his eyes, and perhaps in the eyes of the world, I was hysterical and obsessed; and that I had still been free on Thursday, January the seventeenth. Jack Cross was chewing his lip. He looked concerned but I think he was mainly concerned about me.

'I'd like to help,' he said. 'But . . . look, she's probably in Ibiza.'

'Yes,' I said bitterly. 'Thanks.'

'Have you gone back to work?' he asked.

'Not as such,' I said. 'It's a bit complicated.'

'You should,' he said. 'You need some purpose in your life.'

'My purpose is to stay alive.'

He gave a sigh. 'Yeah, right. If you come across anything I can really deal with, call me.'

'I'm not mad,' I said. 'I might seem mad to you, but I'm not.'

'I'm not mad,' I said to myself, as I lay in the bath with a flannel over my face. 'I'm not mad.'

I put my baggy jeans and red T-shirt back on and wrapped my hair in a towel. I sat cross-legged on the sofa, with the television turned up loud. I hopped through channels. I didn't want silence this evening. I wanted other faces and other voices in the room with me – friendly faces and voices, to make me feel I wasn't so all alone.

Then the doorbell rang again.

Thirteen

There was no need to be frightened. Nobody knew I was here except Cross. I opened the door.

Instantly I knew that I knew him and at the same time I just couldn't think where the hell I'd seen him before.

'Hi,' he said. 'Is Jo . . . ?' And then he recognized me and he saw that I recognized him and he looked completely baffled. 'What the fuck are *you* doing here?'

I responded by slamming the door. He made a feeble attempt to push against it but I pushed hard and it clicked shut. There was a shout from the other side. I put the chain across and leant against the door, panting. I remembered where I'd met him now. It was Ben Brody, the designer. How had he tracked me down? They only had my office number and my mobile. I'd told Carol definitely not to give out my address to anyone. Anyway, she didn't have this address. Terry didn't know either. Nobody knew. Could I have been followed? Could I have left something behind that gave a clue? He was knocking at the door. 'Abbie,' he said. 'Open up.'

'Go away,' I shouted. 'I'm going to call the police.'

'I want to talk to you.'

The chain looked solid enough. What could he do to me through the six-inch-wide gap? He was wearing a dark suit with a white shirt and no tie. On top of that was a long grey coat that hung down below his knees.

'How did you find me?'

'What do you mean how did I find you? I came to see Jo.'

'Jo?' I said.

'I'm a friend of hers.'

'She's not here,' I said.

'Where is she?'

'I don't know.'

He looked more and more confused. 'Are you staying here?'

'Obviously.'

'So how come you don't know where she is?'

My mouth opened but I couldn't quite think of what to say. Then, 'It's a complicated story. You probably wouldn't believe it anyway. Did you have an appointment to meet Jo?'

He gave a short, snappy laugh, and looked to either side as if he couldn't quite believe that he was having this conversation. 'Are you her receptionist? I'm tempted to say that it's none of your business but . . .' He took a deep breath. 'A couple of days ago I was due to meet Jo for a drink and she never showed. I left a couple of messages and she never got back to me.'

'Exactly,' I said. 'That's what I told the police.'

'What?'

'I tried to report Jo missing but they didn't believe me.'

'What's going on here?'

'She might be on holiday,' I continued incoherently.

'Look, Abbie, I don't know what it is you think I'm going to do, but could you let me in?'

'Can't we talk like this?'

'I suppose we can. But why?'

'All right,' I said. 'But we'd better be quick. A detective is coming to see me in a few minutes.'

That was another of my feeble attempts at self-protection.

'What about?'

'To take a statement.'

I unfastened the chain and let him in. He seemed remarkably at home in Jo's flat. He took off his coat and tossed it on to a chair. I removed the towel from my head and rubbed my hair with it.

'Are you and Jo . . . you know?' I said.

'What are you talking about?'

'You seem quite at home here,' I said.

'Not as at home as you are.'

'I just need somewhere to perch.'

He looked at me. 'Are you all right?'

I gave an inward silent groan.

'I know that the all-purpose answer to the question "are you all right?" is "I'm fine". But the short answer is, no, I'm not all right. And the medium-length answer is, it's a long story that you don't want to bother about.'

Ben walked into the kitchen area, filled the kettle and plugged it in. He took two mugs out of the cupboard and placed them on the counter. 'I think I deserve to hear the long version,' he said.

'It's really long,' I said.

'Do you think you've got time?'

'What do you mean?'

'Before your detective gets here.'

I mumbled something unintelligible.

'Are you ill?' he said.

That reminded me. I extracted a couple of pills from the container in my pocket and swallowed them with a gulp of water from the tap. 'I get these headaches still,' I said. 'But that's not really it.'

'So what is really it?'

I sat at the table and put my head in my hands for a moment. Sometimes if I could find the right position for my head the throbbing eased a little. I heard a clattering sound. Ben was making tea. He brought the two mugs across to the table. He didn't sit down. He leant on the arm of Jo's big chair. I sipped at the tea.

'I've become this version of the Ancient Mariner. I trap people in corners and tell them my story. I've started to wonder whether there's really any point. The police didn't believe me. The more I tell it, the less I believe it myself.'

Ben didn't reply. He just looked at me.

'Don't you have a job to go to?' I said.

'I'm the boss,' he said. 'I can come and go when I want.'

So I gave him a faltering, fragmented version of my story. I talked to him about my problems with Jay and Joiner's, some of which he knew about because he had been on the edge of them. I told him about walking out on the job and walking out on Terry. Then I took a deep breath and told him about waking up in that cellar, wherever it was, and those days underground and the escape and the days in hospital and not being believed and being ejected back into the world.

'To anticipate your first question, the one thing I can be really sure about is the bang on my head.' I touched it, just above my ear, very delicately. It still made me flinch. 'So if the bang could erase bits of my life, maybe it could add bits as well. Do you know, I've never actually said that aloud before? I've thought it, late at night, when I wake up and my blood sugar is low and I think about dying. Maybe if you had an accident and banged your head badly, that might very well be the sort of hallucination you'd have. You might fantasize about being trapped underground and a voice talking to you out of the darkness. Don't you think?'

'I don't know,' said Ben. He looked dazed. 'What a nightmare.'

'Perhaps I was mugged somewhere or run over. I might have just been lying somewhere for a few hours. Have you ever had dreams like that? You seem to be living for years, you grow old and then you wake up and it's been a single night. Have you ever had dreams like that?'

'I don't remember my dreams.'

'That's probably a sign of psychological good health. But I do. You know that when I was there, if I was there, I slept and I had dreams and I remember those dreams as well. Lakes, floating in water, a butterfly on a leaf. Does that prove anything? Is it possible to go to sleep and have a dream, and then in that dream go to sleep and have another dream? Is that possible?'

'I design taps and penholders. I don't know much about psychology.'

'It's neurology. I know. I've been seen by a psychologist and by a neurologist. The neurologist was the one who believed me. Anyway, that's my story. I've got this bit missing from my brain and I'm going around to see people who probably think I'm insane trying to fill in the gaps. At the same time I'm taking elaborate precautions to hide from someone who probably isn't looking for me. Did you ever do that as a child? You'd play a game of hide and seek and you'd find the most brilliant hiding place. You'd be there for ages, feeling triumphant at first and then bored, and you'd gradually realize that everyone else has given up the game. And furthermore I've got this feeling that I'm just babbling away like a lunatic and you're just standing there being strong and silent and not saying anything. You were wondering where Jo is and you were wondering what I was doing here. Well, I don't know where Jo is and I don't know what I'm doing here, so you can go back to your workshop now.'

Ben came over and took my mug and walked over to the sink with it. He washed up my mug and his own and laid them upside down on the draining-board. He looked around for a dishtowel. But there wasn't one and he had to shake the water off his hands.

'I think I know what you're doing here,' he said. 'At least, I know how you met Jo.'

'How?'

'I introduced you to her.'

Fourteen

For a moment I felt a wave of excitement as another space of my *terra incognita* was mapped but it quickly became a sickening lurch. 'What are you talking about? Why should you have done that? You didn't seem to know that when you arrived. You were as flabbergasted to see me as I was to see you.'

'I was,' he said. 'But that must have been what happened.' He paused. 'Are you serious? Do you really have no memory of meeting her?'

'I just watched this video that we must have made together of me and her. We seemed to be getting on. I seemed happy. I wish I could remember it. I could do with some happy memories. But, no, I'm sorry, there's nothing there. How did you introduce us? Why?' Ben started to reply and then hesitated. 'You're wondering whether to believe me, aren't you? That's great. The police and the doctors don't believe I was abducted. Now you don't believe that I can have lost my memory. Soon I'll probably meet people who don't believe I'm really Abbie Devereaux. Maybe I'm not. Maybe I'm just impersonating her. It may be a delusion. Maybe I'm really Jo and I'm hallucinating this person called Abbie.'

Ben made an attempt at a smile but then he looked away from me as if he was embarrassed.

'So I met her on Monday?' I said.

'Tuesday,' he said. 'Tuesday morning.'

'I thought you said before that we met on Monday. I'm sure you did.'

'You came back on Tuesday,' he said vaguely. 'With more questions.'

'Oh. And Jo was at your workshop?'

'We went and had a coffee down the road, in a café not so far from here that she goes to regularly. She was on her way to some appointment, I think. I introduced you. We talked for a bit, then I had to run off. If you want me to reconstruct your conversation, I suppose you told her about needing somewhere to stay. She must have said you could stay here. So there's one mystery solved. Nothing sinister.'

'I see.'

'And you think she's missing?'

'I told this detective I . . . I sort of know. He thinks I'm mad. Well, not mad-mad, of course, but wrong. I hope I am too. I don't know what to do. And for some reason I feel responsible for her. Every time I look up and see her photograph, I feel terrible that I'm not doing more. When I was in that place, a prisoner, I kept thinking that people I knew, my friends, would be looking for me and making a great fuss and worrying all the time, and that kept me going. I had to believe it, it was crucial to feel I was alive in people's thoughts, and one of the worst things about coming back again was to realize that no one had missed me at all.'

'I think –' He tried to interrupt.

'No one had noticed I wasn't around, or if they'd noticed it didn't matter much. It was as if I was invisible. Had died. I mean, it wasn't their fault in the slightest, I know that – they're good friends and I think they love me, really, and I'd have done the same in their place. I wouldn't notice if someone wasn't around for a few days – why should I? We come and go in each other's lives, don't we? But I just mustn't do that with Jo. Because I know what it feels like. But I don't know what to do not to do that, if that makes sense. And I'm talking too much and I have this horrible feeling that if I stop talking I may burst into tears.'

I stopped and Ben leant forward and put a hand on my arm. I instinctively jerked away.

'Sorry,' he said, sounding as if he meant it. 'It must make you jumpy, having a strange man in your flat. I should have thought.'

'Kind of, I mean I'm sure that . . . Look, I'm like a person stumbling about in the pitch black, if you see what I mean, with my hands outstretched, trying not to fall off the edge. If there is an edge to fall off anyway. Sometimes I think there's some kind of glimmer at the edge of my vision, and I look round and it goes away. I just keep hoping I'll come into the light again but I don't. Without my memory, it's as if I've lost my map, I'm blundering about and bumping into things, and it's not just that I don't know where I am, I don't know who I am. What is there that's left of me? Especially when other people don't know whether to –' I stopped abruptly. 'I'm gabbling again, aren't I?' He didn't answer. He was staring at me in a way that made me nervous. 'What was I like when we met before?'

'What were you like?' He seemed not to understand the question.

'Yes.'

'Your hair was longer.'

'Well, I know that since it was me who had it cut, but what did I seem like to you? What kind of state was I in?'

'Um.' He looked uncertain and awkward for a moment. 'You seemed quite animated.'

'What did we talk about? Did I tell you anything?'

'Work,' he said. 'Problems at work.'

'Is that all?'

'You said you'd just left your boyfriend.'

'I said that to you?'

'You explained that you were of no fixed address, so you only had a mobile if I needed to call you on business.'

'Anything else? Did I talk about people I'd met recently? Had I met someone else? Did I tell you?'

'Not exactly,' he said. 'But I thought you had. At least, I got that impression.'

'You see, I'm thinking maybe the person I met was, you know, him.'

'Him?'

'The man who grabbed me.'

'I see,' he said, standing up. 'Tell you what, shall we go and have a drink? You'll probably feel safer with me in a crowd.'

'All right,' I said.

'Come on, then.' He picked up his coat from the chair.

'Nice coat.'

He looked down at it, almost with surprise, as if it were an unknown coat that had been put on him without his knowledge. 'It's new.'

'I like those long floppy coats.'

'They're like long cloaks,' Ben said. 'The sort that people used to wear a couple of hundred years ago.'

I frowned. 'Why does hearing that make me feel peculiar?'

'Maybe you agree.'

The pub was reassuringly crowded and full of the fug of cigarette smoke.

'I'm buying,' I said, and fought my way to the bar.

A few moments later, we were sitting at a table, with beer and a packet of crisps between us.

'I don't know where to begin. You're Jo's friend, right?'

'Right.'

'Does she go away a lot?'

'It depends. She does different projects for different publishing companies – trade mags, things like that – and some of them involve research. There was one I remember for a children's encyclopedia and she had to write brief paragraphs about British trees, so she went around visiting three hundred yews, things like that.'

'And she's reliable?'

'Usually very. She depends on her editing work to make ends meet.'

'Does she stand you up much?'

He looked thoughtful. 'As I said, she's reliable.'

'So, she's not here and she should be. She's not on holiday or anything. Something's wrong.'

'Maybe not,' Ben said quietly, staring into his beer. 'She might have gone away somewhere to finish her work. She did that sometimes. Her parents own a cottage in Dorset. Very quiet, no interruptions . . .'

'Can you call her there? Have you got a mobile on you?'

'No interruptions, including no phone.'

'What about her mobile?'

'I've called that number several times already.'

'Oh.'

'Or she might be with her parents. Her father's ill. Cancer. Perhaps he's got worse. Have you tried them?'

'I didn't know about them.'

'And then she's got this on-off boyfriend, Carlo. The last I knew it was off, but maybe it's on again and she's there. Have you tried him?'

I took a deep breath. Was I all right? 'No,' I said. 'I didn't know about him. Or, at least, I don't remember knowing about him. But she would have told you, if you were going to meet her.'

He shrugged. 'I'm just her friend. Friendships can be put on the back burner.'

'Sometimes.'

'Jo gets depressed,' he said slowly, frowning. 'I mean, really depressed, not just down. I thought she was coming out of it.' He finished his beer and wiped his mouth with the side of his hand. 'I'll go back to the flat with you and we can call the people who are close to her – Carlo, her parents – and find out if they've heard from her.' He put his hand in the pocket of his coat and fished out a phone. 'Use this. Ring someone, a friend, a colleague, the police, whatever. Say you're with me. Then we can go and make those calls.'

'This is kind of you . . .' I began.

'It's not kind. Jo's my friend.'

'I don't need to make the call,' I said, while a voice inside me said, 'Oh, yes, you do, you stupid, stupid, *stupid* woman.'

'Suit yourself.'

On the way back, I told him how I'd found Jo's flat because of the receipt and key in the glove compartment of my car.

'It was in the police pound,' I said. 'I had to pay over a hundred pounds to retrieve it, and now it's got a bloody clamp on it. Look.' I pointed, then gawped. It wasn't there any more. There was just a space where it had been. 'It's gone. It's bloody gone again. How is that possible? I thought the whole point of a clamp is you can't move it.'

'It's probably back in the pound.' He was trying not to smile.

'Shit.'

*

231

I opened a bottle of wine. My hands were shaking again, so it took ages to pull out the cork. Ben dialled a number, listened, then spoke. He was clearly not talking to Jo's mother. He put the phone down and turned to me. 'That was the woman who dog-sits for them. They're on holiday and won't be back until the day after tomorrow.'

I poured him a glass of wine but he didn't touch it. He put on his glasses, opened the telephone directory and flicked through it.

'Carlo? Hi, Carlo, it's Ben, Ben Brody . . . Yes, that's right, Jo's friend . . . What? No, I haven't seen her lately, I was rather wondering if you . . . No, no, I won't tell her that from you. No.'

He replaced the phone and turned to me. 'Apparently it's off with Carlo. He wasn't in a very good mood.'

'So what do we do now?' I said, then noticed the 'we' and took a hefty gulp of wine.

'Have you got anything to eat? I'm starving. Jo and I were meant to be going out for a meal tonight.'

I opened the fridge door. 'Eggs, bread, cheese. Lettuce. Pasta, I guess.'

'Shall I make us scrambled eggs?'

'I'd like that.'

He took off his coat and his jacket, and found a pan in the large cupboard, a wooden spoon in the top drawer. He knew where everything was. I sat back and watched him. He took a long time over it; he was very methodical. I drank another glass of wine. I felt exhausted, rather fragile, and a bit drunk. And I was fed up with being scared all the time, of always being on my guard. I couldn't do it any more.

'Tell me what Jo's like,' I said.

'Hang on, one piece of toast or two?'

'One. With lots of butter.'

'Here we are.'

I sat at the kitchen table with him and we ate our scrambled eggs in silence. I drank some more wine.

'She's quite shy until you get to know her,' he said, after his last mouthful. 'Self-reliant. Frugal. She only buys what she needs. Never go shopping with her. She takes ages choosing the tiniest thing then has to compare prices in different shops. Neat, she hates disorder. Better at listening than talking. What else? She grew up in the country, has a younger brother who lives in America and is a sound engineer, is pretty close to her parents, has lots of friends, though usually sees people one-to-one. She doesn't like big groups.'

'What about her relationship with this Carlo?'

'Hopeless, really. He's just a young idiot.' He sounded harshly dismissive, and I must have looked a bit surprised, because he added, 'she could do better. She should meet someone who adores her.'

'We should all do that,' I said, lightly.

'And she's a depressive, I'd say. She has terrible low patches when she can hardly get out of bed. Which is why I'm worried.'

It was late. My day lay behind me like a long, laborious journey – Todd, that spooky telephone call, Inspector Cross, now this. Ben saw me give a giant yawn. He stood up and took his coat from the arm of the sofa. 'I should go,' he said. 'I'll be in touch.'

'Is that all?'

'What d'you mean?'

'Well, she's still missing, isn't she? More missing than ever. So what's next? You can't just leave it like that, can you?'

'No, of course not. I thought I should drive to the

cottage in Dorset. I've been there before and I think I can remember where it is. If she's not there, I'll phone around her friends. Then if nothing comes of that, I'll go and see her parents. After that – well, I guess I'll go to the police.'

'I'd quite like to come with you to the cottage. If that's all right.' I hadn't known that I was going to say that. The words came out in a rush, and he turned a surprised face to look at me. 'When are you thinking of going?'

'Well, now.'

'You mean, right this minute? Drive through the night?'

'I might as well. I'm not tired, and I haven't drunk much. And I've got an important meeting tomorrow afternoon, so I can't go tomorrow. And you've made me anxious.'

'You don't hang about.'

'You don't really want to come, do you?'

I shivered and looked outside, at the cold darkness. I didn't want to, but I didn't want to be here either, lying in bed bathed in my sweat, my heart thumping in my chest, my mouth dry, just waiting for it to be light again when unbearable fear became manageable. Looking at the clock. Falling asleep but then jerking awake a few minutes later. Listening for noises and scared by the wind. Thinking of Jo. Thinking of me. Of him in the darkness, watching me.

'I'll come,' I said. 'Where's your car?'

'Outside my house.'

'Where's your house?'

'Belsize Park. A couple of stops on the tube.'

'Let's get a cab.' I couldn't bear the idea of being underground tonight. I'd had enough scares for one day.

'OK.'

'I'll go and put some warmer clothes on. And this time I will ring someone, to tell them who I'm with and stuff. Sorry.'

Fifteen

As far as I could tell in the darkness, Ben Brody lived in a nice house, just near a park. The street was wide and lined with tall trees that waved their empty branches in the lamplight.

'Why don't you just wait in the car while I grab a few things? You look all in.'

He opened the car door and I climbed into the passenger seat. It was freezing, and the windows were frosted over. It was a very empty, tidy car, just a box of tissues and a road atlas on the floor. I huddled up in my thick jacket, blew curls of breath into the icy air and waited. A light went on in the upstairs room of Ben's house, then a few minutes later it went off again. I looked at the clock on the dashboard; it was nearly two. I asked myself what I was doing there, in the deep of the night, in a part of London I'd never set foot in before, in the car of a man I didn't know. I couldn't come up with an answer that made any sense at all, except that I'd reached breaking point.

'We can go now.'

Ben had opened the door. He was dressed in jeans, a thick speckled jumper and an old leather jacket.

'What've you got there?'

'A torch, a blanket, some oranges and chocolate for the journey. The blanket's for you. Lie on the back seat and I'll cover you up.'

I didn't protest. I clambered over and lay down and he draped me in a thick blanket. He started the engine and turned up the heating. I lay there with my eyes open as we slid away. I saw street lights flick by; tall buildings. Then I saw stars, trees, a distant aeroplane in the sky. I closed my eyes.

I slept and woke through the long drive. At one point I surfaced to hear Ben droning some songs to himself that I didn't recognize. Another time I struggled into a sitting position and looked out of the window. It was still dark and I could see no lights in any direction. No other cars passed us. Ben didn't say anything, but he passed me a couple of squares of chocolate that I nibbled slowly. Then I lay down again. I didn't want to talk.

At half past five we stopped at a garage for petrol. It was still dark, but I could see a smudgy greyness on the horizon. It seemed colder than ever, and I could make out snow on the hilltops. Ben came back carrying two polystyrene cups of coffee. I climbed over into the front seat, dragging the blanket with me, and he handed one to me. I wrapped my hands around its warmth.

'White, no sugar,' he said.

'How did you guess?'

'We had coffee before.'

'Oh. How far is it?'

'Not long now. The cottage is a mile or so from a village called Castleton, on the coast. Take a look on the map if you want – it's on the floor by your feet. I may need you to guide me a bit.'

'Do you think she'll be there?'

He shrugged. 'You always have dark thoughts in the early hours of the morning.'

'It's starting to get light now. You must be tired.'

'Not so bad. It'll hit me later, I expect.'

'In the middle of your meeting.'

'Probably.'

'I can drive if you want.'

'I'm not insured. You'll have to talk to keep me awake.'

'I'll do my best.'

'We passed Stonehenge. I nearly woke you. But we'll go back the same way.'

'I've never seen it.'

'Really?'

'It's amazing the things I haven't seen. I've never been to Stonehenge, or to Stratford, or to Hampton Court or to the Tower of London or to Brighton pier. I've never been to Scotland. Or the Lake District, even. I was going to go to Venice. I'd bought the tickets and everything. When I was in a cellar with a gag over my mouth, I should have been setting off for Venice.'

'You'll go one day.'

'I suppose so.'

'What was the worst thing?' he asked, after a pause.

I looked at him and he looked ahead, at the road and the rolling hills. I took a sip of coffee. I thought about saying that I couldn't talk about it, then I thought that Ben was the first person I had met since I ran barefoot from captivity who wasn't looking at me with an expression of wariness or alarm. He wasn't treating me as if I was pitiable or deranged. So I tried to answer. 'I don't know. I can't say. Hearing him wheeze and knowing he was there beside me. Thinking I couldn't breathe and was going to suffocate, going to drown inside myself. It was . . .' I tried to come up with the right word '. . . *obscene*. Maybe just the waiting in the darkness and knowing I was going to die. I tried to hang on to things so I wouldn't go mad – not things from my own life, because I thought that would be a further way of tormenting myself, of going insane with loneliness and terror. Just images, really, like I told you before. Beautiful pictures of the world outside. I still think of them now, sometimes, when I wake in the night. But I knew I was getting stripped away, bit by bit. I was losing myself. That was the point – or, at least, that's what I think the point was. I was going to shed all the bits that made me into me and in the end I'd just be this ghastly object gibbering on a ledge, half naked, dirty and ashamed.' I stopped abruptly.

'Why don't you peel us both an orange? They're in the bag between us.'

I peeled two oranges and their aroma filled the car. My fingers were sticky with the juice. I handed him his, segment by segment. 'Look,' he said. 'There's the sea now.'

It was silver and empty and still. You could hardly tell where the water ended and the dawn sky began – except to the east, where the sun cast a pale light.

'Tell me where I should be turning off,' he said. 'It must be about now.'

We turned right, away from the sun, along a small road that descended towards the coast. Then left again, along an even smaller road.

'It's just about here, I think,' Ben said, peering ahead.

There was a closed gate and a small track. I got out of the car and opened the gate, waited till Ben had driven through, then closed it again.

'Do Jo's parents come here much?'

'Hardly at all. He's too ill, and it's not very luxurious. So they're always glad to have people use it. It's pretty basic, no heating or anything, and beginning to get rather run down. But from the bedroom you can see the sea. There it is.'

The cottage was tiny and grey-stoned. It had thick

walls and small windows. Tiles had blown off the roof and lay smashed around the front door. It looked shabby and neglected.

'There's no car here,' said Ben. 'No one's here.'

'We should go and look, anyway.'

'I guess so.' He sounded dispirited. I opened the door and got out, and he followed. Our feet crunched over the icy grass. I went up to a window and pressed my face against it, but could see little. I rattled the door, but of course it was locked.

'We have to get inside.'

'Is there any point? You can see no one's been here.'

'You've just driven for four hours to get here. What shall we do? Break a window?'

'I could try getting up to the upstairs window,' he said dubiously.

'How? And, anyway, that looks all locked up as well. Why don't we just break the window that's cracked? We can get it repaired later.'

Before he had time to object, I took off my scarf, wrapped it round my fist, and punched hard and fast against the cracked pane, bringing it back quickly as soon as I felt the impact so that I didn't cut my wrist. I felt rather proud of myself – it was just the way they do it in movies. I picked out the remaining shards of glass and laid them in a pile on the grass. Then I opened the window from inside.

'If I stand on your back, I can climb through,' I said to Ben.

But instead, he put his large hands round my waist and raised me up to the window. The memory of being in the cellar, gripped and lifted down from the ledge, was so powerful that for a moment I thought I would gag or start screaming hysterically. But then I was

240

through the window in an undignified scramble and inside the kitchen. I turned on the lights, noticed that the fireplace was full of wet ashes, and let Ben in through the front door.

In silence, we checked the whole house. It didn't take long – there was just a bedroom and a box room upstairs, a kitchen-living room and a lavatory and shower downstairs. The bed was not made up. The heater for the water was not turned on. The place was chilly and deserted.

'It was a fool's errand,' said Ben dully.

'We had to do it.'

'Maybe.' He prodded the ashes with the toe of his boot. 'I hope she's all right.'

'I'll buy you breakfast,' I said. 'There must be somewhere, by the sea, where they do warm food. You need to have a rest and something to eat before you drive back.'

We got into the car and drove through Castleton, which only had a post office and a pub, to the next small town. We found a little café that was probably full of tourists in the summer months but now was empty. It was open, and they did English breakfasts. I ordered the 'Special' for both of us – sausages, eggs, bacon, mushrooms, grilled tomatoes and fried bread – and a large cafetière of coffee.

We ate the greasy, comforting food in silence.

'We should go if you're going to be in time for your meeting,' I said, after the last mouthful.

We didn't talk much on the way back. There was more traffic on the road, thickening as we approached London into a slow crawl of cars. Ben kept glancing at the clock worriedly.

'You can leave me at an underground station,' I said, but he drove me to the front door and even got out of the car and saw me to the door.

' 'Bye,' I said awkwardly. Our long journey together already seemed unreal. 'Let me know what happens, will you?'

'Of course,' he said. He looked tired and despondent. 'I'll talk to her parents as soon as they're back from their holiday. I can't do anything else till then, can I? And maybe she's with them.'

'I hope your meeting goes well.'

He looked down at his clothes and attempted a smile. 'I don't really look the part, do I? Never mind. Goodbye.' He hesitated as if he was about to say something else, then changed his mind, turned and got back into his car.

Sixteen

I didn't know what to do with myself for the rest of the day. All my plans had petered out and there didn't seem to be any other trails to follow. I had a bath, washed my hair, did my laundry. I played back the messages on the answering-machine. There was only one new one. I opened my laptop and checked for emails. There was one, warning me about a computer virus.

I prowled around the living room, looking at my lists tacked to the wall and trying to focus on what I actually knew. I had been grabbed either on the Thursday evening or on the Friday, Saturday or Sunday. My mobile was being answered by a man. I had had sex with someone. I came to a decision: every time someone rang, I would pick up the phone and speak to them. I would open all her mail. I would try to contact her friends.

I started with the mail. I took the letters I'd left propped up on the mantelpiece and slit them open one by one. She was invited to take part in a time-share in Spain. She was asked to rewrite an educational textbook about the Gunpowder Plot. She was invited to a school reunion. A friend she hadn't seen for years wanted to get back in touch. Another friend sent a newspaper clipping about the pros and cons of Prozac – I wrote down her name and phone number on a scrap of paper, and the phone number of the man who'd sent her an estimate for a new boiler. I looked at the postcards, but they were just scribbles from foreign holidays or thank-you notes.

Then I went through all the messages stored on the answering-machine. I'd already talked to her editor. Few of the callers had left their last names or their numbers. I rang someone called Iris, who turned out to be Jo's cousin, and had a confused conversation with her about dates. She had last seen Jo six months ago. I rang the woman who'd sent the Prozac cutting. Her name was Lucy, she'd known Jo for years, through all her ups and downs. She had seen her on New Year's Eve, when she'd thought Jo had been subdued but more in control of her life. No, she hadn't heard from her since and, no, she had no idea of her plans. She started to sound worried, and I said it was probably fine, not to worry. The boiler-man was out and I left a message on his machine.

I went to Jo's computer, on her desk in the corner of the room, and turned it on. I looked at the files, and wondered if I should call her publisher to say that I was pretty sure that the project she'd been working on for her was here. I clicked on her mailbox and scrolled down the more recent emails. I considered sending out a standard message to all the people in her address file, asking if they had heard from her, but decided to wait for a day or two.

Ben had said Jo was a private person, and I'd invaded that privacy pretty thoroughly by now. I hoped she would understand. He had also said that she was neat. I decided I'd better have a thorough clean-up. I washed the plates we'd used the night before, scrubbed down the bath, put things away. I looked around for the vacuum cleaner and found it in the tall cupboard near the bathroom, along with a cat-litter tray and some unopened cat food, and a black bin-bag which, when I inspected it, had skiing stuff in it. I vacuumed my room and hers. The washing-machine had finished its cycle, so

I hung clothes out on radiators. I made myself another cup of coffee, though I was already feeling twitchy with caffeine and strangeness. I put on some music and sat down on the sofa, but I was restless. Then I heard someone downstairs, shutting a door, and it struck me that I hadn't even done the obvious thing of asking Jo's neighbours when they'd last seen her.

I finished my coffee and went out of the flat and round to the ground-floor entrance. I rang the bell and waited. The door opened a crack and one eye peered out at me.

'Hello, I'm Jo's . . . Jo's flatmate, Abbie, and I . . .'

The door opened wide. 'I know who you are, my love. Jo introduced us. Remember? Peter. You said you'd visit me but you never did, did you?'

He was a tiny old man, much smaller than me. I wondered if he'd shrunk with age or if he'd always been the size of a pre-pubescent schoolboy. He wore a yellow jersey that was unravelling at one sleeve, a checked scarf round his thin neck, and slippers. He had a small amount of grey hair and his face was crumpled and grooved. 'Come inside,' he said. I paused. 'Come on, don't stand outside, come inside. I can make us tea. Sit down. There. Don't mind the cat. Sit down and make yourself comfortable. You'll want biscuits too, I dare say. Sugar? Do you take sugar? You've been rushing around, haven't you? I've seen you come and go. I've got the time to notice these things.'

The room was very hot and scrupulously tidy. Books lined the walls. He had all of Charles Dickens in leathery-looking hardback. I sat on the squashy leather sofa and took the tea he was holding out. The cat twitched in its sleep; it looked like the fat tabby I'd seen out of my window. 'Thanks, Peter. Lovely. Remind me, when did we meet?'

'Wednesday,' he said promptly. 'The day you arrived. I happened to come out on to the pavement, just for a breath of air, when you were taking all your things in and Jo introduced us. I said you should visit if you ever felt at a loose end. But you didn't. And then you went away, of course.'

'When was that? When did we go?'

'Lost your memory, have you?' He laughed cheerily. 'I haven't seen you both around. Been on holiday together, have you?'

'Not exactly.'

'Is Jo back too? Nice girl, Jo. Ever so helpful. She took me to the hospital when I fell over and broke my leg. And came and visited me. No one else did, but she came and she brought flowers.'

'She's not back yet,' I said vaguely.

'I'm eighty-six,' he said. 'Do I look it?'

'No,' I lied.

'My mother lived until she was ninety-five. Ninety-five and then suddenly, one day, boom. She was gone. I still miss her. Silly, isn't it? I'm an old man and I think about my mum every day. I still have her hairbrushes, you know, lovely silver hairbrushes with ivory backs and real horsehair bristles. You don't get things like that nowadays. And her napkin ring, silver with her name on the inside. Pretty.'

'That tea was just what I needed. Thanks a lot.'

'Are you going already? Without a biscuit?'

'I'll come again soon.'

'I'm usually here.'

I was in a deep sleep having a dream in which a fire alarm went off. I couldn't see where the fire was and I couldn't see where the fire exit was. I was paralysed by this ignorance. If I had known where the fire exit was, I could have headed for it. If I'd known where the fire was, I could have run away from it. The fire bell rang again and woke me up. Dimly and stupidly I realized it was the doorbell. I reached for my dressing-gown. My eyes wouldn't open. That was the first problem. They felt as if they were glued together. I pulled the lids apart on one as if I were peeling a grape but even so I had to get myself to the door virtually by touch. Even sleepwalking I made sure that the chain was fastened. I opened the door and the face of a young police officer appeared in the gap. 'Miss Devereaux?' he said.

'What time is it?'

He looked at his watch.

'Three forty-five,' he said.

'In the morning?'

He looked behind him. It was grey and cloudy but very obviously daytime. My mind began to clear. 'If it's about the car,' I said, 'I was planning to get it. It got a ticket, and then it got clamped. I've kept meaning to do something about it but I've been busy. You don't want to know.'

He looked blank. 'I'm not here about a car,' he said. 'Can we come in?'

'I want to see identification.'

He sighed and passed a thin leather wallet through the door. As if I could tell a genuine police identification. 'You can probably buy these on the Net,' I said.

'I can give you a phone number to call, if you're still concerned.'

'To some friend of yours sitting in a bedsit somewhere.'

'Look, Miss Devereaux, I've been sent by DI Cross. He wants to talk to you. If you have some problem with that, could you take it up with him personally?'

247

I unlocked the door. There were two of them. They wiped their feet noisily on the doormat and removed their caps.

'If Cross wants to talk to me, why isn't he here?'

'We've come to collect you.'

I had an impulse to say something angry but at the same time I felt relief. Finally Cross was coming to me. I wasn't the one creating trouble. Five minutes later I was in a police car heading south. When we stopped at traffic lights, I saw people staring in at me. Who was this woman sitting in the back of a police car? Was she a criminal or a detective? I tried to look more like a detective. When we crossed the river, I looked out of the window and frowned. 'This isn't the way,' I said.

'DI Cross is at the Castle Road station.'

'Why?'

There was no answer.

Castle Road was a shiny new police station with lots of plate glass and coloured tubular steel. We drove round to the back and then I was led in quickly through a small door by the car park and up some stairs. Cross was in a small office with another detective, a middle-aged, balding man who offered me his hand and introduced himself as Jim Burrows.

'Thanks for coming,' said Cross. 'How are you doing?'

'Is this about Jo?'

'What?'

'Because I drove down to Dorset and she isn't at the cottage where she normally stays. Also, I've talked to this man who knows her and he's rung other people who know her and nobody knows where she is.'

'Right,' said Cross, looking at Burrows uneasily. It was a see-what-I've-been-talking-about kind of look. 'But there's something else I wanted to ask you. Please sit down.' He gestured me to a chair in front of the desk. 'Do you know a woman called Sally Adamson?'

'No.'

'Are you sure?'

'Who is she?'

'Have you been in touch with Terry Wilmott?'

I suddenly felt a current of cold nausea run through my whole body. It started at the top of my head and ran down to the tips of my toes. Something bad had happened.

'I went round to collect some mail a couple of times.' A thought occurred to me. 'Sally. Is that his girlfriend?'

'His girlfriend?'

'I don't know exactly what the situation is. I've run into her a couple of times. She was arriving as I left. I don't know her second name. I don't know if they're actually together. But I think Terry is one of those people who is psychologically incapable of not being in a relationship. I mean, when we first met . . .' And then I stopped. 'Has something happened?'

The two men looked at each other and Burrows stepped forward. 'She's died,' he said. 'Sally Adamson. She was found dead last night.'

I looked from one man to the other. I had about fifty questions to ask, so I started with the stupidest one. 'Dead?'

'That's right,' said Cross. 'And there's something else. Her body was found under a hedge just inside the front garden of number fifty-four Westcott Street. Strangled, by the way. This wasn't natural causes.'

I shivered. Suddenly I felt cold. 'Terry lives at number sixty-two,' I said.

'Yes,' said Cross.

'Oh, God,' I said. 'Oh, my God.'

'Can we get you something?' Cross said. 'Some coffee?'

I shook my head. 'It's a nightmare,' I muttered. 'It keeps on getting worse. Dear God. Oh, poor Sally. But what do you want *me* for?' Cross didn't answer. He just looked at me and then more realization battered its way into my tired brain.

'No,' I said. 'No and no and no. There's lots of crime around there. A woman on her own, at night, leaving the flat. She could easily be mugged.'

Cross walked across the office to a table in the corner. He returned carrying something in a clear plastic bag. He laid it down on Burrows's desk. 'Sally Adamson's purse,' he said. 'Which we found in Sally Adamson's shoulder-bag, lying next to her body. It contains forty-five pounds in cash. Two credit cards. Several store-cards. It was untouched.'

'No,' I said, more to myself than to the two officers. 'No. It doesn't make any sense. Does Terry know?'

'Terence Wilmott is downstairs,' said Jim Burrows. 'My colleagues are talking to him at the moment.'

'What's he saying?'

'Not much. He has his lawyer with him.'

'You don't seriously think . . . ? You can't . . .' I put my head in my hands, closed my eyes. Perhaps I could go to sleep and when I woke up this would all have faded away, like a dream breaks up into vague, half-remembered images.

Burrows cleared his throat and I lifted my head and looked at him. He picked up a typed piece of paper from his desk and looked at it. 'On at least three occasions in November and December last year, you phoned the police about your boyfriend.'

'That's right,' I said. 'And they didn't do anything about it. They didn't believe me.'

'What did he do?'

'There was nothing complicated about it. Terry gets depressed. He gets angry. He gets drunk. Sometimes he lashes out.'

'He hit you?'

'Look, if you think for a single minute that Terry would murder a woman –'

'Please, Miss Devereaux, we can talk about your opinions later but first can you answer our questions?'

I shut my mouth in what was meant to be an eloquently contemptuous way. 'All right,' I said.

'He hit you?'

'Yes. But –'

'Slapped you?'

'Yes.'

'Did he strike you with a closed hand?'

'You mean a fist? Once or twice.'

'Do you mean just once or twice or that there were one or two occasions on which he used his fists against you?'

I took a deep breath. 'The second. It happened a couple of times.'

'Did he ever use a weapon of any kind?'

I threw up my arms in a wild sort of gesticulation. 'This is all wrong,' I said. 'These yes and no questions aren't right. It was all messier than that.'

Burrows moved closer to me, spoke quietly. 'Did he ever threaten you with anything? Such as a knife?'

'I guess so, yes.'

'You guess so?'

'Yes. He did, I mean.'

'Did he ever hold you around your neck, with his hands or his arm?'

And then I took myself by surprise. I started to cry and cry, helplessly. I fumbled for a tissue but my hands didn't seem to be working properly. I didn't even know why I was crying. I didn't know whether it was because of the wreckage of my life with Terry. Or whether it was because of the fears I had for myself. And then there was Sally. Sally whose second name I hadn't known. I tried to picture her face and couldn't. She was a woman I had probably wished ill towards, if I had thought anything about her at all, and now she had had ill done to her. Did that make me in a small but definite way responsible?

When I came round from my fit of howling, I saw that Cross was standing there holding a paper cup in each hand. He handed me one. It was water and I drank it down in a gulp. The other was coffee, hot and strong, and I sipped at it.

'I want you to make a statement,' he said. 'If you feel able.' I nodded. 'Good. We'll bring in an officer and we'll go through it.'

So, for the next two and a half hours, I drank cup after paper cup of coffee and I talked about all the things in my relationship with Terry that I had wanted to forget. People say that to talk about your bad experiences is therapeutic. For me it was the opposite. I'm a person with good friends, but I'd never talked to them about Terry, not about the worst of it. I'd never spoken the things, never named them. Somehow when I said them aloud, they came alive there in Jim Burrows's office, and they frightened me.

For many months I'd simply thought of myself as being in a relationship with problems, where every so often things got out of control, where we had difficulty communicating. It sounded quite different when I put it into words. The woman typing out what I said was a young uniformed officer. But when I described the evening when Terry, drunk out of his skull, picked up a kitchen knife and waved it at me and then pushed it against my throat, she stopped typing and looked up at me, her eyes wide. He didn't mean it, I said. He would never have done anything to hurt me. WPC Hawkins and Burrows and Cross looked at me and at each other and they didn't bother to say the obvious, which was that he *had* hurt me and who was I trying to fool? Did I have a problem? Was I a natural victim? As I told the story, I began to wonder about the woman who had put up with this for so long. And I thought about the woman I couldn't remember, the woman who had said enough was enough and walked out.

I tried to imagine Sally Adamson, the woman who had told me that we weren't alike, lying cold in a cold front garden. And then I thought of her lying there dead, with Terry's semen inside her, and then I felt so ashamed that my cheeks burned and I thought that Cross would know the terrible thing that had been passing through my mind. I asked who had found her. It was the postman. I thought of her being found by a stranger while the people who knew her and loved her didn't know she was dead. I also started to think: Could Terry really have done this? And if he had, oh, God, if he had, what did that mean about me and my story? No one else had believed me, but until now, I had believed myself. It was all that I'd had to stop me going insane.

Seventeen

When I had finished my statement, I felt as if I had been flayed. The story I'd told was true in all its details, and yet, in a confused way, I felt it wasn't the story I had meant to tell. I felt I needed to add something important to it but I was just too tired. Cross looked through it with occasional nods, like a teacher marking some homework and finding it barely adequate. I signed the statement three times and then WPC Hawkins took the small bundle away. I was thinking about what I was going to do when Cross said he would drive me home. I protested that he didn't have to bother but he said he was going in that direction anyway and I couldn't muster the energy to protest.

For the first part of the drive, through high streets I didn't recognize, I just stared ahead of me and tried to think of nothing. But it was no good. I started to go over it in my mind and in a short time it was there inescapably in front of me.

'Stop,' I said.

'What's wrong?' he said.

'I think I'm going to be sick.'

'Oh, for Christ's sake,' he said, looking around desperately. 'Hang on, we're in a red zone. Wait, I'll find somewhere.'

'You're a policeman, aren't you?'

'Wait, wait, if you're going to throw up, do it out of the window.'

He turned off the main road into a side-street and

pulled up at the kerb. I opened the door and ran out. There was a tall brick wall. It must have been the side of a factory or a warehouse. I put my hands on the rough surface, which was wonderfully cold to the touch. I leant forward and rested my forehead on it. I felt a hand on my back.

'Are you all right?'

A warm sour liquid rose in my throat but I swallowed it and took several deep breaths.

'It's been a difficult day,' Cross said.

'No, no,' I said. 'Well, it has, but that's not it.'

'What do you mean?'

I took a few steps along the pavement, rubbing my arms in an attempt to warm myself. It was dark and my breath was a vapour in front of my face. We were on the edge of an industrial estate. Behind barbed wire there were modern buildings that were already going grimy. Frazer Glass and Glazing Co. Leather Industries Centre. Tippin Memorial Masons.

'This is all wrong,' I said.

'Get back into the car.'

'Wait,' I said. 'You know that I haven't got particularly warm feelings towards Terry at the moment.'

'I can imagine.'

'He's a man with real problems and he probably needs all kinds of help but he didn't do this.'

'Miss Devereaux, Abbie, get back into the car. I'm freezing out here.'

'If we get back into the car, will you answer some questions?'

'Anything. So long as we get out of this.'

We sat in the car in silence for a time.

'Am I keeping you from anything?' I asked.

'Not really,' he said.

'I just have these questions that come into my mind and I can't stop them. I know that you're the expert and I'm just somebody who advises companies about where to put the photocopier and the coffee machine. But it doesn't make sense. For a start, Terry isn't a murderer. And if he was, I don't think he'd pick on a woman he'd just started seeing. And if he had decided to kill her, it would happen in his own flat or her flat. If he was going to go to the trouble of hiding her body, he wouldn't do it three doors down from where he lived.'

Jack Cross's first response, if it can be called a response, was to start the car and drive off.

'I think I can manage this while driving,' he said. 'For a start I should say that Terence Wilmott has not been charged with the murder of Sally Adamson. But he is the obvious suspect and I'm afraid that the obvious suspect usually turns out to be the person who committed the crime. I take your points about Terry –'

'Which means you don't,' I interrupted.

'But the fact is that most people are not killed by strangers who attack them in a dark alley. They are killed by people they know. Women are most at risk from their sexual partners. Terry's history of violence towards his partners – i.e., you – is just further evidence. Compelling evidence, I'd say. As for where he did it, and why, and where he disposed of the body – if he did – all I can say is that there are no rules. People plan murders and they do them on the spur of the moment. Sometimes they don't conceal the body, sometimes they conceal it so perfectly that it's never found, sometimes they half conceal it. He might have killed her, then dumped the body along the road in an attempt to make it look as if she had been mugged while leaving the flat.'

'If he was doing that, why would he leave the purse?

And it would be ridiculously risky to carry the body along the street.'

'Have you ever committed a murder, Abbie?'

'No. Have you?'

'No,' he said, forcing a smile. 'But I know people who have. Imagine the greatest stress you've ever experienced and multiply it by a hundred. You can't breathe, you can't think. People do the strangest things. They make the weirdest mistakes.'

'There's another possibility.'

'There are lots of other possibilities.'

'No. This is really what happened.'

'And what's that?' he asked, with exaggerated patience.

I didn't even want to say this aloud. I had to force myself. 'You know that I've changed my appearance since it all happened.'

'I have noticed.'

'Since you turned me loose and left me without any protection, I've been taking huge precautions not to be followed. And almost nobody knows where I'm staying. I think that one of the only things that that man – the man who grabbed me – knows about me is where I worked and where I lived. I talked about things like that to him. I told him Terry's name. I remember.'

'Yes?'

'Have you ever noticed that when a couple splits up and one of them gets together with somebody else almost straight away, the new partner often looks like a clone of the old one?'

'No, I haven't.'

'It's true. I was struck by it immediately when I bumped into Sally. Ask Terry. I actually mentioned it to them when I met her.'

'Tactful.'

257

'She didn't agree. Well, she wouldn't want to, I suppose. But, anyway, she wouldn't have been able to tell. I'd already changed my appearance so much that we looked completely different. The point I'm trying to make is that the man who kidnapped me knows that I'm out there. Obviously he hasn't been arrested straight away, but still, he doesn't know what I know about him. I'm a risk for him. If he could kill me, he would be safer. One of the only ways he could find me would be to hang around Terry's flat. If he saw Sally coming out in the middle of the night he would obviously have assumed it was me.'

'Go on.'

'He strangled her, thinking she was me. He thought it was my neck. It's the only explanation that really makes sense.'

I looked at Cross. He didn't reply. Suddenly he seemed to be concentrating hard on his driving. And then an idea came to me. 'He thinks he's killed me.'

'What?'

'That man. He thinks I'm dead. He thinks he's safe. He probably didn't realize he had made a mistake. If you could delay announcing the murder, or at least delay revealing the identity of the victim, then that would give me a few days to do something.'

'That's a good idea,' Cross said. 'Unfortunately there's one drawback with it.'

'What's that?'

'It's that I'm living in the real world. We're stuck with a few boring procedural rules. When people are murdered, we're not really supposed to keep it secret. We have to tell their family. And then we're meant to find out who did it.'

We sat in silence for several minutes as we approached Jo's flat. The car pulled up.

'You know what's really funny,' I said.

'No.'

'You don't believe me. You think I'm a fantasist or maybe a chronic liar. You're quite nice and I know you felt a bit worse than the others about cutting me loose, but there we are. But if it had been me lying in that front garden instead of Sally, you would have been sure it was Terry and that man would have got away with it.'

Cross leant over and put his hand on my forearm. 'Abbie, as I have said before, if there is any new evidence, we will open up your case. Of course. And if your friend . . .'

'Jo.'

'If Jo hasn't turned up in the next few days, you should tell me. You know that. I am not dismissing you. We did not cut you loose, as you put it, we had absolutely no evidence of any kind – except that your boyfriend, Terry Wilmott, had beaten you up in the past and had done so just before you lost consciousness. That was all we had to go on. If it had been you we found last night, God forbid, then maybe it would have been Terry who did it. Hasn't that occurred to you? It's my opinion that you were lucky to get away from him.'

'But what about my disappearance? Do you want to blame him for that? He has an alibi, remember?'

Cross's expression hardened. 'He has a story that stands up, that's all. That's all we've got here, lots of stories. Except now we have a dead woman, lying a few yards from the front door of the man who beat you up.'

I opened the door and got out. I bent down and looked at his face, faint in the glow of the street lights. 'Tomorrow Sally's name will be in the papers and he'll know and he'll be after me again. But in the end you'll know I was telling the truth. I've got a way of proving it to you.'

'What's that?'

'You'll know when you find me dead. I'll be strangled in a ditch somewhere and you'll still have Terry locked up and you'll be sorry.'

'You're right,' he said.

'What do you mean?'

'I would be sorry.'

I slammed the door so hard that the car shook.

Eighteen

I looked up at Jo's windows. There were no lights on, and the place seemed very empty and dark. I put the key into the lock. I imagined myself up there, sitting alone through the evening and the long night, picturing Sally's dead body and waiting for the morning to come. Perhaps I should go to Sadie's again, or Sam's, or Sheila's. But the thought of it filled me with despair. I would have to tell them everything that had happened since they'd seen me last, and too much had happened. Though I'd seen them all just a few days ago, they felt too far away. I had fallen out of their world and had become a stranger, and who would know me now?

I couldn't just stand there on the street, an unmoving target. I turned the key and pushed open the door. I looked at the stairs, climbing up to the unlit rooms, and fear rose up in me. I pulled the door shut again and stood for a moment, leaning against it and trying to breathe calmly. A part of me wanted to slide down the door and collapse on the path. I could curl up in a ball, with my arms wrapped around my head, and lie there like a dying animal. Someone else could come and deal with everything. They'd lift me up and carry me somewhere safe and warm and I wouldn't have to go on like this, day after day.

I didn't curl up on the path. I turned back towards the high street, where I flagged down a taxi and asked them to take me to Belsize Park. I didn't know the number of the house but I thought I would remember it once I got there. He probably wouldn't be there, and if he was I didn't know what I would say to him.

I found the house easily. I remembered the tree on the pavement outside, and I somehow knew that it had a wrought-iron fence. There were lights on both downstairs and upstairs. I gave the cab driver a ten-pound note and told him to keep the change. I walked towards the door and my legs felt like jelly and my breath kept catching in my throat. He would probably be in the middle of a dinner party. He'd probably be in bed with someone. I rapped the knocker loudly and stood back. I heard him coming and a little sob escaped me.

'Abbie?'

'Is someone here? Are you in the middle of something?'

He shook his head.

'Sorry,' I said. 'Sorry to bother you like this, but I didn't know what else to do. You're the only person I know who knows everything. If you see what I mean. Sorry.'

'What's happened?'

'I'm scared.'

'Come inside. You must be freezing.' He opened the door and I stepped into the wide hall.

'Sorry.'

'Stop saying sorry, for God's sake. Come on, come into the kitchen, get warm. Here, give me your coat.'

'Thanks.'

He led me into a small kitchen. There were pot plants all along the window-sill and daffodils on the table. I could smell glue, sawdust, varnish.

'Here. Sit down, move that junk. Let me get us something to drink. Tea? Or how about hot chocolate?'

'Lovely.'

He poured milk into a pan and set it on the hob.

'What about food? When did you last eat?'

'This morning, a fry-up. Remember?'

'Was that only this morning? God.'

'Did your meeting go all right?'

'It went, at least. Shall I make you something?'

'Just hot chocolate. That would be very comforting.'

'Comforting,' he said, with a smile.

He spooned chocolate granules into the boiling milk and stirred vigorously, then poured it into a large green mug. 'Drink that, Abbie, and tell me what's happened.'

'Sally died,' I said.

'Sally? Who's Sally?'

'Terry's new girlfriend.' I waited for him to ask who Terry was but he didn't, just nodded and frowned.

'I'm sorry about that, but did you know her well? Was she a friend?'

'I hardly knew her at all. But she was killed.'

'Killed? Someone killed her?'

'Outside Terry's flat. The police are convinced it was Terry.'

'I see,' he said slowly.

'It wasn't. I know it wasn't. But, of course, they just think I'm trapped in some paranoid fantasy. For them, this proves it: Terry bashed me around and I turn it from a squalid tale of domestic abuse into a heroic story of a kidnap. Then he continues the pattern and murders his next girlfriend.'

'But he didn't?'

'No. Terry wouldn't murder anyone.'

'Lots of people who wouldn't murder anyone go and murder someone.'

'That's what the police keep saying. But I know him. Anyway, if he did kill her he would have collapsed with guilt and phoned 999. He certainly wouldn't have dragged her body outside and put it a few doors up. And if he wanted to hide it, which he wouldn't have done, because anyway he wouldn't have done it in the first place, then he would have . . .'

'I'm not the police, you know.'

'No. Sorry. It's just . . . everything. I keep thinking about poor, stupid Terry. And Sally, of course. But there's something more. Sally looked like me. I mean, like I used to look before I got my haircut and stuff.' I watched his face change. 'I just have this horrible feeling that it should have been me.'

'Oh,' he said. 'I see.'

'He's out there, looking for me. He'll find me. I know it.'

'And the police don't take you seriously?'

'No. I don't really blame them. If I wasn't me, I don't know if I would take me seriously. If you see what I mean.'

'I do see what you mean.'

'Do you believe me?'

'Yes,' he said.

'In a big way, I mean? About everything.'

'Yes.'

'Really? You're not just saying that?'

'I'm not just saying it.'

I looked at him. He didn't flinch or look away. 'Thank you,' I said. I picked up my mug of hot chocolate and finished it. I felt better, all of a sudden. 'Can I use your bathroom? Then I'll go home. I shouldn't have come barging in like this, it was stupid of me.'

'Up the stairs, the first room you come to.'

I stood up. My legs felt wobbly as I climbed the stairs. I used the toilet then splashed my blotchy face. I looked like a washed-out schoolgirl. I came out and headed back down the stairs again. It was a nice house; I wondered if a woman lived there. There were pictures on the walls and books in piles. There was a large plant in the alcove where the staircase turned. I stopped dead and looked at it, its old, gnarled trunk and its dark green leaves. I crouched down and pressed a finger against its mossy soil. I sat down beside it and put my head in my hands. I didn't know whether to cry or giggle or scream. I didn't do any of them. I just stood up and went down the rest of the stairs, very slowly. I walked into the kitchen. Ben was still sitting at the table. He wasn't doing anything, just staring into space. He looked tired, as well. Tired and a bit low, perhaps.

Like a person in a dream – my dream, the dream of a life I'd once inhabited, a dream I couldn't remember – I walked round the table and laid one hand against his face. I watched his expression soften. 'Was it like this?' I said. I bent over him and kissed him on the side of his mouth. He closed his eyes and I kissed his eyelids. I kissed him on his mouth until it parted. I felt soft and new. 'Was it?'

'No, it wasn't.'

'So what was it like?'

'You said to me that you felt ugly. You'd been talking about Terry. So I took you by the hand.' He took me by the hand and led me across the room to where there was a full-length mirror hanging on the wall. He placed me in front of it so that I was looking at myself, ragged, blotchy, pale, straggly, worn-out Abigail. He stood behind me and we caught each other's gaze in the mirror. 'I brought you over here and I made you look at yourself. I said that you were beautiful.'

'I look like something you found on a skip.'

'Shut up, Abbie. I'm talking. You were beautiful then and you're beautiful now. I told you that you were lovely and then I couldn't stop myself. I kissed you like this, on your soft neck. Yes, you leant your head just like that.'

'What then?' I said. I felt faint.

'I kissed you like this and rubbed my hands over you, your face and neck. Then I carried on like this.'

He was kissing my neck and at the same time he undid the buttons on the front of my shirt until it opened.

'That right?' I murmured, not very coherently.

He reached under my shirt and unfastened my bra at the back and pulled it up at the front and then his hands were on my breasts. His soft lips were still on my neck, not so much kissing my skin as stroking it.

'Like this,' he said.

I was going to say something but I couldn't speak. His right hand stroked my stomach gently, moving downwards. He deftly snapped open the button at the top of my trousers and opened the zip. He knelt down behind me, kissing his way down my spine as he did so. He put his hands inside the waistband and pulled my trousers and knickers down around my ankles. He stood up again. He was behind me, his arms around me.

'Look at that,' he said, and I looked at my body and in the mirror I looked at him, looking at my body and I looked at my body with his gaze. And I looked into the mirror and thought of my naked body in that mirror, when was it? Two weeks ago?

When I spoke to him my voice was drowsy with arousal. 'I look undignified,' I said.

'You look wonderful.'

'And I can't run away.'

'You can't run away.'

'What did I do after that?'

And then he showed me. I had to hobble, ridiculously, towards his bedroom and I fell over on the bed. I kicked off my shoes and shook off my clothes. They were virtually off anyway. Then he took off his own clothes, taking his time. He reached over to a drawer and took out a condom, opening the packet with his teeth. I helped him put it on. 'I know about this,' I said. 'I found the morning-after pill among my stuff.'

'Oh, God,' he said. 'I'm sorry. We didn't have time.'

'I'm sure I was to blame as well.'

'Yeah,' he said, gasping now. 'You were.'

We looked at each other. He put up one hand and touched my face, my neck, my breasts. 'I thought I'd never touch you again,' he said.

'Was it like this?'

'Yes.'

'This?'

'Yes. Don't stop.'

We didn't stop. We looked at each other the whole time, sometimes smiling at each other. When he came, he cried out like a man in pain. I gathered him to me and held him close. I kissed his damp hair.

'It can't have been better than that,' I said.

He put his lips against the pulse in my throat and then he groaned something into my neck.

'What was that?'

'I said, not an hour's gone by without me missing you.'

'Perhaps I've been missing you, too, but I didn't know it.'

'How did you know?'

'The bonsai tree.' I drew back and glared at him. 'So why the fuck didn't you tell me?'

'I'm sorry, I didn't know what to do. I wanted you to feel something, not be told you had felt it. If that makes sense.'

'I don't know. There's a bit of me waiting to be furious with you. Really furious. That's not a joke. I've been searching and searching for bits of the me that I lost, blundering around like a terrified blind woman, and you knew that, and you could have helped me all along. But you didn't. You chose not to. You knew things about me that I didn't know about me. You still do. You can remember fucking me and I've got no memory at all. You know the other me, the me I keep hidden, and I don't know the other you, do I? What other things do you know about me? How will I know that you've told me everything? I won't. You've got bits of my life. That's not right. Is it?'

'No.'

'Is that all you've got to say?'

'I'm sorry. I didn't know what to do,' he said helplessly. 'I wanted to tell you but what would I have said?'

'The truth,' I said. 'That would have been a good place to start.'

'I'm sorry,' he said again.

I stroked his chest softly. Before I had been grabbed and shut up in a cellar, I had been happy. Everyone had said so. I'd been happy because I'd left a man who beat me up, left a job I disliked, and met Ben. Since coming out of hospital, I had been haunted by the fact that the days I had lost were ones full of lovely memories. I had lost the bits I wanted to keep; I had kept the bits I wanted to let go. Thoughts flitted through my head, or fragments of thoughts. Something about saying yes to life, something about not spending the rest of my life being scared.

Later, we had a bath together. Then he went downstairs and made us both sandwiches, which he brought up on a tray, with a bottle of red wine. I sat against the pillows.

'You're always making me meals,' I said.

'We had oysters before.'

'Did we? I love oysters.'

'I know. That's why we had them. We'll have them again.'

I picked up his hand and kissed it, then bit into the sandwich. 'So it was a Wednesday evening, right?'

'Monday.'

'Monday! You're sure? Straight after we first met?'

'Sure.'

I frowned.

'But you didn't wear a condom?'

'I did.'

'I don't get it. You said earlier . . .'

'You came back.'

'On Wednesday?'

'Yes.'

'You should have fucking well told me that.'

'I know.'

'And you didn't . . .'

'No.'

'Why?'

'You came on an impulse. With the tree. We'd arranged to meet the next evening – Thursday – because I had several people round on the Wednesday. Clients. They were there already and you knocked on the door and handed me the tree. I kissed you.'

'Yes?'

'And then I kissed you some more.'

'Go on.'

'You undid the buttons on my shirt. We could hear my guests talking to each other in the next-door room.'

'And?'

'We went to the bathroom and locked the door and we fucked.'

'Standing up?'

'Yes. It took about thirty seconds.'

'Show me,' I said.

I stayed the night with Ben. In spite of everything, I slept heavily and when I woke in the morning, I could smell coffee and toast. Through the curtains, the sky looked blue. I was frightened by my sudden happiness. It was like the coming of spring.

Nineteen

We had toast in bed. The crumbs spilt on to the sheets, but Ben lay back on the pillows and pulled the duvet under his chin, looking very comfortable.

'Don't you have work to do?' I said.

Ben leant across me to look at the clock by the bed. Funny how quickly you could feel comfortable with another body. 'Eighteen minutes,' he said.

'Won't you be late?'

'I'm already late. But there's someone coming in to see me. He's come all the way from Amsterdam. If I'm not there to meet him, I'll be a bad person as well as late.'

I kissed him. It was meant to be just a peck.

'You'll have to stop doing that,' he said. 'Or I won't be able to go.'

'You see,' I said, whispering it, because my face was almost touching his, 'if I were you and you were me, I'd think that you were mad. Or I was mad. If you see what I mean.'

'You've lost me.'

'If somebody I'd met disappeared and turned up a fortnight later and seemed to have no memory of even having seen me, I'd think they were completely mad. Or a liar. As you know, the police are torn between the two theories.'

'I thought I was mad. Then I thought you were mad. Then I just didn't know.' He stroked my hair. It made me shiver with pleasure. 'I didn't know what to do,' he said. 'It seemed an impossible thing to explain. I suppose I thought that I had to make you like me again. In any case, the idea of me saying to you, "You're attracted to me, or at least you were, you don't remember it but you really were" . . . It didn't sound particularly sane.'

'You don't have hands like a designer,' I said.

'You mean they're rough and scratchy?'

'I like them.'

He contemplated his own hands with curiosity. 'I do a lot of my own manufacturing. Things get spilt on my hands. They get scratched and hammered and scraped, but that's the way I like it. My old man is a welder. He's got a workshop at home and he spends all his weekends taking things apart and putting them back together. When I was younger, if I wanted to communicate with him, the only way was by going in there and passing him the wrench or whatever it was. Getting my hands dirty. That's what I still do, on the whole. I found a way of getting paid for what my dad did as a hobby.'

'It's not quite like that for me,' I said. 'Not with my dad or with my work.'

'You're fantastic at your job. You pulled the whole thing together. You scared us all shitless.'

'Sometimes I can't believe the things I do – or did. You know, risk assessment for an office? You can imagine risk assessment for an oil rig or a polar expedition but the insurance company wanted a risk assessment for the office so I did it. Just at the moment I'm a world expert on every bad thing that can happen to you in an office. Did you know that last year ninety-one office workers in the United Kingdom were injured by typing-correction fluid? I mean, how can you injure yourself with typing-correction fluid?'

'I know exactly how. You use the fluid, you get some on your fingers and then rub your eyes.'

'Thirty-seven people injured themselves with calculators. How do they do that? They only weigh about as much as an egg carton. I could tell them a thing or two about risk.'

It didn't seem so funny any more. I sat up and looked at the clock. 'I guess we both need to get going,' I said.

We took a shower together and we were really very disciplined. We just washed each other and dried each other. We helped each other dress. Putting Ben's clothes on him was almost as exciting as taking them off had been. On the whole it was better for him, no doubt. He had fresh clothes to put on. I had the same ones from the night before. I had to go back to the flat and change. He came over to me, ruffled my hair, kissed my forehead. 'It's a bit creepy seeing you in Jo's clothes, though,' he said.

I shook my head. 'We must have the same taste,' I said. 'These are mine. In fact, this shirt is the one I was wearing when I was kidnapped. I would have thought I'd have thrown it in the bin, or burnt it – but it's quite a nice shirt, and I figured that I'm not going to stop thinking about things just because I set fire to some clothes . . .'

'That shirt was Jo's. She bought it in Barcelona. Unless you've been buying clothes in Barcelona as well.'

'Are you sure?'

'I'm sure.'

I fell silent. I was thinking furiously. That was something. That meant something. But what?

When we were standing on his doorstep, we kissed again. For a moment I felt as if I couldn't let go. I would just stay clinging to him and I would be safe. Then I told myself not to be so stupid. 'I need to go back into the horrible world,' I said.

'What are you going to do?'

'I'm going home – I mean to Jo's – to change. I can't go around in this stuff.'

'I don't mean that.'

'I'm not sure. Today or tomorrow, this man is going to discover that he's killed the wrong woman. He'll start looking for me again. Maybe I'll see if I can find out where Jo has gone. Though I don't know whether that will do any good.' The hope I had felt earlier, lying in bed with Ben eating toast, was fading again.

Ben was fidgeting with his car keys, deep in thought. 'I'll call Jo's parents today,' he said. 'They should be back by now. Then we'll take it from there.'

I kissed Ben. I had to stand on tiptoe to do it. 'That means "thank you",' I said. 'And that you don't have to go out on a limb for me.'

'Don't be stupid, Abbie. I'll call you later.' He handed me a card and then we both laughed at the formality of the gesture. 'You can always reach me at one of those numbers.'

We kissed and I felt his hand on my breast. I put my hand on his hand. 'I'm just thinking of this man from Amsterdam,' I said.

I lay in the bath with the flannel over my face, and I tried to think what he would be thinking. He was about to discover that I was still alive. Perhaps he knew by now. There was another thing as well. There had been that reckless phone call to my own mobile. He had kept it. It was his trophy. And I claimed to be Jo. Did he think I was after him?

274

I dressed in Jo's clothes. I deliberately chose grey cords and a cream-coloured, thick-knitted sweater that were different from anything I had ever worn. Abbie Devereaux had to be dead and gone for the present. I'd just be one of the millions floating around London. How could he find me? But, then, how could I find him?

Next, I did what I should have done before: I picked up the phone and dialled from memory and Terry's father answered. 'Yes?' he said.

'Richard, it's Abbie.'

'Abbie.' His voice was frostily polite.

'Yes, look, I know how awful everything must be at the moment . . .'

'Do you?'

'Yes. And I'm so sorry about Terry.'

'That's rich, coming from you.'

'Has he been released?'

'No. Not yet.'

'I just wanted to say that I know it wasn't him and that I'll do anything to help. Maybe you could tell his solicitor that.'

'Very well.'

'I'll give you my number. Or, no, I'll ring you again, or Terry when he's back. All right?'

'Very well.'

There was a silence, then we both said goodbye.

I stood in the centre of Jo's main room and looked around. It was like that awful stage of looking for something when you start looking again in the places where you've already looked. Even worse than that, I didn't know what I was looking for. A diary would have been useful. I could have discovered if she'd had anything planned. But I had already rifled through her desk. There was nothing like that. I wandered around picking up objects from shelves and putting them down again. There was a pot plant standing on the shelf by the window. My mother would have been able to identify it. She would know its Latin name. But even I could see that it was yellowing. The soil was hard and cracked. I brought a tumbler of water from the kitchen and dribbled the water on to the sad plant. It ran down into the cracks. That was another thing, wasn't it? Would a grown-up responsible young woman like Jo go away on holiday and leave her plant to die? I watered the banyan tree as well.

All of the pieces of evidence I had found were like mirages. They shimmered in the air, but when I ran to clutch them they melted. I had been living in the flat. It might well have been that she went on holiday leaving me in residence. She might have assumed that I would be there watering her plants.

I looked at the pile of mail that I had already filleted in search of anything useful. I flicked through it, for want of anything more sensible. One envelope caught my attention. It was the gas bill that I hadn't paid yet; my own funds had run out. It had one of those transparent windows, so that you could see the name and address inside. I gave a little grunt of surprise when I saw the name: 'Miss L. J. Hooper'. Almost in a dream I found Ben's card and called the number of his mobile. When he answered he sounded busy and distracted, but when he heard my voice, his tone softened. That made me smile. More than smile, it sent a warm feeling through me. It made me feel ridiculously like a fourteen-year-old with a crush. Could you have a crush on someone you had just spent the night with?

'What is Jo's first name?'

'What?'

'I know it's a stupid question. But I was looking at one of her bills and she has an initial. An L before the J. What does it stand for?'

I heard a chuckle on the other end of the line. 'Lauren,' he said. 'Like Lauren Bacall. People used to tease her about it.'

'Lauren,' I repeated, numbly, and I felt my legs tremble. I had to lean against the wall to hold myself up. 'Kelly, Kath, Fran, Gail, Lauren.'

'What?'

'That man, he used to give me a list of names of the women he had killed. Lauren was one of the names.'

'But . . .' There was a long pause. 'It could be a coincidence . . .'

'Lauren? It's not exactly in the top ten.'

'I don't know. There are some funny names in the top ten nowadays. The other problem is that she didn't use the name. She hated it.'

I started murmuring something, more to myself, so that Ben had to ask me what I was saying. 'I'm sorry, I was saying that I know how she might have felt. She might have given that name to him because it was her way of refusing to be beaten by him. It wasn't her, Jo, that he was humiliating and terrifying, but someone else – her public self.'

I put down the phone and forced myself to remember. What had he said about Lauren? Kelly had cried. Gail had prayed. What had Lauren done? Lauren had fought. Lauren hadn't lasted long.

I felt sick. I knew she was dead.

Jack Cross's tone did not soften when he heard my voice. It darkened. It grew weary.

'Oh, Abbie,' he said. 'How are you doing?'

'She was called Lauren,' I said. I was trying not to cry.

'What?'

'Jo. Her first name was Lauren. Don't you remember? Lauren was one of the list of the people he had killed.'

'I'd forgotten.'

'Doesn't that seem significant?'

'I'll make a note of it.'

I told him about the clothes as well, the clothes of Jo's that I'd been wearing. He seemed cautious.

'This is not necessarily significant,' he said. 'We already know that you were living in Jo's flat. Why shouldn't you have been wearing her clothes?'

I looked down at Jo's grey cords that I'd put on, then I shouted, 'For God's sake, what sort of evidence is good enough for you?'

I heard a sigh on the line. 'Abbie, believe me, I'm on your side, and as a matter of fact I was looking through the file just a few minutes ago. I'm even putting one of my colleagues on to it. We haven't forgotten you. But to answer your question, I just need the sort of evidence that will convince someone who doesn't already believe you,' he said.

'Well, you're going to fucking get it,' I said. 'You wait.'

I wanted to slam the phone down but it was one of those cordless phones that you can't slam, so I just pressed the button extra hard.

'Oh, Abbie, Abbie, Abbie, you stupid, stupid thing,' I moaned to myself consolingly.

Twenty

I knew Jo was dead. I didn't care what Cross said, I knew it. I thought of his whispery voice in the darkness: 'Kelly. Kath. Fran. Gail. Lauren.' Lauren was Jo. She had never given him the name that people she loved called her by. She'd given him the name of a stranger. It was her way of staying human, of not going mad. Now he could add another name to his litany: Sally. Although perhaps Sally didn't count for him. She was a mistake. She should have been me. I shivered. Nobody knew where I was except Carol at Jay and Joiner's and Peter downstairs. And Cross and Ben, of course. I was safe, I told myself. I didn't feel safe at all.

I closed the curtains in the main room and listened to the new messages on Jo's phone. There wasn't much; just one from a woman saying that Jo's curtains were ready for collection, and another from someone called Alexis saying hello, stranger, long time no see, and he was back at last, and maybe they should meet soon.

I opened the one letter that had arrived that morning – an invitation to renew her subscription to the *National Geographic*. I did it for her. Then I phoned Sadie, anticipating she wouldn't be there, and left a message saying I wanted us to meet soon and I was missing her, and found as I said it that it was true. I said the same kind of thing on Sheila and Guy's answering-machine. I sent a cheery, vague email to Sam. I didn't want to see or talk to any of them just yet, but I wanted to build bridges.

I made myself an avocado, bacon and mozzarella

sandwich. I wasn't really hungry, but it was comforting to put the sandwich together methodically, then sit on the sofa and chew the soft, salty bread, not really thinking of anything, trying to empty my mind. I found myself seeing the pictures I'd made for myself when I was kept prisoner in the dark: the butterfly, the river, the lake, the tree. I set them against all the ugliness and all the dread. I closed my eyes and let them fill up my mind, beautiful images of freedom. Then I heard myself saying: 'But where's the cat?'

I didn't know where the question had come from. It hung in the quiet room while I considered it. Jo didn't have a cat. The only one I'd seen round here was Peter's downstairs, the tabby with amber eyes that had woken me in the night and spooked me so. But thinking about the question that I'd posed was giving me a peculiar feeling, like a tingling in my brain. It was as if a half-memory was scratching at my consciousness.

Why had I thought of a cat? Because she had things that went with a cat. Things I'd seen without noticing. Where? I went to the kitchen area, pulled open cupboards and drawers. Nothing there. Then I remembered and went to the tall cupboard near the bathroom where I'd come across the vacuum cleaner and Jo's skiing stuff. There, beside the bin-bag full of clothes, was a cat-litter tray, which looked new but might have been merely scrubbed clean, and an unopened pack of six small tins of cat food. I shut the door and went back to the sofa. I picked up the sandwich, put it down again.

So what? Jo had had a cat once. Or maybe she still had a cat and it had gone missing because she'd gone missing and wasn't there to feed and stroke it. Perhaps it's dead, I thought, like . . . I didn't finish that sentence. Or maybe she had been about to get a cat. I went back to the cupboard and took another look at the six tins. They were for kittens. So it looked as if Jo had been about to get a kitten. Why should that matter, apart from being one more poignant detail? I didn't know.

I pulled on my jacket and woollen hat and ran downstairs and out on to the street. I rang Peter's bell and he opened the door as if he'd been watching for me out of his window. His cat was asleep on the sofa, its tail twitching slightly.

'This is a nice surprise,' he said, and I felt a twinge of guilt. 'Tea? Coffee? Perhaps some sherry. Sherry's warming in this weather.'

'Tea would be lovely.'

'There's some I've just made, in the pot. It's as if I knew you were coming. No sugar, is that right?'

'That's right.'

'You'll have a biscuit this time, won't you? Though you're always in a rush. I see you running out of the house, running back in. You should slow down, you know.'

I took a digestive from the tin he held out. It had gone soft. I dunked it into the tea and ate it in three mouthfuls.

'I was wondering if I could get you anything from the shops,' I said. 'You probably don't want to go out much in this weather.'

'That's the beginning of the end,' he said.

'Sorry?'

'When you stop going out and doing things. I go out three times a day. I go in the mornings to the newsagent for my paper. Just before lunch I go for a walk, even if it's raining like today, or icy cold. In the afternoon I go to the shops for my supper.'

'If you ever do need anything . . .'

'It's very kind of you to think of me.'

281

'What's your cat called?' I stroked its stippled back gently and pleasure rippled along its spine. It opened one golden eye.

'Patience. She's nearly fourteen now. That's old for a cat, you know. You're an old lady,' he said to the cat.

'I was wondering, did Jo have a cat too?'

'She wanted one. She said it would be companionship for her. Some people love dogs and some go for cats. She was a cat woman. What are you?'

'I'm not sure. So was she going to get one?'

'She came and asked me where she could find one; she knew I was a cat-lover too, you see. I've always kept them, ever since I was a child.'

'When did she come and see you?'

'Oh, a couple of weeks ago. Just before you arrived, I think. You should know, though.'

'Why should I know?'

'We talked about it together, when I met you on the day you moved all your stuff in.'

'The Wednesday?'

'If you say so. Anyway, don't you remember? She said she was going to get one.'

'When?'

'That afternoon, if she could find one. She seemed very keen on the idea. Said something about needing to set about making changes in her life, starting with the kitty.'

'So what did you say to her, when she asked where she should look?'

'There's all sorts of ways of finding a little kitty. For a start, you can look at the cards in the newsagent's and the post office. That's what most people do, isn't it? There's always something. I noticed a card today, when I was getting my paper.' The telephone started ringing on the table beside him and he said, 'Sorry, dear, will you excuse me. I think it must be my daughter. She lives in Australia, you know.'

He picked up the phone and I stood and put my cup in the sink. I waved at him as I left but he barely looked up.

I wanted to ring Ben and hear his voice. I had felt safe in his house, wrapped up in his warmth. But he was working and there was nothing I needed to say to him except hello, hello, I keep thinking about you.

It was already getting dark, although it was barely four o'clock. It had been the kind of dull, drizzly day when it never seemed to become properly light. I looked out of the window at the street, which had been covered with snow a few days ago. All colour seemed to have drained away. Everything was sepia and charcoal and grey. People walked past like figures in a black-and-white film, heads bowed.

I rewrote my Lost Days.

Friday 11 January: showdown at Jay and Joiner's. Storm out.

Saturday 12 January: row with Terry. Storm out. Go to Sadie's for night.

Sunday 13 January: leave Sadie a.m. Go to Sheila and Guy. Meet Robin for shopping spree and spend too much money. Meet Sam for drink p.m. Go back to Sheila and Guy's.

Monday 14 January: see Ken Lofting, Mr Khan, Ben Brody and Gordon Lockhart. Phone Molte Schmidt. Fill car with petrol. Meet Ben for drink, then meal. Sex with Ben. Phone Sheila and Guy to say not coming back for night. Stay night with Ben.

Tuesday 15 January: Go to café with Ben. Meet Jo.

Ben leaves. Talk to Jo and arrange to move into her flat. Go to Sheila and Guy and leave note saying found somewhere to stay. Collect stuff from there. Go to Jo's flat. Book holiday in Venice. Phone Terry and arrange to collect stuff next day. Order Indian takeaway p.m. Make video?

<u>Wednesday 16 January</u>: collect stuff from Terry's and move it to Jo's. Meet Peter and talk about Jo getting a cat. Phone Todd. Go out and buy bonsai tree. Go to Ben's house p.m. Sex without condom. Go back to Jo's.

<u>Thursday 17 January</u>: Ring Camden police station to say Jo missing. Take first morning-after pill.

I stared at the list. Jo must have gone missing on Wednesday. Searching for a kitten. I wrote 'KITTEN' in large letters under the list and stared at it hopelessly. The telephone rang. It was Carol from Jay and Joiner's.

'Hi, Abbie,' she said, sounding warm. 'Sorry to disturb you.'

'That's all right.'

'I just got a strange phone call from a man who wanted to pass on a message to you.'

'Yes?' My mouth was dry.

'His name was – hang on, I've written it down somewhere. Yes, here we are. Gordon Lockhart.' Relief surged through me. 'He wanted to have your address or your number.'

'You didn't give it to him, did you?'

'No, you told me not to.'

'Thanks. Go on.'

'I said he could write a letter to us and we'd forward it to you. But he said he just wanted to say thank you again.'

'Oh. Right.'

'And he said you should clip the roots every two years to stop it growing. Does that make sense? He went on about it. On and on. In the spring, he said. March or April.'

'Thanks, Carol. It's just about a tree. Keep me posted, will you?'

'Sure. And your old man got in touch all right?'

'My dad?'

'He's probably trying to phone you as we speak.'

'Dad?'

'He said he was trying to track you down. Wants to send you some present, but he's mislaid your new address.'

'Did you give it to him?'

'Well, it was your dad.'

'Fine,' I managed. 'I'll speak to you later. 'Bye.'

I threw the phone down, took a few deep breaths, then picked it up and dialled.

'Hello.'

'Dad? Hi, this is Abbie. Is that you?'

'Course it's me.'

'You rang the office.'

'What office?'

'Just a minute or two ago. You rang Jay and Joiner's.'

'Why should I ring them? I've been doing the garden. The snow pulled down the orange climbing rose. I think I can save it, though.'

I was suddenly cold, as if the sun had gone behind the clouds and an icy wind had sprung up. 'You mean, you didn't ring them?' I said.

'No. I keep saying. You haven't phoned for weeks. How have you been keeping?'

I opened my mouth to reply, and then the doorbell rang, one long, steady peal. I gasped. 'Got to go,' I said, and jumped to my feet. I could hear my father's tiny voice through the phone's mouthpiece. I raced from the sitting room into Jo's bedroom, grabbing my bag and keys as I ran. The bell rang again; two short bursts.

I fumbled with the catch then pulled up the window and leant out. It was only about an eight- or nine-feet drop into Peter's narrow, overgrown garden, but it still looked horribly far and I'd land on concrete. I thought about going back into the living room and dialling the police, but everything in me was telling me to flee. I clambered out on to the window-sill then turned so I was facing backwards. I took a deep breath and pushed off.

I hit the ground hard and felt the shock jarring up my body. I half fell, hands outstretched and scraping along the cold concrete. Then I straightened up and ran. I thought I could hear a sound from the flat. I pounded across the garden's overgrown and sodden lawn. My legs felt like lead as I dragged them over the rotted mulch of leaves; I could barely make them move and it was as if I was running in a dream. A nightmare, where you run and run and never get anywhere.

There was a high wall at the back of the garden. It was full of cracks and in some places the bricks had crumbled and come away. There were brambles with purple stems as wide as hosepipes climbing up it. I found a handhold, a foothold, pulled myself up. I slipped, felt rough brick grazing my cheek; tried again. I could hear myself panting, or sobbing; I couldn't tell which. My hands were on top of the wall, and then I was there, one leg over, the next. I let go and fell into an adjacent garden, landing painfully and twisting my ankles. I saw a woman's face peering out of the downstairs window as I staggered to my feet and limped to the side passage that led out on to the road.

I didn't know which direction to go in. It didn't really matter, so long as I went somewhere. I jogged along the road, each step throbbing in my ankle. I could feel blood trickling down my cheek. A bus drew up at a stop a few yards away and I hobbled towards it and jumped on board as it was drawing away. I went and sat by a middle-aged woman with a shopping basket, even though there were spare seats, and looked back. There was no one there.

The bus went all the way to Vauxhall. I got off at Russell Square and went into the British Museum. I hadn't been there since I was a child and it was all different. There was a great glass roof covering the courtyard and light flooded down on me. I made my way through rooms lined with ancient pottery, and rooms full of great stone sculptures and I saw nothing. I came to a room lined with vast, leatherbound books; some were on stands, opened at illuminated pages. It was softly lit and quiet. People, when they talked, talked in whispers. I sat there for an hour, gazing at the rows of books and seeing nothing. I left when it was closing time; I knew I couldn't go home.

Twenty-one

As I came out on to the steps of the museum I realized that I was freezing. I had escaped from the flat in only a light sweater. So I walked to Oxford Street and went into almost the first clothes shop I came to. I spent fifty pounds on a jacket. It was red and quilted and made me look as if I should be standing on a railway platform taking down train numbers, but it was warm. I took the tube north and walked to Ben's house. He bloody wasn't there. I walked over to a Haverstock Hill café, ordered an expensive frothy coffee and allowed myself to think.

Jo's flat was now out of bounds to me. He'd found me again, and now he'd lost me again, for the time being. I tried to think of another possibility but there was none. A person had obtained my address from Carol by pretending to be my father. I made a feeble attempt to imitate a sceptical policeman. I tried to imagine an angry client or someone I'd hired being so desperate to contact me personally that they would attempt this complicated subterfuge. It was nonsense. It was him. So what would he do? He had found where I was staying. He didn't know I knew that – or maybe he didn't. He might think that I was out and he simply had to wait there for me. If that was so, then I could call the police and they could go and arrest him and it would all be over.

This idea was so tempting that I could hardly stop myself. The snag was that I knew I was about one millimetre away from Jack Cross losing patience with me altogether. If I tried to call out the police because of some suspicion I had, they might simply not come. Or if they did come, they might just find that he wasn't there. And what was I asking them to do? Go up to any man, any man at all, and accost him on suspicion of being my kidnapper?

I finished my coffee and walked back to Ben's flat. The lights were still off. I didn't know what to do so I lurked outside, stamping my feet, rubbing my hands together. What if Ben was in a meeting? What if he had suddenly decided to meet someone for a drink or go out for dinner or a movie? I tried to think of somewhere else to go. I started to compile a list of friends I might drop in on. Abigail Devereaux, the Flying Dutchwoman, wandering from house to house in search of food and a bed for the night. People would be hiding behind their sofas when I rang the bell. By the time Ben walked up the steps, I was feeling thoroughly sorry for myself.

He looked startled as I stepped out of the shadows, and I immediately tried to apologize for being there, and then, in the middle of my apology, I began to cry and was immediately angry with myself for being so pathetic and tried to apologize for crying. So now Ben was standing on the steps outside his flat with a crying woman. Worse and worse. In the midst of it all Ben managed both to put his arm round me and get his keys out of his pocket and unlock the door. I started an explanation of what had happened at Jo's flat but, whether because I was shivering with cold or whether saying it out loud made me realize how frightened I had been, I was unable to speak coherently. Ben just murmured words into my ear and led me up to the bathroom. He turned on the bath taps. He started to pull down zips and unfasten buttons on my clothes.

'I like the jacket,' he said.

'I was cold,' I said.

'No, really.'

He pulled my clothes over my head and eased my trousers down my legs and over my feet. I caught sight of myself in the mirror. Red-faced from the cold, red-eyed from crying. I looked raw, as if my skin had been peeled off with my clothes. The hot water of the bath stung at first, then felt wonderful. I wanted to live in that bath for ever, like a primeval swamp animal. Ben disappeared and came back with two mugs of tea. He placed them both on the side of the bath. He started to take his clothes off. This was nice. He got in with me, entangling his legs with mine, and he behaved like a complete gentleman: he sat at the end with the taps. He draped a flannel over them so that he was able to lie back without being in total discomfort. My mouth was working again and I managed to give him a fairly composed account of my escape, if that's what it had been.

He looked genuinely startled. 'Fuck,' he said, which struck the right note. 'You climbed out of the back window?'

'I didn't open the door and ask him in for tea.'

'You're absolutely sure it was him?'

'I've been desperately trying to think of any other explanation. If you can come up with one, I would be so grateful.'

'It's a pity you didn't get a look at him.'

'Jo's front door doesn't have a peephole. There was the additional problem that I was having a heart-attack from fear. I have to admit that there was a part of me that almost wanted to lie down and wait for him to come and get me so that it would all be over.'

Ben took another flannel and draped it over his face. I heard a sort of murmuring from under it.

'I'm sorry,' I said.

He pulled the flannel away. 'What?' he asked.

'About all this. It's bad enough for me, but I can't do anything about that. I'm sorry that you've been landed with it as well. Maybe we met at the wrong time.'

'You shouldn't say sorry.'

'I should. And I'm also saying it in advance.'

'What do you mean?'

'Because I'm about to ask you for a favour.'

'Go on, then.'

'I was going to ask you to go to Jo's flat and get my stuff for me.' Ben looked so unhappy at this that I immediately rushed into a desperate explanation. 'Because I obviously can't go there myself. I can't go there ever again. He might be watching from outside. But you'll be fine. He's only looking for me. He might assume that he's got the wrong flat.'

'Right,' said Ben, looking even less happy. 'Yes, of course, I'll do it.'

The atmosphere had definitely changed. We didn't talk for a bit.

'Are you all right?' I said, eager to break the silence.

'This wasn't what I planned,' he said.

'I know, I know, it would have been easier for you if you'd met somebody who wasn't involved in something like this.'

'That's not what I meant. I was talking about here, in this bath, now. I was planning to help wash you. I would have rubbed you on your shoulders, and then down over your breasts. We would have gone to bed. But now, instead of that, I'm going to get dressed and go out and probably get murdered myself. Or he might torture me to find out where you are.'

'You don't have to, if you don't want to,' I said.

In the end, Ben phoned up a friend of his, Scud. 'Not his real name,' Ben said. Scud worked with computer graphics, but in his spare time, he played club rugby. 'He's fifteen stone and a lunatic,' Ben said. He managed to persuade Scud to come over straight away. 'Yes, now,' I heard him say on the phone. Scud arrived fifteen minutes later and he was, as advertised, massive. He looked amused to meet a new woman wearing Ben's dressing-gown and he was evidently puzzled by the pared-down version of my story that Ben gave him. But he shrugged and said it would be no problem.

I gave a brief description of where my stuff was.

'And when you leave, make sure you're not followed,' I said.

Scud looked at me, apparently alarmed. I'd forgotten that much of what I said made me sound insane to unprepared normal people. Ben pulled a face.

'You said there'd be no problem.'

'Not for you. But he might think you're connected with me and follow you. Just keep an eye out.'

The two men exchanged glances.

Ben was back in less than an hour, an hour in which I drank a tumbler of whisky and flicked through Ben's glossy magazines. He came in looking as if he had been Christmas shopping. He dumped the bulging carrier-bags on the floor. 'I owe Scud one,' he said.

'What for? Did anything happen?'

'I owe Scud one for dragging him away from his wife and children in order to rummage around the flat of someone he doesn't know. And then possibly involving him in criminal activity.'

'What do you mean?'

'Jo's front door was open. It had been forced.'

'But there's a chain.'

'It must have been kicked in. The whole frame was broken.'

'Jesus.'

'Yes. We weren't sure what to do. It's probably not legal to go round a crime scene helping yourself to things that don't belong to you.'

'He broke in,' I murmured, almost to myself.

'I think I've got everything,' Ben said. 'Clothes, mainly. Some of the odds and ends you asked for. Your pieces of paper, stuff from the bathroom shelf. I can't guarantee that some of this isn't Jo's. In fact, the more I think about this the less legal it seems.'

'Great,' I said, hardly listening.

'And Jo's photograph, like you asked.'

He put it on the table and we both looked at it for a moment.

'I did want to make one comment,' he said. 'In fact, more than one. I assume that you've got nowhere to stay, so I don't want to make a big deal of this or presume on anything but you're welcome to stay here. As long as you want to, basically.'

I couldn't stop myself. I gave him a hug. 'Are you sure?' I said. 'You don't have to, just because I'm in this helpless state. I'm sure I could find somewhere.'

'Don't be stupid.'

'I don't want to be like this dismal, needy woman forcing herself on a man who's too polite to kick her out.'

He put up his hand. 'Stop,' he said. 'Shut up. We should find somewhere to put all this stuff.'

We started going through this odd assortment that I'd gathered over the past days.

'The other thing I wanted to say,' he said, while sorting through my underwear, 'at least I wanted to raise it as a possibility, is that this was just a normal break-in.'

'What about the person who rang work pretending to be my dad?'

'I don't know. There might have been a misunderstanding. Perhaps what you heard at the door was someone breaking in. They rang the door bell, as they do, to check that no one's home. You didn't answer, in your normal style. The villain assumes nobody's home and breaks in. There's so much of that happening in the area. Just a few days ago, these friends of mine round the corner heard a huge crash in the middle of the night. They went downstairs and exactly the same thing had happened. Someone had kicked the door open and grabbed a bag and a camera. It might have been the same thing.'

'Was anything taken?'

'I couldn't tell. A couple of drawers were open. The VCR was still there.'

'Hmmm,' I said sceptically.

Ben looked thoughtful for a moment. He seemed to be thinking so hard that it hurt. 'What do you want for supper?' he said.

I liked that. I liked that so much. In the middle of all I was going through, that question as if we were a couple living together. Which we were, as it turned out.

'Anything,' I said. 'Anything you've got that's left over. But, look, Jo's vanished, someone got my address from Carol under false pretences, there's a knock at the door. I scoot out of the back and he breaks in. It's too much.'

Ben stood like a statue, except it was a statue holding a pair of my knickers. I snatched them from him.

'Tomorrow I'll call the police,' he said. 'Jo's parents should be back tonight. We'll speak to them and then, unless they've got good news, we've got to report her missing.'

I put my hand on his. 'Thanks, Ben.'

'Is that whisky?' he asked, catching sight of my glass. Well, *his* glass, strictly speaking.

'Yes, sorry,' I said. 'I was in urgent need of something.'

He picked up the glass and took a gulp from it. I saw his hand was shaking.

'Are you all right?' I said.

He shook his head. 'You know you said that you thought we might have met at the wrong time? I hope that's wrong. Things feel right in all sorts of ways. But I'm afraid that I'm not really the person who's going to be able to fight anybody off, take a bullet for you. I think I'm afraid, to be honest.'

I kissed him, and our hands felt for each other.

'Most people wouldn't say that,' I said. 'They'd just find an excuse not to have me in the house. But at the moment I'm interested in your plan.'

'What plan?'

'The one that began with you washing my shoulders. We can miss out the washing bit.'

'Oh, that plan,' he said.

Twenty-two

'Listen. I woke up and I couldn't get back to sleep and I've been thinking. You know how it is when you just lie there in the dark and thoughts whirl round and round your head? Anyway, this is how it is. He's after me, but I'm after him too. I've got to get to him before he gets to me. Agreed?' I was sitting at Ben's kitchen table in one of his shirts, dipping brioche into coffee. Outside, there was frost on the grass. The kitchen smelt of fresh bread and hyacinths.

'Maybe,' he said.

'So what does he know about me? He knows my name, what I look like, more or less, where I lived until a couple of weeks ago, where I stayed until yesterday, where I work. Or worked. Right, what do I know about him?' I paused for a moment to drink some coffee. 'Nothing.'

'Nothing?'

'Nothing at all. A blank. Except there's one thing in my favour. He doesn't know that I know he's after me. He thinks he can just creep up behind me, but actually we're like children in that game when you circle round the tree, each pursuing the other and fleeing from them at the same time. But he thinks I don't know he's coming to get me. If you see what I mean.'

'Abbie . . .'

'There's something else too. I'm not just following him, or at least intending to follow him, once I know where to start. I'm following me – the me I can't remember, I mean. Like Grandmother's Footsteps.'

'Hang on . . .'

'Maybe Grandmother's Footsteps isn't quite right. But presumably the me that I can't remember may have tried to find out where Jo was. I would have done, wouldn't I? If I'm doing it now I would have done it then. Don't you think it's a possibility? That's what I was thinking.'

'What time did you wake this morning?'

'About five, I think. My mind was racing. What I need is a piece of solid evidence I can take to Cross. Then they'll start the investigation and protect me and everything will be fine. So if I retrace my footsteps, which were retracing Jo's footsteps, then I may end up where I ended up before.'

'Which, if you remember what happened to you, doesn't sound like a good idea at all.'

'The problem, of course, is that I can't retrace my footsteps because I can't remember them.'

'Do you want some more coffee?'

'Yes, please. And I don't know what Jo's footsteps were either. But, anyway, there was only a small amount of time between when she disappeared and when I was grabbed. I'm sure of that at least, because I know from Peter she was around on Wednesday morning, and I disappeared on Thursday evening.'

'Abbie.' Ben took both of my hands and held them between his own. 'Slow down a bit.'

'Am I gabbling?'

'It's ten past seven and we went to sleep late. I'm not at my sharpest.'

'I've been thinking I need to follow up the cat.'

'Sorry?'

'Jo was going to get a kitten. Her neighbour in the downstairs flat told me that. She'd bought everything for it, and I'm guessing she was just about to get it. If I could find out where she was going to get it from – well, anyway, I can't think of anything else to do. I have to begin somewhere.'

'So now you're planning to track down a cat?'

'I'll ask at the pet shop and the post office, where they pin up notices. The vet, too. They often have notices, don't they? It's probably pointless, but if you've any better ideas I'd love to hear them.'

Ben looked at me for a long, long time. I imagined him thinking: Is this worth it? Because I did have some insight into my condition: I might have been babbling but at least I knew I was babbling.

'I tell you what,' he said. 'I've got to pick up some letters at the office. I'll give some instructions to the guys. I'll be back here mid-morning and we can do it together.'

'Really?'

'I don't like the thought of you wandering around on your own.'

'You don't have to do this, you know. You're not responsible for me or anything.'

'We talked about this last night. Remember?'

'Thank you,' I said. 'Very much.'

'So, what are you going to do while I'm gone?'

'I'm going to call Cross again, though I can't imagine he'll be very pleased to hear from me.'

'You have to, though.'

'I know.'

'I'll call Jo's parents' house from work. There was no reply yesterday evening. We should go and see them before I contact the police.'

'Yes. Oh dear.'

'I know.'

*

Ben left before eight. I had a scalding shower and made myself another cup of coffee. Then I called Cross, but was told he wouldn't be back in his office till the afternoon. I almost cried with impatience. Half a day is a long time when you feel every minute might count.

I had a couple of hours before Ben returned. I cleared up the kitchen and changed the sheets on the bed. His house was more grown-up than anything I was used to. It struck me that Terry and I had lived a bit like students. Everything in our lives had seemed temporary, where and how we lived just arrangements we'd stumbled into. We'd got by, but messily and, in the end, violently. Ben's life was stable and considered. He was doing the job he wanted to do; he lived in a lovely house, where each room was painted a different colour and was full of carefully chosen objects. I opened his wardrobe. He had just two suits, but they looked expensive. His shirts hung neatly on their hangers, above three pairs of leather shoes. Things don't just happen to him, I thought. He chooses them. And he chose me, and he'd missed me when I'd gone. I shivered with pleasure.

He came back just after ten. I was waiting for him, dressed in warm clothes and with a notebook in my bag. I also had the photograph of Jo, which I thought might jog people's memories.

'Jo's parents aren't back till tomorrow,' he said. 'I spoke to the dog-sitter again. They spent an extra night in Paris. We should drive over to their place in the afternoon. It's not far, just on the other side of the M25.'

'That'll be grim.'

'Yes,' he said. For a moment, his face was wiped of all expression. Then he said, with forced cheeriness, 'All right. Cat time.'

'You're sure you're up for this? I mean, it's probably a wild-goose chase. Wrong metaphor.'

'I'll have you for company.' He wrapped an arm round me and we went out to his car. I briefly remembered my own car, stuck in a bloody pound somewhere, but pushed away the thought. I could deal with all of those things later. Friendships, family, work, money (chronic lack of), tax forms, parking tickets, overdue library books, everything had to wait.

We parked in a small street a few hundred yards away from Jo's flat. We'd planned to make a circuit of the area, stopping off at every newsagent's that had cards in the window. It was a boring, frustrating business. The vet's was a dead end. Nobody in the shops recognized Jo's photo, and only a few had cards advertising pets.

After nearly two hours, I had written down three telephone numbers. When we went back to the car, Ben phoned them on his mobile. Two of the cards turned out to have been put up in the last few days so were irrelevant. The other card had been up for longer and, when Ben rang the number, the woman said that there was still one kitten without a home but we probably wouldn't want it.

She lived on the estate just round the corner so we called in on her. The kitten was a tabby and still tiny. The woman, who was very tall and solid, said it had been the runt of the litter and remained fragile. She had to admit that it also seemed to have something wrong with its eyesight. It bumped into things, she said, and stepped in its food. She picked it up and it sat in her large, calloused hand and mewed piteously.

I took Jo's photo out of my bag and showed it to her. 'Did our friend come round here asking about kittens?' I asked.

'What?' She put the tabby on the floor and peered at it. 'No, not that I know of. I'd remember, I'm sure. Why?'

'Oh, it's too long a story,' I said, and she didn't press me. 'We'll be going, then. I hope you find your kitten a home.'

'I won't,' she said. 'Nobody wants a blind cat, do they? I'll just have to take it to the cat sanctuary. Betty'll take her in.'

'Cat sanctuary?'

'Well, it's not really a sanctuary, that sounds too official. But she's cat-mad. Bonkers. She lives for cats; they're all she cares about. She takes in all the strays. She must have about fifty, and they're breeding all the time. Her house is only small as well. It's a sight, really. It must drive her neighbours mad. Maybe you should go there if you're looking for a kitten.'

'Where does she live?' I asked, taking out my notebook.

'Down Lewin Crescent. I don't know the number but you can't miss it. Poky little place and the upstairs windows are all boarded up. It looks deserted.'

'Thanks.'

We went back to the car.

'Lewin Crescent?' asked Ben.

'We may as well, now we're here.'

We found the place on the *A–Z* and drove there. It was wonderfully cosy in the car, but outside it was cold and the wind was a knife. Our breath plumed into the air. Ben took my hand and smiled down at me; his fingers were warm and strong.

The house was certainly dilapidated. There were weeds and frosted, rotten sunflowers by the front door, and the dustbin was overflowing. A wide crack ran up

301

the wall and the paint on the window-ledges was coming away in large flakes. I pressed the bell but couldn't hear it ring, so I knocked hard as well.

'Listen,' said Ben. Through the door I could hear mews, hisses, a strange scratching. 'Have I told you I'm allergic to cats? I get asthma and my eyes go red.'

The door opened on a chain and the sound grew louder. A face peered through.

'Hello,' I said. 'Sorry to bother you.'

'Is it the council?'

'No. We've just come because we were told you have lots of cats.'

The door opened a bit more. 'Come in, then – but be careful they don't get out. Quick!'

I don't know what hit us first, the wall of heat or the smell of meaty cat food, ammonia and shit. There were cats everywhere, on the sofa and the chairs, curled up near the electric heater, lying in soft brown heaps on the floor. Some were washing themselves, some were purring, a couple were hissing at each other, backs arched and tails twitching. There were bowls of food by the kitchen door, and three or four cat-litter trays next to them. It was like an obscene version of a Walt Disney film. Ben hung back by the door, looking appalled.

'It's Betty, isn't it?' I asked. I was trying not to wince. A cat was winding itself round my legs.

'That's right. You should know.'

Betty was old. Her face had folded. Her neck sagged. Her fingers and her wrists were blue. She was dressed in a thick blue shift with several buttons missing, and she was covered in cat hair. She had shrewd brown eyes, peering out from her wrecked face.

'We were told you take in stray cats and that sometimes you give them to people in search of a pet,' I said.

'I have to be sure it's to a good home,' she said sharply. 'I'm not easily satisfied. I don't just give them to anybody, I keep saying.'

'We think a friend of ours might have been here,' I said, and produced the photo of Jo.

'Of course she did.'

'When?' I took a step forward.

'You do go round and round in circles, don't you? But she wasn't right. She seemed to think you can just let a cat wander in and out as they please. Do you know how many cats get killed by cars each year?'

'No,' I said. 'I don't. So you didn't want her to have one of your cats?'

'She didn't seem too keen anyway,' said Betty. 'As soon as I said I had my doubts about her, she was out of the door.'

'And you can't remember when it was?'

'You tell me.'

'Midweek? Weekend?'

'It was the day the bin-men come. They were clattering around outside when she was here.'

'What day's that?'

'That would be a Wednesday.'

'So, a Wednesday,' said Ben, still standing up against the front door. 'Do you know what time?'

'I don't know why you have to be so pushy.'

'It's not that we're –' I began.

'Morning or afternoon?' asked Ben.

'Afternoon,' she said grudgingly. 'They usually come when I'm giving the cats their tea. Don't they, pussies?' she added, addressing the room at large, which seemed to shift and ripple with the movement of cats.

'Thank you,' I said. 'You've been very helpful.'

'That's what you said last time.'

I froze with my hand on the door handle. 'Did I come here before?'

'Of course you did. On your own, though.'

'Betty, can you tell me when I came?'

'No need to speak so loudly, I'm not deaf. Or stupid. The day after, that's when you came. Lost your memory, have you?'

'Home?' said Ben.

'Home,' I agreed, then blushed violently at the word. He noticed and laid a hand on my knee. I turned and we kissed each other very gently, our lips hardly grazing. We kept our eyes open and I could see myself reflected in his pupils.

'Home,' he said again. 'Home to toast and tea.'

Toast and tea, and making love in an unlit room, while outside it grew colder and darker and we held each other for comfort. And for a while we didn't talk about sombre things, but did what all new lovers do, which was to ask about each other's past. At least, I asked him.

'I've already told you,' he said.

'Have you? You mean, before?'

'Yes.'

'Isn't that odd, to think that I'm carrying all these things inside me – things that were done to me, things you've said to me, secrets, gifts – and I don't know what they are? If I don't know, is it the same as it never having happened, do you think?'

'I don't know,' he said. I traced his mouth with one finger; he was smiling in the darkness.

'You'll have to tell me again. Who was before me?'

'Leah. An interior designer.'

'Was she beautiful?'

'I don't know. In a way. She was half Moroccan, very striking.'

'Did she live here?' I asked.

'No. Well, not really.'

'How long were you together?'

'Two years.'

'Two years – that's a long time. What happened?'

'Nearly a year ago now, she fell in love with someone else and left me.'

'Stupid woman,' I said. 'Who could ever leave you?' I stroked his soft hair. It was still only afternoon, and here we were, lying under the duvet as if we were in a small cave, while outside the world closed in. 'Were you very hurt?'

'Yes,' he said. 'I suppose I was.'

'But you're all right now? Are you?'

'Now I am.'

'We need to talk about Jo,' I said, after a bit.

'I know. I feel I shouldn't be so happy.' He leant across, switched on the bedside lamp and we both blinked in the sudden dazzle. 'So she was looking for a cat on Wednesday afternoon, and you were looking for her on Thursday.'

'Yes.'

'You're following yourself.'

'Like that mad cat woman said – round and round in circles.'

Twenty-three

Ben went out to buy food for supper, and on a sudden impulse I rang Sadie.

'Hi there,' I said. 'Guess who?'

'Abbie? God, Abbie, where've you disappeared to? Do you realize I don't even have a phone number for you? I was at Sam's yesterday evening; he was having a little birthday get-together, and we all said how odd it was you weren't with us. We even toasted you. Well, we toasted absent friends, and that was mainly you. But nobody knew how to get hold of you. It's as if you've fallen off the face of the earth.'

'I know, I know. And I'm sorry. I miss all of you, but, well – I can't explain now. I should have remembered his birthday; I've never forgotten it before. But things are, well, rather dramatic.'

'Are you all right?'

'Kind of. In a way yes and in a way no.'

'Very mysterious. When can I see you? Where are you staying?'

'At a friend's,' I said vaguely. 'And we'll meet soon. I just need to sort things out first. You know.' What I wanted to say was: I just need to save my life first. But that sounded insane. It even felt insane, here in Ben's house, with the lights on and the radiators humming and from the kitchen the sound of the dishwasher.

'Yes, but listen, Abbie, I've talked to Terry.'

'Have you? Is he all right? Have the police let him go yet?'

'Yup, finally. I think they kept him as long as they were legally entitled to, though.'

'Thank God for that. Is he all over the place?'

'You could say that. He's been trying to get hold of you.'

'I'll call him. At once. But is he still under suspicion, or what?'

'I don't know. He wasn't being exactly rational when I talked to him. I think he was a bit pissed.'

'Sadie, I'll go now. I'll call Terry at once. And I'll come and see you soon, very soon.'

'Do that.'

'Is Pippa well?'

'She's gorgeous.'

'Well, I know that. You are too, Sadie.'

'What?'

'Gorgeous. You're gorgeous. I'm lucky to have friends like you. Tell everyone I love them.'

'Abbie?'

'Everyone. Tell Sheila and Guy and Sam and Robin and – well, everyone. When you see them, tell them I . . .' I suddenly caught sight of myself in the mirror over the fireplace. I was waving my hand around hysterically, like an opera singer. 'Well, you know. Send my love, at least.'

'You're sure you're all right?'

'It's all so weird, Sadie.'

'Listen –'

'I've got to go. I'll call you.'

I called Terry. The phone rang and rang, and just as I was about to give up, he answered.

'Hello.' His voice was slurred.

'Terry? It's me, Abbie.'

'Abbie,' he said. 'Oh, Abbie.'

'They've let you go.'

'Abbie,' he repeated.

'I'm so sorry, Terry. I told them it couldn't be you. Did your dad tell you I rang? And I'm so sorry about Sally. I can't tell you how sorry.'

'Sally,' he said. 'They thought I killed Sally.'

'I know.'

'Please,' he said.

'What? What can I do?'

'I need to see you. Please, Abbie.'

'Well, it's difficult right now.' I couldn't go to his house – he might be waiting there for me.

The front door opened and Ben came in, with two carrier-bags.

'I'll call you back,' I said. 'In a few minutes. Don't go away.' Putting the phone down, I turned to Ben and said, 'I have to see Terry. He sounds terrible and it's because of me, all of this. I owe him.'

He sighed and put his bags on the floor. 'There was I, planning a romantic dinner for two. Stupid.'

'I have to, don't I? You do see?'

'Where?'

'Where what?'

'Where do you want to meet him?'

'Not at his place, that's for sure.'

'No. Here?'

'That would be too odd.'

'Odd? Well, we can't have odd, can we?'

'Maybe a café or something is better. Not a pub – he sounded as if he'd drunk quite enough already. Tell me somewhere near here.'

'There's one on Belmont Avenue, at the park end of the road. The something Diner.'

'Ben?'

'What?'

'Will you come with me?'

'I'll drive you there and wait outside in the car.'

'Ben?'

'Yes, Abbie.'

'I appreciate it.'

'Then that makes it all worthwhile,' he said drily.

Forty-five minutes later I was sitting in the Diner (it was just called the Diner), drinking cappuccino and watching the door. Terry arrived ten minutes later, muffled up in an old greatcoat and a woollen hat. He was slightly unsteady on his feet and his face had a wild look about it.

He came over to my table and sat down too noisily. He pulled off his hat. His hair was a bit greasy and his cheeks, red with cold or drink, had a new gaunt look to them.

'Hello, Terry,' I said, and put my hands over his.

'Your hair is growing back.'

'Is it?'

'Oh, God.' He closed his eyes and leant back in his chair. 'Oh, God, I'm knackered. I could sleep for a hundred hours.'

'What can I get you?'

'Coffee.'

I gestured to the waitress. 'A double espresso, please, and another cappuccino.'

Terry took out his cigarette packet and shook one out. His hands were trembling. He lit it and sucked ferociously, making his face look even more hollow.

'I told the police you didn't do it, Terry. And if you need me to, I'll talk to your solicitor. It's all a mistake.'

'They went on and on about me being a violent man.' The waitress put the coffee down on the table, but he took no notice. 'It was like my head filling up with blood. I never would have hurt you. They made it sound as if I was an evil fucker. They said I'd sent you over the edge . . .'

'Did they now?'

'And Sally . . . Sally . . . Oh, shit.'

'Terry. Don't.'

He started crying. Fat tears rolled down his cheeks and into his mouth. He tried to pick up his coffee but his hands were shaking so much that he spilt great splashes of it over the table.

'I don't know what's happened,' he said, mopping ineffectually at the puddle with a napkin. 'Everything was going along normally, and then it all went to hell. I kept thinking I'd wake up and it would be a bad dream and you'd be there, or Sally would be there. Someone, anyway. Someone would be there. But instead you're here and Sally's dead and the police still think it was me. I know they do.'

'The main thing is that they've let you go,' I said. 'It wasn't you and they can't say it was. You'll be all right now.'

But he wasn't listening. 'I feel so fucking lonely,' he said. 'Why me?'

I felt a spasm of irritation at his self-pity. 'Or why Sally?' I said.

The next morning Ben phoned Jo's parents. They were back from holiday and I could hear the mother's voice. No, they hadn't seen Jo since before their holiday; she hadn't come with them. And, yes, they'd be delighted to see Ben if he was in the area and of course it was fine if he brought a friend with him. Ben's face was tight, his mouth drawn down as if he'd eaten something sour. He said we'd be there by eleven.

We drove in silence through north London, to their house in Hertfordshire. It was foggy and damp; the shapes of trees and houses loomed up at us as we passed. They lived just outside a village, in a low white house at the end of a gravelled drive. Ben stopped at the top of it for a few seconds. 'I feel completely sick,' he said angrily, as if it was my fault. Then he drove on.

Jo's mother was called Pam, and she was a handsome, robust woman with a firm handshake. Her father, though, was skeletally thin and his face was etched with lines. He looked decades older than his wife and when I shook his hand it was like grasping a bundle of bones. We sat in the kitchen and Pam poured us tea and produced some biscuits. 'So tell me, Ben, how's everything going? It's been ages since Jo brought you over to see us.'

'I've come for a reason,' he said abruptly.

She put down her mug and looked at him. 'Jo?' she said.

'Yes. I'm worried about her.'

'What's wrong with her?'

'We don't know where she is. She's disappeared. You've heard nothing at all?'

'No,' she said in a whisper. Then, louder, 'But you know how it is with her, she's always gadding off without telling us. She can go weeks without getting in touch.'

'I know. But Abbie was sharing her flat and Jo just went missing one day.'

'Missing,' she repeated.

'You have no idea where she might be?'

'The cottage?' she said, and her face brightened with hope. 'She sometimes goes and camps out there.'

'We went there.'

'Or that boyfriend of hers?'

'No.'

'I don't understand,' said Jo's father. 'How long has she been missing?'

'Since about January the sixteenth,' I said. 'We think.'

'And today's what? February the sixth? That's three weeks!'

Pam stood up. She stared down at us and said, 'But we must start looking! At once!'

'I'm going to the police now,' said Ben, rising too. 'As soon as we leave here. We've already talked to them about this – well, Abbie has anyway, but they don't take it seriously for the first week or so. Unless it's a child.'

'What shall I do? I can't just sit here. I'll ring round everyone. There'll be a simple explanation. Who have you talked to?'

'It might mean nothing,' said Ben helplessly. 'She might be fine. People are always going missing then turning up.'

'Yes. Of course,' said Pam. 'Of course that's true. The thing is not to panic.'

'We'll go straight to the police now,' said Ben. 'I'll ring you later. All right?' He put his hands on Pam's shoulders and kissed her on both cheeks. She clutched at him briefly then let him go. Jo's father was still sitting at the table. I looked at his parchment skin, the liver spots on his brittle hands.

'Goodbye,' I said. I didn't know what else to say. There wasn't anything.

★

'Ben, this is Detective Inspector Jack Cross. This is Ben Brody. He's a friend of Josephine Hooper, who I told you about last –'

'I know. I visited her flat, remember? And you told me about wearing her clothes, and you told me her name's Lauren.'

'I'm glad you let Terry go,' I said. 'Now you know he's not guilty, you must realize there's someone out there who is, and maybe Jo . . .'

'I can't comment on that,' Cross said warily.

'Shall we begin by telling Detective Inspector Cross what we actually know for certain, Abbie?'

Cross looked at him with faint surprise. Perhaps he had thought that anyone connected with me was bound to be mad: contamination by association.

Much of it I had told him before, of course, but then the words had sounded like yet more confirmation of my paranoia. They sounded more plausible when it wasn't me saying them.

We went over everything, several times. It was very technical, like filling in a complicated tax return. I wrote down the times and dates that I'd worked out for the missing week, both for myself and for Jo. I handed over Jo's photograph. Ben gave him the telephone numbers for her parents and her ex-boyfriend and told him which companies she regularly worked for.

'What do you think?' I asked.

'I'll consider this,' Cross replied. 'But I'm not –'

'The thing is . . .' I stopped and looked at Ben, then resumed. 'The thing is, I'm very scared that if I'm right about Jo being grabbed by the same man as me, then, well, she's very likely, she's probably, you know . . .' I couldn't say the word, not with Ben sitting beside me. I couldn't even remember meeting Jo; he'd known her half his life.

A series of expressions chased across Cross's face. When he had first met me, he had believed my story without hesitation. I was a victim. Then he had been persuaded not to believe me at all, and I had become a victim of my own delusions; an object of pity. Now he was filled with shifting doubts.

'We'll just take it bit by bit,' he said. 'We'll contact Ms Hooper's parents. Where are you staying?'

'With me,' said Ben.

Cross looked at him for a few seconds, then nodded. 'All right,' he said, standing up. 'I'll be in touch.'

'He's beginning to believe me, isn't he?'

Ben picked up my hand and twisted the ring on my little finger round. 'Do you mean about you or about Jo?'

'Is there a difference?'

'I don't know,' he said.

'I'm so sorry about Jo, Ben. I'm really, really sorry. I don't know how to say it.'

'Sorry?' he said. 'I still hope the phone will ring and it will be her.'

'That would be nice,' I said.

He poured us both some more wine. 'Do you think a lot about the days when you were his prisoner?'

'Sometimes it just feels like a terrible nightmare and then I even think, Maybe I did dream it, after all. But then other times – usually in the night, or when I'm on my own and feel especially vulnerable – it comes back to me as if I was actually reliving it. As if I was actually *in* it again, and had never escaped, and all this' – I waved my hand around the brightly lit kitchen, the plates and wine glasses on the table – 'was the dream. Everything's jumbled up, what I remember and what I imagine and what I fear. You know when I wake in the early hours, when everything seems grim and sad, what I sometimes think? I think that I'm on a wheel, going round and round. And that I've done all this before – because in a way I have, haven't I, searching for Jo, falling in love with you? – and I'm about to disappear into the darkness again.'

'It'll soon be over now.'

'Do you really think so?'

'Yes. The police will deal with it – and, God, they'll want to get it right this time. You can just lie low for a few days, here with me, and then the nightmare will be over. I'm sure of it. You'll be off your wheel.'

Twenty-four

Ben was at work and I was in his shower in the middle of the morning. That was one of the many good bits about Ben's house. It was modern and technological and things functioned in a way I had hardly even imagined before. The so-called shower at Terry's was like a dripping tap six feet above the bath. You stood under it and it drip-drip-dripped on to you. Even when the water was hot, the drops got cold on the way down. Ben's shower, on the other hand, was a real machine, with an apparently inexhaustible supply of hot water and the power and concentration of a fire hose. And it wasn't in the bath. It had an entire space to itself with a door. I crouched in a corner and I imagined that I was on a planet that was perpetually bombarded with hot rain. Of course, such a planet would have had its disadvantages when you wanted to eat or sleep or read a book, but just then it felt fine. A jet of hot water hitting my head with considerable force was a good way of stopping myself thinking.

I'd like to have stayed in there until spring, or until the man was caught, but I finally switched off the shower and dried myself with the slowness and attention to detail of a woman without a pressing appointment. I wandered through to Ben's bedroom and dressed myself largely in his clothes: tracksuit bottoms and a floppy blue T-shirt many sizes too big for me. And some huge football socks and a pair of slippers I found in the back of his cupboard. In the kitchen I boiled the kettle and made half a pot of coffee for myself.

One day I was going to have to start thinking about taking my career out of its current state of abeyance, but that could wait. Everything could wait.

I drank my coffee then made some half-hearted attempts at cleaning and tidying. I didn't know Ben's house well enough to do much. I didn't know what implement went into which drawer or on which hook and I wasn't keen enough to scrub the floor or anything extreme like that so I contented myself with doing the dishes, wiping surfaces, straightening out the duvet and generally putting things in neat piles. Even that took less than an hour and left me with an empty day stretching out until Ben came back. I had a chance to spend time in the way I'd always planned to but never had the time. I could flop on a sofa and drink coffee and listen to music and read and be a woman of leisure.

Women of leisure wouldn't listen to the jangly pop music that made up the bulk of my own collection. They would want something more sophisticated. I browsed through Ben's CDs until I found something that looked jazzy and mellow. I put it on. It sounded very grown-up. More like a soundtrack than something you would actually listen to, but that was fine. I was going to be reading and sipping coffee and I just wanted something in the background. The problem with having an entire day of leisure was settling on a particular book to read. I wasn't in the mood to tackle a proper serious book and there was no point in starting a big fat thriller. In fact, as I took books out of the shelves and inspected them, it quickly became clear that I wasn't quite in the mood to be an authentic woman of leisure. Despite my long shower and my empty schedule, I was still very agitated. I couldn't concentrate on anything. I couldn't stop thinking about the one thing I wanted to avoid.

Ben had a stack of photography books and I sat flicking through them, unable to settle on one in particular. I lasted the longest with a collection of photographs from the nineteenth century. There were exotic landscapes and dramatic events, battles and revolutions and disasters, but what I looked at were the faces. There were men and women and children. Some were distracted, terrified. Others were celebrating at fairs and fiestas. Sometimes a face would look round at the camera with a conspiratorial smile.

That was what struck me most. The strangeness of those faces. I thought, and I couldn't stop thinking, that all of those people, the beautiful and the ugly, the rich and the poor, the lucky and the benighted, the evil and the virtuous, the religious and the godless, now had one thing in common: they were dead. Each of them, singly, utterly alone, in a street or on a battlefield or in a bed, had died. All of the people in that world were gone. I thought about that but I didn't just think about it. I felt it like toothache. This was part of what I had to get over. I looked at the higher shelves at the spines of the smaller books, which wouldn't have any pictures in them. Poetry. That was what I needed. I've probably only read about eight poems in the years since I left school but I suddenly felt the need to read a poem. It would also have the extra advantage of being short.

Ben obviously wasn't much of a poetry reader either but there were a few of the sort of anthologies that grandparents and godparents give you when all inspiration fails. Most of them looked too much like textbooks for me or else they were poems on subjects that didn't interest me, like the countryside or the sea or nature in general. But then my eye fell on a volume called *Poems of Longing and Loss*, and even though I felt like an alcoholic reaching for a bottle of vodka, I couldn't resist it. I sat with my coffee and dipped into the book. I was hardly aware of tracing the meaning of individual poems. Instead, there was a blur of grief and regret and absence and grey landscapes. It was like being at a party of depressives, but in a good way. Trying to pretend that I was happy and relaxed had been a mistake. It was much better to find that there were other lost souls who felt the way I did. I was among friends, and after a while I found I was smiling with recognition.

I liked the book and turned to the beginning to see who had compiled this wonderfully bleak anthology and I saw that a message had been scrawled on the title page. I experienced the tiniest flash of an impulse that it was wrong to read the message. I ignored it. It wasn't as if I had rifled through Ben's desk and found his diary or some old love letters. An inscription in a book is like a postcard that has been pinned to a wall. Even if it's addressed to a single person, it's still a sort of public declaration. At least, that's what I told myself in that fraction of a second, and when I saw the first three words of the inscription, which were 'Dearest darling Ben', I began to suspect that this wasn't really a public declaration but by that time I was reading it and this is what I read: 'Dearest darling Ben. Here are some sad words which are better at saying what I feel than I am myself. I am so so sorry about all this and you are probably right but I feel torn apart and terrible in different ways. And this is a hell of a message to write in a book. All of my love, Jo.' It was dated November 2001.

And there wasn't even the tiniest bit of me that even tried to believe that this could be some other Jo. I had been living in Jo's flat for days and her writing was all over the place, on shopping lists, memos, on the covers of videos, and I knew it almost as well as I knew my own. I felt scalding hot all through my body, through my hands and my feet, and then I shivered uncontrollably. Fucking Ben. Fucking fucking Ben. He'd told me all about that bloody Leah. He'd been all sensitive about that relationship and how beautiful she'd been and every-thing, and he'd just omitted to mention the minor little detail that after he'd split up with her he just happened to have been fucking the woman whose flat I was living in, the woman who just happened to have disappeared. I thought of him casually ringing her doorbell. They were friends, it was no big deal. We had spent huge amounts of time wondering where Jo was. Or, at least, I had been wondering. What had he been thinking? I feverishly went over conversations I had had with him. What had he said about her? He had fucked her in the same bed that he had fucked me. He hadn't thought to mention it. But, then, he hadn't mentioned to me that he had already fucked me. What other secrets did he have?

I tried to think of the innocent reasons he might have had for not telling me. He didn't want to upset me. It might have been awkward. But the other reasons kept intruding. I needed to think about this. I needed to sort it out in my head. But not here. I was starting to tell myself different stories in my head, and all of them definitely required that I get out of Ben's house as soon as possible. I looked at my watch. The day didn't seem so long any more. I ran into his bedroom and took my clothes off – his clothes – as if they were contaminated. I started to mutter to myself like a madwoman. I wasn't sure I could get it to make sense but the one thing that Jo and I had in common was that we had been sexually involved with Ben. There was no doubt about that. Not only that, we had both been sexually involved with him just before we disappeared. I quickly pulled on my own clothes. I just couldn't get it to make sense. I had to think about it somewhere else, somewhere safe and quiet. Because I wasn't safe here any more. The quietness of the house closed round me.

Once I was dressed I moved quickly around the flat retrieving what I absolutely needed. Shoes, bag, sweater, purse, my horrible warm red jacket. What was he playing at with me? He'd lied to me, or sort of lied, or omitted to tell the full truth, and I wasn't going to sit here and wait for him to come home. I tried to remember that voice out of the dark. I'd heard Ben's voice in the dark as well, next to me in bed, murmuring in my ear, groaning, telling me he adored me. Could it be the same voice?

I ran over to Ben's desk and started rummaging through the drawers. I pushed files and notebooks aside impatiently until I found what I was after. A strip of passport-sized photographs of Ben. I contemplated it for a moment. Oh, God, he was a handsome man. I had asked whether people had seen Jo. But I had never asked – had never thought to ask – whether they had seen Ben. I had been tracking myself tracking Jo. I might consider tracking Ben. I hesitated, then picked up his mobile phone. I needed it more than he did. I opened his front door and before leaving I turned and looked back, as if to say goodbye to a place where I had been briefly happy.

I couldn't rely on anyone now. I had to be quick. I was running out of safe places.

Twenty-five

I was running. Running down the road, bitter wind on my cheeks and my feet slipping on the icy pavement. Where was I going? I didn't know, I just knew I was going, leaving, moving on to somewhere else, something else. I'd closed the door on the warm house that smelt of sawdust and I hadn't even taken a key. I was on my own again, out here in the winter weather. It occurred to me that I was very visible, in my red jacket, but the thought flitted vaguely through my head like a snowflake then melted. I just kept running, my heart thumping in my chest and my breath coming in gasps, and the houses and trees and cars and the faces of other people were a blur.

At the bottom of the road I forced myself to stop and look around. My heart slowed down. Nobody seemed to be taking any notice of me, though you never know. Think, Abbie, I told myself; think now. Think for your life. But I couldn't think, not at first. I could only feel and see. I saw pictures in my head. Ben and Jo together, holding each other. I closed my eyes and saw darkness, and it felt like the darkness of my lost time, folding around me again. Eyes in the pitch black; eyes watching Jo, watching me. A butterfly on a green leaf, a tree on a hill, a shallow stream, then clear deep water. I opened my eyes and the harsh grey world came back into focus.

I started moving again, walking this time, not really knowing where I was going. I walked past the park and down the hill. I walked towards Jo's flat, though I knew I mustn't go there. On the main road, which was full of traffic and lined with shops selling pastries, hats, candles, fish, I saw Jo's face. I blinked and stared and of course it wasn't her. It was just a woman, going about her day, with no sense of how blessed she was.

I knew I had traced Jo to within the last couple of hours of her freedom, Wednesday afternoon, and she'd been looking for a kitten. She had disappeared on a Wednesday afternoon, and the next day I too had gone. After all this time of blundering around chasing for clues, that was all I had. A pathetic shred.

I turned on my track and went down the high street and left on to a road that led to Lewin Crescent. I walked up the narrow street until I came to the dingy house with its boarded-up windows and knocked on the door. I listened and I could hear miaows; I even thought I caught a faint whiff of urine. Then I heard shuffling footsteps on the other side of the door. The door opened a chink on its chain and her eyes peered suspiciously out at me. 'Yes?'

'Betty?'

'Yes?'

'It's Abbie. I came to see you – two days ago. I asked you about my friend.'

'Yes?' she said again.

'Can I come in?'

The chain slid and the door opened. I stepped into the hot, stale room, with its moving carpet of cats. The smell caught in my nostrils. Betty was wearing the same blue shift with its missing buttons and covering of cat hairs, and the same ratty slippers and thick brown tights. I thought at least some of the ammonia smell came from her. She was so thin that her arms were like sticks and her fingers twigs. Her skin gathered in pouches on her small face.

'So it's you again. Can't keep away, can you?'

'There was something I forgot to ask you.'

'What?'

'You said you'd seen my friend? Jo?' She didn't answer. 'The one who came about having a kitten and you said she couldn't have one because . . .'

'I know who you mean,' she said.

'I didn't ask about the man I was with. Hang on.' I fumbled in my bag and took out the strip of passport photos of Ben. 'Him.'

She glanced briefly down. 'Well?'

'Do you recognize him?'

'I think so.'

'No, I mean, *did* you recognize him? Before.'

'You're a very confused young lady,' she said. She held out a hand to the ginger cat that was butting against her legs and it leapt up and nuzzled its chin against her fingers, purring like a tractor.

'What I want to know is, had you seen him before he came here with me?'

'Before?'

'Have you seen this man more than the once?' I asked desperately.

'When did I see him?'

'Yes.'

'What?'

'I mean, yes, when did you see him?' I was starting to feel slightly sick.

'I said that to you. I said, when did I see him? "Yes" isn't an answer.'

I rubbed my eyes. 'I just wanted to know if you'd seen him before two days ago. That's all.'

'All sorts of people come here. Is he from the council?'

'No, he's –'

'Because if he's from the council, I won't let him into my house.'

'He's not from the council.'

'Cats are naturally clean animals, you know.'

'Yes,' I said dully.

'And some people think it's not nice, the way they hunt. But it's just their nature.'

'I know.'

'I don't give my kitties to homes where they're allowed to go outside. That's what I told your friend. When she said she'd let a cat outside, I told her it wasn't a fit place. It would just get run over.'

'Yes. Thank you. I'm sorry to have bothered you.' I turned to go.

'Not like the hippie lot, mind.'

'The hippie lot?'

'Yes. They don't make proper checks.' She sniffed disapprovingly.

'These, um, these hippies have lots of cats, like you?'

'Not like me,' she said. 'No.'

'Did you tell Jo about them?'

'Maybe,' she said.

'Betty, where do they live?'

I don't know why I felt I was in such a hurry. It was as if I was scared the trail would go cold. I knew where Jo had gone after Betty's – or, at least, I knew where she might have gone, and that was enough for me. Now I was in the final hour or two of her final day. Everything else had faded and all I could see was her receding shape and I was stumbling along in her footsteps. But who was coming behind me? Who was following me?

Betty had called them hippies, but I guessed from what she'd said about them – their dreadlocked hair and patched clothes – that they were New Age travellers. She had told me that they lived in an abandoned church over in Islington, and I prayed that they hadn't moved on. I jogged back to the high street and flagged down a taxi. Because I didn't know the exact address although I knew the general area, I told the woman driver to take me to the Angel. I could walk from there. I kept glancing over my shoulder. I kept looking for a face I'd seen before. I saw nobody, but still the sickening sense remained that I didn't have much time left. I sat on the edge of my seat, impatient with traffic jams and red lights.

It was starting to get dark by the time we reached the Angel – or, at least, the colour was draining from the day. I had lost all track of time and I couldn't even think what day it was. It was a weekday, I knew that. Most people were at work, sitting in heated offices, drinking coffee from vending machines, having meetings that they liked to think were important. I paid the driver and got out, side-stepping a half-frozen puddle. Out of the low, dulling sky a few flakes of snow fell. I pulled up the collar of my jacket and started walking.

Some of the church had been painted in primary colours, and there was an asymmetrical rainbow over the large wooden-ribbed door. A rusty pink-sprayed bicycle leant against the wall, beside an old pram full of wood and another full of tin cans. By the side of the church was a van decorated with swirls and flowers, and with blinds drawn down over all of its windows. A large, dun-coloured dog was nosing its tyres.

I lifted the knocker and let it fall with a heavy rap on to the door, which was already open a crack.

'Just push and come in,' shouted a female voice.

The interior of the church was dim and hazy with smoke from a fire burning on the floor, in a makeshift fireplace of bricks. Round it a group of people sat or squatted, wrapped in blankets or coiled in sleeping-bags. One was holding a guitar, although he was making no attempt to play it. I saw the shapes of other figures towards the back of the church, where there were still a few pews. There were mattresses and bags over the floor. A great crack ran down the stained-glass window.

'Hi,' I said uncertainly. 'Sorry to butt in.'

'You're welcome here,' said a woman with cropped hair and studs in her eyebrow, nose, lips and chin. She leant forward and thick copper bangles cascaded down her arm.

'I'm Abbie,' I said, and shook her mittened hand. 'I just wanted to ask . . .'

'Well, we know you're Abbie – at least, I do. Some of us haven't been here for more than a few days. I'm Crystal – remember? You've cut your hair, haven't you? Anyway, sit down,' said Crystal. 'Do you want tea? Boby's just made some. Boby! Another tea – we've got a visitor. You don't take sugar, do you? See, I always remember.'

Boby came over with mud-coloured tea in a pewter mug. He was small and skinny and had a white, nervous face. His combat trousers hung off him and his neck looked thin in the chunky knit of his sweater.

'Thanks,' I said. 'I've been here before, have I?'

'We've got some beans spare. Do you want some?'

'I'm fine,' I said. 'Thanks.'

The man with the guitar ran his fingers over the neck of the instrument to produce a few broken chords. He grinned at me and I saw that his mouth was full of black, broken teeth. 'I'm Ramsay,' he said. 'Ram for short. I came yesterday from the bypass protest. My first night for weeks on the solid ground. Where've you come from?'

I realized I looked like a runaway. I'd become one of them. I didn't have to struggle to make sense here. I slid down by the fire and took a gulp of my tepid, bitter tea. The smoke from the fire stung my eyes.

'I don't know where I've come from, really,' I said. 'But Betty told me about you lot.'

'Betty?'

'The old woman with all the cats,' said Crystal. 'You told us about her last time.'

I nodded, feeling oddly peaceful. The fight had gone out of me. Perhaps it wouldn't matter, being dead. 'I probably did,' I said. 'I probably asked you about my friend Jo.'

'That's right. Jo.'

'I asked if she'd come here.'

'D'you want a roll-up?' said Boby.

'All right,' I said. I took the thin cigarette that he held out and Ram lit it for me. I inhaled and coughed. Nausea swept over me. I took another drag. 'Did she come here?'

'Yup,' said Crystal. She looked at me. 'Are you OK?'

'Yes.'

'Here. Have some beans.' She picked up one of the tins of baked beans that was by the fire, stuck in a plastic spoon and handed it over. I took a mouthful: disgusting. Then another. I sucked on the roll-up and pulled acrid smoke into my lungs.

'Great,' I said. 'Thanks. So Jo came here, did she?'

'Yeah. But I told you.'

'I can't remember things,' I said.

'I get like that too,' said Ram, and made another stab

at a chord. A man opened the door of the church and came in pushing the pram. He tossed some more wood on the fire then bent over and kissed Crystal. They kissed for a long time.

'So she came here looking for a kitten?' I said finally.

'Because that crazy Betty thinks we keep cats here.'

'Don't you?'

'Can you see cats?'

'No.'

'I mean, we have had a few strays, because we give them milk and food. And some of us were in a raid that released cats from a laboratory the other month.'

'I dunno how she heard about us, though.'

'Nor do I,' I said. 'So did she just go away?'

'Jo?'

'Yes.'

'She gave us some money for our projects. A fiver, I think.'

'And that was it?'

'Yup.'

'Oh, well,' I said. I looked around. Perhaps I could join them and become a traveller and eat baked beans and sleep on stone floors and up trees and make roll-ups until my fingers were stained yellow. That would be different from designing offices.

'Except I said she could always try Arnold Slater.'

'Arnold Slater?'

'He's the man we gave some of the strays to. When the dogs started chasing them. He's in a wheelchair but he looks after them anyway.'

'So did she go there?'

'She said she might. So did you – last time, I mean. Weird, eh? Like *déjà vu*. Do you believe in *déjà vu*?'

'Of course. Round and round and round I go,' I said.

I threw the end of the roll-up into the fire and drained my tea. 'Thanks,' I said. I turned suddenly to Boby. 'You have a big tattoo of a spider, don't you?'

He blushed violently then pulled up his thick jumper and on his flat white stomach was a tattooed web that stretched out of sight round his back. 'There,' he said.

'But where's the spider gone?' I asked.

'That's what you said before.'

'Clearly I'm a very consistent person,' I said.

It was really dark when I left the church, even though it wasn't evening yet. I could make out the ghost of a moon behind the clouds. Arnold Slater lived two minutes from here and he was old and in a wheelchair and Jo had thought she might go to see him and I had thought I might follow Jo and go to see him . . . I stepped out into the road, and at that moment the mobile I'd grabbed as I left Ben's started to ring, making me jump violently. Backing on to the pavement, I put my hand in my pocket and pulled it out. Without thinking, I pressed the 'call' button.

'Hello?' I said.

'Abbie! Where the fuck are you, Abbie? What are you up to? I've been out of my mind worrying. I've been calling the house all day and you didn't reply so I came back and you weren't here . . .'

'Ben,' I said.

'So I waited and waited. I thought you might have gone to the shops or something, and then I saw my mobile wasn't on the charger any longer, so I rang it on the off-chance. When are you coming home?'

'Home?'

'Abbie, when are you coming back?'

'I'm not coming back,' I said.

'What?'

'You and Jo. I know about Jo. I know you were with her.'

'Listen to me now, Abbie –'

'Why didn't you tell me? Why, Ben?'

'I was scared that –'

'*You* were scared,' I said. '*You*.'

'Christ, Abbie –' he said, but I pressed the off-button. I held the phone cradled in my hand and stared down at it as if it could bite. Then I scrolled down the names in its memory bank. I didn't know any of them until I came to Jo Hooper. I recognized the number, because it belonged to her flat. But then there was another Jo Hooper (mobile). I pressed 'call' and heard the sound of ringing and just as I was about to give up, someone said, 'Hello,' in a whisper. So quiet I could hardly hear and, anyway, whispers in the dark all sound the same.

I didn't say a word. I stood with the mobile pressed to my cheek. I tried not to breathe. I heard him breathing very softly. In and out, in and out. There was a coldness in my veins. I closed my eyes and listened. He didn't say anything else. I had the strongest feeling that he knew it was me, and that he knew I knew it was him. I could feel him smiling.

Twenty-six

I felt that I was in a dream running down a slope that was becoming steeper and steeper so that I was unable to stop. There was nothing in the street that I recognized – not the stunted tree with a broken branch flapping down, not the huge wooden buttresses propping up one ramshackle stretch of houses. There was just a smell about it. I had the impression of footsteps sounding ahead of me. Jo's. My own. If I moved more quickly, I would catch them.

I'd written Arnold Slater's number on the back of my hand. Twelve. The far end of this insalubrious street. But I was going to the house of an old man in a wheelchair. He couldn't be the one. I wouldn't have stopped anyway, now that I was almost scraping at Jo's heels. I thought of her walking along this street, impatient. Could it be so difficult to get a bloody cat? The street was the familiar mixture of the restored, the abandoned and the neglected. Number twelve wasn't so bad. It must have been owned by the council because quite elaborate work had been done to enable a wheelchair to get to the front door. There was a concrete ramp and some heavy-duty handrails. I rang the bell.

Arnold Slater wasn't in his wheelchair. I could see it folded up in the hall behind him. But he was no kind of threat to anyone who could move faster than a tortoise. He was an old man in an outdoor coat, blinking at the daylight and holding the door handle as if for support. He looked at me with a frown. I was trying to remember him. Was he trying to remember me?

'Hello,' I said brightly. 'Are you Arnold Slater? I've heard that you might have a cat for sale.'

'Bloody hell,' he said.

'Sorry,' I said. 'Don't you have cats?'

He shuffled aside to leave a space. 'A few,' he said, with a throaty chuckle. 'Come in.'

I looked at his thin, sinewy wrists protruding from his raincoat. I assured myself once more that this man couldn't do me any harm and stepped inside.

'I've got cats,' he said. 'There's Merry. And Poppy. And Cassie and, look, there's Prospero.'

A mustard-coloured shape darted down the hallway and disappeared into the gloom. I suddenly had an image of a secret society, a freemasonry, of cat nuts dotted around London, linked by their obsession like the secret rivers that run beneath London.

'Nice names,' I said.

'Cats have their own names,' he said. 'You've just got to recognize them.'

I was in a fever. His words seemed to come from a long way away and take a long time to reach me. I was like someone who was drunk and trying not to show it. I was doing my best possible impersonation of a cheerful young woman who was terribly eager to have a discussion about cats. 'Like children, I guess.'

He looked offended. 'They're not like children. Not like *my* children. These ones can look after themselves.'

My head was buzzing and I was moving from one foot to another in impatience. 'I was sent by the people in the church. They said you had cats for sale.'

Another scratchy laugh, like he had something stuck in his throat. 'I don't have cats for sale. Why would I want to sell a cat? Why do people keep thinking that?'

'That's part of what I wanted to talk to you about.

Have you had other people coming here wanting to buy cats from you?'

'They're mad. I've taken the odd cat off their hands and then they send people on to me as if I was a pet shop.'

'What sort of people?'

'Stupid women wanting a cat.'

I forced myself to laugh. 'You mean women have been pitching up here trying to buy a cat? How many?'

'A couple of them. I told them both that they weren't for sale.'

'That's funny,' I said, as casually as I could manage, 'because I think a friend of mine may have been one of the people who was sent to you. Could this be her?' I had been fingering the photograph of Jo in my jacket pocket. Now I took it out and showed it to Arnold.

Immediately he looked puzzled and suspicious. 'What's this? What do you want to know for?'

'I was wondering if she was one of the women who came here looking for a cat.'

'What do you want to know for? I thought *you* wanted a cat. What's all this about? You some sort of police or something?'

My thoughts were scattered all over, I could almost hear my brain humming inside my head. I felt in a rush, escaping something and chasing something both at the same time, and now I had to think of some half-way plausible explanation of what on earth I was up to.

'I'm looking for a cat as well,' I said. 'I just wanted to make sure I'd come to the same place she had.'

'Why don't you ask her?'

I wanted to scream and howl. What did it matter? This wasn't a checkpoint on the Iraqi border. It was a house in Hackney with four mangy cats. I just needed to move on to the next square in the ridiculous game I was playing and he was the only one who could help me. I tried to think. It was so hard. Poor Jo hadn't got her cat here, that was obvious enough.

'I'm sorry, Mr Slater,' I said. 'Arnold. I just have this need to get a cat.'

'That's what they all say.'

'Who?'

'That woman in the picture.'

'Thank God,' I said to myself.

'They've all got to have a cat and they've got to have it today. Can't wait until tomorrow.'

'I know the feeling. You get the idea of something in your head, like a hamburger, and you've just got to have one. You won't rest.'

'A hamburger?'

'Now, Mr Slater, if I was to come to you and ask you for a cat, which in fact I have done, and you were to say that yours aren't for sale, as they aren't, what would you recommend? Where would you steer me?' Arnold Slater's attention was still on Jo's photograph. I put it back in my pocket. 'Arnold,' I said, more quietly and urgently, 'where did you send her?'

'Who was the other one?'

He was looking at me with a keener expression. He may have been starting to remember me. I paused but it was no good. I couldn't think of any possible way of telling him anything like the truth.

'It doesn't matter. It's not a big deal, Arnold. It's only a cat. I just want to know where you sent them.'

'There's pet shops,' he said. 'Ads in the paper. That's the best way.'

'Oh,' I said. Was this it? The blind alley.

'I just sent them round the corner.'

335

I bit my lip and tried to stay calm as if it was all terribly unimportant. 'That sounds good,' I said. 'Did you hear back from her?'

'I just sent her on.'

'So she probably got her cat, then.'

'I dunno. I didn't hear back.'

'So it sounds like the place for me,' I said. 'Sounds like a good place for cats.'

'I dunno about that,' he said. 'It's just a place round the corner. They sell all different stuff. Christmas trees at Christmas. I bought logs there for my fire. He dropped them round. He had some kittens. I didn't know if they'd gone.'

'What's its name, Arnold?'

'Hasn't got a name. It was a greengrocer's and then they put up the rent and then it was different shops, and then it was Vic Murphy.'

'Vic Murphy,' I said.

'That's right. I sent them to Vic. But the shop still says Greengrocer's on the sign. Well, not Greengrocer's. Buckley's Fruit and Vegetables.'

'How do I get there?'

'It's just a couple of minutes' walk.'

But it took more than a couple of minutes for Arnold to explain the route to me and then I left him there with his cats and his baffled expression. He must have still been thinking about the photograph and wondering what on earth I was up to. I glanced at my watch. It was just after six thirty. I wouldn't do anything reckless. I would just go and have a look from a safe distance. I looked like a different person. It would be fine. Still, I found it difficult to breathe. My chest felt tight.

To get there, I had to walk up a long, dull street, full of houses that had been boarded up. I knew the street.

At first I thought a part of my lost memory was returning, but then I saw the street sign. Tilbury Road. It was from here that my car had been towed away. I walked in a daze of dread and unreality.

It was a row of shabby shops in a mainly residential street. There was a launderette, a food shop with veg-etables and fruit on racks outside, a betting shop and the Buckley's Fruit and Vegetables shop. It was closed. Very closed. Green metal shutters were pulled down in front of it and looked as if they hadn't been opened for weeks. Posters had been plastered on it and names and insignia sprayed across. I stepped close up and pushed uselessly against it. There was a letter-box. I looked through and I could see a large pile of mail inside on the floor. I walked into the food shop next door. Behind the counter were two Asian men. The younger of them was filling the cigarette rack. The other was older, white-bearded, reading the evening newspaper.

'I'm looking for Vic Murphy,' I said to him.

He shook his head. 'Don't know him,' he said.

'He used to run the shop next door. The one selling logs and Christmas trees.'

The man gave a shrug. 'He's gone. Shut up.'

'Do you know where?'

'No. It's a rubbish shop. Different people come but they all end up closing down.'

'It's really important I find Vic Murphy,' I said.

The men grinned at each other. 'Owe you money?'

'No,' I said.

'I think he went without paying a few bills. A few of them came round after him. But he was long gone.'

'So there's no way of tracking him down?'

Another shrug. 'Not unless you want to ask the bloke who moved his stuff for him.'

'Who's that?'

'That'd be George.'

'Have you got his number?'

'No. I know where he lives, though.'

'Can you tell me?'

'Baylham Road. Number thirty-nine, I reckon.'

'What was Vic Murphy like?'

'Pretty weird,' the man said. 'But you've got to be pretty weird to run a shop there. I mean, logs and Christmas trees. I reckon he just got a batch of logs and wanted to flog them and move on.'

'Did he have any cats?'

'Cats?'

'I want to buy a cat.'

'You want a pet shop, love.'

'I heard that Vic Murphy sold cats.'

'I don't know. He may have had a cat. There's always cats around. But you never know who they belong to, do you?'

'I've never really thought about it,' I said.

'They like whoever feeds them, cats.'

'Really?' I said.

'Not like dogs. You'd be better off with a dog. A dog's a real friend.'

'I'll bear it in mind.'

'Protection as well.'

'Yes.'

'I don't think you'll get your money back.'

'What?'

'From that Vic Murphy.'

'I already told you, he doesn't owe me money.'

'That's what the other one said. They say they're friends. Don't want to scare him off.'

I took my photograph of Jo out of my pocket.

'Was this girl one of them?' I asked.

The man looked at the picture. 'She's a woman,' he said.

'That's right.'

'They were all men. Except you.'

Twenty-seven

I set off once more. People had left their offices now and were trudging home through the cold, dark streets. Men and women with their heads down against the wind, just thinking about being some place warm. I wasn't thinking about anything except getting the address. I knew I was no longer following in Jo's footsteps and my own. At the same time everything had been so tantalizingly close, and I was grimly determined to follow the last lead.

A van roared past, splashing icy mud from the puddles in the road over me. I cursed and wiped the mud from my face. Perhaps I should just go home? Where was home? I'd have to go back to Sadie's. Except I simply couldn't bear the thought of turning up there again, coming full circle and ending up right back at the nightmarish beginning, with nothing achieved except dread, fear, danger, deceit.

I took Ben's mobile out of my pocket and held it for a minute, standing still in the middle of the pavement while people surged round me. I turned it on. There were twelve new messages and I played them back. Three were to Ben, from people I'd never heard of. Eight were from Ben to me, each sounding more frantic than the one before. The eighth just said, 'Abbie.' That was all. 'Abbie.' Like someone calling to me from a long way off.

There was another message to me, from Cross. 'Abbie,' he said, in a stern voice. 'Listen to me. I have just spoken to Mr Brody, who seems very concerned about your whereabouts. Can I suggest to you that, at the very least, you let us know where you are and that you are safe? Please call me as soon as you get this message.' There was a pause, then he added: 'I'm serious, Abbie. Get in touch. Now.'

I turned off the mobile and put it into my pocket. Jack Cross was quite right. I had to call him at once and tell him what I'd discovered. Across the road was a pub, the Three Kings. It'd be warm in there, full of smoke and laughter and spilt beer and gossip. I'd go quickly to this person with the van, find out the address where Vic Murphy had gone. Then go into the pub, order a drink and some crisps, and call Cross to tell him what I'd found. He could take it from there. I'd call Ben, too. I had to give him his mobile back, at least. And after that . . . but I didn't want to think about what I would do after, because that was like staring across a stretch of dead brown water.

I felt cheered by this decision. An address, then it would be over. But it was so savagely cold. My toes ached with it, my fingers were turning numb, and my face felt tight and raw as if there was grit in the wind, scraping at my skin. The pavement glinted with frost; parked cars were becoming covered with a thin layer of ice. I walked quicker, breath curling up out of my mouth. My nose stung. I could sleep on Sadie's sofa tonight then go flat-hunting in the morning. I had to get a job, begin again. I urgently needed the money and, even more, I needed the sense of purpose and normality. I'd buy an alarm clock tomorrow and set it for seven thirty. I'd have to collect clothes from Ben's, and get Cross to escort me to Jo's flat for the rest of my stuff. My life was scattered in little fragments around London. I had to get it back.

I turned left, up a narrower, darker street. The sky

was clear and there was a thin, cold moon and glittering white stars above me. Curtains were closed on the houses I passed, and through them shone the bright lights of other people's lives. I'd done all I could, I thought. I'd searched for Jo and I'd searched for me, and I hadn't found either of us. We were lost and I no longer believed that Cross would find us, but he might find him and I might be safe.

I didn't believe anything any more, not really. I could no longer imagine that I was in peril, or that I'd been grabbed and held in a dark place, and escaped. The remembered time and the lost time seemed to merge in my head. The Ben I'd known and forgotten seemed inseparable from the Ben I'd rediscovered then lost again. The Jo I'd once met and laughed with was gone, gone even from my memory. Everything was as insubstantial as everything else. I just put one foot in front of the other, because that was what I'd told myself I had to do.

With fingers that felt like frozen claws, I took the instructions out of my pocket and peered at the writing. I took the second turn on the right: Baylham Road, which had speed humps along it, and high privet hedges. The road led up a small hill then down, houses on either side. Lights were on in their front rooms; some had smoke rising from the chimneys, blissful bits of other people's lives. I trudged on.

They'd said at the shop that it was number thirty-nine, which was on the left side of the road, just at the bottom of the rise. From a distance, I could see no lights on and although I hadn't really expected anything my dismal sense of having gone astray increased. I trailed down the hill and stopped in front of number thirty-nine.

It was different from the other houses, because it was set back from the road, and accessible by a rotting double gate, which hung loosely from its hinges and creaked every time the wind gusted. I pushed it open. This was my last task. In a few minutes, I would be through with this; I would have done everything that I could. Inside was a yard, full of iced-up potholes. It was littered with objects that loomed out at me in the darkness – a pile of sawdust, a wheelbarrow, a rusty trailer, a stack of rubber tyres, a couple of what looked like storage heaters, a chair, lying on its back with a leg missing. The house was to the left of the yard – a two-storey, red-brick building, with a small porch over its front door. There was a broken terracotta pot in the porch, and a pair of large rubber boots, which for a moment made me hope that the man was in after all. I pressed the bell at the side of the door but couldn't hear the sound of its ring, so I hammered with my fists instead, and waited, stamping my feet to keep the feeling in them. Nothing. No one came. I pressed my ear to the door and listened. I couldn't hear a sound.

So that was the end of that. I turned round again to face the yard, which I looked at properly for the first time. I realized that this was an old stableyard. Under the clear sky, I could just make out the individual horseboxes and, when I looked closer, there were still names written above each doorway in fading capital letters. Spider, Bonnie, Douglas, Bungle, Caspian, Twinkle. But there were no horses here any longer, and obviously hadn't been for a long time. Many of the doors were missing. Instead of straw and manure, I could smell oil, paint, mechanical things. An upper door of one of the horse-boxes hung open; inside it was dank, full of objects – paint tins, planks, panes of glass. Instead of the whinny and snort of horses, there was thick silence.

Then I heard a sound. I thought it came from the low

building at the other side of the yard, opposite the house. Perhaps the landlord was here, after all. I took a few steps in the direction of the sound. I still wasn't scared. Not really.

'Hello?' I called. 'Hello, is anyone home?'

Nobody replied. I stood still and listened. I could hear cars in the distance; somewhere music was playing, the faint pulse of its bass quivering in the night air.

'Hello?'

I went across to the building and stood outside, hesitating. It was made of breeze blocks and wood and had no windows. The tall door was held shut by a heavy latch. There was another sound, like a long hum or groan. I held my breath and heard it again.

'Is anyone there?' I called.

I lifted the latch and pushed the heavy door till it swung open enough for me to peer inside. But it was cold and dark – almost pitch black, out of the moonshine. There was no one in here, after all, except perhaps an animal. I thought about bats, and mice, and then I thought about rats, always nearby, growing large and bloated on rotten food and dead animals, creeping about under the floorboards, with their sharp yellow teeth and thick tails . . . I heard the sound again as the door creaked, blown by the wind.

Gradually I could make out dim shapes inside the building: straw bales heaped up at one end, a machine like an old plough near me. Something indistinguishable at the end. What was it? I edged forward. The door shut behind me and I put out my hands. There was damp straw under my feet now.

'Hello,' I said again. My voice sounded small and wavery; it floated in the air. There was a smell in my nostrils now; a smell of shit and piss.

344

'I'm here,' I said. 'I'm here.' I took a few more steps, on legs that felt as weak as bits of string and weighed down by the boulder of terror in my chest. 'Jo?' I said. 'Jo? It's me, Abbie.'

She was seated on straw bales at the end of the building, just a dark outline in the dark air. I felt for her: thin shoulder beneath my hands. She smelt rank – of fear and shit and stale sweat. I put my hands higher and felt the rough fabric where her face should be. She was making small noises through the cloth, and her body jerked at my touch. I put my hand up to her throat and felt the wire there. I felt round her back and there was stiff, cold rope twisted around her wrists and leading back away from her body, towards the wall behind her. When I tugged violently at it, it pulled taut but didn't give. She had been tethered like a horse.

'Ssh,' I murmured. 'It's OK.' A high noise came out of her shrouded face. 'Don't struggle, don't do anything. I'll do it. I'll rescue you. Oh, please, please, stay still.'

I pulled at the hood. My fingers were shaking so badly that I couldn't do it at first, but eventually I tugged it up, over her head. I couldn't see her face in the darkness and her hair was just a greasy tangle under my fingers. Her cheeks were icy and wet with tears. She kept making the same high-pitched noise, like an animal stuck fast in a trap.

'Sssh,' I hissed. 'Keep quiet, please, shut up. I'm trying.'

I untwisted the wire round her throat. It seemed to be attached from the ceiling or something, so she had to keep her head tilted backwards. Because I couldn't see what I was doing, it took ages, and at first I twisted it in the wrong direction, making it tighter. I could feel the sharp pulse in her throat. I kept whispering that everything would be all right, but we could both hear the hissing terror in my voice.

Her ankles were tied together, rope wound round and round her calves so she was trussed. But this time it was easier than I'd expected. Soon her legs were free, and she kicked out like a drowning person kicks for the surface. Her left foot thumped into my stomach and her right clipped my elbow. I got my arms around her knees like a rugby player and held her. 'Sit completely still,' I begged. 'I'm doing my fucking best.'

Next I found the knot behind her back. As far as I could feel, it was absolutely tight. I pulled and tugged uselessly at it, my nails tearing, and it didn't give. I knelt down and dug my teeth into the rope, which tasted oily. I remembered the taste of oil, I remembered the smell of shit and piss that was in the room and on her skin and in my lungs. And the smell of fear. And the way my heart banged against my ribs and my breath came in shattered gasps and bile rose up in my throat and there was darkness in every direction . . .

'Hang on,' I said. 'I'm going to see if I can untie it from the other end. Don't worry. I'm not going. Please, please, please, don't make that noise. For God's sake.'

I followed the rope from her wrists to the wall, where it was tied to what felt like an iron hoop. If only I could see something. I felt in my pocket, in case I might miraculously find matches, a lighter, anything. There was none, but I did bring out my old car keys. I dug the end of the key into the bulge of the knot and worked it in deeper, wriggled it around until I felt the faint creaking give of the rope. My fingers were stiff with cold. At one point I dropped the key and had to scramble around among the straw on the floor to retrieve it, my fingers scraping on the rough surface. She started to make muffled screams inside her gag again and then she half stood up, before collapsing across the bales.

'Shut up,' I hissed. 'Shut up shut up shut up shut up! Oh, shit, don't tug on the rope like that, it'll only tighten the knot. Keep still! Let the rope go slack. Oh, Christ! Please please please.'

I worked away with the key. I could feel the knot loosening, bit by bit, but, oh, God, it took a long time; such a long time. Sweat was gathering on my forehead and turning clammy there. I could just run away, I thought. Now! Run and call for help. Why the fuck didn't I run into the road and stand there howling and screeching for help? I could hammer at doors and flag down every car. I had to leave, at once. I mustn't, mustn't, mustn't be here. The rope eased further.

'Nearly,' I gasped. 'A few minutes more and you'll be free. Ssssh, please.'

Done! I stood up and pulled the gag from her mouth and a terrible wailing sound escaped from her.

'Jo?' I whispered. 'Are you Jo?'

'I'm Sarah. Sarah. Help me. Please help me. Oh God, oh God, oh God, godgodgodgod.'

I felt winded with disappointment, except there was no time for that now. No time for anything except flight.

'Get up!' I said, grabbing her by the forearm.

She half rose, falling against me in her weakness.

'Listen! What's that?' I gasped.

Someone was outside. There were footsteps in the yard. The clank of something metal in the distance.

I shoved Sarah down on the bales. I stuffed the gag back in her mouth, stifling the gurgling sound that she was making. She started struggling, but feebly.

'Sarah! Our only chance. Let me. Fucking *let* me. I'm here, Sarah. I'll save you. All right?'

Her eyes flickered at me, terrified. I found the wire dangling above me like a giant spider's thread, and pulled it over her head, pulling it tighter. The footsteps were coming nearer. I wrapped the rope clumsily round her legs. The wrists. I had to find the rope. I bent down and swam my hands over the gritty floor until I picked it up. Now the footsteps were getting nearer. A wheezy cough. There was a scream burning in the back of my throat and I swallowed it back. Nausea. Blood hammering in my eardrums. I felt for the hood on the floor and then the bales beside the seated, shuddering figure, and when I found it, I jammed it back over her head roughly, feeling her neck jerk.

'Wait,' I hissed, and hurtled over to the other side of the room, behind a metal object that ripped my shin, my heart like a violent drum beat he would surely hear, my breath like sobs that he had to hear, as soon as he lifted the latch, opened the door, came inside.

Twenty-eight

I had retreated into a corner right at the back, away from the door. I was deep in the shadow, behind an incomprehensible, rusting machine, an assembly of wheels and cogs and bolts, connected to nothing. Even if he looked in my direction he probably wouldn't be able to see me. Probably. That was the difficult word. I shuffled back as far as I could. I felt the chill damp of the wall on my neck, on my scalp through my short hair. And now he was there. I had found him by accident. I felt a plunging, plummeting sensation of nausea as I fell back into my nightmare.

And then, as I saw him, my first feeling was: there must be a mistake. When he had been a voice out of the darkness, I had thought of him as huge and powerful, a monster. He had been the foul god who was going to punish me and reward me and feed me and starve me and decide whether I lived or died.

Now I saw flashes of him as he caught the light. Just a detail here and there, a rough coat, and straggled, greying hair, combed across his balding head. I could hardly see his face at all. It was largely covered by a flowery woman's scarf. To a stranger it might have looked like a protection against dust. But I knew what it was. It was to disguise his voice. He came in muttering to himself, carrying a galvanized bucket, which he tossed on the floor with a clatter. I couldn't connect my memories with this shambling, down-at-heel, insignificant man. He looked like the person you don't notice who has come to clean the windows or sweep the floor. He talked to Sarah as if she were a slightly troublesome pig that needed mucking out.

'How are you doing?' he said, arranging things around her in ways I couldn't see. 'Sorry I've been away a bit. Been busy. But I'll be here for a bit now. I've made time for you.'

He walked out and for a wild moment I considered flight. But almost at once, he returned with something that he placed on the ground with a clatter. It might have been a tool-box. He came and went, came and went, carrying and hauling in objects from the yard outside. Most of them were hidden in the gloom but I caught sight of an unlit lantern, a blow-torch and some empty vinyl bags, the sort that people carry their sports kit in. And all I could do was crouch in the darkness, trying not to move, not to breathe. The straw rustled against my foot when I shifted position. I gulped when I swallowed. Surely he could hear the thunder of my heart, the rush of my blood, the scream in my throat?

During one of his brief absences I reached into my pocket and my fingers closed around Ben's mobile phone. Softly, oh, so slowly, I took it out and brought it close to my face. I wrapped my fingers around it and pressed a button to illuminate the tiny screen. There was the tiniest of beeps. It sounded like the ringing of a bell. Had he heard it? There was no chance of talking but could I send a text message or just dial 999? I looked at the screen. How could he not see that light in the darkness? Up the right-hand side of the screen there were three broken lines, which showed that the battery was almost full. On the left-hand side there should have been what looked like four flowers, or goblets, on top of each other to indicate the strength of reception. But there was one, indicating no reception at all. There was no chance. I couldn't make a call and I couldn't receive a call. I slipped the phone back into my pocket.

I wanted to cry and curse and scratch my fingernails on the stone. As soon as I had seen Sarah, I should have got out and called for help. It would have been so simple. Instead, I had followed myself back into the trap. I was cursed and blighted. I looked across at him, silhouetted against the faint light from the space outside.

I went over options in my mind. I could make a run for the door and try to escape and bring help. That was completely hopeless. He was by the door. Even with the advantage of surprise, I would have no chance. I could attack him, smash him over the head, knock him out. Could I get to him without him hearing? Could I take him by surprise? It didn't seem likely. No, my only chance was to wait and hope he would leave and I would have my chance.

The thought of that, of having to stay silent in the shadows, made me want to lie on the cold floor and weep. I felt so very tired. I wanted to sleep. Perhaps I didn't want to die, but I was close to wanting to be dead. At least the dead are cut off from pain and fear. What was the point of even fighting against it?

And then, almost without realizing it, I started to feel different. Looking at him bustling casually around with that poor girl trussed up on the straw bales, I began to feel that I was looking at myself. I remembered those days when I had been the one with the wire around my neck and the hood over my face. I had been there, with my toes over the edge of the abyss, waiting to be slaughtered, and I remembered what I had felt. I had given up all hope of surviving. What I had prayed for was a chance to go for him, tear an eye out, scratch him,

351

just do some sort of damage to him, before I died. Now I had been given that opportunity. I couldn't defeat him. That was too much to ask. But if he found me, at least I would do him some damage. I needed something. I felt a small whimper of regret. I would have given everything I had ever owned for a kitchen knife or an aerosol spray. Then I made myself not mind about that. I was here. I had nothing. Anything I could put in my hand would be something.

I crouched and started to feel around me in the darkness, very delicately, praying that I wouldn't knock anything over. My right hand touched something cold. A tin, by its size a paint tin. I pushed at it experimentally. It was empty, useless to me. Next to it my fingers closed around a handle. This was more promising but it turned out to be a paint brush with stiff, clogged bristles. There was nothing. No chisel. No screwdriver. No steel pole. Nothing I could hold. I stood up again, feeling my knees creak. How could he not hear that? I just had to wait until he had gone. Then I could go outside and call the police. Release Sarah.

The man was arranging things. I couldn't make out exactly what he was doing but I could hear him muttering lightly to himself. He reminded me of my father at the weekend, the only happy part of his life, when he would be repairing the fence in the garden, painting a window-frame, putting up a bookshelf.

The man was unfastening the wire around Sarah's neck. Oh, yes, the bucket. The hooded figure was pulled forward, her trousers tugged down, she crouched over the bucket, his hands around her neck. I heard the splashing in the bucket.

'Well done, my beauty,' he murmured, pulling her trousers back up.

With the casualness of long practice, he refastened the wire around her neck until she was helpless once more, but there was a tenderness about it. He seemed to like her more than he had liked me. He had never called me his beauty. The language had always been hostile. He had always been breaking me down.

'You've slimmed down,' he said. 'I think we're ready. You're lovely, Sarah. Lovely. Not like all of them.'

He stood back, in contemplation of her. I heard a metallic rasping sound and a flicker of light. He had lit the lantern. Light was splashed across the room and I shrank back behind the machinery. He examined Sarah with approving murmurs, feeling her naked arms, running his fingers along them, the way you might feel a horse to check if its fever had subsided. He laid the lantern on the floor. He lifted his arms, with his hands behind his head. He looked like someone who was newly awake, yawning and stretching and then I saw he was unfastening his scarf. It required some complicated tugging and fiddling with the tight knot and then he pulled the scarf away and there, for the first time, in the shifting orange light of the lantern, I saw his face.

It meant nothing to me. I didn't recognize it. I didn't know him. And, suddenly and strangely, it was as if a small turn had been made to the dial and everything had come into focus. The edges were sharp and hard, even in that flickering lantern light. My fever had gone. Even my fear had gone. What I had wanted was to know, and now I knew. Even my thoughts were clear now, and hard-edged. I didn't remember. My memory had not been restored. The sight of his drab face provoked no shock of recognition. But I knew what I needed to know.

I'd thought it was about me. There I had been in my fucked-up life, my stupid job and my disastrous relationship, and I had thought and fantasized and feared that he – that man over there – had recognized it in me. I had been heading for disaster and I had brought it willingly on myself. He had recognized it in me and we had been made for each other, needed each other. I had wanted to be destroyed.

Now I knew that this wasn't true. Maybe I had been careless, frantic, deranged, but I had blundered into his path. Not even that. I could never know for sure, but I guessed that it was Jo who had encountered him, eager, vulnerable, desperate, a perfect victim for him. I had been concerned for Jo and had followed in her footsteps and encountered him in turn. That pathetic loser over there had nothing to do with my life. He was the meteor that had fallen on me. He was the earthquake that had opened up under my feet. And that was the funny thing. There, cowering in the darkness and knowing I was trapped, I felt free of him.

I couldn't remember what had happened. I would never be able to. But now I sort of knew what had happened those weeks ago. I'd been out there, in the land of the living, and then by mistake I had wandered into his territory, into his hobby. What do they say about a fight? I had read or heard or been told that the winner was the person who struck the first blow. I think I could guess what must have happened. I was looking for Jo. This man, this unmemorable man, was part of the background, part of the furniture. Suddenly he had leapt into the foreground. He'd pulled me out of my world into his world. It had nothing to do with my world except that I was going to die in it. I imagined myself being taken by surprise by this man I had hardly noticed and fighting back too late, my head banged against the wall, or clubbed.

I made myself think: If he sees me, what will I do? I made myself remember what he had done to me. All the terrible memories that I had spent weeks trying to suppress I now dragged out to the forefront of my mind. They were like a terrible inflamed, rotting, infected tooth around which I pushed my tongue as hard as I could to remind myself of what pain could be like. And then I looked at that man, fussing around Sarah, as if she were a sheep being crammed into a stall, slapping at her, muttering endearments, setting out tools in preparation. He was both the patient, fussing lover and the busy, dispassionate slaughterman.

There was apparently some resistance from her because he cuffed her lightly.

'What's that, my love?' he said. There must have been some sort of groan from inside the hood, but I couldn't hear it. 'Am I hurting you? What? What is it? Hang on a moment, love.'

I heard his breathing, oh, yes, I remembered that hoarse breathing, as he struggled to release the gag.

'What's this?' he said. 'You been trying to get free.'

She coughed as she was released from the gag, coughed and heaved.

'There, there, my darling, mind your neck now.'

'I was choking,' she said. 'I thought I was going to die.'

'Is that all?'

'No, no.'

A suspicion started to spread in me like a stain. I knew what was going to happen now and I wasn't afraid. I had died already. It didn't matter.

'So what is it?'

'I don't want to die,' she said. 'I'll do anything to stay alive.'

'You stupid little bitch. I've told you. I don't want anything. They didn't pay the ransom. Did I tell you that? They didn't pay the ransom. You know why? 'Cause I didn't ask for one. Hur hur hur.' He laughed at his own joke.

'If I told you something. Something really important. Would you let me live?'

'Like what?'

'But would you?'

There was a few seconds' silence now. He was troubled.

'Tell me first,' he said in a softer tone.

Sarah didn't speak. She just gave a sob.

'Fucking tell me.'

'Do you promise? Do you promise to let me live?'

'Tell me first,' he said. 'Then I'll let you go.'

A long pause. I could count Sarah's gasps as I waited for what I knew she was going to say.

'There's someone here. Now let me go.'

'What the fuck?'

He stood up and looked around at the very moment that I stepped forward towards him, out of the shadow. I had thought of flying at him but that would be no good. He was almost ten yards away. He had too much time. I looked beyond him at the doorway. It might as well have been on the moon. He narrowed his eyes with the effort of making me out in the shadow at the back, way away from the door.

'You?' he said, his mouth open in bafflement. 'Abbie. How the fuck did you . . . ?'

I took a step towards him. I didn't look at Sarah. I looked him right in the eyes.

'I found you,' I said. 'I wanted to find you. I couldn't stay away.'

'I've been fucking looking for you,' he said. He looked around, obviously disconcerted. Was there anybody else here?

'I'm on my own,' I said. I held up my hands to him. 'Look. I've got nothing.'

'What the fuck are you doing here?' he said. 'I've got you now. You fucking got away. I've got you.'

I smiled. I felt so calm now. Nothing mattered. I thought again of those days in the dark. My tongue pushing at the rotting tooth. Remembering. Reliving.

'What do you mean you've "got me"?' I said. 'I've come back. I wanted to come back.'

'You'll regret this,' he said. 'You'll fucking regret this.'

I took another step forward. 'What do you want with her?' I said. 'I was listening to you both.' I took another step forward. We were just a few feet apart now. 'I heard you calling her your love. I felt that should have been me. Isn't that funny?'

He looked wary again. 'It's not funny,' he said.

I took another step forward. 'I missed you,' I said.

'You fucking ran away,' he said.

'I was scared,' I said. 'But afterwards I thought about it. You understood me. You dominated me. Nobody ever understood me the way you understood me. I want to understand you.'

He smiled. 'You're mad, you are.'

'It doesn't matter,' I said. 'I'm here. I'm in your hands. There's just one thing.' Another step forward. We were quite close now.

'What's that?'

'All that time, when we were together, you were just this voice in the dark, looking after me, feeding me. I used to think about you all the time, wonder what you were like. Will you let me kiss you just once?' I moved

357

my face closer to his. He smelt of something bad. Sweet and chemical. 'Just once. It won't matter.' Close up, it was such an ordinary face. Nothing frightening about it. Nothing special. 'Look at me,' I said, holding my hands out, open and empty. 'I'm just here, in front of you. Just one touch.' As I leant over I thought of him not as a man but as a sheep's head. That was important. I imagined a dead sheep's head that had been cut away from the body. 'Just one kiss. We're both lonely. So lonely. Just one.' I softly touched his lips with mine. Nearly now. Nearly. Slowly. 'I've waited for that.' Another kiss. I brought my hands up to his face, gently touching the side of his face with my palms. Wait. Wait. A dead sheep's head. Tongue on the rotten tooth. My face moved back. I looked at him wistfully and then I pushed my thumbs into his eyes. They were only the eyes in the skull of a dead sheep. A dead sheep who had kept me in the dark and tortured me. I knew that the nails on my thumbs were long. I gripped on the side of his head with my other fingers like claws and the thumbnails gouged into his eyes and I saw with interest that my thumbs, as they pushed into his head and scraped in the sockets, were now streaked with liquid, a watery liquid streaked with yellow, like pus.

I thought he would grab me. I thought he would kill me. Tear me into pieces. He didn't even touch me. I was able to step back and pull my sludgy thumbs out. A strange scream came from deep inside him, a howl, and his hands went up to his face, and his body folded up and he lay wriggling on the floor, spluttering and whimpering.

I took a step back, out of the reach of this grub-like creature, squirming and squeaking on the floor. I took a tissue from my pocket and wiped my thumbs. I took some deep breaths, filling my lungs. I felt like a drowning swimmer who had reached the surface and was breathing in the beautiful clean life-giving air.

Twenty-nine

There was the moon still, and there were the stars. Frost on the surface of everything, a glitter in the semi-darkness. A world of ice and snow and stillness. The cold cut into my face. I breathed in, quite steadily, and felt clean air in my mouth, and streaming down my throat. I breathed out again and watched how my breath hung in the air.

'Oh-oh-ohhh, nu-nu.'

Sarah made a sound like an animal, a piteous, high-pitched tangle of syllables. I couldn't make out the words. I put my arm more firmly around her shoulders to hold her up and she hung off me, whimpering. Her body felt tiny against me and I wondered how old she was. She looked like a snotty, unwashed little kid. She crumpled and put her head on my chest and I could smell her greasy hair and her sour sweat.

I put my hand in the pocket of my jacket and pulled out Ben's mobile. There was just enough power now. I dialled 999. 'What service, please?' a woman's voice demanded. I was stumped for a moment. All of them really, except the fire brigade. I said there were serious injuries and a serious crime. We would need two ambulances, and also the police.

I put the phone back and looked at Sarah; her small, slightly flat face was a ghastly white, with spots all over her forehead and a swollen mouth. Her lips were pulled back in a terrified, silent snarl. She looked like a trapped animal. I could make out a bruise on her neck where the wire had been. Her whole body was shaking. She was only wearing a long-sleeved T-shirt and some cotton trousers, thick socks but no shoes.

'Here,' I said, and took off my quilted jacket and put it round her. I pulled the collar up high so her face was protected from the air. 'You're wearing my shirt,' I said and put my arm back round her.

A sound came from her shivering body. I couldn't make out what she was saying.

'They'll be here soon,' I said. 'You're safe now.'

'Sorrysorrysorrysorry.'

'Oh, that.'

'It wasn't me. Not me. Mad. I thought I was going to die.' She started to weep. 'I knew I was about to die. I was mad.'

'Yes,' I said. 'I've been mad like that too. But I'm not any more.'

The blue lights and sirens came over the hill. Two ambulances and two police cars. Doors swung open. People jumped out and hurried towards us. There were faces looking down at us, hands separating us. Stretchers were laid on the ground. I sent a couple of people inside. I could hear Sarah beside me, sobbing and sobbing, till her sobs turned into a raw, retching sound. I could hear voices being soothing. The word 'Mummy' cut through the babble. 'Where's Mummy?'

A blanket was draped over my shoulder.

'I am perfectly all right,' I said.

'Lie down here now.'

'I can walk.'

There were shouts from inside. One of the men in green overalls ran out and whispered to a young policeman.

'Jesus Christ,' the policeman said, and looked at me hard.

'He's a killer,' I said.

'A killer?'

'But it's quite safe. He can't see anything. He's not dangerous any more.'

'Let's get you into the ambulance, my dear.' The voice soothed me as if I was hysterical with shock.

'You should call Detective Inspector Jack Cross,' I continued. 'My name is Abigail Devereaux. Abbie. I put out his eyes. He'll never look at me again.'

They drove Sarah away first. I clambered into the second ambulance with the blanket still around me. Two people climbed in with me, a paramedic and a female police officer. Somewhere behind me I was aware of a growing clamour, voices shouting urgently, the wail of a third ambulance coming down the road. But I didn't need to bother with that any more. I sat back and closed my eyes, not because I was tired – I wasn't, I felt quite clear-headed, as if I'd slept for a long time – but to block out the lights and the clutter around me and to stop all the questions.

Oh, I was so clean and so warm. I had shampooed hair and scrubbed skin, and my fingernails and toenails were clipped to the quick. I'd brushed my teeth three times, then gargled with some green concoction that made my breath feel minty right down to my lungs, I sat up in bed, wearing an absurd pink nightie and cov- ered in stiff, hygienic sheets and layers of thin, scratchy blankets, and drank tea and ate toast. Three cups of scalding hot sugared tea and a piece of limp white buttered toast. Or margarine, probably. They don't have butter in hospital. There were daffodils in a plastic jug on my locker.

Different hospital, different room, different view, different nurses bustling around with thermometers and bedpans and trolleys, different doctors with their clip charts and their tired faces, different policemen staring at me nervously then looking away. Same old Jack Cross, though, hunched in the chair like an invalid himself, with his hand around his cheek as if he had a toothache, and staring at me as if I frightened him.

'Hello, Jack,' I said.

'Abbie . . .' he started, and then stopped, working his hand round so his fingers covered his mouth. I waited and eventually he tried again. 'Are you all right?'

'Yes,' I said.

'The doctors said . . .'

'I'm all right. They just want to keep me under observation for a couple of days.'

'I'm not surprised, I don't know where to begin. I . . .' He shifted in his chair and rubbed his eyes. Then he sat up straighter and took a deep breath. He looked me straight in the eyes. 'We were wrong. There's no excuse.' I could see him thinking about putting forward all the reasons and excuses, then swallowing them back. Good. 'I can't believe you did that.' He slumped into the chair again and put his face back into his hand. 'What a fucking balls-up from start to finish. You can take us all to the cleaners, you know.'

'Is he dead?'

'He's in the ITU.'

'Oh.'

'Do you know what you did to him?'

'Yes.'

'His eyes.' He said this in a whisper. I couldn't tell if

363

he was looking at me with admiration or horror and disgust. 'You pushed them half-way into his brain. I mean, fuck.'

'With my thumbs,' I said.

'But, Jesus, Abbie, you must be . . .'

'I didn't have anything else.'

'We'll need to take a formal statement later.'

'Of course. Is Sarah all right?'

'Sarah Maginnis is shocked, malnourished. The way you were. She'll be all right. Do you want to see her?'

I thought about that for a minute. 'No.'

'She's very sorry, Abbie.'

'You know?'

'She can't stop talking about it.'

I shrugged.

'Maybe I was lucky,' I said. 'He was going to kill her. He'd taken his scarf off. I don't know what I would have done. I don't know if I would have just stood there and watched him do it. Nobody would have blamed me, would they? Poor, traumatized Abbie.'

'I don't think you'd have just stood there.'

'Is there any news about Jo? Has he said anything?'

'I don't think he'll be talking for a bit. We're beginning our investigation into Miss Hooper's disappearance.'

'You're too late,' I said.

He lifted his hands but then let them fall back on to his lap. We sat in silence for a few minutes. A nurse came in and said someone had left me flowers at Reception. She laid a damp bunch of anemones on my locker. I picked them up and sniffed them. They smelt of freshness; there were droplets of water on their bright petals. I laid them back on the locker. Cross's face was grey with fatigue.

'Tell me what you know about him,' I said.

'We've only just begun. His name is George Ronald Sheppy. Fifty-one years old. His only conviction was for animal cruelty, years ago. Slap-on-the-wrist job. We don't know much more yet, we've talked to a few neighbours. He was an odd-job man – a bit of this and a bit of that. Removals, fairground mechanic, lorry driver. Doesn't seem much, really.'

'What about the other women?'

'The other names,' said Cross. 'We'll keep on looking, of course, especially now – try to match missing people with areas he worked. Maybe when we know more . . .' He gave a helpless shrug. 'I'm just saying, don't expect too much.'

So the names were still only syllables spoken to me in the darkness.

'Are you seeing someone?' he asked.

'Several doctors, but I'm fine.'

'No – I meant someone to help you. Who you can talk to. After what you've been through.'

'I don't need help.'

'Abbie, I've been in there, I've seen what's left of him.'

'Do you expect me to be traumatized?'

'Well . . .'

'I put his eyes out.' I held up both hands and stared at my fingers. 'I put my thumbs against his eyeballs and I gouged his eyes out. That's not a trauma, Jack. The trauma was being grabbed. The trauma was being held in a cellar with a hood over my head and a gag in my mouth and eyes watching me in the darkness, hands touching me in the darkness. That was trauma. Knowing I was going to die and no one could help me. That was trauma. Escaping and finding out no one believed me. That was trauma. Being in danger all over again, when I should have been safe. That was trauma. This was not.

This was me surviving. This was me staying alive. No, I don't think I need help any more. Thank you.'

He leant back as I was talking, as if I was pummelling him. When I'd finished speaking, he nodded and left.

Ben came at lunchtime – his lunchtime, that is. Hospital lunch is at about half past eleven. Supper is at five. Then the evening stretches on and on until it becomes night, and then the night stretches on and on until it edges into morning again. He leant over me to kiss me awkwardly on the cheek with cold lips. He was wearing his lovely floppy overcoat. He held out a box of chocolates and I took it and put it on the pillow. He sat down and we looked at each other.

'I brought this as well,' he said, and pulled a smooth wooden oval out of his pocket. It was honey-coloured, veined with darker contours. 'Hornbeam,' he said. 'A special wood. I made it for you last night in the work-shop, when I was waiting for you and hoping you'd come back.'

I closed my fist around it. 'It's beautiful. Thank you very much.'

'Do you want to talk about it yet?'

'Not really.'

'Have you remembered anything?'

'No.'

There was a silence between us.

'I'm sorry about Jo,' I added. 'She's dead.'

'You don't know that. Not for sure.'

'She's dead, Ben.'

He stood up and went and looked out of the small closed window at the blue sky above the rooftops. He stayed like that for several minutes. I think perhaps he was crying.

366

'Abbie,' he said, at last, turning back to the bed, 'I was out of my mind with worry. I wanted to help you. I didn't want you to be on your own like that. Whatever you felt about me and Jo, you shouldn't have run off, as if you thought I was the murderer or something. I know you were upset with me. I understand that. But you could have died. And it wasn't right, Abbie,' he said. 'It wasn't well done.'

'Ben.'

'All right, all right . . . Look, I'm sorry about me and Jo – at least, I'm sorry you found out like that. I'm not saying I'm sorry we had an affair. That's something different and, if you want, one day I can tell you about it. And I'm not even saying I was completely wrong not to tell you. We started right in the deep end, us two. We didn't have the proper order to our relationship, did we? In the normal run of things, we would have got to know each other, and gradually given each other our confessions. We hardly knew each other and suddenly there you were living in my house and scared for your life, and everything was all so momentous and so out in the open. I didn't want to start our relationship by laying all my cards on the table, all at once. I was scared of losing you again.'

'So instead you started our relationship off with a lie,' I said.

'It wasn't a lie.'

'Not technically. Morally.'

'I'm sorry that I lied,' he said. He sat down beside me again and I lifted my hand to stroke his nice soft hair.

'And I'm sorry that I ran off like that,' I answered. 'Have a chocolate.'

'No, thanks.'

I took one. Caramel.

'There are words now that hold different meanings for me than they do for, say, you,' I said. 'Darkness. Silence. Winter.' I took another chocolate. 'Memory,' I added, and put the chocolate into my mouth.

Ben picked up my hand, the one that wasn't wrapped round his wooden egg. He held it against his face. 'I do love you,' he said.

'I think I was mad for a bit. That's all over.'

'You look different,' he said. 'Beautiful.'

'I feel different.'

'What are you going to do next?'

'Earn some money. Grow my hair. Go to Venice.'

'Do you want to come back?'

'Ben . . .'

'I'd like you to.'

'No. I mean, no, you probably wouldn't like me to although it's very nice of you to ask. And, no, I won't.'

'I see.' He put my hand on the bed and smoothed its fingers, one by one, not looking at me.

'You could ask me out,' I said. 'We could go on a date. See a movie. Drink cocktails. Eat swanky meals in restaurants.'

He started to smile at me, eager and uncertain. It made his eyes crinkle up. He was a nice man, really. I'd invented all the rest.

'Spring is coming,' I said. 'You never know what may happen.'

There was someone else who came to see me. Well, of course, lots of people came to see me. My friends, singly or in groups, clutching flowers, tearful or giggly or embarrassed. I hugged people until my ribs hurt. It was like a non-stop party in my room. It was like the party I'd thought I would have the first time I returned from the dead, only to enter instead a world of silence and shame – yet now I found that I was a stranger at my party, looking in on the fun, laughing but not really getting the joke.

But someone else came, too. He knocked on the door, even though it was half open, and stood on the threshold until I told him to come in.

'I don't know if you remember me,' he said. 'I'm . . .'

'Of course I remember,' I said. 'You told me that I had a very good brain. You're Professor Mulligan, the memory man, the only person I really want to see.'

'I didn't bring flowers.'

'That's good, because I'm leaving here this afternoon.'

'How are you?'

'Fine.'

'Well done,' he said.

I remembered from before the sense of approval he brought with him. It made me feel warm. 'Jack Cross told me you stood up for me.'

'Well . . .' He waved his hands vaguely in the air.

'You walked out of the meeting.'

'It didn't do any good. Tell me, did your memory come back at all?'

'No. Not really,' I said. 'Sometimes I think there's something there, just on the fringes of my consciousness, but I can't catch it and if I turn my head it's gone. And sometimes I think that the lost time is like a tide that flooded me and that's now ebbing away. It's so infinitesimally slow that I can't possibly detect it and perhaps I'm imagining it. Or maybe, bit by bit, memory will return. Do you think that's possible?'

He leant forward and looked at me. 'Don't count on it,' he said. 'Anything's possible but everything's a mystery.'

'For a long time I thought that there would be an answer in the end,' I said. 'I thought if I saw him I would remember. I thought that the things that were lost could be found again. But it's not going to happen like that, is it?'

'What did you want to find?'

'I wanted to find me.'

'Ah. Well, then.'

'I'll never get that lost me back, will I?'

Professor Mulligan took one of the flowers and sniffed it. He tore off the end of the stalk and inserted it into his lapel.

'Do you mind?' he said. I smiled and shook my head. 'Try not to dwell on what you don't remember. Think of the things that you do.'

Things I don't remember. I count them up on my fingers: leaving Terry, meeting Jo, meeting Ben, meeting him. I still think of him as nameless, just 'him', the man, a dark shape, a voice in the darkness. I don't remember falling in love. I don't remember that week of being simply and gloriously happy. I don't remember being snatched out of my life. I don't remember losing myself.

Things I do remember: a hood on my head, a wire on my neck, a gag in my mouth, a sob in my throat, a voice in the night, a laugh in the darkness, invisible hands touching me, eyes watching me, terror, loneliness, madness, shame. I remember dying and I remember being dead. And I remember the sound of my beating heart, the sound of my continuing breath, a yellow butterfly on a green leaf, a silver tree on a small hill, a calm river, a clear lake; things I haven't seen and will never forget. Being alive. I remember.

Read on for a taste of

SECRET SMILE

By Nicci French

Coming in hardback in March 2004

(Michael Joseph, priced £16.99)

I

I've had a dream recently, the same dream, over and over again, and each time I think it's real. I'm back at the ice rink on the afternoon I first met Brendan. The cold stings my face, I can hear the scrape of the blades on the ice and then I see him. He's glancing over at me with that funny look of his, as if he's noticed me and he's got something else on his mind. I see all over again that he's good-looking in a way that not everybody would notice. His hair is glossy black like a raven's wing. His face is oval and his cheekbones and chin are prominent. He has an amused expression on his face as if he has seen the joke before anybody else, and I like that about him. He looks at me and then gives me a second look and he's coming over to say hello. And in my dream I think: *Good. I've been given another chance. It doesn't have to happen. This time I can stop it now, here, before it's even begun.*

But I don't. I smile at what he says to me, and I say things back to him. I can't hear the words and I don't know what they are, but they must be funny because Brendan laughs and says something, and then I laugh. And so it goes, back and forwards. We're like actors in a long-running show. We can say our lines without thinking, and I know what's going to happen to this boy and this girl. They have never met before, but he is a friend of a friend of hers and so they are surprised that this is the first time they have come across each other. I'm trying to stop myself, in this dream which I both know and don't know is a dream. An ice rink is a good place for a boy and a girl to meet, especially when neither of them can skate. Because they have to lean against each other for support and it's almost compulsory for the boy to put his steadying arm around the girl and they help each other up and laugh at their joint predicament. Her laces are frozen together and he helps her to untie them, her foot in his lap for convenience. When the group starts to break up, it's only natural that the boy asks the girl for her phone number.

The girl is surprised by a moment of reluctance. It's been fun, but does she need something like this at the moment? She looks at the boy. His eyes are shining from the cold. He is smiling at her expectantly. It seems easier just to give him the number and so she does, even though I am shouting for her not to. But the shouting is silent and in any case she is me and she doesn't know what is going to happen – but I do.

I'm wondering how it is that I know what is going to happen. I know they are going to meet twice – a drink, a movie – and then, on her sofa, she'll think, well, why not? And so I'm thinking, if I know what's going to happen, it must mean that I can't change it. Not a single detail. I know they'll sleep together twice more, or is it three times? Always in the girl's flat. After the second time she sees a strange toothbrush in the mug next to hers. A moment of confusion. She will have to think about that. She will barely have time. Because the next afternoon, her mind will be made up for her. It's at about that moment – the girl coming home from work, opening the door of her flat – that I wake up.

After weeks of greyness and drizzle, it was a beautiful autumn afternoon. A blue sky just beginning to lose its electric glare, a sharp wind that was shaking bright leaves from the trees. It had been a long day, and I'd spent most of it up a ladder painting a ceiling, so my neck and right arm ached and my whole body felt grimy and sore, and there were splashes of white emulsion over my knuckles and in my hair. I was thinking about an evening alone: a hot bath, supper in front of the TV in my dressing gown. Cheese on toast, I thought. Cold beer.

So I opened the door to my flat and walked in, letting my bag drop to the floor. And then I saw him. Brendan was sitting on the sofa or, rather, lying back with his feet up. There was a cup of tea on the floor beside him, and he was reading something that he closed as I came in.

'Miranda.' He swung his legs off the cushion and stood up. 'I thought you'd be back later than this.' And he took me by the shoulders and kissed me on the lips. 'Shall I pour you some tea? There's some in the pot. You look all in.'

I could hardly think which question to ask first. He barely knew what job I did. What was he doing, thinking about when I finished work? But most of all, what was he doing in my flat? He looked as if he had moved in.

'What do you think you're doing?'

'I let myself in,' he said. 'I used the keys under the flowerpot. That's all right, isn't it? You've got paint in your hair, you know.'

I bent down and picked up the book from the sofa. A worn, hard-backed exercise book, a faded red, the spine split. I stared at it. It was one of my old diaries.

'That's private,' I said. 'Private!'

'I couldn't resist,' he said with his roguish smile. He saw my expression and held up his hands. 'Point taken, I'm sorry, it was wrong. But I want to know all about you. I just wanted to see what you were like before I met you.' He reached a hand out and gently touched my hair where the paint was, as if to scratch it away. I pulled away.

'You shouldn't have.'

Another smile.

'I won't do it again then,' he said in a playfully apologetic tone. 'All right?'

I took a deep breath. No. I didn't think it was all right.

'It's from when you were seventeen,' he said. 'I like to think of you at seventeen.'

I looked at Brendan and already he seemed to be receding into the distance. He was on the platform and I was on the train which was pulling away and leaving him behind for ever. I was thinking how to say it, as cleanly and finally as possible. You can say, 'I don't think this is working any more,' as if the relationship was a machine that has stopped functioning, some vital bit having gone missing. Or, 'I don't think we should continue,' as if you were both on a road together and you've looked ahead and seen that the road forks, or peters out in rocks and brambles. You can say, 'I don't want to keep on seeing you.' Only of course you don't mean *see*, but touch, hold, feel, want. And if they ask why – 'Why is it over?' 'What have I done wrong?' – then you don't tell them: 'You get on my nerves,' 'Your laugh suddenly irritates me,' 'I fancy someone else.' No, of course you say, 'You haven't done anything. It's not you, it's me.' These are the things we all learn.

Almost before I knew what I was about to do, I said the words. 'I don't think we should go on with this.'

For a moment, his expression didn't alter. Then he stepped forwards and laid his hand on my shoulder. 'Miranda,' he said.

'I'm sorry, Brendan.' I thought of saying something else, but I stopped myself.

His hand was still on my shoulder.

'You're probably exhausted,' he said. 'Why don't you have a bath and put on some clean clothes.'

I stepped away from his hand.

'I mean it.'

'I don't think so.'

'What?'

'Are you about to get your period?'

'Brendan . . .'

'You're due about now, aren't you?'

'I'm not playing games.'

'Miranda.' He had a coaxing tone to his voice, as if I were a frightened horse and he was approaching me with sugar on his outstretched palm. 'We've been too happy for you to just end it like this. All those wonderful days and nights.'

'Eight,' I said.

'What?'

'Times we met. Is it even that many?'

'Each time special.'

I didn't say, not for me, although it was the truth. You can't say that it really didn't mean much after all. It was just one of those things that happened. I shrugged. I didn't want to make a point. I didn't want to discuss things. I wanted him to leave.

'I've arranged for us to meet some mates of mine for a drink this evening. I told them you were coming.'

'What?'

'In half an hour.'

I stared at him.

'Just a quick drink.'

'You really want us to go out and pretend we're still together?'

'We need to give this time,' he said.

It sounded so ridiculous, so like a marriage guidance counsellor giving glib advice to a couple who had been together for years and years and had children and a mort-gage that I couldn't help myself. I started to laugh, then stopped myself and felt cruel. He managed a smile that wasn't really a smile at all, but rather lips stretched tight over teeth, a grimace or a snarl.

'You can laugh,' he said at last. 'You can do this and still laugh.'

'Sorry,' I said. My voice was still shaky. 'It's a nervous kind of laugh.'

'Is that how you behaved with your sister?'

'My sister?' The air seemed to cool around me.

'Yes. Kerry.' He said the name softly, musing over it. 'I read about it in your diary. I know. Mmm?'

I walked over to the door and yanked it open. The sky was still blue and the breeze cooled my burning face.

'Get out,' I said.

'Miranda.'

'Just go.'

So he left. I pushed the door shut gently, so he wouldn't think I was slamming it behind him, and then I suddenly felt nauseous. I didn't have the meal in front of the TV I'd been looking forward to so much. I just had a glass of water and went to bed and didn't sleep.

My relationship with Brendan had been so brief that my closest friend, Laura, had been on holiday while it was going on and missed it completely. And it was so entirely over and in the past that when she got back and rang to tell me about what a great time she and Tony had had – well, after all that, I didn't bother to tell her about Brendan. I just listened as she talked about the holiday and the weather and the food. Then she asked me if I were seeing someone and I said no. She said that was funny because she'd heard something and I said, well, nothing much and anyway it was over. And she giggled and said she wanted to hear all about it and I said there was nothing to tell. Nothing at all.